BROWN RIVER, WHITE OCEAN

BROWN RIVER,

WHITE OCEAN

*An Anthology of Twentieth-Century
Philippine Literature in English*

EDITED AND WITH AN INTRODUCTION BY
LUIS H. FRANCIA

Rutgers University Press

New Brunswick, New Jersey

Library of Congress Cataloging-in-Publication Data

Brown river, white ocean : an anthology of twentieth-century
Philippine literature in English / edited and with an introduction
by Luis H. Francia.
     cm.   cm.
    Includes bibliographical references and index.
    ISBN 0-8135-1989-6 (cloth)—ISBN 0-8135-1999-3 (pbk.)
    1. Philippine literature (English) 2. Philippines—Literary
collections. 3. English literature—20th century. I. Francia,
Luis, 1945–
PR9550.5.B76 1993
820.8'09599—dc20   92-46381
                                   CIP

British Cataloging-in-Publication information available

CONTENTS

Introduction

MR. AND MRS. ENGLISH TRAVEL WITH A RATTAN SUITCASE

Luis H. Francia

When I first mentioned to American friends that I was editing an anthology of Philippine literature in English, most assumed that it would be literature *translated* into English. That they should have assumed so didn't surprise me. Years ago, when I first came to New York, I thought somewhat naively that everyone knew Filipinos spoke English, not as a borrowed tongue but as one they grew up with. My settling in Manhattan quickly disabused me of that notion. I learned early on, living in a country that once occupied my own, that former colonizers rarely know much about the histories of their ex-colonies beyond the superficial, the exotic. The reverse was true, of course: the vanquished quickly learn the victors' customs and quirks. In a sense, our voyage here reflects an artificial nostalgia, a remembrance of what we never actually had. Initially, I was puzzled when people I met on different occasions often remarked about how fluent my English was, wondering innocently where I had picked it up. My reply was usually a flippant "on the plane coming here." It didn't take me long to realize however that, while uninformed, the question was perfectly innocent.

In fact, English is spoken throughout the archipelago that is the Philippines. A good number of Filipinos grow up bilingual and even trilingual, not uncommon considering that approximately eighty-seven indigenous languages exist in the country. This linguistic bonus may be the only advantage to having been colonized, although, strange as it may seem, Spanish is no longer widely spoken. Although modern Tagalog (or Pilipino, as the national tongue is now termed) has a large, Spanish-derived vocabulary, and although the Southeast Asian nation was part of New Spain for three and a half centuries, Spanish never took hold the way it did in Latin America, or the way that the Spanish form of Catholicism did. Not being a linguist, I can only hazard a guess. In 1898, when the USS *Maine* was blown up while anchored off Havana, the United States of America, spoiling for a fight, quickly declared war on Spain and brought the hostilities to its colonies: the Philippines, Puerto Rico, and Cuba. With that martial embrace, the United States permanently altered Philippine history, forever delaying the emergence of Philippine Spanish as a full-grown language.

That emergence, that flowering, would have come earlier had the Spanish proved to be as fervent educators as they were proselytizers.

The conquistador and the friar constituted a formidable duo, implanting the fear of God in brown breasts, teaching the *indios* prayering charms to ward off the devil but lacking the same zeal in educating the masses. Higher education was reserved for the wellborn, the *ilustrados,* scions of transplanted Spanish families and of prominent creole clans. Old World imperialists that they were, the Spanish disdained any notion of democracy, horrified by the thought of a brown-skinned people ever identifying with them. Whatever their faults they always made it perfectly clear how unattractive cross-cultural pollination was to them.

Such unabashed elitism did little to blunt a burgeoning nationalist consciousness. There were at least two hundred revolts before 1896, when the Katipunan, a secret revolutionary society determined to oust the Spanish, launched a successful revolution, the first in colonial Asia. But victory, however sweet, was short-lived. Another victor had emerged, more powerful than the fledgling republic. The United States had easily defeated Spain and, in a betrayal of its alliance with the Philippine revolutionaries, struck an onerous bargain in Paris in December 1898, paying the Spanish government $20 million for the privilege of being the new plantation master.

The Yankee embrace quickly turned into a stranglehold. In a little-known guerrilla war that prefigured Vietnam by more than fifty years and may have claimed a million Filipino lives, the Philippine revolutionary government under the leadership of General Emilio Aguinaldo resisted this New World strain of imperialism for five years before succumbing to superior arms.

Of the U.S. colonial adventure, Mark Twain, in his essay "The Philippine Incident," portrayed a Filipino "sitting in darkness" who tells himself: "There must be two Americas: one that sets the captive free, and one that takes a once-captive's new freedom away from him, and picks a quarrel with him with nothing to found it on; then kills him to get his land."[1] These Caesars proved to be slier and more efficient than the Spanish. Urged on by both the missionary zeal of Manifest Destiny—a patently racist policy based on the Kiplingesque idea of the White Man's Burden—and self-interest, the Yankees realized very quickly that it would be easier for their values to take hold if their subjects—or, as we were referred to patronizingly in those days, "little brown brothers"—learned their language. As poet and critic Bienvenido Lumbera points out, "Although there was some debate as to whether or not a language native to the Filipinos ought to be the language of education, the architects of the colonial educational system quickly decided it would be to the advantage of the U.S. to make English the medium of instruction in all Philippine schools.... English opened the floodgates of colonial values through the conduits of textbooks originally intended for American children."[2]

So it was that six hundred American teachers arrived in 1901, on board the USS *Thomas* (from then on, all the colonial-era teachers were called "Thomasites") to spread the gospel according to Thomas Jefferson & Co., and later to make us forever imagine the ethereal beauty of white Christmases, Coca-Cola bottles in hand. The Philippine Normal School was founded the same year, so Filipinos could be trained as teachers. In the meantime, a nationwide public school system was being set in place. Having been denied mass public education by the Spanish, Filipinos took to learning their ABCs and nursery rhymes like the proverbial ducks to water, water of a distinctive New England character. By enabling Filipinos of proletarian background to go not just to grammar school but all the way to university, the American occupiers seemed downright revolutionary. Where Filipino intellectuals had previously come from the ranks of the affluent, now they came as well from the poorer socioeconomic classes. An American-inspired education gave them, in theory anyway, the means toward economic and social mobility. In a feudal society, however, dependent on clan and blood ties, the notion of mobility ultimately proved to be a cruel illusion.

Although Spanish continued to be taught formally in schools through to the early 1970s, English quickly supplanted it as the language not just of the literati but of businessmen and politicians as well. In short, it took hold in every arena of the public sector. Students learned schoolroom Spanish but chose instead to mimic American accents and slang. Today, except in certain boardrooms and bedrooms, Spanish hardly figures in any significant public or private discourse. If the most enduring legacy of the Spaniard was his religion, that of the Yankee was his language, not, as some claim, democratic institutions. The Americans may have set these up, but they never allowed unfettered discourse, certainly not radical criticism of their rule. And they continued to accommodate the same narrow interests as had existed under the Spanish. As a result, democracy in the Philippines has always been subject to a great deal of instability. But the language of administration remains. As in India, it has also served as a unifying language: people from different linguistic regions often communicate much better with each other through English. Of course, it is English filtered through regional accents, just as it is elsewhere.

As with most Filipinos who get an education, I grew up with three languages: English, Spanish, and Pilipino. The order in which I list them indicated for a very long time each tongue's social standing. And of the three, I am most fluent in English, reflecting both the conditions of a home where our parents spoke to us in English and the middle-class society I was reared in, as attuned to the mores of the Western world as to those of its own milieu. And my education at the hands of American Jesuits guaranteed an assiduous cultivation of the language at the expense of Pilipino, referred to by our teachers as the "dialect." In high school, we were forbidden to speak "dialect" on the premises, and if caught indulging in it by a teacher or a school monitor (a student who performed the equivalent func-

tions of a jail trusty) had to undergo "Post"—a form of corporal punishment whereby we had to perform numbing calisthenics after school.

Except for classes in Pilipino at the primary school level, my education was thoroughly Western and almost as thoroughly colonial. The very name of the Jesuit university I attended—Ateneo de Manila, Spanish for Athens of Manila—reflected its European origins. Naturally, the texts we studied were from the traditional Western canon of literary and philosophical classics, from *Beowulf* and Virgil's *Aeneid* to Milton's *Paradise Lost,* from T. S. Eliot's *Four Quartets* to Ernest Hemingway's stories, from the pre-Socratics to Kant and Martin Buber, from James Joyce's *Dubliners* to the plays of Albee and Beckett. It was fashionable to be given over to bouts of doubt, of angst, to have, in other words, in a way only the young possess, the dissolute airs of resolute iconoclasts. And the juvenile rebellions we indulged in were the sincerest form of flattery we could give the Western authors we so revered. The Thomasites and their successors had succeeded beyond their wildest dreams.

Given the slant of our education, not a single class in Philippine literature in English, or in any of the country's major languages, was ever taught. (That situation has since been remedied—proof that a sense of nationalism has finally made some impact on the private school system.) So I knew it only through my own intermittent readings outside of school, and through meeting some of its authors. In hindsight that might have been best, for then I approached the texts with no preconceptions whatsoever. Still, Philippine literature in English deserved a place in the curriculum, although its body of works was understandably slim compared to that of the English and the Americans.

Steeped as I and my peers were in Western literature, we looked upon our own literature in English as a poor relative, to be visited from time to time as an act of charity. Our indifference was inevitable. Had our educators not been so slavish in their singular imitation of the West, there was absolutely no reason then, as there is none now, not to appreciate more than one body of literature. This mistaken, patronizing attitude which we confused with hipness unfortunately extended to the other arts as well. Thus, for instance, we much preferred Hollywood films to Filipino ones—sneeringly labeled *bakya,* a word meaning "wooden clogs" (footwear for the peasantry) and, in the cultural jargon of the day, used as a pejorative for any manifestation of popular art. The beauty of the local screen goddesses had to have Caucasian antecedents. The more *mestiza* the better.

Our education, alleged to attune us to the complexities of a heavily Western, heavily modern world, really served as a wedge between what was native to our soil and what we were in the process of becoming: stand-ins for our American and Americanized mentors. More than anything else, our postcolonial education revealed vividly that school was really more about the process of socialization. We were expected to embody the store of traditions that mark a society. The irony of course was that many of these so-called traditions had been transplanted and considered superior to native ones by that very fact. No more fitting epigraph exists about our condition, our altered state, than what Edward Said, discussing Jean Genet's late works, wrote: "Imperialism is the export of identity."[3]

Sometimes there were funny consequences. I remember a classmate and friend of mine who was the only soul on campus who owned a surfboard. He was a devotee of the Southern California life-style, from his Beach Boys haircut to his sockless feet in penny loafers. Sometimes there were pathetic results: classmates who spoke very little Pilipino and when they did, spoke it with difficulty. Most of us, however, straddled the cultural divide quite easily, blending both worlds unconsciously. Even my surfer friend (he spoke Pilipino fluently), to his credit, had enough of a sense of the absurd to laugh at himself. This balancing act was an art, honed over the centuries by a people continually visited by stranger after stranger, each with fixed ideas as to who we were.

Only after graduating from university did I begin to methodically read the works of writers who were homegrown, marked with the same cultural influences, and who used English in a manner I could instinctively identify with. Not only was the tongue familiar; so too were the writers. I've always resented the lack of formal studies of Philippine literature in English, and when the chance came to do this anthology, I took it readily. My preparation for it has been a second education, a rereading of much of what I had read before and a getting to know works I had hitherto not read. If the idea of a literature in English other than American or British was lodged somewhat amorphously in my brain, work on this anthology has shaped it up, and given the word flesh, so to speak. It has also stripped away certain misplaced expectations. Simply for the reason that Philippine literature in English has existed for barely nine decades, it would be unwise and unfair to think of it along the same lines as those of English and American literatures, which both have the advantage of time and which originate in sources different from those of Philippine culture. It would be more appropriate to compare it, say, to Indian literature in English, or to other literatures whose midwife was colonialism: the Caribbean countries, Kenya, Singapore, Malaysia, and the rest.

Yet it would be a great mistake to view the literatures produced during and after the colonial era as merely expressions of a foreign culture in native disguise. Certainly there are in these literatures works that simply mimic, often artfully, the (as it were) "mother" literature. But most of the writers, having subsumed English as an expressive vehicle, have long cast it in their image, shedding the mantle of imitation and self-consciousness. Not surprisingly, the complex, even Byzantine, web of relations between the colonizer and the colonized, and the discourse between different cultures, often figure as prominent themes in these literatures, with their characters embodying cultural contradictions, North–South, East–West.

We have often been accused of not knowing ourselves, of lacking a clear-cut, well-defined cultural sensibility. It is an accusation born of the belief that culture is a neat package, convenient for handling and weighing. This concept, intrinsically related to ideas of racial purity and a defensive insularity, is the complete antithesis of living Philippine culture, an attempt to pasteurize and sterilize it. And many of us are forever attempting to be irreducibly pure when what we really want to be is irreducibly Filipino. In the Philippine context, what is foreign and what is indigenous has always been a tricky and ultimately impossible subject. For better or worse, Filipinos have unconsciously perfected the art of mixing the two up, confounding definitions and scholars. To be a purist in such a situation is not just to be a hopeless romantic but to turn away from the modern Filipino as he or she is: Malayan, Chinese, Indian, Hispanic, and American—somewhat like a Cubist painting with blurry lines. As in the painting, a synthesis is involved, a recognition, an acceptance, of a confusion that can be seen in positive terms. Poet Rolando Tinio hits it right on the head when he declares, "I mean, somehow, the idea of cultural confusion appeals to me, and I hope that it happens everywhere else even as I suspect that it happened to the Greeks and Romans and the Europeans. The trouble is that we look at the past and the present through the eyes of scholarship, and scholarship being in love with death, it necessarily kills what it brings to light."[4] This hodgepodge quality of Philippine society is deliberately reflected in the works of many of our writers, imparting an idiosyncratic flavor and a layered complexity to their works. Thus, in her novel *Dogeaters,* Jessica Hagedorn captures the *mestizo* nature and soap-operatic flair of Manila society. The two main characters, Rio and Joey, are of mixed blood, as is their milieu which has everything, from Hollywood icons and Pacific island languor to Catholic rituals and macho posturing.

In terms of a genuinely Philippine literary tradition, the past nine decades of Philippine writing in English form part of its core. There are other, older streams forming this river of tradition: Tagalog, Visayan, Spanish, among others. A parallel situation obtains here in the United States, the quintessential immigrant society: the Anglo tradition may be the most prominent, but it certainly isn't the only one. There are African-American, Hispanic-American, Asian-American and—the oldest— Native American traditions. English in the Philippines may have come from a feared Anglo America, but it has since blended with the landscape. The poet Gemino Abad declares that "the Filipino writer of English is enabled to transform, to mold unto his own image and sensibility, the ideology or the way of seeing and feeling which the alien language secretes. English in Filipino hands, under the pressure of his own circumstances and choices, becomes not English but Filipino. If he is at first possessed, he comes also in time to possess both the medium and the message *in his own way,* by the language of his blood."[5]

I believe writers write primarily for self-knowledge, to try to understand the mystery of being, and of being themselves, perhaps in relation to others—to society—or simply in relation to their own ideas and perceptions of who they are. Apart from style, what differentiates two writers from different backgrounds is language and culture. The process of exploration, of writing, of language itself, cannot be separated from the cultural process. Nick Joaquin, then, or Ninotchka Rosca is no more American than the Caribbean poet Derek Walcott or the Indian writer R. K. Narayan is English. Language—as filtered through a particular culture—and writer always interact, each language offering a distinct if stubborn landscape, the writer seeking to alter its contours to fit, more or less, the geography of his or her experience, real or imagined. Whatever Philippine writers write about, whether they intend to or not, reveals them as being ineluctably Filipino.

In a postcolonial society such as ours, the question of cultural identity is a crucial one, particularly since our sense of a collective self tends to be fragmented. Social distinctions in an industrial society normally presuppose a distance between "I" and "Thou"—and an even greater one between "I" and "We," with the "I" holding the preeminent spot. We take this automization for granted; but from all indications, precolonial Philippine society—a geographic grouping of different kingdoms and tribes—stressed the communal over the individual. And it was a sense of communality that embraced strangers as long as these weren't hostile. It was an extremely hospitable embrace: a semitropical climate, volcanic soil, and fertile waters meant abundance was the rule rather than the exception. We could afford to be generous to a fault and so were. Such generosity was manipulated by the Westerner, rendering us victims of our own hospitality.

Behind our legendary open arms is a deeper reason than sheer bonhomie. Good that the newcomer feels relaxed but make no mistake: the paroxysms of generosity and friendliness are essentially masks to conceal our inner selves. Seduced by kindness, the stranger will be less inclined to probe further and inquire about the secret compartments every people possesses. When Octavio Paz in his study of the Mexican character, *The Labyrinth of Solitude*, describes his typical compatriot as "a person who shuts himself away to protect himself: his face is a mask and so is his smile," he could have been describing the Filipino.[6] Our masks of kindness have helped us survive, as the apt and familiar phrase in Manila goes, four hundred years in a convent and fifty in Hollywood.

Filipinos have been so good at hiding their selves that these are in danger of being lost. It has been fashionable for a while now to speak of the "Other": one hears this notion incessantly discussed in panel after panel, often with predictable rhetoric substituting

for insight. For most Westernized Filipinos—and I certainly can be categorized as such—the "Other" exists but as a rudimentary reminder of what the pre-Western inhabitant of the archipelago was like, or was imagined to be like. Here ultimately lies the cruel legacy of colonialism: the Other refers to what was once our familiar but now has become foreign; and what was once foreign has now become our familiar. If the idea of the Other appears as an exoticized objectification of the alien in contemporary Western society, in the Philippines what has been exoticized and commodified has been the deepest part of our selves. The chroniclers of our history who were known to the world were invariably Westerners; these wrote about us as though "us" were distant. No wonder then that between the chronicled and the chronicler there existed a tremendous gap. Even today, in a supposedly postcolonial age, colonial images of the Philippines—for that matter, of Third World countries—linger on in global discourse like an invincible virus, spread by "experts" who, like their predecessors, happen for the most part to be white and male. Inheritors of that formalist history (as opposed to living, unwritten traditions) occupy the exact same spot where stood the original observers and with the same bent: viewing themselves as though they were Other, perpetuating a decidedly painful colonial hangover.

Literary texts being historical texts as well, i.e., written at precise moments in a country's evolution, they can help the process of commodification, or they can expose it. Apart from their literariness they tell us a great deal about ourselves. Even more, they can give us back our "selves." In a sense, many of our Filipino writers in English are engaged in the literary equivalent of guerrilla warfare, using the very same weapon that had been employed to foist another set of foreign values upon a ravished nation, but now as part of an arsenal meant for conscious self-determination and the unwieldy process of reclaiming psychic territory from the invader. In the process, as we have grown more assured, no longer self-conscious in the use of what was once a foreign tongue, we have become much more aware of—no, much more comfortable with—the many disparate strands of a collective self.

Imagine, then, English in the Philippines as an American-made train, its luggage racks and boxcars crammed with American baggage and freight. Imagine the train rolling out of the depot and across the country, picking up Filipino passengers along the way. As the train's racks and freight cars are filled with what to the Filipino are strange-looking suitcases, portmanteaus, and various other items, it becomes readily apparent that there is no place for his or her own luggage. In a supreme act of accommodation, many chuck their goods out the window and cheerfully appropriate what is already there. But as the train goes deeper and deeper into the countryside, more and more passengers come aboard until eventually one or two or three start to toss out the strange-looking suitcases, portmanteaus, and various other items and replace them with their own, but made of bamboo, rattan, buri. And almost everyone follows suit, until finally the train's metamorphosis is complete, and it becomes indisputably Philippine.

The stories and poems in this anthology are portmanteaus of a unique society, containing images drawn from different social strata, different time periods, different locales. Businessmen, doctors, soldiers, farmers, workers, slum dwellers, immigrants, artists, students—they're all here. And the themes are as varied: incest, the burdens of tradition, reincarnation, the horror of tyranny, young love, exile, among others. From Paz Marquez Benitez's short story "Dead Stars" (the earliest story included here) and Amador Daguio's poem "Man of Earth" to Rowena Tiempo-Torrevillas's story, "Prodigal Season," and Emmanuel Lacaba's poem "Open Letters to Filipino Artists," this collection of short stories and poetry should give the American reader—and, for that matter, any reader of English—more than aesthetic pleasure, even though that is the main intent here. It should also give the reader a view of

Philippine society, past and present, different from what could otherwise be obtained.

Because this is a single volume, I have limited its scope to the short story and to poetry; my choices are based on an exhaustive reading of works published since Philippine literature in English began. As is probably true of other anthologies, I selected more than could finally fit this one-volume format. The subsequent and painful task of eliminating stories and poems was solely mine so, yes, I am to blame for this book's omissions, no one else.

———

When we consider that English was brought in at the turn of this now-ending century and that recognizably serious literary efforts started to emerge in the 1920s, the results in literature have been remarkable. For one thing, many of the pioneers in Philippine literature in English are still with us. And we benefit from their recollections, especially on their early literary influences. Bienvenido Santos, now in his early eighties, says at the beginning of his career that he was "impressed by Hemingway, Sherwood Anderson. I liked, I loved, Anderson. . . . It was a tribute to the way Sherwood Anderson wrote, I really like Anderson better than Hemingway. Later, of course, I even liked Faulkner better than Hemingway." The poet Angela Manalang Gloria remembers reading Edna St. Vincent Millay, Sara Teasdale, and Elizabeth Barrett Browning, although she "preferred Spanish poetry, which cast a heady spell over me."[7]

Inevitably the way most of the early Philippine writers used English indicated that it had come from the outside. This couldn't be helped. They grew up in a society that, while governed by English-speakers, was still very much Hispanic. Describing those early efforts, critic Pura Santillan-Castrence points out: "Indeed, Spanish was the language which the predecessor-writers used. . . . Much of that Spanish psychology has clung to the writing of some of them, as well as the Spanish floridness of expression, the flowery turn of phrase, perhaps also some of the bombast."[8] So we had a Filipino, steeped in a Catholic, Spanish tradition, articulating the creative impulse in an Anglo-Saxon tongue.

In literary endeavors, the first known Filipino poem in English, Justo Juliano's "Sursum Corda," was printed in 1907, six years from the arrival of the Thomasites. In 1920, the first collection of poems was published, *Never Mind and Other Poems,* by Procopio Solidum. But as early as 1899 there existed English-language newspapers, and in 1900 the *Daily Bulletin* (now the *Manila Bulletin*) was founded. As was to be expected, initial literary expressions were stiff, betraying the still-heavy influence of Spanish. Thus for instance these lines, from Maximo Kalaw's "The Parting Year":

> But no! O no! leave that alone—
> Awakening love! I have it hid
> Within me deep; leave it unknown
> Till it o'ergrows and flies unbid.[9]

The early short stories in English, which favored romances and adventures as themes, displayed the same awkward characteristics.[10] By the mid-1920s, however, stories were beginning to shed the mantle of imitation and, with the publication of Paz Marquez Benitez's "Dead Stars" in 1925, the Philippine short story in English had arrived. A tale of loss and disillusionment, "Dead Stars" is simply constructed but gives a convincing portrait of a man's inner conflict, born of a kind of romantic idealism, and his attempts to resolve it.[11] There is little dialogue, and the author skillfully situates the reader squarely in the middle of the protagonist Alfredo's romantic turmoil.

In poetry Luis Dato, born during the early years of American rule, was among the first poets to create work that, like "Dead Stars," established its own identity, its own place. "Day on the Farm," written in 1934 and following the classical sonnet form with its ABAB rhyme scheme, isn't really about farm life but about the poet's beloved whose "smiles have died." While romantic, it avoids the exaggerated rhetorical flourish typical of the lines above. And the couplet, with its gentle remonstrance, is distinctly modernist in tone.

Unquestionably, English has been ingrained into our writers' consciousness as yet another language in which to express themselves. Yet, though no longer in an overbearing way, an unmistakable Spanish flavor lingers in much of contemporary Philippine literature in English. As many have remarked, our fiction bears a strong resemblance to South America's. And why not? With our Hispanic roots we could very well be a displaced Latin American country, Southeast Asia's odd man.

But it is precisely the tensions and contradictions that result from two or more cultures coexisting within the same social framework that give much of our literature its impetus. The best example is Nick Joaquin, one of the country's most gifted writers. Joaquin, who has written in both Spanish and English, represents a bridge between a Hispanic Philippines and an Americanized archipelago. His subjects have included the *ilustrados* as well as young modern couples very much attuned to Yankee ways. But it is in his stories of the dying class of Hispanicized Filipinos that Joaquin is at his best. Such masterpieces as "The Summer Solstice" and "Mayday Eve" could only have been penned by a Filipino of a certain generation steeped in the Hispanic traditions, especially Catholicism, that took root in the islands.

His stories of predominantly creole characters form a collective romantic elegy, infused with a bittersweet tone, on the grandeur of the colonial Spanish era. Often, Joaquin reveals how pre-Hispanic and Hispanic ways are a curious and in the end contrapuntal conjunction. In "The Summer Solstice," the upper-class Don Paeng and Doña Lupeng have all the affectations of Spanish gentry, but Doña Lupeng gets drawn into a pre-Hispanic pagan ritual, the *Tadtarin,* where only women are allowed to participate and which ultimately asserts the supremacy of the female principle.

It is something the domineering husband cannot understand, so distant is he from native traditions, but in a powerful ending, he submits to her totally.

This tug between two cultures is a common note sounded by many of our writers, such as Carlos Bulosan, Bienvenido Santos, F. Sionil José, Sinai Hamada, and Rowena Tiempo-Torrevillas. The stories of Bulosan and Santos in particular very often deal with the confluence and conflict of Philippine and American values. Bulosan is especially concerned with the social dimensions of this uneasy exchange, expressing his concerns mostly in comedy and satire. Santos favors an understated emotionalism, and records the psychological toll years of exile take on womenless *manongs,* or aging Filipino men. Both Bulosan's and Santos's characters embody the inequities and loneliness of being a person of color in a predominantly white society.

In Philippine poetry in English, with themes that are even more varied, the cultural tug is not so evident simply because of poetry's elliptical nature. But a debate began in the 1930s, between art for art's sake and art informed by social causes, continues to be an influential one. That was the decade when José Garcia Villa—the best-known Philippine poet in English—first declared meaning anathema to poetry, or at the very least irrelevant. He stressed craft and the supremacy of language and music over content. Because Villa, who has lived most of his life in New York, acquired an international reputation, his pronouncements have had a seminal influence on younger generations of Philippine writers. His credo—formalist, abstract, experimental—broke with tradition, a tradition created by Tagalog and Spanish works written from the nineteenth century to the 1920s. Prior to 1946, when we gained our independence from the United States, writers drew principally from this tradition, fueled by the 1896 Revolution, in their drive for the Filipinos' right to self-determination. Accompanying the clamor for independence was a campaign "to make Americans aware of the cultural legacy of the Filipino people, as this was concretized in the folklore, history and literature of the Philippines."[12]

It was precisely this tradition and the agrarian and social unrest of the 1930s (an unrest even greater today) that prompted Villa's contemporary, the critic and educator Salvador P. Lopez, to repudiate the poet's aesthetics as the meaningless result of a writer, "a decadent aesthete who stubbornly confuses literature with painting and refuses to place words in the employ of man and his civilization." For Lopez, the writer ignored society and its political and social struggles only at the risk of becoming irrelevant, of being read solely in elitist circles. Lopez favored the creation of works in service of political and social change—in a word, proletarian literature.[13]

The advent of New Criticism as an influential critical theory, with its overriding emphasis on the text as a thing-in-itself (whether as object of scrutiny or in the making), meant that appreciating literature apart from its social context was not merely permissible but necessary as well, if writers were to be artistically effective. The supremacy given to the text swung the debate in favor of Villa's nontraditional aesthetics.[14] While New Criticism meant the short end of the stick for social issues (although this wasn't true of writing in Pilipino), it did force writers to pay close attention to craft, to the "literariness" of their works. But since the fundamental changes wrought in the national consciousness by the martial law regime of Ferdinand Marcos, from the 1970s to the mid-eighties, and the aggravation of persistent social and political problems, the debate has been rekindled.

Nevertheless, it would be reductive thinking to categorize the poems one way or the other. Good poets, natural subverters of dogma, render the debate, and any pigeonholing, superfluous. The best example I can think of is Emmanuel Lacaba who, having joined the communist New People's Army in the 1970s after acquiring a Byronic reputation in Manila, was at the age of twenty-seven treacherously shot by a military patrol after his capture in 1976. His early works are evidence of a tremendously gifted bard; they can also be easily seen as the writings of an "aesthete." However, the works composed after he went underground (many of which were written in Pilipino) retain a lyrical tone even as they grapple with highly political issues. His last poem, "Open Letters to Filipino Artists," a magnificent three-part work finished two months before his death, is also his best, a moving testament to the revolutionary spirit of the poet himself and of the masses. The third and last section, with its brief quote from Robert Frost's "The Road Not Taken," is unrivaled for the way it seamlessly weaves lyrical intensity and political fervor. There can be no question that as the poet wrote this he was for one transcendent moment both the incarnation of past Filipino revolutionaries *and* a modern man schooled in the ways and tongue of the West.

=====

The flux that characterizes Philippine society today is as great as any that has gripped it in the past. It will certainly affect the future of English in the Philippines but precisely in what way is extremely difficult to predict. Change, as the recent tumultuous events on the global stage have shown, has a way of thumbing its nose at prediction. Certainly as a language English has set down roots. Just as there is "Spanglish," there is also "Taglish"—a conversational mode where speakers shuttle effortlessly between Tagalog and English and where English words have been Filipinized. The use of English may have begun, as Francisco Arcellana points out, as a "historical mistake," but by the thirties "the Filipino writer in English may be said to have mastered the language well enough to enable him to observe the life around him without the language interfering. . . . he felt he had sufficient control of it to be able to look at his material with a clear vision, unobstructed by language only partially possessed." He goes on to note that "the writer is a writer exactly because he sees *with* language, not just with his eyes: only that has been which has been verbalized. The harsh truth is that the writer is a writer exactly because he lives *with* words: until experience is transfigured into words, it is not experience."[15]

Many nationalists would eliminate this "historical mistake" altogether, relying on arguments traditionally used against Spanish that appeal to a vision of the Filipino as untainted by foreign influences. More pragmatic nationalists simply point to the enormous gulf that separates the mass of readers of Pilipino and other indigenous languages from English-language readers. The latter is a strong argument, but it is an argument not so much against the use of English as for a wider use—and appreciation—of the various main languages of the archipelago such as Tagalog, Cebuano, and Ilocano. Indeed, it is not uncommon for many of our writers to write in two languages, including English. If after all it is the writer's prerogative to use the language(s) most suited to his or her temperament, then the question isn't so problematic as it seems. I quite agree with Tinio when he writes, "And . . . the best thing for the Filipino writer in English is to write in English. If tomorrow I suddenly decide to read nothing but Tagalog poems, perhaps even to write Tagalog poems—well, isn't that nice? Perhaps I will, and perhaps I won't, but whatever I choose to do is certainly nobody else's business."[16]

Ironically, a significant portion of the literature that contributed to the debate on nationalism, or served to fan its flames, has been written either in Spanish or English, from the anticlerical Spanish novels of the nineteenth-century reformist and genius José Rizal (he was executed by the Spanish in 1896) to the continuing critiques in English of Philippine society by nationalist historian Renato Constantino.

The debate over language and identity continues. Personally, I find the idea of cultural diversity appealing, although it may seem like pointless confusion to others. And perhaps, having been raised in a multicultural society, I am making a virtue out of a historical condition. Still, as boundaries disappear and cultures become more fluid than ever, diversity will be the keynote of a global community even as it strives to become unified. In the case of the Philippines, by wishing our intracultural differences weren't so pronounced, we strain after a false homogeneity. Is it that we lack, or that we have too much? The daunting challenge of a twice-colonized people is to assimilate constructive aspects of the past and forge a new identity that unstintingly acknowledges history, but in ways that liberate rather than constrict us.

One thing is evident: Philippine writers in English know better than to expect a mass audience in their home country, partly for reasons discussed and partly because of the absence of a viable publishing industry. The books in English published in the Philippines stand little chance of international distribution. There are a few distributors here and there, but these cater to a specialized audience. Being published outside of the country, then, is prized not so much for its cachet as for the opportunity of tapping into a much greater reading public. Of course, to be shut off from a wider audience is not the mere result of market mechanisms but more precisely of a lack of empowerment, the consequences of which the late great film director Luis Buñuel in his autobiography, *My Last Breath*, clearly saw: "It seems clear to me that without the enormous influence of the canon of American culture, Steinbeck would be an unknown, as would Dos Passos and Hemingway. If they'd been born in Paraguay or Turkey, no one would ever have read them, which suggests the alarming fact that the greatness of a writer is in direct proportion to the power of his country. Galdós, for instance,

is often as remarkable as Dostoevsky, but who outside Spain ever reads him?"[17]

This anthology is a small but, I believe, important gesture toward addressing the disparities in dissemination that exist between Third World literatures and those of the West. It also represents in some way a creative subversion of the Thomasites' efforts, in a way they never dreamed of. The language they brought with them almost a century ago is not the language that exists today. Language survives and flourishes as a mutable form, or not at all.

In the long run, what endures in the physical language is the language of the spirit. Surely it is enough that the creative minds behind these stories, these poems, are leaving their unique imprints to be noticed and remarked upon by the society they lived in, and by the society that will come after. I hope the reader who comes to these works fresh will be enlivened and pleased, and that the reader already familiar with them will have memory not only delightfully rekindled but added to.

I would like to thank the following individuals and institutions for lending me hard-to-find books or for facilitating access to certain libraries: Reynaldo Alejandro, Luis Cabalquinto, Nick Deocampo, Linda Faigao-Hall, Alberto Florentino, Jessica Hagedorn, Prospero Hernandez of Rutgers University Press, the Philippine Center, Ninotchka Rosca, Jack Salzman and Ian Moulton of the Center for American Culture Studies, Bart Suretsky, and Ted Tanoue.

My gratitude as well to my editor Kenneth Arnold, and to David Friedman and Virgilio Reyes for their invaluable comments on the draft of my Introduction.

NEW YORK CITY
NOVEMBER 1992

NOTES

1. Mark Twain, "The Philippine Incident," quoted in *The Atlantic Monthly* (April 1992), 50.

2. Bienvenido Lumbera and Cynthia Nograles-Lumbera, *Philippine Literature: A History and Anthology* (Manila: National Book Store, 1982), pp. 109–110.

3. Edward Said, "On Jean Genet's Late Works," *Grand Street* **9**, no. 4 (1990), 38.

4. Rolando Tinio, "Period of Awareness: The Poets," in *Brown Heritage,* ed. Antonio Gella Manuud (Manila: Ateneo de Manila University Press, 1967), p. 618.

5. Gemino H. Abad, "Reading Past Writ," in *Man of Earth: An Anthology of Filipino Poetry and Verse from English, 1905 to the Mid-50s,* ed. G. H. Abad and E. Z. Manlapaz (Manila: Ateneo de Manila University Press, 1989), p. 9.

6. Octavio Paz, *The Labyrinth of Solitude* (New York: Grove Press, 1985), p. 29.

7. Edilberto N. Alegre and Doreen G. Fernandez, *The Writer and His Milieu* (Manila: De La Salle University Press, 1984), p. 63.

8. Pura Santillan-Castrence, "The Period of Apprenticeship," in *Brown Heritage,* ed. Manuud, p. 548.

9. Abad and Manlapaz, eds., *Man of Earth,* p. 30.

10. Richard Croghan, S. J., *The Development of Philippine Literature in English* (Quezon City: Alemar-Phoenix Publishing House, 1975), p. 6.

11. Santillan-Castrence, "The Period of Apprenticeship," p. 551.

12. Lumbera and Nograles-Lumbera, *Philippine Literature,* p. 103.

13. Herbert Schneider, S. J., "The Period of Emergence of Philippine Letters (1930–1944)," in *Brown Heritage,* ed. Manuud, p. 583.

14. Lumbera and Nograles-Lumbera, *Philippine Literature,* p. 235ff.

15. Francisco Arcellana, "Period of Emergence: The Short Story," in *Brown Heritage,* ed. Manuud, pp. 607–608.

16. Tinio, "Period of Awareness," p. 619.

17. Luis Buñuel, *My Last Breath* (London: Fontana, 1985), p. 222.

SHORT STORIES

Paz Marquez Benitez

DEAD STARS

Through the open window the air-steeped outdoors passed into his room, quietly enveloping him, stealing into his very thought. Esperanza, Julia, the sorry mess he had made of life, the years to come even now beginning to weigh down, to crush—they lost concreteness, diffused into formless melancholy. The tranquil murmur of conversation issued from the brick-tiled *azotea* where Don Julian and Carmen were busy puttering away among the rose pots.

"Papa, and when will the 'long table' be set?"

"I don't know yet. Alfredo is not very specific, but I understand Esperanza wants it to be next month."

Carmen sighed impatiently. "Why is he not a bit more decided, I wonder. He is over thirty, is he not? And still a bachelor! Esperanza must be tired waiting."

"She does not seem to be in much of a hurry either," Don Julian nasally commented, while his rose scissors busily snipped away.

"How can a woman be in a hurry when the man does not hurry her?" Carmen returned, pinching off a worm with a careful, somewhat absent air. "Papa, do you remember how much in love he was?"

"In love? With whom?"

"With Esperanza, of course. He has not had another love affair that I know of," she said

with good-natured contempt. "What I mean is that at the beginning he was enthusiastic—flowers, serenades, notes, and things like that—"

Alfredo remembered that period with a wonder not unmixed with shame. That was less than four years ago. He could not understand those months of a great hunger that was not of the body nor yet of the mind, a craving that had seized on him one quiet night when the moon was abroad and under the dappled shadow of the trees in the plaza, man wooed maid. Was he being cheated by life? Love—he seemed to have missed it. Or was the love that others told about a mere fabrication of perfervid imagination, an exaggeration of the commonplace, a glorification of insipid monotonies such as made up his love life? Was love a combination of circumstances, or sheer native capacity of soul? In those days love was, for him, still the eternal puzzle; for love, as he knew it, was a stranger to love as he divined it might be.

Sitting quietly in his room now, he could almost revive the restlessness of those days, the feeling of tumultuous haste, such as he knew so well in his boyhood when something beautiful was going on somewhere and he was trying to get there in time to see. "Hurry, hurry, or you will miss it," someone had seemed to urge in his ears. So he had avidly seized on the shadow of Love and deluded himself for a long while in the way of humanity from time immemorial. In the meantime, he became very much engaged to Esperanza.

Why would men so mismanage their lives? Greed, he thought, was what ruined so many. Greed—the desire to crowd into a moment all the enjoyment it will hold, to squeeze from the hour all the emotion it will yield. Men commit themselves when but half-meaning to do so, sacrificing possible future fullness of ecstasy to the craving for immediate excitement. Greed—mortgaging the future—forcing the hand of Time, or of Fate.

"What do you think happened?" asked Carmen, pursuing her thought.

"I supposed long-engaged people are like that; warm now, cool tomorrow. I think they are oftener cool than warm. The very fact that an engagement has been allowed to prolong itself argues a certain placidity of temperament—or of affection—on the part of either, or both." Don Julian loved to philosophize. He was talking now with an evident relish in words, his resonant, very nasal voice toned down to monologue pitch. "That phase you were speaking of is natural enough for a beginning. Besides, that, as I see it, was Alfredo's last race with escaping youth—"

Carmen laughed aloud at the thought of her brother's perfect physical repose—almost indolence—disturbed in the role suggested by her father's figurative language.

"A last spurt of hot blood," finished the old man.

Few certainly would credit Alfredo Salazar with hot blood. Even his friends had amusedly diagnosed his blood as cool and thin, citing incontrovertible evidence. Tall and slender, he moved with an indolent ease that verged on grace. Under straight recalcitrant hair, a thin face with a satisfying breadth of forehead, slow, dreamer's eyes, and astonishing freshness of lips—indeed Alfredo Salazar's appearance betokened little of exuberant masculinity; rather a poet with wayward humor, a fastidious artist with keen, clear brain.

He rose and quietly went out of the house. He lingered a moment on the stone steps; then went down the path shaded by immature acacias, through the little tarred gate which he left swinging back and forth, now opening, now closing on the gravel road bordered along the farther side by madre cacao hedge in tardy lavender bloom.

The gravel road narrowed as it slanted up to the house on the hill, whose wide, open porches he could glimpse through the heat-shrivelled tamarinds in the Martinez yard.

Six weeks ago that house meant nothing to him save that it was the Martinez house, rented and occupied by Judge del Valle and his family. Six weeks ago Julia Salas meant nothing to him; he did not even know her name; but now—

One evening he had gone "neighboring" with Don Julian; a rare enough occurrence, since he made it a point to avoid all appearance of currying favor with the Judge. This particular evening however, he had allowed himself to be persuaded. "A little mental relaxation now and then is beneficial," the old man had said. "Besides, a judge's good will, you know"; the rest of the thought—"is worth a rising young lawyer's trouble"—Don Julian conveyed through a shrug and a smile that derided his own worldly wisdom.

A young woman had met them at the door. It was evident from the excitement of the Judge's children that she was a recent and very welcome arrival. In the characteristic Filipino way formal introductions had been omitted—the Judge limiting himself to a casual "Ah, ya se conocen?"—with the consequence that Alfredo called her Miss del Valle throughout the evening.

He was puzzled that she should smile with evident delight every time he addressed her thus. Later Don Julian informed him that she was not the Judge's sister, as he had supposed, but his sister-in-law, and that her name was Julia Salas. A very dignified rather austere name, he thought. Still, the young lady should have corrected him. As it was, he was greatly embarrassed, and felt that he should explain.

To his apology, she replied, "That is nothing. Each time I was about to correct you, but I remembered a similar experience I had once before."

"Oh," he drawled out, vastly relieved.

"A man named Manalang—I kept calling him Manalo. After the tenth time or so, the young man rose from his seat and said suddenly, 'Pardon me, but my name is Manalang, Manalang'. You know, I never forgave him!"

He laughed with her.

"The best thing to do under the circumstances, I have found out," she pursued, "is to pretend not to hear, and to let the other person find out his mistake without help."

"As you did this time. Still, you looked amused every time I—"

"I was thinking of Mr. Manalang."

Don Julian and his uncommunicative friend, the Judge, were absorbed in a game of chess. The young man had tired of playing appreciative spectator and desultory conversationalist, so he and Julia Salas had gone off to chat in the vine-covered porch. The lone piano in the neighborhood alternately tinkled and banged away as the player's moods altered. He listened, and wondered irrelevantly if Miss Salas could sing; she had such a charming speaking voice.

He was mildly surprised to note from her appearance that she was unmistakably a sister of the Judge's wife, although Doña Adela was of a different type altogether. She was small and plump, with wide brown eyes, clearly defined eyebrows, and delicately modeled lips—a pretty woman with the complexion of a baby and the expression of a likable cow. Julia was taller, not so obviously pretty. She had the same eyebrows and lips, but she was much darker, of a smooth rich brown with underlying tones of crimson which heightened the impression she gave of abounding vitality.

On Sunday mornings after mass, father and son would go crunching up the gravel road to the house on the hill. The Judge's wife invariably offered them beer, which Don Julian enjoyed and Alfredo did not. After a half hour or so, the chessboard would be brought out; then Alfredo and Julia Salas would go out to the porch to chat. She sat in the low hammock and he in a rocking chair and the hours—warm, quiet March hours—sped by. He enjoyed talking with her and it was evident that she liked his company; yet what feeling there was between them was so undisturbed that it seemed a matter of course. Only when Esperanza chanced to ask him indirectly about those visits did some uneasiness creep into his thoughts of the girl next door.

Esperanza had wanted to know if he went straight home after mass. Alfredo suddenly realized that for several Sundays now he had not waited for Esperanza to come out of the church as he had been wont to do. He had been eager to go "neighboring."

He answered that he went home to work. And, because he was not habitually untruthful, added, "Sometimes I go with Papa to Judge del Valle's."

She dropped the topic. Esperanza was not prone to indulge in unprovoked jealousies. She was a believer in the regenerative virtue of institutions, in their power to regulate feeling as well as conduct. If a man were married, why, of course, he loved his wife; if he were engaged, he could not possibly love another woman.

That half-lie told him what he had not admitted openly to himself; that he was giving Julia Salas something which he was not free to give. He realized that; yet something that would not be denied beckoned imperiously, and he followed on.

It was so easy to forget up there, away from the prying eyes of the world, so easy and so poignantly sweet. The beloved woman, he standing close to her, the shadows around, enfolding.

"Up here I find—something—"

He and Julia Salas stood looking out into the quiet night. Sensing unwanted intensity, she laughed, woman-like, asking, "Amusement?"

"No; youth—its spirit—"

"Are you so old?"

"And heart's desire."

Was he becoming a poet, or is there a poet lurking in the heart of every man?

"Down there," he had continued, his voice somewhat indistinct, "the road is too broad, too trodden by feet, too barren of mystery."

"Down there" beyond the ancient tamarinds lay the road, upturned to the stars. In the darkness the fireflies glimmered, while an errant breeze strayed in from somewhere, bringing elusive, faraway sounds as of voices in a dream.

"Mystery—" she answered lightly, "that is so brief—"

"Not in some," quickly. "Not in you."

"You have known me a few weeks; so the mystery."

"I could study you all my life and still not find it."

"So long?"

"I should like to."

Those six weeks were now so swift-seeming in the memory, yet had they been so deep in the living, so charged with compelling power and sweetness. Because neither the past nor the future had relevance or meaning, he lived only the present, day by day, lived it intensely, with such a willful shutting out of fact as astounded him in his calmer moments.

Just before Holy Week, Don Julian invited the Judge and his family to spend Sunday afternoon at Tanda where he had a coconut plantation and a house on the beach. Carmen also came with her four energetic children. She and Doña Adela spent most of the time indoors directing the preparation of the merienda and discussing the likeable absurdities of their husbands—how Carmen's Vicente was so absorbed in his farms that he would not even take time off to accompany her on this visit to her father; how Doña Adela's Dionisio was the most absentminded of men, sometimes going out without his collar, or with unmatched socks.

After the merienda, Don Julian sauntered off with the Judge to show him what a thriving young coconut looked like—"plenty of leaves,

close set, rich green"—while the children, convoyed by Julia Salas, found unending entertainment in the rippling sand left by the ebbing tide. They were far down, walking at the edge of the water, indistinctly outlined against the gray of the out-curving beach.

Alfredo left his perch on the bamboo ladder of the house and followed. Here were her footsteps, narrow, arched. He laughed at himself for his black canvas footwear which he removed forthwith and tossed high up on dry sand.

When he came up, she flushed, then smiled with frank pleasure.

"I hope you are enjoying this," he said with a questioning inflection.

"Very much. It looks like home to me, except that we do not have such a lovely beach."

There was a breeze from the water. It blew the hair away from her forehead, and whipped the tucked-up skirt around her straight, slender figure. In the picture was something of eager freedom as of wings poised in flight. The girl had grace, distinction. Her face was not notably pretty; yet she had a tantalizing charm, all the more compelling because it was an inner quality, an achievement of the spirit. The lure was there, of naturalness, of an alert vitality of mind and body, of a thoughtful, sunny temper, and of a piquant perverseness which is sauce to charm.

"The afternoon has seemed very short, hasn't it?" Then, "This, I think, is the last time—we can visit."

"The last? Why?"

"Oh, you will be too busy perhaps."

He noted an evasive quality in the answer.

"Do I seem especially industrious to you?"

"If you are, you never look it."

"Not perspiring or breathless, as a busy man ought to be."

"But—"

"Always unhurried, too unhurried, and calm." She smiled to herself.

"I wish that were true," he said after a meditative pause.

She waited.

"A man is happier if he is, as you say, calm and placid."

"Like a carabao in a mud pool," she retorted perversely.

"Who? I?"

"Oh, no!"

"You said I am calm and placid."

"That is what I think."

"I used to think so too. Shows how little we know ourselves."

It was strange to him that he could be wooing thus: with tone and look and covert phrase.

"I should like to see your home town."

"There is nothing to see—little crooked streets, yunut roofs with ferns growing on them, and sometimes squashes."

That was the background. It made her seem less detached, less unrelated, yet withal more distant, as if that background claimed her and excluded him.

"Nothing? There is you."

"Oh, me? But I am here."

"I will not go, of course, until you are there."

"Will you come? You will find it dull. There isn't even one American there!"

"Well—Americans are rather essential to my entertainment."

She laughed.

"We live on Calle Luz, a little street with trees."

"Could I find that?"

"If you don't ask for Miss del Valle," she smiled teasingly.

"I'll inquire about—"

"What?"

"The house of the prettiest girl in the town."

"There is where you will lose your way." Then she turned serious. "Now, that is not quite sincere."

"It is," he averred slowly, but emphatically.

"I thought you, at least, would not say such things."

"Pretty-pretty—a foolish word! But there is none other more handy. I did not mean that quite—"

"Are you withdrawing the compliment?"

"Re-enforcing it, maybe. Something is pretty when it pleases the eye—it is more than that when—"

"If it saddens?" she interrupted hastily.

"Exactly."

"It must be ugly."

"Always?"

Toward the west, the sunlight lay on the dimming waters in a broad, glinting streamer of crimsoned gold.

"No, of course you are right."

"Why did you say this is the last time?" he asked quietly as they turned back.

"I am going home."

The end of an impossible dream!

"When?" after a long silence.

"Tomorrow. I received a letter from Father and Mother yesterday. They want me to spend Holy Week at home."

She seemed to be waiting for him to speak.

"That is why I said this is the last time."

"Can't I come to say good-bye?"

"Oh, you don't need to!"

"No, but I want to."

"There is no time."

The golden streamer was withdrawing, shortening, until it looked no more than a pool far away at the rim of the world. Stillness, a vibrant quiet that affects the senses as does solemn harmony; a peace that is not contentment but a cessation of tumult when all violence of feeling tones down to the wistful serenity of regret. She turned and looked into his face, in her dark eyes a ghost of sunset sadness.

"Home seems so far from here. This is almost like another life."

"I know. This is Elsewhere, and yet strange enough, I cannot get rid of the old things."

"Old things?"

"Oh, old things, mistakes, encumbrances, old baggage." He said it lightly, unwilling to mar the hour. He walked close, his hand sometimes touching hers for one whirling second.

Don Julian's nasal summons came to them on the wind.

Alfredo gripped the soft hand so near his own. At his touch, the girl turned her face away, but he heard her voice say very low, "Good-bye."

II

Alfredo Salazar turned to the right where, farther on, the road broadened and entered the heart of the town—heart of Chinese stores sheltered under low-hung roofs, of indolent drug stores and tailor shops, of dingy shoe-repairing establishments, and a cluttered goldsmith's cubbyhole where a consumptive bent over a magnifying lens; heart of old brick-roofed houses with quaint hand-and-ball knockers on the door; heart of grass-grown plaza reposeful with trees, of ancient church and convento, now circled by swallows gliding in flight as smooth and soft as the afternoon itself.

Into the quickly deepening twilight, the voice of the biggest of the church bells kept ringing its insistent summons. Flocking came the devout with their long wax candles, young women in vivid apparel (for this was Holy Thursday and the Lord was still alive), older women in sober black skirts. Came too the young men in droves, elbowing each other under the talisay tree near the church door.

The gaily decked rice-paper lanterns were again on display while from the windows of the older houses hung colored glass globes, heirlooms from a day when grasspith wicks floating in coconut oil were the chief lighting device.

Soon a double row of lights emerged from the church and uncoiled down the length of the street like a huge jewelled band studded with glittering clusters where the saints' platforms were. Above the measured music rose the untutored voices of the choir, steeped in incense and the acrid fumes of burning wax.

The sight of Esperanza and her mother sedately pacing behind Our Lady of Sorrows suddenly destroyed the illusion of continuity and broke up those lines of light into component individuals. Esperanza stiffened self-consciously, tried to look unaware, and could not.

The line moved on.

Suddenly, Alfredo's slow blood began to beat violently, irregularly. A girl was coming down the line—a girl that was striking, and vividly alive, the woman that could cause violent commotion in his heart, yet had no place in the completed ordering of his life.

Her glance of abstracted devotion fell on him and came to a brief stop.

The line kept moving on, wending its circuitous route away from the church and then back again, where, according to the old proverb, all processions end.

At last Our Lady of Sorrows entered the church, and with her the priest and the choir, whose voices now echoed from the arched ceiling. The bells rang the close of the procession.

A round orange moon, "huge as a winnowing basket," rose lazily into a clear sky, whitening the iron roofs and dimming the lanterns at the windows. Along the still densely shadowed streets the young women with their rear guard of males loitered and, maybe, took the longest way home.

Toward the end of the row of Chinese stores, he caught up with Julia Salas. The crowd had dispersed into the side streets, leaving Calle Real to those who lived farther out. It was past eight, and Esperanza would be expecting him in a little while: yet the thought did not hurry him as he said "Good evening" and fell into step with the girl.

"I had been thinking all this time that you had gone," he said in a voice that was both excited and troubled.

"No, my sister asked me to stay until they are ready to go."

"Oh, is the Judge going?"

"Yes."

The provincial docket had been cleared, and Judge del Valle had been assigned elsewhere. As lawyer—and as lover—Alfredo had found that out long before.

"Mr. Salazar," she broke into his silence, "I wish to congratulate you."

Her tone told him that she had learned, at last. That was inevitable.

"For what?"

"For your approaching wedding."

Some explanation was due her, surely. Yet what could he say that would not offend?

"I should have offered congratulations long before, but you know mere visitors are slow about getting the news," she continued.

He listened not so much to what she said as to the nuances in her voice. He heard nothing to enlighten him, except that she had reverted to the formal tones of early accquaintance. No revelation there; simply the old voice—cool, almost detached from personality, flexible and vibrant, suggesting potentialities of song.

"Are weddings interesting to you?" he finally brought out quietly.

"When they are of friends, yes."

"Would you come if I asked you?"

"When is it going to be?"

"May," he replied briefly, after a long pause.

"May is the month of happines, they say," she said, with what seemed to him a shade of irony.

"They say," slowly, indifferently. "Would you come?"

"Why not?"

"No reason. I am just asking. Then you will?"

"If you will ask me," she said with disdain.

"Then I ask you."

"Then I will be there."

The gravel road lay before them; at the road's end the lighted windows of the house on the hill. There swept over the spirit of Alfredo Salazar a longing so keen that it was pain, a wish that, that house were his, that all the bewilderments of the present were not, and that this woman by his side were his long-wedded wife, returning with him to the peace of home.

"Julita," he said in his slow, thoughtful manner, "did you ever have to choose between something you wanted to do and something you had to do?"

"No!"

"I thought maybe you had had that experience; then you could understand a man who was in such a situation."

"You are fortunate," he pursued when she did not answer.

"Is—is this man sure of what he should do?"

"I don't know, Julita. Perhaps not. But there is a point where a thing escapes us and rushes downward of its own weight, dragging us along. Then it is foolish to ask whether one will or will not, because it no longer depends on him."

"But then why—why—" her muffled voice came. "Oh, what do I know? That is his problem after all."

"Doesn't it—interest you?"

"Why must it? I—I have to say good-bye, Mr. Salazar; we are at the house."

Without lifting her eyes she quickly turned and walked away.

Had the final word been said? He wondered. It had. Yet a feeble flutter of hope trembled in his mind though set against that hope were three years of engagement, a very near wedding, perfect understanding between the parents, his own conscience, and Esperanza herself—Esperanza waiting, Esperanza no longer young, Esperanza the efficient, the literal-minded, the intensely acquisitive.

He looked attentively at her where she sat on the sofa, appraisingly, and with a kind of aversion which he tried to control.

She was one of those fortunate women who have the gift of uniformly acceptable appearance. She never surprised one with unexpected homeliness nor with startling reserves of beauty. At home, in church, on the street, she was always herself, a woman past first bloom, light and clear of complexion, spare of arms and of breast, with a slight convexity to thin throat; a woman dressed with self-conscious care, even elegance; a woman distinctly not average.

She was pursuing an indignant relation about something or other, something about Calixta, their note-carrier, Alfredo perceived, so he merely half-listened, understanding imperfectly. At a pause he drawled out to fill in the gap: "Well, what of it?" The remark sounded ruder than he had intended.

"She is not married to him," Esperanza. insisted in her thin, nervously pitched voice. "Besides, she should have thought of us. Nanay practically brought her up. We never thought she would turn out bad."

What had Calixta done? Homely, middle-aged Calixta?

"You are very positive about her badness," he commented dryly. Esperanza was always positive.

"But do you approve?"

"Of what?"

"What she did."

"No," indifferently.

"Well?"

He was suddenly impelled by a desire to disturb the unvexed orthodoxy of her mind. "All I say is that it is not necessarily wicked."

"Why shouldn't it be? You talked like an—immoral man. I did not know that your ideas were like that."

"My ideas?" he retorted, goaded by a deep, accumulated exasperation. "The only test I wish to apply to conduct is the test of fairness. Am I injuring anybody? No? Then I am justified in my conscience. I am right. Living with a man to whom she is not married—is that it? It may be wrong, and again it may not."

"She has injured us. She was ungrateful." Her voice was tight with resentment.

"The trouble with you. Esperanza, is that you are—" he stopped, appalled by the passion in his voice.

"Why do you get angry? I do not understand you at all! I think I know why you have been indifferent to me lately. I am not blind, or deaf; I see and hear what perhaps some are trying to keep from me." The blood surged into his very eyes and his hearing sharpened to points of acute pain. What would she say next?

"Why don't you speak out frankly before it is too late? You need not think of me and of what people will say." Her voice trembled.

Alfredo was suffering as he could not remember ever having suffered before. What people will say—what will they not say? What

don't they say when long engagements are broken almost on the eve of the wedding?

"Yes," he said hesitatingly, diffidently, as if merely thinking aloud, "one tries to be fair—according to his lights—but it is hard. One would like to be fair to one's self first. But that is too easy, one does not dare—"

"What do you mean?" she asked with repressed violence. "Whatever my shortcomings, and no doubt they are many in your eyes, I have never gone out of my way, of my place, to find a man."

Did she mean by this irrelevant remark that he it was who had sought her; or was that a covert attack on Julia Salas?

"Esperanza—" a desperate plea lay in his stumbling words. "If you—suppose I—" Yet how could a mere man word such a plea?

"If you mean you want to take back your word, if you are tired of—why don't you tell me you are tired of me?" she burst out in a storm of weeping that left him completely shamed and unnerved.

The last word had been said.

III

As Alfredo Salazar leaned against the boat rail to watch the evening settling over the lake, he wondered if Esperanza would attribute any significance to this trip of his. He was supposed to be in Sta. Cruz whither the case of the People of the Philippine Islands vs. Belina et al had kept him, and there he would have been if Brigida Samuy had not been so important to the defense. He had to find that elusive old woman. That the search was leading him to that particular lake town which was Julia Salas' home should not disturb him unduly. Yet he was disturbed to a degree utterly out of proportion to the prosaicalness of his errand. That inner tumult was no surprise to him; in the last eight years he had become used to such occasional storms. He had long realized that he could not forget Julia Salas. Still, he had tried to be content and not to remember too much. The climber of mountains who has known the back-break, the lonesomeness, and the chill, finds a certain restfulness in level paths made easy to his feet. He looks up sometimes from the valley where settles the dusk of evening, but he knows he must not heed the radiant beckoning. Maybe, in time, he would cease even to look up.

He was not unhappy in his marriage. He felt no rebellion: only the calm of capitulation to what he recognized as irresistible forces of circumstance and of character. His life had simply ordered itself; no more struggles, no more stirring up of emotions that got a man nowhere. From his capacity of complete detachment he derived a strange solace. The essential himself, the himself that had its being in the core of his thought, would, he reflected, always be free and alone. When claims encroached too insistently, as sometimes they did, he retreated into the inner fastness, and from that vantage he saw things and people around him as remote and alien, as incidents that did not matter. At such times did Esperanza feel baffled and helpless; he was gentle, even tender, but immeasurably far away, beyond her reach.

Lights were springing into life on the shore. That was the town, a little up-tilted town nestling in the dark greenness of the groves. A snubcrested belfry stood beside the ancient church. On the outskirts the evening smudges glowed red through the sinuous mists of smoke that rose and lost themselves in the purple shadows of the hills. There was a young moon which grew slowly luminous as the coral tints in the sky yielded to the darker blues of evening.

The vessel approached the landing quietly, trailing a wake of long golden ripples on the dark water. Peculiar hill inflections came to his ears from the crowd assembled to meet the boat—slow, singing cadences, characteristic of the Laguna lake-shore speech. From where he stood he could not distinguish faces, so he had no way of knowing whether the presidente was there to meet him or not. Just then a voice shouted.

"Is the abogado there? Abogado!"

"What abogado?" someone irately asked.

That must be the presidente, he thought, and went down to the landing.

It was a policeman, a tall pock-marked individual. The presidente had left with Brigida Samuy—Tandang "Binday"—that noon for Santa Cruz. Señor Salazar's second letter had arrived late, but the wife had read it and said, "Go and meet the abogado and invite him to our house."

Alfredo Salazar courteously declined the invitation. He would sleep on board since the boat would leave at four the next morning anyway. So the presidente had received his first letter? Alfredo did not know because that official had not sent an answer. "Yes," the policeman replied, "but he could not write because we heard that Tandang Binday was in San Antonio so we went there to find her."

San Antonio was up in the hills! Good man, the presidente! He, Alfredo, must do something for him. It was not every day that one met with such willingness to help.

Eight o'clock, lugubriously tolled from the bell tower, found the boat settled into a somnolent quiet. A cot had been brought out and spread for him, but it was too bare to be inviting at that hour. It was too early to sleep: he would walk around the town. His heart beat faster as he picked his way to shore over the rafts made fast to sundry piles driven into the water.

How peaceful the town was! Here and there a little tienda was still open, its dim light issuing forlornly through the single window which served as counter. An occasional couple sauntered by, the women's chinelas making scraping sounds. From a distance came the shrill voices of children playing games on the street—tubigan perhaps, or "hawk-and-chicken." The thought of Julia Salas in that quiet place filled him with a pitying sadness.

How would life seem now if he had married Julia Salas? Had he meant anything to her? That unforgettable red-and-gold afternoon in early April haunted him with a sense of incompleteness as restless as other unlaid ghosts. She had not married—why? Faithfulness, he reflected, was not a conscious effort at regretful memory. It was something unvolitional, maybe a recurrent awareness of irreplaceability. Irrelevant trifles—a cool wind on his forehead, far-away sounds as of voices in a dream—at times moved him to an oddly irresistible impulse to listen as to an insistent, unfinished prayer.

A few inquiries led him to a certain little tree-ceilinged street where the young moon wove indistinct filigrees of light and shadow. In the gardens the cotton tree threw its angular shadow athwart the low stone wall; and in the cool, stilly midnight the cock's first call rose in tall, soaring jets of sound. Calle Luz.

Somehow or other, he had known that he would find her house because she would surely be sitting at the window. Where else, before bedtime on a moonlit night? The house was low and the light in the sala behind her threw her head into unmistakable relief. He sensed rather than saw her start of vivid surprise.

"Good evening," he said, raising his hat.

"Good evening. Oh! Are you in town?"

"On some little business," he answered with a feeling of painful constraint.

"Won't you come up?"

He considered. His vague plans had not included this. But Julia Salas had left the window, calling to her mother as she did so. After a while, someone came downstairs with a lighted candle to open the door. At last—he was shaking her hand.

She had not changed much—a little less slender, not so eagerly alive, yet something had gone. He missed it, sitting opposite her, looking thoughtfully into her fine dark eyes. She asked him about the home town, about this and that, in a sober, somewhat meditative tone. He conversed with increasing ease, though with a growing wonder that he should be there at all. He could not take his eyes from her face. What had she lost? Or was the loss his? He felt an impersonal curiosity creeping into his gaze. The girl must have noticed, for her cheek darkened in a blush.

Gently—was it experimentally?—he pressed her hand at parting; but his own felt undisturbed and emotionless. Did she still care? The answer to the question hardly interested him.

The young moon had set, and from the uninviting cot he could see one half of a star-studded sky.

So that was all over.

Why, had he obstinately clung to that dream?

So all these years—since when?—he had been seeing the light of dead stars, long extinguished, yet seemingly still in their appointed places in the heavens.

An immense sadness as of loss invaded his spirit, a vast homesickness for some immutable refuge of the heart far away where faded gardens bloom again, and where live on in unchanging freshness, the dear, dead loves of vanished youth.

Arturo B. Rotor

ZITA

Turong brought him from Pauambang in his small sailboat, for the coastwise steamer did not stop at any little island of broken cliffs and coconut palms. It was almost midday; they had been standing in that white glare where the tiniest pebble and fluted conch had become points of light, piercing-bright—the municipal president, the parish priest, Don Eliodoro who owned almost all the coconuts, the herb doctor, the village character. Their mild surprise over when he spoke in their native dialect, they looked at him more closely and his easy manner did not deceive them. His head was uncovered and he had a way of bringing the back of his hand to his brow or mouth; they read behind that too, it was not a gesture of protection. "An exile has come to Anayat... and he is so young, so young." So young and lonely and sufficient unto himself. There was no mistaking the stamp of a strong decision on that brow, the brow of those who have to be cold and haughty, those shoulders stooped slightly, less from the burden that they bore than from a carefully cultivated air of unconcern; no common school-teacher could dress so carelessly and not appear shoddy.

They had prepared a room for him in Don Eliodoro's house so that he would not have to walk far to school every morning, but he gave nothing more than a glance at the big stone building with its Spanish azotea, its arched doorways, its flagged courtyard. He chose instead Turong's home, a shaky hut near the sea. Was the sea rough and dangerous at times? He did not mind it. Was the place far from the church and the schoolhouse? The walk would do him good. Would he not feel lonely with nobody but an illiterate fisherman for a companion? He was used to living alone. And they let him do as he wanted, for the old men knew that it was not so much the nearness of the sea that he desired as its silence so that he might tell it secrets he could not tell anyone else.

They thought of nobody but him; they talked about him in the barber shop, in the cockpit, in the sari-sari store, the way he walked, the way he looked at you, his unruly hair. They dressed him in purple and linen, in myth and mystery, put him astride a black stallion, at the wheel of a blue automobile. Mr. Reteche? Mr. Reteche! The name suggested the fantasy and the glitter of a place and people they never would see; he was the scion of a powerful family, a poet and artist, a prince.

That night, Don Eliodoro had the story from his daughter of his first day in the classroom; she perched wide-eyed, low-voiced, short of breath on the arm of his chair.

"He strode into the room, very tall and

serious and polite, stood in front of us and looked at us all over and yet did not seem to see us.

" 'Good morning, teacher,' we said timidly.

"He bowed as if we were his equals. He asked for the list of our names and as he read off each one we looked at him long. When he came to my name, Father, the most surprising thing happened. He started pronouncing it and then he stopped as if he had forgotten something and just stared and stared at the paper in his hand. I heard my name repeated three times through his half-closed lips, 'Zita. Zita. Zita.'

" 'Yes sir, I am Zita.'

"He looked at me uncomprehendingly, inarticulate, and it seemed to me, Father, it actually seemed that he was begging me to tell him that that was not my name, that I was deceiving him. He looked so miserable and sick I felt like sinking down or running away.

" 'Zita is not your name; it is just a pet name, no?'

" 'My father has always called me that, sir.'

" 'It can't be; maybe it is Pacita or Luisa or—'

"His voice was scarcely above a whisper, Father, and all the while he looked at me begging, begging. I shook my head determinedly. My answer must have angered him. He must have thought I was very hard-headed, for he said, 'A thousand miles, Mother of Mercy... it is not possible.' He kept on looking at me; he was hurt perhaps that he should have such a stubborn pupil. But I am not really so, Father?"

"Yes, you are, my dear. But you must try to please him, he is a gentleman; he comes from the City. I was thinking... Private lessons, perhaps, if he won't ask too much." Don Eliodoro had his dreams and she was his only daughter.

Turong had his own story to tell in the barber shop that night, a story as vividly etched as the lone coconut palm in front of the shop that shot up straight into the darkness of the night, as vaguely disturbing as the secrets that the sea whispered into the night.

"He did not sleep a wink, I am sure of it. When I came from the market the stars were already out and I saw that he had not touched the food I had prepared. I asked him to eat and he said he was not hungry. He sat by the window that faces the sea and just looked out hour after hour. I woke up three times during the night and saw that he had not so much as changed his position. I thought once that he was asleep and came near, but he motioned me away. When I awoke at dawn to prepare the nets, he was still there."

"Maybe he wants to go home already." They looked up with concern.

"He is sick. You remember Father Fernando? He had a way of looking like that, into space, seeing nobody, just before he died."

Every month there was a letter that came for him, sometimes two or three; large, blue envelopes with a gold design in the upper left hand corner, and addressed in broad, angular, sweeping handwriting. One time Turong brought one of them to him in the classroom. The students were busy writing a composition on a subject that he had given them, "The Things That I Love Most." Carelessly he had opened the letter, carelessly read it, and carelessly tossed it aside. Zita was all aflutter when the students handed in their work for he had promised that he would read aloud the best. He went over the pile two times, and once again, absently, a deep frown on his brow, as if he were displeased with their work. Then he stopped and picked up one. Her heart sank when she saw that it was not hers, she hardly heard him reading:

"I did not know any better. Moths are not supposed to know; they only come to the light. And the light looked so inviting, there was no resisting it. Moths are not supposed to know, one does not even know one is a moth until one's wings are burned."

It was incomprehensible, no beginning, no end. It did not have unity, coherence, emphasis. Why did he choose that one? What did he see in it? And she had worked so hard, she had wanted to please, she had written about the flowers that she loved most. Who could have written what he had read aloud? She did not know that any of her classmates could write so, use such words, sentences, use a blue paper to write her lessons on.

But then there was little in Mr. Reteche that the young people there could understand. Even his words were so difficult, just like those dark and dismaying things that they came across in their readers, which took them hour after hour in the dictionary. She had learned like a good student to pick out the words she did not recognize, writing them down as she heard them, but it was a thankless task. She had a whole notebook filled now, two columns to each page:

esurient .... greedy.
amaranth .... a flower that never fades.
peacock .... a large bird with lovely
gold and green feathers.
mirash ....

The last word was not in the dictionary.

And what did such things as original sin, selfishness insatiable, actress of a thousand faces mean, and who were Sirse, Lorelay, other names she could not find anywhere? She meant to ask him someday, someday when his eyes were kinder.

He never went to church, but then, that always went with learning and education, did it not? One night Bue saw him coming out of the dim doorway. He watched again and the following night he saw him again. They would not believe it, they must see it with their own eyes and so they came. He did not go in every night, but he could be seen at the most unusual hours, sometimes at dusk, sometimes at dawn, once when it was storming and the lightning etched ragged paths from heaven to earth. Sometimes he stayed for a few minutes, sometimes he came twice or thrice in one evening. They reported it to Father Cesareo but it seemed that he already knew. "Let a peaceful man alone in his prayers." The answer had surprised them.

The sky hangs over Anayat, in the middle of the Anayat Sea, like an inverted wineglass, a glass whose wine had been spilled, a purple wine of which Anayat was the last precious drop. For that is Anayat in the crepuscule, purple and mellow, sparkling and warm and effulgent when there is a moon, cool and heady and sensuous when there is no moon.

One may drink of it and forget what lies beyond a thousand miles, beyond a thousand years; one may sip it at the top of a jagged cliff, nearer peace, nearer God, where one can see the ocean dashing against the rocks in eternal frustration, more moving, more terrible than man's; or touch it to his lips in the lush shadows of the dama de noche, its blossoms iridescent like a thousand fireflies, its bouquet the fragrance of flowers that know no fading.

Zita sat by her open window, half asleep, half dreaming. Francisco B. Reteche; what a name! What could his nickname be. Paking, Frank, Pa.... The night lay silent and expectant, a fairy princess waiting for the whispered words of a lover. She was not a bit sleepy; already she had counted three stars that had fallen to earth, one almost directly into that bush of dama de noche at their garden gate, where it had lighted the lamps of a thousand fireflies. He was not so forbidding now, he spoke less frequently to himself, more frequently to her; his eyes were still unseeing, but now they rested on her. She loved to remember those moments she had caught him looking when he thought she did not know. The knowledge came keenly, bitingly, like the sea breeze at dawn, like the prick of the rose's thorn, or—yes, like the purple liquid that her father gave the visitors during pintakasi which made them red and noisy. She had stolen a few drops one day, because she wanted to know, to taste, and that little sip had made her head whirl.

Suddenly she stiffened; a shadow had emerged from the shrubs and had been lost in the other shadows. Her pulses raced, she strained forward. Was she dreaming? Who was it? A lost soul, an unvoiced thought, the shadow of a shadow, the prince from his tryst with the fairy princess? What were the words that he whispered to her?

They who have been young once say that only youth can make youth forget itself; that life is a river bed; the water passes over it, sometimes it encounters obstacles and cannot go on, sometimes it flows unencumbered with a song in every bubble and ripple, but always it goes forward. When its way is obstructed it burrows deeply or swerves aside and leaves its impression, and whether the impress will be shallow and transient, or deep and searing, only God determines. The people remembered the day when he went up Don Eliodoro's house, the light of a great decision in his eyes, and finally accepted the father's request that he teach his daughter "to be a lady."

"We are going to the City soon, after the next harvest perhaps; I want her not to feel like a 'Provinciana' when we get there."

They remembered the time when his walks by the seashore became less solitary, for now of afternoons, he would draw the whole crowd of village boys from their game of leapfrog or patintero and bring them with him. And they would go home hours after sunset with the wonderful things that Mr. Reteche had told them, why the sea is green, the sky blue, what one who is strong and fearless might find at that exact place where the sky meets the sea. They would be flushed and happy and bright-eyed, for he could stand on his head longer than any of them, catch more crabs, send a pebble skimming over the breast of Anayat Bay farthest.

Turong still remembered those ominous, terrifying nights when he had got up cold and trembling to listen to the aching groan of the bamboo floor, as somebody in the other room restlessly paced to and fro. And his pupils still remember those mornings he received their flowers, the camia which had fainted away at her own fragrance, the kampupot, with the night dew still trembling in its heart; receive them with a smile and forget the lessons of the day and tell them all about those princesses and fairies who dwelt in flowers; why the dama de noche must have the darkness of the night to bring out its fragrance; how the petals

of the ylang-ylang, crushed and soaked in some liquid, would one day touch the lips of some wondrous creature in some faraway land whose eyes were blue and hair golden.

Those were days of surprises for Zita. Box after box came in Turong's sailboat and each time they contained things that took the words from her lips. Silk as sheer and perishable as gossamer, or heavy and sheeny and tinted like the sunset sky; slippers with bright stones which twinkled with the least movement of her feet; a necklace of green, flat, polished stone, whose feel against her throat sent a curious choking sensation there; perfume that she must touch her lips with. If only there would always be such things in Turong's sailboat, and none of those horrid blue envelopes that he always brought. And yet—the Virgin have pity on her selfish soul—suppose one day Turong brought not only those letters but the writer as well? She shuddered, not because she feared it but because she knew it would be.

"Why are these dresses so tight fitting?" Her father wanted to know.

"In society, women use clothes to reveal, not to hide." Was that a sneer or a smile in his eyes? The gown showed her arms and shoulders and she had never known how round and fair they were, how they could express so many things.

"Why do these dresses have such bright colors?"

"Because the peacock has bright feathers."

"They paint their lips...."

"So that they can smile when they do not want to."

"And their eyelashes are long."

"To hide deception."

He was not pleased like her father; she saw it, he had turned his face toward the window. And as she came nearer, swaying like a lily atop its stalk, she heard the harsh, muttered words:

"One would think she'd feel shy or uncomfortable, but no... oh no... not a bit... all alike... comes naturally."

There were books to read; pictures, names

to learn; lessons in everything; how to polish the nails, how to use a fan, even how to walk. How did these days come, how did they go? What does one do when one is so happy, so breathless? Sometimes they were a memory, sometimes a dream.

"Look, Zita, a society girl does not smile so openly; her eyes don't seek one's so—that reveals your true feelings."

"But if I am glad and happy and I want to show it?"

"Don't. If you must show it by smiling, let your eyes be mocking; if you would invite with your eyes, repulse with your lips."

That was a memory.

She was in a great drawing room whose floor was so polished it reflected the myriad red and green and blue lights above, the arches of flowers and ribbons and streamers. All the great names of the capital were there, stately ladies in wonderful gowns who walked so, waved their fans so, who said one thing with their eyes and another with their lips. And she was among them and every young and good-looking man wanted to dance with her. They were all so clever and charming but she answered: "Please, I am tired." For beyond them she had seen him alone, he whose eyes were dark and brooding and disapproving and she was waiting for him to take her.

That was a dream. Sometimes though, she could not tell so easily which was the dream and which the memory.

If only those letters would not bother him now, he might be happy and at peace. True he never answered them, but every time Turong brought him one, he would still become thoughtful and distracted. Like that time he was teaching her a dance, a Spanish dance, he said, and had told her to dress accordingly. Her heavy hair hung in a big, carelessly tied knot that always threatened to come loose but never did; its dark, deep shadows showing off in startling vividness how red a rose can be, how like velvet its petals. Her earrings—two circlets of precious stones, red like the pigeon's blood—almost touched her shoulders. The heavy Spanish shawl gave her the

most trouble—she had nothing to help her but some pictures and magazines—she could not put it on just as she wanted. Like this, it revealed her shoulder too much; that way, it hampered the free movement of the legs. But she had done her best; for hours she had stood before her mirror and for hours it had told her that she was beautiful, that red lips and tragic eyes were becoming to her.

She'd never forget that look on his face when she came out. It was not surprise, joy, admiration. It was as if he saw somebody there whom he was expecting, for whom he had waited, prayed.

"Zita!" It was a cry of recognition.

She blushed even under her rouge when he took her in his arms and taught her to step this way, glide so, turn about; she looked half questioningly at her father for disapproval, but she saw that there was nothing there but admiration too. Mr. Reteche seemed so serious and so intent that she should learn quickly; but he did not deceive her, for once she happened to lean close and she felt how wildly his heart was beating. It frightened her and she drew away, but when she saw how unconcerned he seemed, as if he did not even know that she was in his arms, she smiled knowingly and drew close again. Dreamily she closed her eyes and dimly wondered if his were shut too, whether he was thinking the same thoughts, breathing the same prayer.

Turong came up and after his respectful "Good evening" he handed an envelope to the school teacher. It was large and blue and had a gold design in one corner; the handwriting was broad, angular, sweeping.

"Thank you, Turong." His voice was drawling, heavy, the voice of one who has just awakened. With one movement he tore the unopened envelope slowly, unconsciously, it seemed to her, to pieces.

"I thought I had forgotten," he murmured dully.

That changed the whole evening. His eyes lost their sparkle, his gaze wandered from time to time. Something powerful and dark had come between them, something which shut out the light, brought in a chill. The tears came to her eyes for she felt utterly powerless. When her sight cleared she saw that he was sitting down and trying to piece the letter together.

"Why do you tear up a letter if you must put it together again?" rebelliously.

He looked at her kindly. "Someday, Zita, you will do it too, and then you will understand."

One day Turong came from Pauambang and this time he brought a stranger. They knew at once that he came from where the teacher came—his clothes, his features, his politeness—and that he had come for the teacher. This one did not speak their dialect, and as he was led through the dusty, crooked streets, he kept forever wiping his face, gazing at the wobbly, thatched huts and muttering short, vehement phrases to himself. Zita heard his knock before Mr. Reteche did and she knew what he had come for. She must have been as pale as her teacher, as shaken, as rebellious. And yet the stranger was so cordial; there was nothing but gladness in his greeting, gladness at meeting an old friend. How strong he was; even at that moment he did not forget himself, but turned to his class and dismissed them for the day.

The door was thick and she did not dare lean against the jamb too much, so sometimes their voices floated away before they reached her.

"... like children ... making yourselves ... so unhappy."

"... happiness? Her idea of happiness ..."

Mr. Reteche's voice was more low-pitched, hoarse, so that it didn't carry at all. She shuddered as he laughed, it was that way when he first came.

"She's been ... did not mean ... understand."

"... learning to forget ..."

There were periods when they both became excited and talked fast and hard; she heard somebody's restless pacing, somebody sitting down heavily.

"I never realized what she meant to me until I began trying to seek from others what she would not give me."

She knew what was coming now, knew it before the stranger asked the question:

"Tomorrow?"

She fled; she could not wait for the answer.

He did not sleep that night, she knew he did not, she told herself fiercely. And it was not only his preparations that kept him awake, she knew it, she knew it. With the first flicker of light she ran to her mirror. She must not show her feeling, it was not in good form, she must manage somehow. If her lips quivered, her eyes must smile, if in her eyes there were tears.... She heard her father go out, but she did not go; although she knew his purpose, she had more important things to do. Little boys came up to the house and she wiped away their tears and told them that he was coming back, coming back, soon, soon.

The minutes flew, she was almost done now; her lips were red and her eyebrows penciled; the crimson shawl thrown over her shoulders just right. Everything must be like that day he had first seen her in a Spanish dress. Still he did not come, he must be bidding farewell now to Father Cesareo; now he was in Doña Ramona's house; now he was shaking the barber's hand. He would soon be through and come to her house. She glanced at the mirror and decided that her lips were not red enough; she put on more color. The rose in her hair had too long a stem; she tried to trim it with her fingers and a thorn dug deeply into her flesh.

Who knows? Perhaps they would soon meet again in the City; she wondered if she could not wheedle her father into going earlier. But she must know now what were the words he had wanted to whisper that night under the dama de noche, what he had wanted to say that day he held her in his arms; other things, questions whose answers she knew. She smiled. How well she knew them!

The big house was silent as death; the little village seemed deserted, everybody had gone to the seashore. Again she looked at the mirror. She was too pale, she must put on more rouge. She tried to keep from counting the minutes, the seconds, from getting up and pacing. But she was getting chilly and she must do it to keep warm.

The steps creaked. She bit her lips to stifle a wild cry there. The door opened.

"Turong!"

"Mr. Reteche bade me give you this. He said you would understand."

In one bound she had reached the open window. But dimly, for the sun was too bright, or was her sight failing?—she saw a blur of white moving out to sea, then disappearing behind a point of land so that she could no longer follow it; and then, clearly against a horizon suddenly drawn out of perspective, "Mr. Reteche," tall, lean, brooding, looking at her with eyes that told her somebody had hurt him. It was like that when he first came,

and now he was gone. The tears came freely now. What matter, what matter? There was nobody to see and criticize her breeding. They came down unchecked and when she tried to brush them off with her hand, the color came away too from her cheeks, leaving them bloodless, cold. Sometimes they got into her mouth and they tasted bitter.

Her hands worked convulsively; there was a sound of tearing paper, once, twice. She became suddenly aware of what she had done when she looked at the pieces, wet and brightly stained with uneven streaks of red. Slowly, painfully, she tried to put the pieces together and as she did so a sob escaped deep from her breast—a great understanding had come to her.

Loreto Paras Sulit

HARVEST

He first saw her in his brother's eyes. The palay stalks were taking on gold in the late afternoon sun, were losing their trampled, wind-swept look and stirring into little, almost inaudible whispers.

The rhythm of Fabian's strokes was smooth and unbroken. So many palay stalks had to be harvested before sundown and there was no time to be lost in idle dallying. But when he stopped to heap up the fallen palay stalks he glanced at his brother as if to fathom the other's state of mind in that one, side-long glance.

The swing of Vidal's figure was as graceful as the downward curve of the crescent-shaped scythe. How stubborn, this younger brother of his, how hard-headed, fumed Fabian as he felled stalk after stalk. It is because he knows how very good-looking he is, how he is so much run-after by all the women in town. The obstinate, young fool! With his queer dreams, his strange adorations, his wistfulness for a life not of these fields, not of their quiet, colorless women and the dullness of long nights of unbroken silence and sleep. But he would bend . . . he must bend . . . one of these days.

Vidal stopped in his work to wipe off the heavy sweat from his brow. He wondered how his brother could work that fast all day without pausing to rest, without slowing in the rapidity of his strokes. But that was the reason the master would not let him go; he could harvest a field in a morning that would require three men to finish in a day. He had always been afraid of this older brother of his; there was something terrible in the way he determined things, how he always brought them to pass, how he disregarded the soft and the beautiful in his life and sometimes how he crushed, trampled people, things he wanted destroyed. There were flowers, insects, birds of boyhood memories, what Fabian had done to them. There was Tinay . . . she did not truly like him, but her widowed mother had some lands. . . . he won and married Tinay.

I wonder what can touch him. Vidal thought of miracles, perhaps a vision, a woman . . . But no . . . he would overpower them . . . he was so strong with those arms of steel, those huge arms of his that could throttle a spirited horse into obedience.

"Harvest time is almost ended, Vidal." (I must be strong also, the other prayed). "Soon the planting season will be on us and we shall have need of many carabaos. Milia's father has five. You have but to ask her and Milia will accept you any time. Why do you delay . . ."

He stopped in surprise for his brother had sprung up so suddenly and from the look on his face it was as if a shining glory was smiling shyly, tremulously in that adoring way of his that called forth all the boyishness of his nature. There was the slow crunch, crunch of footsteps on dried soil and Fabian sensed the presence of people behind him. Vidal had taken off his wide, buri hat and was twisting and untwisting it nervously.

"Ah, it is my model! How are you, Vidal?" It was a voice too deep and throaty for a woman but beneath it one could detect a gentle, smooth nuance, soft as silk. It affected Fabian very queerly, he could feel his muscles tensing as he waited for her to speak again. But he did not stop in work nor turn to look at her.

She was talking to Vidal about things he had no idea of. He could not understand why the sound of her voice filled him with this resentment that was increasing with every passing minute. She was so near him that when she gestured perhaps as she spoke, the silken folds of her dress brushed against him slightly, and her perfume, a very subtle fragrance, was cool and scented in the air about him.

"From now on he must work for me every morning, possibly all day."

"Very well. Everything as you please." So it was the master who was with her.

"He is your brother, you say, Vidal? Oh, your elder brother." The curiosity in her voice must be in her eyes. "He has very splendid arms."

Then Fabian turned to look at her.

He had never seen anyone like her. She was tall, with a regal unconscious assurance in her figure that she carried so well, and pale as though she had just recovered from a recent illness. She was not exactly very young nor very beautiful. But there was something disquieting and haunting in the unsymmetry of her features, in the queer reflection of the dark blue-blackness of her hair, in her eyes, in that mole just above her nether lips, that tinged her whole face with a strange loveliness. For, yes, she was indeed beautiful. One discovered it after a second, careful glance. Then the whole plan of the brow and lip and eye was revealed; one realized that her pallor was the ivory-white of rice grain just husked,

that the sinuous folds of silken lines were but the undertones of the grace that flowed from her as she walked away from you.

The blood rushed hot to his very eyes and ears as he met her grave, searching look that swept him from head to foot. She approached him and examined his hot, moist arms critically.

"How splendid! How splendid!" she kept on murmuring.

Then "Thank you," and taking and leaning on the arm of the master she walked slowly away.

The two brothers returned to their work but to the very end of the day did not exchange a word. Once Vidal attempted to whistle but gave it up after a few bars. When sundown came they stopped harvesting and started on their way home. They walked with difficulty on the dried rice paddies till they reached the end of the rice fields.

The stillness, the peace of the twilit landscape was maddening to Fabian. It augmented the spell of that woman that was still over him. It was queer how he kept on thinking about her, on remembering the scent of her perfume, the brush of her dress against him and the look of her eyes on his arms. If he had been in bed he would be tossing painfully, feverishly. Why was her face always before him as though it were always focused somewhere in the distance and he was forever walking up to it?

A large moth with mottled, highly colored wings fluttered blindly against the bough, its long, feathery antennae quivering sensitively in the air. Vidal paused to pick it up, but before he could do so his brother had hit it with the bundle of palay stalks he carried. The moth fell to the ground, a mass of broken wings, of fluttering wing-dust.

After they had walked a distance, Vidal asked, "Why are you that way?"

"What is my way?"

"That—that way of destroying things that are beautiful like moths ... like ..."

"If the dust from the wings of a moth should get into your eyes, you would be blind."

"That is not the reason."

"Things that are beautiful have a way of hurting. I destroy it when I feel a hurt."

To avoid the painful silence that would surely ensue Vidal talked on whatever subject entered his mind. But gradually, slowly the topics converged into one. He found himself talking about the woman who come to them this afternoon in the fields. She was a relative of the master. A cousin, I think. They call her Miss Francia. But I know she has a lovely, hidden name . . . like her beauty. She is convalescing from a very serious illness she has had and to pass the time she makes men out of clay, of stone. Sometimes she uses her fingers, sometimes a chisel.

One day Vidal came into the house with a message for the master. She saw him. He was just the model for a figure she was working on; she had asked him to pose for her.

"Brother, her loveliness is one I cannot understand. When one talks to her forever so long in the patio, many dreams, many desires come to me. I am lost . . . I am glad to be lost."

It was merciful the darkness was up on the fields. Fabian could not see his brother's face. But it was cruel that the darkness was heavy and without end except where it reached the little, faint star. For in the deep darkness, he saw her face clearly and understood his brother.

On the batalan of his home, two tall clay jars were full of water. He emptied one on his feet, he cooled his warm face and bathed his arms in the other. The light from the kerosene lamp within came in wisps into the batalan. In the meager light he looked at his arms to discover where their splendor lay. He rubbed them with a large, smooth pebble till they glowed warm and rich brown. Gently he felt his own muscles, the strength, the power beneath. His wife was crooning to the baby inside. He started guiltily and entered the house.

Supper was already set on the table. Tinay would not eat; she could not leave the baby, she said. She was a small, nervous woman still with the lingering prettiness of her youth. She was rocking a baby in a swing made of a blanket tied at both ends to ropes hanging from the ceiling. Trining, his other child, a girl of four, was in a corner playing siklot solemnly all by herself.

Everything seemed a dream, a large spreading dream. This little room with all the people inside, faces, faces in a dream. That woman in the fields, this afternoon, a colored, past dream by now. But the unrest, the fever she had left behind . . . was still on him. He turned almost savagely on his brother and spoke to break these two grotesque, dream bubbles of his life. "When I was your age, Vidal, I was already married. It is high time you should be settling down. There is Milia."

"I have no desire to marry her nor anybody else. Just—just—for five carabaos." There! He had spoken out at last. What a relief it was. But he did not like the way his brother pursed his lips tightly. That boded not defeat. Vidal rose, stretching himself luxuriously. On the door of the silid where he slept he paused to watch his little niece. As she threw a pebble into the air he caught it and would not give it up. She pinched, bit, shook his pants furiously while he laughed in great amusement.

"What a very pretty woman Trining is going to be. Look at her skin; white as rice grains just husked; and her nose, what a high bridge. Ah, she is going to be a proud lady . . . and what deep, dark eyes. Let me see, let me see. Why, you have a little mole on your lips. That means you are very talkative."

"You will wake up the baby. Vidal! Vidal!" Tinay rocked the child almost despairingly. But the young man would not have stopped his teasing if Fabian had not called Trining to his side.

"Why does she not braid her hair?" he asked his wife.

"Oh, but she is so pretty with her curls free that way about her head."

"We shall have to trim her head. I will do it before going out to work tomorrow."

Vidal bit his lips in anger. Sometimes. . . . well, it was not his child anyway. He retired to his room and fell in a deep sleep unbroken till after dawn when the sobs of a child awakened him. Peering between the bamboo slats of the floor he could see dark curls falling from a child's head to the ground.

He avoided his brother from that morning. For one thing he did not want repetitions of the carabao question with Milia to boot. For another there was the glorious world and new life opened to him by his work in the master's house. The glamour, the enchantment of hour after hour spent on the shadow-flecked ylang-ylang scented patio where she molded, shaped, reshaped many kinds of men, who all had his face from the clay she worked on.

In the evening after supper he stood by the window and told the tale of that day to a very quiet group. And he brought that look, that was more than a gleam of a voice made weak by strong, deep emotions.

His brother saw and understood. Fury was a high flame in his heart . . . If that look, that quiver of voice had been a moth, a curl on the dark head of his daughter . . . Now more than ever he was determined to have Milia in his home as his brother's wife . . . that would come to pass. Someday, that look, that quiver would become a moth in his hands, a frail, helpless moth.

When Vidal, one night, broke out the news Fabian knew he had to act at once. Miss Francia would leave within two days; she wanted Vidal to go to the city with her, where she would finish the figures she was working on.

"She will pay me more than I can earn here, and help me get a position there. And shall always be near her. Oh, I am going! I am going!"

"And live the life of a—a servant?"

"What of that? I shall be near her always."

"Why do you wish to be near her?"

"Why? Why? Oh, my God! Why?"

That sentence rang and resounded and vibrated in Fabian's ears during the days that followed. He had seen her closely only once and only glimpses thereafter. But the song of loveliness had haunted his life thereafter. If by a magic transfusing he, Fabian, could be Vidal

and . . . and . . . how one's thoughts can make one forget of the world. There she was at work on a figure that represented a reaper who had paused to wipe off the heavy sweat from his brow. It was Vidal in stone.

Again—as it ever would be—the disquieting nature of her loveliness was on him so that all his body tensed and flexed as he gathered in at a glance all the marvel of her beauty.

She smiled graciously at him while he made known himself; he did not expect she would remember him.

"Ah, the man with the splendid arms."

"I am the brother of Vidal." He had not forgotten to roll up his sleeves.

He did not know how he worded his thoughts, but he succeeded in making her understand that Vidal could not possibly go with her, that he had to stay behind in the fields.

There was an amusement rippling beneath her tones. "To marry the girl whose father has five carabaos. You see, Vidal told me about it."

He flushed again a painful brick-red; even to his eyes he felt the hot blood flow.

"That is the only reason to cover up something that would not be known. My brother has wronged this girl. There will be a child."

She said nothing, but the look in her face protested against what she had heard. It said, it was not so.

But she merely answered, "I understand. He shall not go with me." She called a servant, gave him a twenty-peso bill and some instruction. "Vidal, is he at your house?" The brother on the patio nodded.

Now they were alone again. After this afternoon he would never see her, she would never know. But what had she to know? A pang without a voice, a dream without a plan . . . how could they be understood in words.

"Your brother should never know you have told me the real reason why he should not go with me. It would hurt him, I know."

"I have to finish this statue before I leave. The arms are still incomplete. Would it be too much to ask you to pose for just a little while?"

While she smoothed the clay, patted it and molded the vein, muscle, arm, stole the firmness, the strength, of his arms to give to this lifeless statue, it seemed as if life left him, left his arms that were being copied. She was lost in her work and noticed neither the twilight stealing into the patio nor the silence brooding over them.

Wrapped in that silver-grey dusk of early night and silence she appeared in her true light to the man who watched her every movement. She was one he had glimpsed and crushed all his life, the shining glory in moth and flower and eyes he had never understood because it hurt with its unearthly radiance.

If he could have the whole of her in the cup of his hands, drink of her strange loveliness, forgetful of this unrest he called life, if . . . but his arms had already found their duplicate in the white clay beyond . . .

When Fabian returned Vidal was at the batalan brooding over a crumpled twenty-peso bill in his hands. The haggard tired look in his young eyes was as grey as the skies above.

He was speaking to Tinay jokingly. "Soon all your sampaguitas and camias will be gone, my dear sister-in-law because I shall be seeing Milia every night . . . and her father." He watched Fabian cleansing his face and arms and later wondered why it took his brother that long to wash his arms, why he was rubbing them as hard as that . . .

Paz Latorena

DESIRE

She was homely. A very broad forehead gave her face an unplesant, masculine look. Her eyes, which were small, slanted at the corners and made many of her acquaintances wonder if perchance she had a few drops of celestial blood in her veins. Her nose was broad and flat, and its nostrils were always dilated, as if breathing were an effort. Her mouth, with its thick lips, was a long, straight gash across her face made angular by her unusually big jaws.

But Nature, as if ashamed of her meanness in fashioning the face, moulded a body of unusual beauty. From her neck to her small feet, she was perfect. Her bust was full, and her breast rose up like twin roses in full bloom. Her waist was slim as a young girl's her hips seemed to have stolen the curve of the crescent moon. Her arms were shapely, ending in small hands with fine, tapering fingers that were the envy of her friends. Her legs with their trim ankles reminded one of those lifeless things seen in shop windows displaying the latest silk stockings.

Hers was a body a sculptor, athirst for glory, might have dreamt of and moulded in a feverish frenzy of creation, with hands atremble with a vision of the fame in store for him. Hers was a body that might have been the delight and despair of a painter whose faltering brush tried in vain to depict on the canvas such a beautiful harmony of curves and lines. Hers was a body a poet might have raved over and immortalized in musical, fanciful verses. Hers was a body men would gladly have gone to hell for.

And they did. Men looked at her face and turned their eyes away; they look at her body and were enslaved. They forgot the broad masculine forehead, the small eyes that slanted at the corners, the unpleasant mouth, the aggressive jaws. All they had eyes for was that body, those hips that had stolen the curve of the crescent moon.

But she hated her body—hated that gift which Nature, in a fit of remorse for the wrong done to her face, had given her. She hated her body because it made men look at her with an unbeautiful light in their eyes—married eyes, single eyes.

She wanted love, was starved for it. But she did not want the love that her body inspired in men. She wanted something purer... cleaner.

She was disgusted. And hurt. For men told other women that they loved them looking into their eyes to the souls beneath, their voices low and soft, their hands quivering with the weight of their tenderness. But men told her that they loved her body with eyes that made her feel as if she were naked, stripped bare for their sinful eyes to gaze upon. They told her that with voices made thick by desire, touched her with hands afire, that seared her flesh, filling her with scorn and loathing.

She wanted to be loved as other women were loved. She was as good, as pure as they. And some of them were as homely as she was. But they did not have beautiful bodies. And so they were loved for themselves.

Deliberately she set out to hide from the eyes of men the beautiful body that to her was a curse rather than a blessing. She started wearing long, wide dresses that completely disfigured her. She gave up wearing the Filipino costume which outlined her body with startling accuracy.

It took quite a time to make men forget that body that had once been their delight. But after a time they became accustomed to the disfiguring dresses and concluded she had become fat and shapeless. She accomplished the desired result.

And more. For there came a time when men looked at her and turned their eyes away, not with the unbeautiful light of former day but with something akin to pity mirrored there—pity for a homely face and a shapeless mass of flesh.

At first she was glad. Glad that she had succeeded in extinguishing that unbeautiful light in the eyes of men when they looked at her.

After some time, she became rebellious. For she was a woman and she wanted to be loved and to love. But it seemed that men would not have anything to do with a woman with a homely face and an apparently shapeless mass of flesh.

But she became reconciled to her fate. And rather than bring back that unbeautiful light in men's eyes, she chose to go on . . . with the farce.

She turned to writing to while away the long nights spent brooding all alone.

Little things. Little lyrics. Little sketches. Sometimes they were the heart-throbs of a woman who wanted love and sweet things whispered to her in the dark. Sometimes they were the ironies of one who sees all the weaknesses and stupidities of men and the world through eyes made bitter by loneliness.

She sent them to papers which found the little things acceptable and published them. "To fill space," she told herself. But she continued to write because it made her forget once in a while how drab her life was.

And then he came into her life—a man with white blood in his veins. He was one of those who believed in the inferiority of colored races. But he found something unusual in the light, ironic tirades from the pen of the unknown writer. Not in the little lyrics. No, he thought that those were superfluous effusions of a woman belonging to a race of people who could not think of writing about anything except love. But he liked the light airy sketches. They were like those of the people of his race.

One day, when he had nothing to do, he sent her, to encourage her, a note of appreciation. It was brief. But the first glance showed her that it came from a cultured man.

She answered it, a light, nonsensical answer that touched the sense of humor of the white man. That started a correspondence. In the course of time, she came to watch for the mail carrier for the grey tinted stationery that was his.

He asked to see her—to know her personally. Letters were so tantalizing. Her first impulse was to say no. A bitter smile hovered about her lips as she surveyed her face before the mirror. He would be so disappointed, she told herself.

But she consented. They would have to meet sooner or later. The first meeting would surely be a trial and the sooner it was over, the better.

He, the white man, coming from a land of fair, blue-eyed women, was shocked. Perhaps, he found it a bit difficult to associate this homely woman with the one who could write such delightful sketches, such delightful letters.

But she could talk rather well. There was a light vein of humor, faintly ironical at times, in everything she said. And that delighted him.

He asked her to come out with him again. By the shore of Manila Bay one early evening, when her homely face was softened by the darkness around them, he forgot that he was a white man, that she was a brown maiden— a homely and to all appearances, shapeless creature at that. Her silence, as with half closed eyes she gazed at the distance, was very soothing and under the spell of her understanding sympathy, he found himself telling her of his home way over the seas, how he loved the blue of the sea on early mornings because it reminded of the blue of the eyes of the women of his native land. He told her his love for the sea, for the waves that dashed against the rocks in impotent fury, how he could spend his life on the water, sailing on and on, to unknown and uncharted seas.

She listened to him silently. Then he woke up from the spell and, as if ashamed of the outburst of confidence, added irrelevantly:

"But you are different from the other women of your race," looking deep into her small eyes that slanted at the corners.

She smiled. Of course she was, the homely and shapeless mass of flesh that he saw her to be.

"No, I do not mean that," he protested, divining her thoughts, "you do not seem to care much for conventions. No Filipino girl would come out unchaperoned with a man, a white man at that."

"A homely woman can very well afford to break conventions. Nobody minds her if she does. That is one consolation of being homely," was her calm reply.

He laughed.

"You have some very queer ideas," he observed.

"I should have," she retorted. "If I didn't nobody would notice me with my face and my ... my ... figure," she hated herself for stammering the last words.

He looked at her impersonally, as if trying to find some beauty in her.

"But I like you," was his verdict, uttered with the almost brutal frankness of his race. "I

have not come across a more interesting girl for a long time."

They met, again. And again. Thoughts, pleasant thoughts, began to fill her mind. Had she at last found one who liked her sincerely? For he liked her, that she was ready to believe. As a friend, a pal who understood him. And the thought gave her happiness—a friend, a pal who understood him—such as she had never experienced before.

One day, an idea took hold of her—simply obsessed her. He was such a lover of beautiful things—of beauty in any form. She noticed that in all his conversations, in every look, every gesture of his. A desire to show him that she was not entirely devoid of beauty which he so worshipped came over her.

It would not do any harm, she told herself. He had learned to like her for herself. He had learned to value their friendship, homely as she was and shapeless as he thought her to be. Her body would matter not at all now. It would please the aesthete in him perhaps, but it certainly would not matter much to the man.

From the bottom of a very old trunk, she unearthed one of those flimsy, shapely things that had lain their unused for many years. As she looked at herself in the mirror before the appointment, she grudgingly admitted that her body had lost nothing of its hated beauty.

He was surprised. Pleasantly so.

Accustomed as he was to the beautiful bodies of the women of his race, he had to confess that here was something of unusual beauty.

"Why have you been hiding such a beautiful figure all this time," he demanded in mock anger.

"I did not know it was beautiful," she lied.

"Pouff! I know it is not polite to tell a young lady she is a liar so I won't do it. But ... but ......"

"But ....." fear was beginning to creep into her voice.

"Well.... Let us talk of something else."

She heaved a deep sigh. She was right. She had found a man to whom her body mattered little if anything at all. She need not take warning. He had learned to like her for herself.

At their next meeting she wore a pale rose of Filipino dress that softened the brown of her skin. His eyes lighted up when they rested on her, but whether it was the unbeautiful light that she dreaded so much, she could not determine for it quickly disappeared. No, it could not be the unbeautiful light. He liked her for herself. This belief she treasured fondly.

They had a nice long ride out in the country, where the winds were soft and faintly scented and the bamboo trees sighed love to the breeze. They visited a little out of the way nipa chapel by the roadside where a naked Man, nailed to the Cross, looked at them with eyes which held the tragedy and the sorrow of the world—for the sins of sinning men.

She gazed at the figure feeling something vague and incomprehensible stirring within her. She turned to him for sympathy and found him staring at her . . . at her body.

He turned slightly red. In silence they left the little chapel. He helped her inside the car but did not start it at once.

"I . . . . I . . . . love . . . . . ." he stammered after some moments, as if impelled by an irresistible force. Then he stopped.

The small eyes that slanted at the corners were almost beautiful with a tender, soft light as she turned them on him. So he loved her. Had he learned not only to like her but to love her. For herself. And the half finished confession found an echo in the heart of the woman who was starved for love.

"Yes . . . . ." there was a pleading note in her voice.

He swallowed hard. "I love . . . your body," he finished with a thick voice. And the blue eyes flared with the dreaded, hateful light.

She uttered an involuntary cry of protest, of pain, of disillusion. And then a sob escaped her.

And dimly the man from the West realized that he had wronged this little brown maiden with the homely face and the beautiful body as she never had been wronged before. And he felt sorry, infinitely so.

When they stopped before the door of her house, he got out to open the door for her.

"I am sorry," was all he said.

There was a world of regret in the eyes she turned on him.

"For what?" she asked in a tired voice. "You have just been yourself . . . like other men." He winced.

And with a weary smile she passed within.

Manuel Arguilla

HOW MY BROTHER LEON BROUGHT HOME A WIFE

She stepped down from the carretela of Ca Celin with a quick delicate grace. She was lovely. She was tall. She looked up to my brother with a smile, and her forehead was on a level with his mouth.

"You are Baldo," she said and placed her hand lightly on my shoulder. Her nails were long, but they were not pointed. She was fragrant like a morning when papayas are in bloom. And a small dimple appeared momently high up on her right cheek.

"And this is Labang of whom I have heard so much." She held the wrist of one hand with the other and looked at Labang, and Labang never stopped chewing his cud. He swallowed and brought up to his mouth more cud and the sound of his insides was like a drum.

I laid a hand on Labang's massive neck and said to her:

"You may scratch his forehead now."

She hesitated and I saw that her eyes were on the long curving horns. But she came and touched Labang's forehead with her long fingers, and Labang never even stopped chewing his cud except that his big eyes half closed. And by and by, she was scratching his forehead very daintily.

My brother Leon put down the two trunks on the grassy side of the road. He paid Ca Celin twice the usual fare from the station to the edge of Nagrebcan. Then he was standing beside us, and she turned to him eagerly. I watched Ca Celin, where he stood in front of his horse, and he ran his fingers through its forelock and could not keep his eyes away from her.

"Maria—," my brother Leon said.

He did not say Maring. He did not say Mayang. I knew then that he had always called her Maria, and that to us all she would be Maria; and in my mind I said—"Maria"—and it was a beautiful name.

"Yes, Noel."

Now where did she get that name? I pondered the matter quietly to myself, thinking Father might not like it. But it was only the name of my brother Leon said backwards and it sounded much better that way.

"There, is Nagrebcan, Maria," my brother Leon said, gesturing widely toward the west.

She moved close to him and slipped her arm through his. And after a while she said quietly:

"You love Nagrebcan, don't you, Noel?"

Ca Celin drove away hi·yi·ing to his horse loudly. At the bend of the *camino real* where the big duhat tree grew, he rattled the handle of his braided rattan whip against the spokes of the wheel.

We stood alone on the roadside.

The sun was in our eyes for it was dipping into the bright sea. The sky was wide and deep and very blue above us; but along the saw-tooth rim of the Katayaghan hills to the southwest flamed huge masses of clouds. Before us the fields swam in a golden haze through which floated big purple and red and yellow bubbles when I looked at the sinking sun. Labang's white coat which I had washed and brushed that morning with coconut husk, glistened like beaten cotton under the lamplight and his horns appeared tipped with fire. He faced the sun and from his mouth came a call so loud and vibrant that the earth seemed to tremble under-foot. And far away in the middle of the fields a cow lowed softly in answer.

"Hitch him to the cart, Baldo," my brother Leon said, laughing, and she laughed with him a bit uncertainly, and I saw that he had put his arm around her shoulders.

"Why does he make that sound?" she asked. "I have never heard the like of it."

"There is not another like it," my brother Leon said. "I have yet to hear another bull call like Labang. In all the world there is no other bull like him."

She was smiling at him, and I stopped in the act of tying the *sinta* across Labang's neck to the opposite end of the yoke, because her teeth were very white, her eyes were so full of laughter, and there was the small dimple high up on her right cheek.

"If you continue to talk about him like that, either I shall fall in love with him or become greatly jealous."

My brother Leon laughed and she laughed and they looked at each other and it seemed to me there was a world of laughter between them and in them.

I climbed into the cart over the wheel and Labang would have bolted for he was always like that, but I kept a firm hold on his rope. He was restless and would not stand still, so that my brother Leon had to say "Labang" several times. When he was quiet again, my brother Leon lifted the trunks into the cart, placing the smaller on top.

She looked down once at her high-heeled shoes, then she gave her left hand to my brother Leon, placed a foot on the hub of the wheel, and in one breath she had swung up into the cart. Oh, the fragrance of her. But Labang was fairly dancing with impatience and it was all I could do to keep him from running away.

"Give me the rope, Baldo," my brother Leon said. "Maria, sit down on the hay and hold on to anything." Then he put a foot on the left shaft and that instant Labang leaped forward. My brother Leon laughed as he drew himself up to the top of the side of the cart and made the slack of the rope hiss above the back of Labang. The wind whistled against my cheeks and the rattling of the wheels on the pebbly road echoed in my ears.

She sat up straight on the bottom of the cart, legs bent together to one side, her skirts spread over them so that only the toes and heels of her shoes were visible. Her eyes were on my brother Leon's back; I saw the wind on her hair.

When Labang slowed down, my brother Leon handed to me the rope. I knelt on the straw inside the cart and pulled on the rope until Labang was merely shuffling along, then I made him turn around.

"What is it you have forgotten now, Baldo?" my brother Leon said.

I did not say anything but tickled with my fingers the rump of Labang; and away we went—back to where I had unhitched and waited for them. The sun had sunk and down from the wooded sides of the Katayaghan hills shadows were stealing into the fields. High up overhead the sky burned with many slow fires.

When I sent Labang down the deep cut that would bring us to the dry bed of the Waig which could be used as a path to our place during the dry season, my brother Leon laid a hand on my shoulder and said sternly:

"Who told you to drive through the fields tonight?"

His hand was heavy on my shoulder, but I did not look at him nor utter a word until we were on the rocky bottom of the Waig.

"Baldo you fool, answer me before I lay the

rope of Labang on you. Why do you follow the Waig instead of the *camino real?*"

His fingers bit into my shoulder.

"Father, he told me to follow the Waig tonight, *Manong.*"

Swiftly, his hand fell away from my shoulder and he reached for the rope of Labang. Then my brother Leon laughed, and he sat back, and laughing still, he said:

"And I suppose Father also told you to hitch Labang to the cart and meet us with him instead of with Castaño and the *calesa.*"

Without waiting for me to answer, he turned to her and said, "Maria, why do you think Father should do that, now?" He laughed and added, "Have you ever seen so many stars before?"

I looked back and they were sitting side by side, leaning against the trunks, hands clasped across knees. Seemingly but a man's height above the tops of the steep banks of the Waig, hung the stars. But in the deep gorge, the shadows had fallen heavily, and even the white of Labang's coat was merely a dim grayish blur. Crickets chirped from their homes in the cracks in the banks. The thick unpleasant smell of dangla bushes and cooling sun-heated earth mingled with the clean, sharp scent of arrais roots exposed to the night air and of the hay inside the cart.

"Look Noel, yonder is our star!" Deep surprise and gladness were in her voice. Very low in the west, almost touching the ragged edge of the bank, was the star, the biggest and brightest in the sky.

"I have been looking at it," my brother Léon said. "Do you remember how I would tell you that when you want to see stars you must come to Nagrebcan?"

"Yes, Noel," she said. "Look at it," she murmured, half to herself. "It is so many times bigger and brighter than it was at Ermita beach."

"The air here is clean, free of dust and smoke."

"So it is, Noel," she said, drawing a long breath.

"Making fun of me, Maria?"

She laughed then and they laughed together and she took my brother Leon's hand and put it against her face.

I stopped Labang, climbed down, and lighted the lantern that hung from the cart between the wheels.

"Good boy, Baldo," my brother Leon said as I climbed back into the cart, and my heart sang.

Now the shadows took fright and did not crowd so near. Clumps of andadasi and arrais flashed into view and quickly disappeared as we passed by. Ahead, the elongated shadow of Labang bobbed up and down and swayed drunkenly from side to side, for the lantern rocked jerkily with the cart.

"Have we far to go yet, Noel?" she asked.

"Ask Baldo," my brother Leon said, "we have been neglecting him."

"I am asking you, Baldo," she said.

Without looking back, I answered, picking my words slowly:

"Soon we will get out of the Waig and pass into the fields. After the fields is home—*Manang.*"

"So near already."

I did not say anything more, because I did not know what to make of the tone of her voice as she said her last words. All the laughter seemed to have gone out of her. I waited for my brother Leon to say something, but he was not saying anything. Suddenly he broke out into song and the song was "Sky Sown with Stars"—the same that he and Father sang when we cut hay in the fields of nights before he went away to study. He must have taught her the song because she joined him, and her voice flowed into his like a gentle stream meeting a stronger one. And each time the wheels encountered a big rock, her voice would catch in her throat, but my brother Leon would sing on, until, laughing softly, she would join him again.

Then we were climbing out into the fields, and through the spokes of the wheels the light of the lantern mocked the shadows. Labang quickened his steps. The jolting became more frequent and painful as we crossed the low dikes.

"But it is so very wide here," she said. The light of the stars broke and scattered the darkness so that one could see far on every side, though indistinctly.

"You miss the houses, and the cars, and the people and the noise, don't you?" My brother Leon stopped singing.

"Yes, but in a different way. I am glad they are not here."

With difficulty, I turned Labang to the left, for he wanted to go straight on. He was breathing hard, but I knew he was more thirsty than tired. In a little while, we drove up the grassy side onto the *camino real.*

"—you see," my brother Leon was explaining, "the *camino real* curves around the foot of the Katayaghan hills and passes by our house. We drove through the fields, because—but I'll be asking Father as soon as we get home."

"Noel," she said.

"Yes, Maria."

"I am afraid. He may not like me."

"Does that worry you still, Maria?" my brother Leon said. "From the way you talk, he might be an ogre, for all the world. Except when his leg that was wounded in the Revolution is troubling him, Father is the mildest-tempered, gentlest man I know."

We came to the house of Lacay Julian and I spoke to Labang loudly, but Moning did not come to the window, so I surmised she must be eating with the rest of her family. And I thought of the food being made ready at home and my mouth watered. We met the twins, Urong and Celin, and I said "Hoy," calling them by name. And they shouted back and asked if my brother Leon and his wife were with me. And my brother Leon shouted to them and then told me to make Labang run; their answers were lost in the noise of the wheels.

I stopped Labang on the road before our house and would have gotten down, but my brother Leon took the rope and told me to stay in the cart. He turned Labang into the open gate and we dashed into our yard. I thought we would crash into the bole of the camachile tree, but my brother Leon reined

in Labang in time. There was light downstairs in the kitchen, and Mother stood in the doorway, and I could see her smiling shyly. My brother Leon was helping Maria over the wheel.

The first words that fell from his lips after he had kissed Mother's hand were:

"Father, where is he?"

"He is in his room upstairs," Mother said, her face becoming serious. "His leg is bothering him again."

I did not hear anything more because I had to go back to the cart to unhitch Labang. But I had hardly tied him under the barn when I heard Father calling me. I met my brother Leon going to bring up the trunks. As I passed through the kitchen, there were Mother and my sister Aurelia and Maria and it seemed to me they were crying, all of them.

There was no light in Father's room. There was no movement. He sat in the big armchair by the western window, and a star shone directly through it. He was smoking, but he removed the roll of tobacco from his mouth when he saw me. He laid it carefully on the window-sill before speaking.

"Did you meet anybody on the way?" he asked.

"No, Father," I said. "Nobody passes through the Waig at night."

He reached for his roll of tobacco and hitched himself up in the chair.

"She is very beautiful, Father."

"Was she afraid of Labang?" My father had not raised his voice, but the room seemed to resound with it. And again I saw her eyes on the long curving horns and the arm of my brother Leon around her shoulders.

"No, Father, she was not afraid."

"On the way—"

"She looked at the stars, Father. And Manong Leon sang."

"What did he sing?"

" 'Sky Sown with Stars.' She sang with him."

He was silent again. I could hear the low voices of Mother and my sister Aurelia downstairs. There was also the voice of my brother Leon, and I thought that Father's voice must have been like it when he was young. He had laid the roll of tobacco on the window-sill once more. I watched the smoke waver faintly upward from the lighted end and vanish slowly into the night outside.

The door opened and my brother Leon and Maria came in.

"Have you watered Labang?" Father spoke to me.

I told him that Labang was resting yet under the barn.

"It is time you watered him, my son," my father said.

I looked at Maria and she was lovely. She was tall. Beside my brother Leon, she was tall and very still. Then I went out, and in the darkened hall the fragrance of her was like a morning when papayas are in bloom.

Carlos Bulosan

THE ROMANCE OF MAGNO RUBIO

Magno Rubio. Filipino boy. Four-foot six inches tall. Dark as a coconut. Head small on a body like a turtle. Magno Rubio. Picking peas on a California hillside for twenty-five cents an hour. Filipino boy. In love with a girl he had never seen. A girl twice his size sideward and upward, Claro said...

I was listening to their heated discussion.

"I love her," he said.

"But how could you?" Claro asked. "She's twice your size sideward and upward."

"Has size got anything to do with love?"

"That's what I've heard from my uncle."

"Your uncle could be wrong."

"My uncle was never wrong, God bless his soul."

"Was he an educated man?"

"Not in the book sense but in the life sense."

"I don't know," he said, screwing up his fish-eyes. Then he saw me. "You went to college, Nick?"

"Yes."

"How many years?"

"Enough to understand a few things, Magno."

"Now tell me," he said. "Has size got anything to do with love? I mean real love, an honest love?"

"I don't think so."

He brightened up. He turned to Claro. "That's what I thought," he concluded.

"But," Claro protested, "he hasn't seen the girl he's supposed to be in love with?"

He looked at me hopefully.

"The object of love may be an idea, a dream, a reality," I explained. "The love is there. And it grows—depending, of course, on the ability of the lover to crystallize the beloved."

He opened his black mouth, showing rotten teeth. He jumped to his feet like a monkey. "That's it!" he cried. "I don't understand all your words, Nick. But I get it that it's possible for me to love a girl I've never seen!"

"That's exactly what I mean, Magno."

"Nick, you saved my life!"

"It's all wrong," Claro said, grabbing the long neck of his jug of red wine on the table. His throat gargled. His stomach rumbled. "Words, words, words! They don't mean a thing. My uncle couldn't be wrong: he was a gentleman!"

They were sitting directly opposite each other. They were pushing the jug of wine back and forth across the bare dining table in the smoky kitchen of our bunkhouse. It was early spring and the sun outside was glittering on the dew-laden hills, where the royal crowns of eidelweiss, the long blue petals of lupines and multicolored poppies were shaking slightly in the wind. It was morning and we had no work. Some members of our crew were sleeping in their straw beds, some playing cards in a corner of the bunkhouse, some playing musical instruments on the porch. We were pursuing the daily routine of our lives when we had no work. But the three of us were thinking of Magno Rubio's romance with a girl in the mountains of Arkansas. A girl he had been corresponding with but never seen.

"Will you help me, Nick?" he asked me suddenly.

"Sure, Magno."

He looked at Claro with displeasure. "Please go away," he told him.

"This illiterate peasant tells me to go away," Claro said contemptuously. "This ignoramus tells a man who has gone to the second grade to go away! Listen, peon—"

"Here's a dollar," he said, disregarding the insult. "Now go away. Drink the wine in your room. I was crazy to pay for it anyway."

"Look, Igorot—"

"Here's two dollars. Be a gentleman like your uncle."

Claro looked tentatively at the money. He picked up the crisp bills on the table. He grabbed the jug of wine and went to his room.

"What is it, Magno?" I asked.

"I like you to write a letter for me, Nick."

"Where to?'

"My girl in Arkansas."

"I thought you've been writing to her."

"In a way."

"I can't express your feelings, Magno."

"Sure you can. I'll dictate in our dialect and you translate it into English." He looked in the direction of Claro's room, where a bed was squeaking like a dozen little pigs. He turned to me and frowned. "You see, he has been writing my letters. But he's very expensive. Very, Nick."

"You paid him?"

"And how!"

"How much per letter?"

"No, no, no!" he protested. "It's very complicated. At first there was only a gallon of wine. Later he thought of making some money. I don't know where he had stolen the idea, but it must have been from the movies. He demanded a flat rate of five dollars per letter."

"That's reasonable, Magno. After all he spent some money when he went to the second grade."

"But it's not that, Nick! You see, I wrote to my girl every day. I earn only two dollars fifty cents a day. Still, I had to write to her. I love her. You understand, Nick?"

"I understand. I was in love once."

"You see what I mean?"

I nodded my head. I said, "Five dollars per letter. That's more than I earn a day as a bookkeeper for our crew."

"That's not the end of it, Nick." He leaned toward me, his fish-eyes shining like mud. "Realizing that I truly love the girl, that I can't live in the world without her, he demanded one cent per word!"

"One cent per word? It's robbery!"

"Yes! And do you know what, Nick! He wrote long letters that I couldn't understand. And he used big words. How would I know if he wasn't writing for himself?"

"It's hard to say."

"However, I'm not worried about that part of the deal," he said, showing his protruding rotten teeth. He bit at a twisted chunk of chewing tobacco, rolled it from cheek to cheek and said: "I've confidence in myself. But some men use their education to enslave others. I thought education is meant to guide the uneducated. Did some educated man lie about this thing called education, Nick?"

"I don't think so, Magno. Education is what you said: for the educated to guide the uneducated. And it's more than that. Education is a periscope through which a common ground of understanding should be found among men."

He coughed up the slimy wad of tobacco in his mouth, licked the brown shreds of saliva dripping down his thick lips with the tip of his serrated tongue. He banged the splintery table with a fist and said, "The thief! He acts like an exploiter, always squeezing the last drop of my blood! You know what he did to enslave me for a lifetime if you didn't come along, Nick?"

I looked at his coconut head. I looked at his turtle neck. "No," I said.

"Later he charged me ten cents per word!"

"What?"

"You heard me right, Nick! I paid him twenty dollars per letter! Sometimes more! There!"

I studied his monkey face. I said, "It's unbelievable, Magno!"

He bit another chunk of tobacco, swallowed his saliva and bared his ugly teeth. He said, "I didn't mind paying him that much money. But the words were too long and deep for me. And again I say: how would I know if he hadn't been writing for himself? Do you think he's that low, Nick?"

"Some men are capable of anything, Magno. Some men could crawl on their bellies on human filth to earn a dollar."

"I didn't know that, Nick." He was disappointed. "I thought we were all born honest."

"We were all born honest, Magno. But along the way some of us lost our honesty."

"I didn't lose my honesty."

"Keep it, Magno. Honesty is the best policy."

"That's what I've heard. Still . . ."

"You heard right, Magno."

"I will, Nick." He brushed off a scab on his flat nose. "But I'm free now because I've you. Will you write for me from now on, Nick?"

"Sure, Magno."

"What would you like to have? You don't drink like Claro. You don't go after girls like our foreman. You don't gamble like the hoodlums in the poolroom in town. You don't smoke like the whores at the Elite Hotel. You don't chew tobacco like—"

I stopped him. I said, "Don't start anything, Magno. I'll do it because I like to help you. Maybe I'll need your help some day."

"That's what I like about you, Nick. You use your college education in the right direction."

"By the way, Magno," I said. "How do you know your girl in Arkansas is tall and big on the beam?"

"She wrote to me about the matter."

"You mean Claro told you that's what she wrote?"

"Exactly."

"Did she send you a picture of herself?"

He fumbled in his pockets and produced an old wallet. He extracted a snapshot from a bunch of bills and magazine clippings.

"This is it, Nick."

I looked at the snapshot. It was faded due to too much handling. It was impossible to determine the girl's age and shape and height.

"How tall is she according to Claro?"

"Five-foot eleven inches," he said. "But I don't mind. I really don't. I like tall girls."

"Everybody does, Magno," I told him. Who is short like you, I almost added. Instead I asked him, "And how heavy is she, according to Claro?"

"One hundred ninety-five pounds on bare feet," he said. "But I don't care about that either. I like heavy girls. I really do."

"Everybody does, Magno," I said. Who is a featherweight like you, I almost added. Instead I told him, "It doesn't really matter how tall she is and how much she weighs if you love her."

His flat nose flared up. "I love her, Nick," he said.

"I know you do."

"Will you write a letter now?"

"Sure, Magno."

He ran to his room. He came back with a pencil and a pad of notepaper. Plus a big dictionary, I didn't know why. He put his hands behind his back, walked around the table a few times, stopped in front of me and screwed up his monkey face. Then he began to dictate in our dialect.

Magno Rubio. Four-foot six inches tall. Dark as a coconut. Head small on a body like a turtle. Filipino boy. In love with a girl five-foot eleven inches tall. One hundred ninety-five pounds of flesh and bones on bare feet. A girl twice his size sideward and upward, Claro said . . .

"How did you know Clarabelle?" I asked him.

"I found her in a magazine," he said.

"How?"

"You know, one of those magazines that advertised the names and addresses of girls for one dollar."

"A Lonely Hearts magazine."

"I guess so."

"But you can't read, Magno?"

"Claro read it for me."

"And he found the name for you?"

"He did."

"And of course you gave him the dollar."

He nodded his turtle head. He inserted a finger in his hairy nostril to extricate a slab of dried mucus. He made a face when he pulled it out, looked at a minute, flung it aside and wiped his hand on his trousers.

"How long have you been writing to her?" I asked him.

"Three months. Do you remember the time when we were picking tomatoes and I didn't want to work? That was the time when I found Clarabelle."

"I remember, Magno."

"For a long time I had nobody to work for, Nick," he explained. "But when I found Clarabelle..." He grunted because he had swallowed the wad of tobacco in his cheek, bringing tears to his dull eyes. "You know what I mean, Nick."

"I do."

"Well, that's why I've been working every day ever since. And I don't regret it, either."

"That's the spirit, Magno."

He put his chin between his hands. I looked at him and wondered what was transpiring in his bird brain. But I recalled, about three months before, he used to stay in the bunkhouse all day. I saw him looking with dreamy eyes at the pages of dime magazines. I knew he couldn't read, but the magazines were illustrated with the photographs of nude and semi-nude girls. I was tempted to teach him the alphabet, which I did for a few days, but he lacked concentration. And his memory was bad because his mind was taken up by the enticing photographs. So he made excuses that he was either ill or too busy to study.

But he was not ill. Of course, he was ill with love. The foreman scolded him once for staying out of the work, but he complained that he was suffering from arthritis. The foreman left it at that because, if Magno Rubio had the illness that he claimed, it would be dangerous for him to work in the cold weather. It was winter then, and the tomatoes were almost frozen. But the crop was saved by our industry and endurance.

And he was not busy, either. He had nothing to do in the bunkhouse, because we had a cook who cooked our food and cleaned the place. Magno Rubio seldom washed his clothes, if he ever did. He had the same rags on him all the time, even when he was in bed. It was insufferable to sit beside him at the dining table. He smelled of mud, sweat and filth, and more, he smelled like a skunk. He was not lazy of course, but he just didn't know how to be clean. He had forgotten that some human beings had a sensitive sense of smell, and unlike him, he who had been a peon and a companion of pigs and goats all his life.

But now he had Clarabelle. He was in love for the first time in his life. And also for the first time in his life the filthy rags clinging on his back were discarded. I recalled that when he burned them in the back yard, I dashed out of the house to the foothill for fresh air. But even then my stomach betrayed me, and made me curse the ugliness of some human beings. However, it was all over. Magno Rubio was a human being again. And he was in love.

It was in the middle of spring and we were picking peas on the hillsides near our bunkhouse. Magno Rubio and I were working side by side, astride neighboring rows that began from the slope of the hills and ended atop a stony plateau, where goats and sheep were let loose by farmers to eat the destructive loco weeds. We worked up and down the hills, crawling on our knees like brown beetles.

I threw a handful of pea pods into my can and looked at him. "What are your plans for Clarabelle?" I asked.

"I want to marry her, Nick," he said.

"Would you like to say that in your next letter?"

"That's what I've been planning to tell you."

"Well, you should propose to her. How much money have you already spent on her?"

He counted it on his fingers, his thick lips moving the while. "A little over two hundred dollars, Nick. There was the engagement ring. Seventy-five dollars. The wrist-watch. Eighty dollars. A pair of suede shoes, some clothes, a diamond bracelet. One hundred twenty-nine. It's over three hundred dollars, Nick!"

"That's plenty of money, Magno."

"It's worth it."

"If you think so."

"I spent every cent I earned for her. I also borrowed some money from the foreman with interest."

I studied his flaring flat nose. It was caked with dirt and mucus.

"But it's worth it, Nick."

"Of course, Magno. Would you like me to write a letter of proposal of marriage tonight?"

"Yes, Nick. The sooner the better."

"Suppose she'll change her mind when she arrives in California?"

There was a flicker of momentary doubt in his monkey face. "I don't think Clarabelle will do that. She's a good girl."

"I hope you are right."

"I've confidence in her."

So I wrote the letter of proposal. She answered immediately saying that she was accepting his proposal, but, unfortunately, she had to stay home for a while because of her sick mother. However she urged him to send her the ticket money and some extra for expenses, in abeyance, since she expected the old woman to get well.

The money was sent. Several days passed. Two weeks passed. Three weeks, and a letter arrived from Clarabelle. I read it and gave the translation to Magno Rubio. Clarabelle said, in resume, that her mother died from a lingering disease and she had to spend the money on her funeral. And not only that, she wrote sobbingly: now she had to take care of her little brothers and sisters, all under ten. But, she added, her heart was with him: she was looking forward to the day when she would be free from her family obligations.

"Poor girl," Magno Rubio commented sadly. And that was all he said, nothing more. So we kept on writing to her. Sometimes we sent her money when she asked for it, sometimes we sent clothes for her brothers and sisters. Magno Rubio never complained. Not one word of protest. The plight of the girl in Arkansas made him more industrious and frugal. He even cut down his expenses on chewing tobacco, which made him look like a Moro juramentado about to go beserk among Christians so he could go to heaven an honored heathen. And of course he was back to his rags.

He worked and worked. He worked like a carabao but lived like a dog. Then the pea season was over. We had a rest for a week, before we started planting celery and carrots. Then the lettuce season came. We thinned and irrigated the seedlings. So the months passed, the seasons came and went. And a year passed by uneventfully, sadly, for Magno Rubio.

A stream of letters flowed from Arkansas to California. Clarabelle was still supporting her little brothers and sisters. And poor Magno Rubio, he didn't suspect anything wrong. He was still looking forward to her coming to California.

"Will you wait?" This was her constant plea in every letter.

"I'll wait," Magno Rubio said to himself.

And he waited. It was now two years and a half since he first contacted her through Claro. Then the third year passed, and he still waited. What sustains a man to have such patience? What quality of soul does he possess to have so much faith in something he has never seen?

I don't know. But Magno Rubio had the patience and the faith. Where most men would have given up long ago, he kept on beyond belief and all reason.

"I'll wait," he said every day.

Magno Rubio. Filipino boy. Four-foot six inches tall. Dark as a coconut. Head small on a body like a turtle. Picking tomatoes on a California hillside for twenty-five cents an hour. In love with a girl he had never seen. A girl five-foot eleven inches tall. One hundred ninety-five pounds of flesh and bones on bare feet. Filipino boy. In love with a girl twice his size sideward and upward, Claro said...

"What are you giving Clarabelle for Christmas, Magno?" I asked him.

He grinned like a goat. He was carrying a big bundle under one arm. "I'm giving her a radio," he said. "A combination radio-phonograph. It costs me nearly two hundred dollars."

"That's good, Magno."

"Let's send it right away, Nick."

We did. And we waited in vain for her letter. Then Christmas day came.

We were all in the bunkhouse. The foreman and two others were playing poker in a corner of the kitchen. Claro was drinking wine at the dining table. Magno Rubio was oiling his hair near a window, where he had propped up a broken mirror. He was grinning like a monkey. He was in love.

"So Clarabelle will know I'm clean tonight," he explained.

"It doesn't make any difference to her," I said. "She's too far away to appreciate your cleanliness."

He stopped combing his oily black hair and turned to me. "We'll tell her about it in the next letter, Nick."

"Sure, Magno."

"You see, Nick. I'm clean in my soul, thinking of her."

I stopped playing solitaire. I studied his monkey face, and somehow felt that a pure soul was hidden by his flat nose and fish-eyes. I glanced over at Claro. He was getting drunk. Saliva was dripping down the corners of his twisted mouth. His eyes were popping red, like frozen tomatoes.

"Don't you have a girl, Nick?" Magno Rubio suddenly asked me.

I turned my face away from Claro and looked at Magno. "No," I said.

"You should have. You are a college man."

"Education has nothing to do with love."

"You really don't have a girl anywhere in the wide world?" I shook my head vigorously.

"If I were you I would write to all the pretty girls. There must be a girl somewhere for you, Nick."

"I don't think so, Magno."

"How come pretty girls fall for an uneducated guy like me, huh?"

"You tell me, Magno."

"Now take Clarabelle. Why didn't she fall for you, Nick?"

"You found her first."

"If you found her first and I horned in, would she still fall for me?"

"I guess so, Magno."

He laughed like a horse. Claro banged on the table with both fists and leaped to his feet.

"Listen, you peon!" He pointed a finger at Magno. "What are you laughing about?"

"He's happy, Claro," I said. "He has a girl, that's why he's happy."

"I got Clarabelle," Magno said.

"Clarabelle, my eye!" Claro screamed.

"What do you mean by that foolishness?" Magno asked. He put the comb in his shirt pocket and advanced toward Claro. "Will you clarify your statement?"

"You mean to tell me that a girl like Clarabelle loves a donkey like you?"

"What's wrong with me?"

"What's wrong with me?" Claro imitated him. "Don't you know, peasant?"

Magno advanced closer to his adversary. I stopped playing solitaire.

"Don't you know that you look like a monkey?" Claro continued his tirade. His voice was becoming hysterical, his eyes redder, and his mouth was foaming. "Don't you know that besides being a peasant you are also illiterate! Girls like Clarabelle don't fall for your kind, illiterate peasant!"

"You are also a peasant."

"An educated peasant! There, monkey-faced dog peasant!"

"What's the difference?"

"What's the difference?" Claro imitated him again.

"I don't care what you say. Clarabelle loves me."

"Prove it, dog eater!"

Calmly Magno produced his old wallet. He threw a lock of hair on the table.

"Here's the absolute proof. She sent it to me. It's from her own head."

"You think you are the only man with a lock of hair from Clarabelle?" Claro also produced a lock of hair and flung it upon the table. "There, monkey! That's the real proof. And it's not from her head, either!"

Magno Rubio was astonished. He leaned over the two locks of hair, examining one and then the other. Then the two of them were leaning over the table, examining the two locks of hair in all their minutiae, as though they were looking down the magnificent lens of a microscope. And they were growing suspicious of each other, their heads bent close together, their eyes popping like over-ripe guavas. But, finally, Magno Rubio calmed down. He didn't want any violence. His soul was clean and beautiful.

"Your lock of hair doesn't prove anything," he told Claro. Carefully he put Clarabelle's faded snapshot on the table. "But this proves something definite," he added.

Claro sneered. He flung a snapshot beside Magno's face down and said, "Proof, my ass! This is the irrefutable proof! Look for yourself, pig!"

Magno Rubio reached for the snapshot. Claro snatched it away. I had a quick glance of it. I hoped Magno wouldn't see it, because it was the picture of a pretty girl, quite young and proportionately shaped. But he was aroused.

"Let me see!" he demanded.

"Go to hell!" Claro shouted.

The coconut head sunk into the turtle body. The fish-eyes shone. The flat black nose flared. The ugly mouth snarled. Then the gorilla legs leaped. Then they were rolling on the floor. Then Magno Rubio was on top of Claro, beating his face into pulp with his whirlwind fists.

I jumped to my feet. I grabbed Magno Rubio's hands. But he was strong. He was like a mad dog. I looked toward the poker players.

"You guys!" I called. "Help me!"

They looked in our direction for a minute, then continued their game. I changed my tactics on the mad dog. I squeezed his neck and kept on squeezing until he released Claro. He gasped for air, while Claro scrambled to his feet and dashed outside. I went back to my game of solitaire.

Magno Rubio walked straight to a wall. He began beating it with his fists, weeping at the same time. He kept beating the wall until his fists began to bleed. Then he sank exhausted in a corner of the kitchen, while Claro shouted obscenities from the porch.

Magno Rubio. Filipino boy. Four-foot six inches tall. Dark as a coconut. Head small like a turtle. Magno Rubio. Cutting celery for twenty-five cents an hour. In love with a girl in the mountains of Arkansas. Filipino boy. In love with a girl he had never seen. A girl twice his size sideward and upward, Claro said...

"Have you heard from Clarabelle, Magno?" I asked him one day.

"No."

"We should write to her."

He looked at me. His serrated tongue darted out of the black pit of his mouth. Then he yawned, and the orifice at the root of his tongue revealed its yellowish membrane.

"It's no use, Nick," he said finally. "Claro fouled up everything."

"I don't think so," I consoled him. "Besides he's gone."

"He's a louse."

"How do you know?"

"He's been writing to her."

"Well, the best man wins, Magno. And you are the best man."

"Do you think so?"

"Don't you?"

He sighed. "We'll write to her tonight."

"Are you sure you didn't get a letter from her since—?"

He did not let me finish. "I have, Nick," he confessed. "Ten letters in all. I didn't want to show them to you. The letters are in my room."

"Why didn't you let me know?"

"I thought Clarabelle—"

"Of course you were wrong, Magno," I finished it for him.

"Will you read them tonight, Nick? And write a letter for me?"

"Sure, Magno."

We were packing lettuce in the shade. It was May again and the crop was good. It was now three years and four months since he had first written to her. I read all of Clarabelle's letters in translation to him. They were arranged chronologically; he had stacked them in an empty cigar box as they arrived. Clarabelle's plea of love became more fervent in every letter, for it seemed that her responsibilities were diminishing. Magno Rubio nodded his head. A genuine smile decorated his black face. When we came to the last letter, I couldn't believe its message. But it was true. Clarabelle was coming to California. She was already on the way.

"When did you get this letter?" I asked him.

"This morning."

"Clarabelle is on the way."

His dull fish-eyes shone for the first time. "Did she say she's coming to marry me?"

"That's what she says, Magno. Did you save enough money for this emergency?"

"I've fifty dollars."

"That's not enough."

"But I thought—"

"You'll have to get out of the state to get married, you know."

"Can't we get married in town?"

"You can't marry here, Magno," I explained. "You can't marry in the whole state of California. You must go to New Mexico or Washington. These are the nearest states where you can get married. And you'll need at least two hundred dollars for the whole affair."

"I didn't know it would cost that much to get married."

"It's only the beginning, Magno."

"You mean there are other expenses?"

"Well, later."

Dreams of glory misted his eyes. "I know what you mean, Nick."

"I know you."

"I'll borrow some more from the foreman."

"You are mortgaging your whole future," I told him.

"It's worth it, Nick." Dreams of glory crossed his face again. "When is she arriving?"

"Saturday around noon, the letter says. Today is Thursday. You've barely two days to prepare. You are supposed to meet her at the bus station."

"Will you come with me, Nick?"

"Sure, Magno."

He licked his thick lips and turned away from me. "Will you lend me a hundred, Nick?"

"I'm very sorry, Magno."

"I understand. I'll go to the foreman . . ."

"I'm sure he'll help you."

"Do you think she wrote to Claro?"

"I don't know."

"I will kill him."

We were loading the crates of lettuce in the waiting trucks when a telegram came for Magno Rubio. It was from Clarabelle. She was arriving in town sooner than she had expected, at five o'clock Friday afternoon. And it was already Friday noon. He had only four hours to prepare, and we had five more trucks to load. He was stunned for a moment. Then he started throwing the loaded crates into the trucks, working like two men. I followed him, hoping we would finish the job before the momentous hour arrived.

We did. We rushed to the bunkhouse and took a quick shower, changed our clothes, borrowed the pickup from the foreman and drove into town.

Clarabelle was waiting in the bus station. I knew her right away. I had seen the snapshot in Claro's wallet. He didn't recognize her. He was expecting a girl five-foot eleven inches tall, one hundred ninety-five pounds of flesh and bones on bare feet. I pulled his arm. I propelled him toward her.

"Clarabelle?" I greeted her.

"Yes," she said. "Are you Claro?"

Magno Rubio winced.

"No," I said.

"I wonder why he didn't meet me. Are you his brother?"

"Claro is gone," I told her. "Claro has no brother. My name is Nick."

"Glad to meet you, Nick. Where did he go?"

"Alaska."

"Why did he go there of all places?"

"He's working in the fish canneries."

"He didn't tell me about it. Will he be gone long?"

"He left suddenly, Clarabelle. He'll probably be gone for several months. Maybe longer. I can't tell."

She looked like a prospector who had reached the promised hill in vain. The hill was there all right, but the gold—

"What a way to treat a lady," she complained.

I grabbed Magno's arm. "This is Magno Rubio, Clarabelle."

Her blue eyes flickered. The promised hill of gold reappeared. The rose mouth unfolded sweetly. The dying prospector murmured a prayer: the vein of gold was not a mirage after all.

"Yes, yes!" She grabbed his hand. "How are you, Magno?"

He blushed. He muttered something. She turned to me for help.

"May I speak to him for a minute?" she asked me.

I nodded my head. They went to a corner. I walked to the restaurant and ordered a cup of coffee. Then I saw him motioning to me. I left my cup and went to him.

"She's trying to tell me something, Nick," he said. "But I can't understand her. Will you help me?"

I followed him in silence. "What is it, Clarabelle?" I asked her.

"It's difficult for me to make him understand," she explained. "This is what I like to tell him: I must check in a hotel before we talk things over. He understands the marriage part of our conversation. But I need some rest. Explain it to him, Nick."

I explained it to him in our dialect.

"Tell him," Clarabelle added, "that I need some expense money."

I told him.

"And tell him that I sold our engagement ring. Tell him that I need another ring."

"He can't do it today, Clarabelle," I said. "The banks are closed now."

She looked at the big clock on the wall. "Tomorrow will be okay."

I told him. He gave her fifty dollars.

"Now that everything is arranged properly," Clarabelle said, "let's look for a hotel."

He carried her small suitcase. We walked a block and found a hotel. I followed her to the desk, while he sat in a chair near the door. She signed her name on the registry and turned to me.

"Too bad you are not interested," she said in a low tone of voice. "I like you, Nick."

I shook my head.

"I suppose not," she said. "Will you come with him tomorrow?"

"I will, Clarabelle."

She threw a kiss at Magno and walked to the waiting elevator. We went out the lobby. He was the happiest man on earth. He hopped and jumped like a little boy. He was in love.

The next day he borrowed two hundred fifty dollars from the foreman. Then we went to town again. He bought a diamond ring for one hundred dollars. I phoned Clarabelle, and she met us at the door of her hotel. He gave her the ring, and she put it on her finger. Then she kissed him. On the tip of his small flat nose.

"We'll get married tomorrow, Magno," she said.

He understood. He nodded his head.

"Have you got a car, Magno?" Her voice was like a song.

He shook his head.

"It doesn't matter," she said. "How about my expense money, Magno?"

He opened his wallet and gave her two hundred dollars. Clarabelle kissed him again. On the tip of his small flat black nose. She looked at me for a moment trying to say something with her blue eyes. One gesture— and a life was broken forever. One word—and it could have been mended.

"You understand, Nick," she told me at last.

"Yes."

"Thanks."

"You should at least be alone with him."

"But I can't do that, Nick."

"I know."

"I'll see you both tomorrow," she said.

We left her. We rode back to our bunkhouse. Magno Rubio couldn't sleep even when midnight came. I heard him prowling restlessly in his room. He knocked at my door when daylight struck the windows.

"This is the day, Nick!" he greeted me. He was carrying a small suitcase.

"Where are you going to get married?" I asked him.

"New Mexico. It's the nearest place."

"You have enough money?"

"I borrowed some more from the foreman. I'm the luckiest man in the world!"

I followed him to the pickup. We drove into town. We parked outside Clarabelle's hotel and both went into the lobby. We went to the clerk, and I asked for Clarabelle.

"She just checked out," the clerk informed me. "Her husband came for her."

"Her husband?"

The clerk looked at me with eyes that said more than the whole words in the dictionary.

Magno Rubio was beginning to understand. He pulled at my arm. We went outside in silence.

We were walking down the street when we saw Clarabelle in a car pulling out from the curb. She was sitting beside a man with brown hair and thin mustache. She was laughing. He was laughing, too.

Magno Rubio watched the car pull away. He was speechless for a moment. Then he understood everything. He brushed his eyes with a finger and took my arm.

"I guess we'll start picking the tomatoes next week, Nick," he said.

"Yeah," I said.

"Well, what are we waiting for? Let's hurry back to the bunkhouse. Those guys will eat all the chicken!"

Why does everybody make it difficult for an honest man like Magno Rubio to live in the world?

Magno Rubio. Filipino boy. Four-foot six inches tall. Dark as a coconut. Head small on a body like a turtle. Magno Rubio. Picking tomatoes on a California hillside for twenty-five cents an hour. Filipino boy. In love with a girl one hundred ninety-five pounds of flesh and bones on bare feet. A girl twice his size sideward and upward, Claro said . . .

Bienvenido N. Santos

THE DAY THE DANCERS CAME

As soon as Fil woke up, he noticed a whiteness outside, quite unusual for the November mornings they had been having. That fall, Chicago was sandman's town, sleepy valley, drowsy gray, slumbrous mistiness from sunup till noon when the clouds drifted away in cauliflower clusters and suddenly it was evening. The lights shone on the avenues like soiled lamps centuries old and the skyscrapers became monsters with a thousand sore eyes. Now there was a brightness in the air and Fil knew what it was and he shouted, "Snow! It's snowing!"

Tony, who slept in the adjoining room, was awakened.

"What's that?" he asked.

"It's snowing," Fil said, smiling to himself as if he had ordered this and was satisfied with the prompt delivery. "Oh, they'll love this, they'll love this."

"Who'll love that?" Tony asked, his voice raised in annoyance.

"The dancers, of course," Fil answered. "They're arriving today. Maybe they've already arrived. They'll walk in the snow and love it. Their first snow, I'm sure."

"How do you know it wasn't snowing in New York while they were there?" Tony asked.

"Snow in New York in early November?" Fil said. "Are you crazy?"

"Who's crazy?" Tony replied. "Ever since

you heard of those dancers from the Philippines, you've been acting nuts. Loco. As if they're coming here just for you."

Tony chuckled. Hearing him, Fil blushed, realizing that he had, indeed, been acting too eager, but Tony had said it. It felt that way—as if the dancers were coming here only for him.

Filemon Acayan, Filipino, was fifty, a U.S. citizen. He was a corporal in the U.S. Army, training at San Luis Obispo, on the day he was discharged honorably, in 1945. A few months later, he got his citizenship papers. Thousands of them, smart and small in their uniforms, stood at attention in drill formation, in the scalding sun, and pledged allegiance to the flag and the republic for which it stands. Soon after he got back to work. To a new citizen, work meant many places and many ways: factories and hotels, waiter and cook. A timeless drifting; once he tended a rose garden and took care of a hundred-year-old veteran of a border war. As a menial in a hospital in Cook County, all day he handled filth and gore. He came home smelling of surgical soap and disinfectant. In the hospital, he took charge of a row of bottles on a shelf, each bottle containing a stage of the human embryo in preservatives, from the lizard-like fetus of a few days, through the newly born infant, with its position unchanged, cold and cowering and afraid. He had nightmares through the years of himself inside a bottle. That was long ago. Now he had a more pleasant job as special policeman in the post office.

He was a few years younger than Tony— Antonio Bataller, a retired Pullman porter— but he looked older in spite of the fact that Tony had been bedridden most of the time for the last two years, suffering from a kind of wasting disease that had frustrated doctors. All over Tony's body, a gradual peeling was taking place. At first, he thought it was merely *tinia flava*, a skin disease common among adolescents in the Philippines. It had started around the neck and had spread to his extremities. His face looked as if it was healing from severe burns. Nevertheless, it was a young face, much younger than Fil's, which had never looked young.

"I'm becoming a white man," Tony had said once, chuckling softly.

It was the same chuckle Fil seemed to have heard now, only this time it sounded derisive, insulting.

Fil said, "I know who's nuts. It's the sick guy with the sick thoughts. You don't care for nothing but your pain, your imaginary pain."

"You're the imagining fellow. I got the real thing." Tony shouted from the room. He believed he had something worse than the whiteness spreading on his skin. There was a pain in his insides, like dull scissors scraping his intestines. Angrily, he added, "What for I got retired?"

"You're old, man, old, that's what, and sick, yes, but not cancer," Fil said turning towards the snow-filled sky. He pressed his face against the glass window. There's about an inch now on the ground, he thought, maybe more.

Tony came out of his room looking as if he had not slept all night. "I know what I got," he said, as if it were an honor and a privilege to die of cancer and Fil was trying to deprive him of it. "Never a pain like this. One day, I'm just gonna die."

"Naturally. Who says you won't?" Fil argued, thinking how wonderful it would be if he could join the company of dancers from

the Philippines, show them around, walk with them in the snow, watch their eyes as they stared about them, answer their questions, tell them everything they wanted to know about the changing seasons in this strange land. They would pick up fistfuls of snow, crunch it in their fingers or shove it into their mouths. He had done just that the first time, long, long ago, and it had reminded him of the grated ice the Chinese sold near the town plaza where he had played *tatching* with an older brother who later drowned in a squall. How his mother had grieved over the death, she who had not cried too much when his father died, a broken man. Now they were all gone, quick death after a storm, or lingeringly, in a season of drought, all, all of them he had loved.

He continued, "All of us will die. One day. A medium bomb marked Chicago and this whole dump is *tapus*, finished. Who'll escape then?"

"Maybe your dancers will," Tony answered, now watching the snow himself.

"Of course, they will," Fil retorted, his voice sounding like a big assurance that all the dancers would be safe in his care. "The bombs won't be falling on this night. And, when the dancers are back in the Philippines..."

He paused, as if he was no longer sure of what he was going to say. "But maybe, even in the Philippines the bombs gonna fall, no?" he said, gazing sadly at the falling snow.

"What's that to you?" Tony replied. "You got no more folks ove'der, right? I know it's nothing to me. I'll be dead before that."

"Let's talk about something nice," Fil said, the sadness spreading on his face as he tried to smile. "Tell me, how will I talk, how am I gonna introduce myself?"

He would go ahead with his plans, introduce himself to the dancers and volunteer to take them sight-seeing. His car was clean and ready for his guests. He had soaped the ashtrays, dusted off the floor boards and thrown away the old mats, replacing them with new plastic throw rugs. He had got himself soaking wet while spraying the car, humming, as he worked, faintly remembered tunes from the old country.

Fil shook his head as he waited for Tony to say something. "Gosh, I wish I had your looks, even with those white spots, then I could face every one of them," he said, "but this mug."

"That's the important thing, your mug. It's your calling card. It says, Filipino. Countryman," Tony said.

"You're not fooling me, friend," Fil said. "This mug says, Ugly Filipino. It says, old-timer, *muchacho*. It says Pinoy, *bejo*."

For Fil, time was the villain. In the beginning, the words he often heard were: too young, too young; but all of a sudden, too young became too old, too late. What had happened in between? A weariness, a mist covering all things. You don't have to look at your face in a mirror to know that you are old, suddenly old, grown useless for a lot of things and too late for all the dreams you had wrapped up well against a day of need.

"It also says sucker," Tony said. "What for you want to invite them? Here? Aren't you ashamed of this hole?"

"It's not a palace, I know," Fil answered, "but who wants a palace when they can have the most delicious *adobo* here and the best stuffed chicken . . . yum . . . yum . . ."

Tony was angry. "Yum, yum, you're nuts," he said, "plain and simple loco. What for you want to spend? You've been living on loose change all your life and now on a treasury warrant so small and full of holes, still you want to spend for these dancing kids who don't know you and won't even send you a card afterwards."

"Never mind the cards," Fil answered. "Who wants cards? But don't you see, they'll be happy; and then, you know what? I'm going to keep their voices, their words and their singing and their laughter in my magic sound mirror."

He had a portable tape recorder and a stack of recordings, patiently labeled, songs and speeches. The songs were in English, but most of the speeches were in the dialect, debates between him and Tony. It was evident Tony was the better speaker of the two in English, but in the dialect, Fil showed greater mastery. His style, however, was florid, sentimental, poetic.

Without telling Tony, he had experimented on recording sounds, like the way a bed creaked, doors opening and closing, rain or sleet tapping on the window panes, footsteps through the corridor. He played all the sounds back and tried to recall how it was on the day or night the sounds had been recorded. Did they bring back the moment? He was beginning to think that they did. He was learning to identify each of the sounds with a particular mood or fact. Sometimes, like today, he wished that there was a way of keeping a record of silence because it was to him the richest sound, like snow falling. He wondered as he watched the snow blowing in the wind, what took care of that moment if memory didn't. Like time, memory was often a villain, a betrayer.

"Fall, snow, fall," he murmured and, turning to Tony, said, "As soon as they accept my invitation, I'll call you up. No, you don't have to do anything, but I'd want you to be here to meet them."

"I'm going out myself." Tony said. "And I don't know what time I'll be back." Then he added, "You're not working today. Are you on leave?"

"For two days. While the dancers are here," Fil said.

"It still don't make sense to me," Tony said. "But good luck, anyway."

"Aren't you going to see them tonight? Our reserved seats are right out in front, you know."

"I know. But I'm not sure I can come."

"What? You're not sure?"

Fil could not believe it. Tony was indifferent. Something must be wrong with him. He looked at him closely, saying nothing.

"I want to, but I'm sick, Fil. I tell you, I'm not feeling so good. My doctor will know today. He'll tell me," Tony said.

"What will he tell you?"

"How do I know?"

"I mean, what's he trying to find out?"

"If it's cancer," Tony said. Without saying another word, he went straight back to his room.

Fil remembered those times, at night, when Tony kept him awake with his moaning. When he called out to him, asking, "Tony, what's the matter?" his sighs ceased for a while, but afterwards, Tony screamed, deadening his cries with a pillow against his mouth. When Fil rushed to his side, Tony drove him away. Or he curled up in the bedsheets like a big infant suddenly hushed in its crying. The next day, he would look all right. When Fil asked him about the previous night, he would reply, "I was dying," but it sounded more like disgust over a nameless annoyance.

Fil had misgivings, too, about the whiteness spreading on Tony's skin. He had heard of leprosy. Every time he thought of that dreaded disease, he felt tears in his eyes. In all the years he had been in America, he had not had a friend until he met Tony whom he liked immediately and, in a way, worshipped, for all the things the man had which Fil knew he himself lacked.

They had shared a lot together. They made merry on Christmas, sometimes got drunk and became loud. Fil recited poems in the dialect and praised himself. Tony fell to giggling and cursed all the railroad companies of America. But last Christmas, they hadn't gotten drunk. They hadn't even talked to each other on Christmas day. Soon, it would be Christmas again.

The snow was still falling.

"Well, I'll be seeing you," Fil said, getting ready to leave. "Try to be home on time. I shall invite the dancers for luncheon or dinner maybe, tomorrow. But tonight, let's go to the theater together, ha?"

"I'll try," Tony answered, adding after a pause, "Oh, Fil, I can't find my boots. May I wear yours?" His voice sounded strong and healthy.

"Sure, sure!" Fil answered. He didn't need boots. He loved to walk in the snow.

The air outside felt good. Fil lifted his face to the sky and closed his eyes as the snow and a wet wind drenched his face. He stood that way for some time, crying, more, more! to himself, drunk with snow and coolness. His car was parked a block away. As he walked towards it, he plowed into the snow with one foot and studied the scar he made, a hideous shape among perfect footmarks. He felt strong as his lungs filled with the cold air, as if just now it did not matter too much that he was the way he looked and his English the way it was. But perhaps, he could talk to the dancers in his dialect. Why not?

A heavy frosting of snow covered his car and as he wiped it off with his bare hands, he felt light and young, like a child at play, and once again, he raised his face to the sky and licked the flakes, cold and tasteless on his tongue.

———

When Fili arrived at the Hamilton, it seemed to him the Philippine dancers had taken over the hotel. They were all over the lobby on the mezzanine, talking in groups animatedly, their teeth sparkling as they laughed, their eyes disappearing in mere slits of light. Some of the girls wore their black hair long. For a moment, the sight seemed too much for him who had all but forgotten how beautiful Philippine girls were. He wanted to look away, but their loveliness held him. He must do something, close his eyes perhaps. As he did so, their laughter came to him like a breeze murmurous with sounds native to his land.

Later, he tried to relax, to appear inconspicuous. True, they were all very young, but there were a few elderly men and women who must have been their chaperons or well-wishers like him. He would smile at everyone who happened to look his way. Most of them smiled back, or rather, seemed to smile, but it was quick, without recognition, and might not have been for him but for someone else near or behind him.

His lips formed the words he was trying to phrase in his mind: *Ilocano ka? Bicol? Ano na, paisano? Comusta?* Or should he introduce himself? How? For what he wanted to say, the words didn't come too easily, they were unfamiliar, they stumbled and broke on his lips into a jumble of incoherence.

Suddenly, he felt as if he was in the center of a group where he was not welcome. All the things he had been trying to hide now showed: the age in his face, his horny hands. He knew it the instant he wanted to shake hands with the first boy who had drawn close to him, smiling and friendly. Fil put his hands in his pocket.

Now he wished Tony had been with him. Tony would know what to do. He would charm these young people with his smile and his learned words. Fil wanted to leave, but he seemed caught up in the tangle of moving bodies that merged and broke in a fluid strangle hold. Everybody was talking, mostly in English. Once in a while he heard exclamations in the dialect right out of the past, conjuring up playtime, long shadows of evening on the plaza, barrio fiestas, *misa de gallo.*

Time was passing and he had yet to talk to someone. Suppose he stood on a chair and addressed them in the manner of his flamboyant speeches recorded in his magic sound mirror?

"Beloved countrymen, lovely children of the Pearl of the Orient Seas, listen to me. I'm Fil Acayan. I've come to volunteer my services. I'm yours to command. Your servant. Tell me where you wish to go, what you want to see in Chicago. I know every foot of the lakeshore drive, all the gardens and the parks, the museums, the huge department stores, the planetarium. Let me be your guide. That's what I'm offering you, a free tour of Chicago, and finally, dinner at my apartment on West Sheridan Road—pork *adobo* and chicken *relleno,* name your dish. How about it, *paisanos?*"

No. That would be a foolish thing to do. They would laugh at him. He felt a dryness in his throat. He was sweating. As he wiped his face with a handkerchief, he bumped against a slim, short girl who quite gracefully stepped aside, and for a moment he thought he would swoon in the perfume that enveloped him. It was fragrance long forgotten, essence of *camia,* of *ilang-ilang,* and *dama de noche.*

Two boys with sleek, pomaded hair were sitting near an empty chair. He sat down and said in the dialect, "May I invite you to my apartment?" The boys stood up, saying, "Excuse us, please," and walked away. He mopped his brow, but instead of getting discouraged, he grew bolder as though he had moved one step beyond shame. Approaching another group, he repeated his invitation, and a girl with a mole on her upper lip, said, "Thank you, but we have no time." As he turned towards another group, he felt their eyes on his back. Another boy drifted towards him, but as soon as he began to speak, the boy said, "Pardon, please," and moved away.

They were always moving away. As if by common consent, they had decided to avoid him, ignore his presence. Perhaps it was not their fault. They must have been instructed to do so. Or was it his looks that kept them away? The thought was a sharpness inside him.

After a while, as he wandered about the mezzanine, among the dancers, but alone, he noticed that they had begun to leave. Some had crowded noisily into the two elevators. He followed the others going down the stairs. Through the glass doors, he saw them getting into a bus parked beside the subway entrance on Dearborn.

The snow had stopped falling; it was melting fast in the sun and turning into slush.

As he moved about aimlessly, he felt someone touch him on the sleeve. It was one of the dancers, a mere boy, tall and thin, who was saying, "Excuse, please." Fill realized he was in the way between another boy with a camera and a group posing in front of the hotel.

"Sorry," Fil said, jumping away awkwardly.

The crowd burst out laughing.

Then everything became a blur in his eyes, a moving picture out of focus, but gradually the figures cleared, there was mud on the pavement on which the dancers stood posing, and the sun threw shadows at their feet.

Let them have fun, he said to himself,

they're young and away from home. I have no business messing up their schedule, forcing my company on them.

He watched the dancers till the last of them was on the bus. The voices came to him, above the traffic sounds. They waved their hands and smiled towards him as the bus started. Fil raised his hand to wave back, but stopped quickly; aborting the gesture. He turned to look behind him at whomever the dancers were waving their hands to. There was no one there except his own reflection in the glass door, a double exposure of himself and a giant plant with its thorny branches around him like arms in a loving embrace.

———

Even before he opened the door to their apartment, Fil knew that Tony had not yet arrived. There were no boots outside on the landing. Somehow he felt relieved, for until then he did not know how he was going to explain his failure.

From the hotel, he had driven around, cruised by the lakeshore drive, hoping he would see the dancers somewhere, in a park perhaps, taking pictures of the mist over the lake and the last gold on the trees now wet with melted snow, or on some picnic grounds, near a bubbling fountain. Still taking pictures of themselves against a background of Chicago's gray and dirty skyscrapers. He slowed down every time he saw a crowd, but the dancers were nowhere along his way. Perhaps they had gone to the theater to rehearse. He turned back before reaching Evanston.

He felt weak, not hungry. Just the same, he ate, warming up some left-over food. The rice was cold, but the soup was hot and tasty. While he ate, he listened for footfalls.

Afterwards, he lay down on the sofa and a weariness came over him, but he tried hard not to sleep. As he stared at the ceiling, he felt like floating away, but he kept his eyes open, willing himself hard to remain awake. He wanted to explain everything to Tony when he arrived. But soon his eyes closed against a weary will too tired and weak to fight back

sleep—and then there were voices. Tony was in the room, eager to tell his own bit of news.

"I've discovered a new way of keeping afloat," he was saying.

"Who wants to keep afloat?" Fil asked.

"Just in case. In a shipwreck, for example," Tony said.

"Never mind shipwrecks. I must tell you about the dancers," Fil said.

"But this is important," Tony insisted. "This way, you can keep floating indefinitely."

"What for indefinitely?" Fil asked.

"Say in a ship . . . I mean, in an emergency, you're stranded without help in the middle of the Pacific or the Atlantic, you must keep floating till help comes . . ." Tony explained.

"More better," Fil said, "find a way to reach shore before the sharks smells you. You discover that."

"I will," Tony said, without eagerness, as though certain that there was no such way, that, after all, his discovery was worthless.

"Now you listen to me," Fil said, sitting up abruptly. As he talked in the dialect, Tony listened with increasing apathy.

"There they were." Fil began, his tone taking on the orator's pitch, "who could have been my children if I had not left home—or yours, Tony. They gazed around them with wonder, smiling at me, answering my questions, but grudgingly, edging away as if to be near me were wrong, a violation in their rule book. But it could be that every time I opened my mouth, I gave myself away. I talked in the dialect, Ilocano, Tagalog, Bicol, but no one listened. They avoided me. They had been briefed too well: Do not talk to strangers. Ignore their invitations. Be extra careful in the big cities like New York and Chicago, beware of the old-timers, the Pinoys. Most of them are bums. Keep away from them. Be on the safe side—stick together, entertain only those who have been introduced to you properly.

"I'm sure they had such instructions, safety measures, they must have called them. What then could I have done, scream out my good intentions, prove my harmlessness and my love for them by beating my breast? Oh, but I loved them. You see, I was like them once. I, too, was nimble with my feet, graceful with my hands; and I had the tongue of a poet. Ask the village girls and the envious boys from the city—but first you have to find them. After these many years, it won't be easy. You'll have to search every suffering face in the village gloom for a hint of youth and beauty or go where the graveyards are and the tombs under the lime trees. One such face... oh, God, what am I saying?

"All I wanted was to talk to them, guide them around Chicago, spend money on them so that they would have something special to remember about us here when they return to our country. They would tell their folks: We met a kind, old man, who took us to his apartment. It was not much of a place. It was old—like him. When we sat on the sofa in the living room, the bottom sank heavily, the broken springs touching the floor. But what a cook that man was! And how kind! We never thought that rice and *adobo* could be that delicious. And the chicken *relleno!* When someone asked what the stuffing was—we had never tasted anything like it—he smiled saying, 'From heaven's supermarket,' touching his head and pressing his heart like a clown as if heaven were there. He had his tape recorder which he called a magic sound mirror, and he had all of us record our voices. Say anything in the dialect, sing, if you please, our *kundiman,* please, he said, his eyes pleading, too. Oh, we had fun listening to the playback. When you're gone, the old man said, I shall listen to your voices with my eyes closed and you'll be here again and I won't ever be alone, no, not anymore, after this. We wanted to cry, but he looked very funny, so we laughed and he laughed with us.

"But, Tony, they would not come. They thanked me, but they said they had no time. Others said nothing. They looked through me. I didn't exist. Or worse, I was unclean. *Basura.* Garbage. They were ashamed of me. How could I be Filipino?"

The memory, distinctly recalled, was a rock on his breast. He gasped for breath.

"Now, let me teach you how to keep afloat," Tony said, but it was not Tony's voice.

Fil was alone and gasping for air. His eyes opened slowly till he began to breathe more easily. The sky outside was gray. He looked at his watch—a quarter past five. The show would begin at eight. There was time. Perhaps Tony would be home soon.

The apartment was warming up. The radiators sounded full of scampering rats. He had a recording of that in his sound mirror.

Fil smiled. He had an idea. He would take the sound mirror to the theater, take his seat close to the stage, and make tape recordings of the singing and the dances.

Now he was wide-awake and somehow pleased with himself. The more he thought of the idea, the better he felt. If Tony showed up now... He sat up, listening. The radiators were quiet. There were no footfalls, no sound of a key turning.

═══

Late that night, back from the theater, Fil knew at once that Tony was back. The boots were outside the door. He, too, must be tired, and should not be disturbed.

He was careful not to make any noise. As he turned on the floor lamp, he thought that perhaps Tony was awake and waiting for him. They would listen together to a playback of the dances and the songs Tony had missed. Then he would tell Tony what happened that day, repeating part of the dream.

From Tony's bedroom came the regular breathing of a man sound asleep. To be sure, he looked into the room and in the half-darkness, Tony's head showed darkly, deep in a pillow, on its side, his knees bent, almost touching the clasped hands under his chin, an oversized fetus in the last bottle. Fil shut the door between them and went over to the portable. Now. He turned it on to low. At first nothing but static and odd sounds came through, but soon after there was the patter of feet to the rhythm of a familiar melody.

All the beautiful boys and girls were in the room now, dancing and singing. A boy and a girl sat on the floor holding two bamboo poles by their ends flat on the floor, clapping them together, then apart, and pounding them on the boards, while dancers swayed and balanced their lithe forms, dipping their bare brown legs in and out of the clapping bamboos, the pace gradually increasing into a fury of wood on wood in a counterpoint of panic among the dancers and in a harmonious flurry of toes and ankles escaping certain pain—crushed bones, and bruised flesh, and humiliation. Other dances followed, accompanied by songs and live with the sounds of life and death in the old country; Igorot natives in G-strings walking down a mountainside; peasants climbing up a hill on a rainy day; neighbors moving a house, their sturdy legs showing under a moving roof; lovers at Lent hiding their passion among wild hedges, far from the crowded chapel; a distant gong sounding off a summons either to a feast or a wake. And finally, prolonged ovation, thunderous, wave upon wave . . .

"Turn that thing off!" Tony's voice was sharp above the echoes of the gongs and the applause settling into silence.

Fil switched off the dial and in the sudden stillness, the voices turned into faces, familiar and near, like gesture and touch that stayed on even as the memory withdrew, bowing out, as it were, in a graceful exit, saying, thank you, thank you, before a ghostly audience that clapped hands in silence and stomped their feet in a sucking emptiness. He wanted to join the finale, such as it was, pretend that the curtain call included them, and attempt a shamefaced imitation of a graceful adieu, but he was stiff and old, incapable of grace; but he said, thank you, thank you, his voice sincere and contrite, grateful for the other voices and the sound of singing and the memory.

"Oh, my God . . ." the man in the other room cried, followed by a moan of such anguish that Fil fell on his knees, covering the sound mirror with his hands to muffle the sounds that had started again, it seemed to him, even after he had turned it off.

Then he remembered.

"Tony, what did the doctor say? What did he say?" he shouted and listened, holding his breath, no longer able to tell at the moment who had truly waited all day for the final sentence.

There was no answer. Meanwhile, under his hands, there was a flutter of wings, a shudder of gongs. What was Tony saying? That was his voice, no? Fil wanted to hear, he must know. He switched dials on and off, again and again, pressing buttons. Suddenly, he didn't know what to do. The spools were live, they kept turning. His arms went around the machine, his chest pressing down on the spools. In the quick silence, Tony's voice came clear.

"So they didn't come after all?"

"Tony, what did the doctor say?" Fil asked, straining hard to hear.

"I knew they wouldn't come. But that's okay. The apartment is old anyhow. And it smells of death."

"How you talk. In this country, there's a cure for everything."

"I guess we can't complain. We had it good here all the time. Most of the time, anyway."

"I wish, though, they had come. I could . . ."

"Yes, they could have. They didn't have to see me, but I could have seen them. I have seen their pictures, but what do they really look like?"

"Tony, they're beautiful, all of them, but especially the girls. Their complexion, their grace, their eyes, they were what we call talking eyes, they say things to you. And the scent of them!"

There was a sigh from the room, soft, hardly like a sigh. A louder, grating sound, almost under his hands that had relaxed their hold, called his attention. The sound mirror had kept going, the tape was fast unravelling.

"Oh, no!" he screamed, noticing that somehow, he had pushed the eraser.

Frantically, he tried to rewind and play back the sounds and the music, but there was nothing now but the dull creaking of the tape on the spool and meaningless sounds that somehow had not been erased, the thud of dancing feet, a quick clapping of hands, alien voices and words: *in this country... everything... all of them... talking eyes... and the scent...* a fading away into nothingness, till about the end when there was a screaming, senseless kind of finale detached from the body of a song in the background, drums and sticks and the tolling of a bell.

"Tony! Tony!" Fil cried, looking towards the sick man's room, "I've lost them all."

Biting his lips, Fil turned towards the window, startled by the first light of dawn. He hadn't realized till then the long night was over.

Amador T. Daguio

WEDDING DANCE

Awiyao reached for the upper horizontal log which served as the edge of the head-high threshold. Clinging to the log, he lifted himself with one bound that carried him across to the narrow door. He slid back the cover, stepped inside, then pushed the cover back in place. After some moments during which he seemed to wait, he talked to the listening darkness.

"I'm sorry this had to be done. I am really sorry. But neither of us can help it."

The sound of the *gangsas* beat through the walls of the dark house like muffled roars of falling waters. The woman, who had moved with a start when the sliding door opened, had been hearing the *gangsas* for she did not know how long. The sudden rush of the rich sounds when the door opened was like a sharp gush of fire in her. She gave no sign that she heard Awiyao but continued to sit unmoving in the darkness.

But Awiyao knew that she heard him and his heart pitied her. He crawled on all fours to the middle of the room; he knew exactly where the stove was. With bare fingers he stirred the covered smoldering embers and blew into them. When the coals began to glow, Awiyao put pieces of pine on them, then full round logs as big as his arms. The room brightened.

"Why don't you go out," he said, "and join the dancing women?" He felt a pang inside him, because what he said was really not the right thing to say and because the woman did not stir. "You should join the dancers," he said, "as if—as if nothing has happened." He looked at the woman huddled in a corner of the room, leaning against the wall. The stove fire played with strange moving shadows and lights upon her face. She was partly sullen, but her sullenness was not because of anger or hate.

"Go out—go out and dance. If you really don't hate me for this separation, go out and dance. One of the men will see you dance well; he will like your dancing; he will marry you. Who knows but that, with him, you will be luckier than you were with me?"

"I don't want any man," she said sharply. "I don't want any other man."

He felt relieved that at least she talked. "You know very well that I don't want any other woman, either. You know that, don't you?"

She did not answer him.

"You know it, Lumnay, don't you?" he repeated.

"Yes, I know," she said weakly.

"It is not my fault," he said, feeling relieved. "You cannot blame me: I have been a good husband to you."

"Neither can you blame me," she said. She seemed about to cry.

"No, you have been very good to me. You

have been a good wife. I have nothing to say against you." He set some of the burning wood in place. "It's only that a man must have a child. Seven harvests is just too long to wait. Yes, we have waited too long. We should have another chance before it is too late for both of us."

This time the woman stirred, stretched her right leg out, and bent her left leg in. She wound the blanket more snugly around herself.

"You know that I have done my best," she said. "I have prayed to Kabunyan much. I have sacrificed many chickens in my prayers."

"Yes, I know."

"You remember how angry you were once, when you came home from your work in the terrace because I butchered one of our pigs without your permission. I did it to appease Kabunyan, because, like you, I wanted to have a child. But what could I do?"

"Kabunyan does not see fit for us to have a child," he said. He stirred the fire. The sparks rose through the crackles of the flame. The smoke and soot went up to the ceiling.

Lumnay looked down and unconsciously started to pull at the rattan that kept the split bamboo flooring in place. She tugged at the rattan flooring. Each time she did this the split bamboo went up and came down with a slight rattle. The gongs of the dancer clamorously called in her ears through the walls.

Awiyao went to the corner where Lumnay sat, paused before her, looked at her bronzed and sturdy face, then turned to where the jars of water stood piled one over the other. Awiyao took a coconut cup and dipped it in the top jar and drank. Lumnay had filled the jars from the mountain creek early that evening.

"I came home," he said, "because I did not find you among the dancers. Of course, I am not forcing you to come, if you don't want to join my wedding ceremony. I came to tell you that Madulimay, although I am marrying her, can never become as good as you are. She is not as strong in planting beans, not as fast in cleaning water jars, not as good in keeping a

house clean. You are one of the best wives in the whole village."

"That has not done me any good, has it?" she said. She looked at him lovingly. She almost seemed to smile.

He put the coconut cup aside on the floor and came closer to her. He held her face between his hands and looked longingly at her beauty. But her eyes looked away. Never again would he hold her face. The next day she would not be his any more. She would go back to her parents. He let go of her face, and she bent to the floor again and looked at her fingers as they tugged softly at the split bamboo floor.

"This house is yours," he said. "I built it for you. Make it for your own, live in it as long as you wish. I will build another house for Madulimay."

"I have no need for a house," she said slowly. "I'll go to my own house. My parents are old. They will need help in the planting of the beans, in the pounding of the rice."

"I will give you the field that I dug out of the mountain during the first year of our marriage," he said.

"You know I did it for you. You helped me to make it for the two of us."

"I have no use for any field," she said.

He looked at her, then turned away, and became silent. They were silent for a time.

"Go back to the dance," she said finally. "It is not right for you to be here. They will wonder where you are, and Madulimay will not feel good. Go back to the dance."

"I would feel better if you could come and dance—for the last time. The *gangsas* are playing."

"You know that I cannot."

"Lumnay," he said tenderly. "Lumnay, if I did this it is because of my need for a child. You know that life is not worth living without a child. The men have mocked me behind my back. You know that."

"I know it," she said. "I will pray that Kabunyan will bless you and Madulimay."

She bit her lips now, then shook her head wildly and sobbed.

She thought of the seven harvests that had passed, the high hopes they had in the beginning of their new life, the day he took her away from her parents across the roaring river on the other side of the mountain, the trip up the trail which they had to climb, the steep canyon which they had to cross—the waters boiled in her mind in foams of white and jade and roaring silver; the waters rolled and growled, resounded in thunderous echoes through the walls of the stiff cliffs; they were far away now but loud still and receding; the waters violently smashed down from somewhere on the tops of the other ranges, and they had looked carefully at the buttresses of rocks they had to step on—a slip would have meant death.

They both drank of the water and rested on the other bank before they made the final climb to the other side of the mountain.

She looked at his face with the fire playing upon his features—hard and strong and kind. He had a sense of lightness in his way of saying things, which often made her and the village people laugh. How proud she had been of his humor. The muscles were taut and firm, bronze and compact in their hold upon his skull—how frank his bright eyes were. She looked at his body that carved out of the mountains five fields for her; his wide and supple torso heaved as if a slab of shining lumber were heaving; his arms and legs flowed down in fluent muscles—he was strong, and for that she had lost him.

She flung herself upon his knees and clung to them. "Awiyao, Awiyao, my husband!", she cried. "I did everything to have a child," she said passionately in a hoarse whisper. "Look at me," she cried. "Look at my body. Then it was full of promise. It could dance; it could work fast in the fields; it could climb the mountains fast. Even now it is firm, full. But Awiyao, Kabunyan never blessed me. Awiyao, Kabunyan is cruel to me. Awiyao, I am useless. I must die."

"It will not be right to die," he said, gathering her in his arms. Her whole warm naked breast quivered against his own; she clung now to his neck, and her head lay upon his right shoulder; her hair flowed down in cascades of gleaming darkness.

"I don't care about the fields," she said. "I don't care about the house. I don't care for anything but you. I'll have no other man."

"Then you'll always be fruitless."

"I'll go back to my father. I'll die."

"Then you hate me," he said. "If you die it means you hate me. You do not want me to have a child. You do not want my name to live in our tribe."

She was silent.

"If I do not try a second time," he explained, "it means I'll die. Nobody will get the fields I have carved out of the mountains; nobody will come after me."

"If you fail—if you fail this second time—" she said thoughtfully. Then her voice was a shudder. "No—no, I don't want you to fail."

"If I fail," he said. "I'll come back to you. Then both of us will die together. Both of us will vanish from the life of our tribe."

The gongs thundered through the walls of their house, sonorous and far away.

"I'll keep my beads," she said. "Awiyao, let me keep my beads," she half-whispered.

"You will keep the beads. They come from far-off times. My grandmother said they came from way up North, from the slant-eyed people across the sea. You keep them, Lumnay. They are worth twenty fields."

"I'll keep them because they stand for the love you have for me," she said. "I love you. I love you and have nothing to give." She took herself away from him, for a voice was calling out to him from outside. "Awiyao! O Awiyao! They are looking for you at the dance!"

"I am not in a hurry."

"The elders will scold you. You had better go."

"Not until you tell me that it is all right with you."

"It is all right with me."

He clasped her hands. "I do this for the sake of the tribe," he said.

"I know," she said.

He went to the door.

"Awiyao!"

He stopped as if suddenly hit by a spear. In pain he turned to her. Her face was agony. It pained him to leave. She had been wonderful to him. What was it that made a man wish for a child? What was it in life, in the work in the fields, in the planting and harvest, in the silence of the night in the communings with husband and wife, in the whole life of the tribe itself that made a man wish for the laughter and speech of a child? Suppose he changed his mind? Why did the unwritten law demand, anyway, that a man, to be a man, must have a child to come after him? And if he was fruitless—but he loved Lumnay. It was like taking away half of his life to leave her like this.

"Awiyao," she said, and her eyes seemed to smile in the light. "The beads!"

He turned back and walked to the farthest corner of their room, to the trunk where they kept their worldly possessions—his battle-axe and spear points, her betel nut box and her beads. He dug out from the darkness the beads which had been given to him by his grandmother to give to Lumnay on the day of his marriage. He went to her, lifted her head, put the beads on, and tied them in place. The white and jade and deep orange obsidians shone in the firelight. She suddenly clung to him, clung to his neck, as if she would never let him go.

"Awiyao! Awiyao, it is hard!" she gasped, and she closed her eyes and buried her face in his neck.

The call for him from the outside was repeated.

His grip loosened, and he hurried out into the night.

Lumnay sat for some time in the darkness. Then she went to the door and opened it. The moonlight struck her face; the moonlight spilled itself upon the whole village.

She could hear the throbbing of the *gangsas* coming to her through the caverns of the other houses. She knew that all the houses were empty, that the whole tribe was at the dance. Only she was absent. And yet was she

not the best dancer in the village? Did she not have the most lightness and grace? Could she not, alone among all the women, dance like a bird tripping for grains on the ground, beautifully timed to the beat of the *gangsas?* Did not the men praise her supple body and the women envy the way she stretched her hands like the wings of the mountain eagle now and then as she danced? How long ago did she dance at her own wedding? Tonight all the women who counted, who once danced in her honor, were dancing now in honor of another whose only claim was that perhaps she could give her husband a child.

"It is not right. It is not right!" she cried. "How does she know? How can anybody know? It is not right," she said.

Suddenly she found courage. She would go to the dance. She would go to the chief of the village, to the elders, to tell them it was not right. Awiyao was hers; nobody could take him away from her. Let her be the first woman to complain, to denounce the unwritten rule that a man may take another woman. She would break the dancing of the men and women. She would tell Awiyao to come back to her. He surely would relent. Was not their love as strong as the river?

She made for the other side of the village where the dancing was. There was a flaming glow over the whole place; a great bonfire was burning. The *gangsas* clamored more loudly now and it seemed they were calling to her. She was near at last. She could see the dancers clearly now. The men leaped lightly with their *gangsas* as they circled the dancing women decked in feast garments and beads, tripping on the ground like graceful birds, following their men. Her heart warmed to the flaming call of the dance; a strange beat in her blood welled up, and she started to run.

But the flaming brightness of the bonfire commanded her to stop. Did anybody see her approach? She stopped. What if somebody had seen her coming? The flames of the bonfire leaped in countless sparks which spread and rose like yellow points and died out in the night. The blaze reached out to her like a spreading radiance. She did not have the courage to break into the wedding feast.

Lumnay walked away from the dancing ground, away from the village. She thought of the new clearing of beans which Awiyao and she had started to make only four moons before. She followed the trail above the village.

When she came to the mountain stream, she crossed it carefully. Nobody held her hands, and the stream water was very cold. The trail went up again, and she was in the moonlight shadows among the trees and shrubs. Slowly she climbed the mountain.

When Lumnay reached the clearing, she could see from where she stood the blazing bonfire at the edge of the village, where the dancing was. She could hear the far-off clamor of the gongs, still rich in their sonorousness, echoing from mountain to mountain. The sound did not mock her; they seemed to call far to her, speak to her in the language of unspeaking love. She felt the pull of their clamor, almost the feeling that they were telling her their gratitude for her sacrifice. Her heartbeat began to sound to her like many *gangsas.*

Lumnay thought of Awiyao as the Awiyao she had known long ago—a strong, muscular boy carrying his heavy loads of fuel logs down the mountains to his home. She had met him one day as she was on her way to fill her clay jars with water. He had stopped at the spring to drink and rest; and she had made him drink the cool mountain water from the coconut shell. After that it did not take him long to decide to throw his spear into the stairs of her father's house in token of his desire to marry her.

The mountain clearing was cold in the freezing moonlight. The wind began to cough and stir the leaves of the bean plants. Lumnay looked for a big rock on which to sit down. The bean plants now surrounded her, and she was lost among them.

A few more weeks, a few more months, a few more harvests—what did it matter? She would be holding the bean flowers, soft in texture, silken almost, but moist where the dew got into them, silver to look at, silver on the light blue, blooming whiteness, when the morning came. The stretching of the bean pods full length from the hearts of the wilting petals would go on.

Lumnay's fingers moved a long, long time among the growing bean pods.

Sinai Hamada

TANABATA'S WIFE

Fas-Sang first came to Baguio by way of the Mountain Trail. When at last she emerged from her weary travel over the mountains, she found herself just above the Trinidad Valley. From there, she overlooked the city of Baguio itself.

Baguio was her destination. Along with three other women, she had planned to come thither and work on the numerous roads that were being built around the city. Native women were given spades to shovel earth from the hillsides, and so make way for the roads that were being cut.

They had almost arrived. Yet Fas-Sang knew no place where she could abide in the city while waiting to be taken in as laborer. Perhaps, she would stay in the workers' camp and be picked with the other laborers in their smelly quarters. She had heard a lot about the tiered beds, the congestion in the long, low-roofed house for the road workers.

It was mid-afternoon. The four women and three men, new immigrants from Bontoc, walked on the long straight road of the Trinidad Valley. They had never before, in their lives, seen a road as long and as straight. After the regular up and down journey over hill and dell, the level road was tedious and slow to travel on.

Plodding at snail's pace, they left the valley behind, passed through the narrow gap of the Trinidad River, and entered Lucban valley. All along the road, the sight was a succession of cabbage plots, more and more.

And when they passed Lucban valley and came to Kisad valley, still there were rows and rows of cabbages. But now, the sun was sinking low behind the brown hills in the west. And the company thought of their abode for the night. For they had one more steep hill to climb till the city laborers' camp, so they had been told. And their feet ached most painfully. Was there no door open for them among the thatched homes in the valley?

It was then that they came to the house of Tanabata-san. The Japanese gardener was looking out through his tiny window as they were about to pass on. He halted them.

"Are you looking for work?" the gardener called out in his broken dialect.

"Indeed we are, my lord," one of the strangers replied.

"If you like, I have work for two women in my garden," Tanabata offered.

The men looked questioningly at the women. "Which of you would like to stay?" one man asked.

Only Fas-Sang was willing to consider the gardener's offer. She stepped forward. "How much would you give me?" she demanded.

"Ten pesos."

Fas-Sang asked for twelve, but Tanabata would not agree to that. Wherefore, Fas-Sang again reflected for a moment, and then confided to her companions, "I guess I'll stay. There is but a difference of two pesos between what I'll get here and my wage if I became a road worker. My lot here may even be better."

One of the remaining two women was also persuaded to stay after Fas-Sang had made her decision. Tanabata was smiling as he watched the two make up their minds.

The rest of the company were going on their way. "So, you two shall stay," the eldest of the group said, affecting a superior air. "Well if you think it is best for both of you, then it is all right. You need not worry over us, for we shall proceed and reach the camp early tonight."

In this way, Fas-Sang first lent herself to Tanabata. She was at the height of her womanhood then. Her cheeks were ruddy, though not so rosy as in her childhood. She had a buxom breast, the main charm of her sturdy self. As she walked, her footsteps were heavy. But anyone would admit she was indeed pretty.

II

Tanabata had had no wife. For a long time now, he had been looking for one among the native women, hoping he would find one who might consent to be his spouse. But none did he ever find, until Fas-Sang, guided by fate, came. He had almost sent for a Japanese wife from his homeland. He had seen her picture. But it would have cost him much.

Would Fas-sang, perchance, learn to like him and later agree to their marriage? This was only a tiny thought hatched in the mind of Tanabata as he sat one evening looking wistfully at Fas-Sang. She was washing her feet by the outer ditch in front of the house. Every now and then, she lifted her skirt above her knees, and Tanabata saw her clear, bright skin, tempting him.

After a time, Fas-Sang herself would watch Tanabata. As they sat before their supper, she would cast furtive glances at him across the low, circular table. He was bearded. Sometimes, he let his beard grow for three days, and his unshaven, hairy face was ugly to look at. Only with a clean countenance and in his blue suit did Fas-Sang like him at all.

Well-dressed, Tanabata-san would walk on Sundays to the market fair. Close behind would follow one of his laborers, carrying two heavy baskets over his shoulder. The basket overflowed with the minor products of the garden, such as strawberries, celery, tomatoes, spinach, radishes, and "everlasting" flowers. Fas-Sang, arrayed in her gayest Sunday dress, would trail in the rear. She was to sell the garden products at the market.

In the afternoon, the fair would be over. Fas-Sang would go home with a heavy handbag. She would arrive to find Tanabata, usually drunk, with a half-emptied bottle still before him on the table.

Fas-Sang would lay the bag of money on his crossed legs. "That is the amount the vegetables have brought us," she would report.

"Good." And Tanabata would release a happy smile. He always said gracias after that, showing full trust in Fas-Sang. He would pick out two-peso pieces and give them to her. "Here, take these. They are for you. Buy yourself whatever you like with them." For he was a prosperous, generous gardener.

On week days, there was hard and honest work in the gardens. The other native woman had gone away when she saw that she was not so favored as Fas-Sang was. So, Fas-Sang, when she was not cooking, stayed among the cabbage rows picking worms. All that Tanabata did was to care for the seedlings in the shed house. Also, he did most of the transplanting, since he alone had the sensitive fingers that could feel the animate touch of the soil. He had but a little area to superintend, and only three farm hands to look after.

New life! Fas-Sang liked the daily turns that were her lot. Little by little, she learned to do the domestic chores. Early in the morning, she rose up to cook. Before noon, she cooked again. And in the evening, likewise. In the daytime, the plates were mounted on a platerack and sunned. She washed clothes occasionally, more often when the laundress came irregularly. She swept the house. And, of course, she never forgot to leave a tea kettle steaming over live embers. Anytime, Tanabata might come in and sip a cup of tea.

III

Immediately after noon on week days, when the sun was hot and the leaves were almost wilting, Tanabata liked to stroll and visit his neighbor, Okamoto-san. They were of the same province in Japan, Hiroshimaken. Okamoto had a Benguet woman for a wife. Kawane was an industrious and amiable companion. The only fault Okamoto found in Kawane was her ignorance. She had no idea of the world beyond her small valley.

One afternoon, Tanabata as usual paid his friend a visit. This was of great consequence, for he had in mind to ask Okamoto if he thought Fas-Sang could be a fit wife for him. Tanabata was slow in broaching the subject to his friend, but he was direct:

"I think I shall marry that woman," Tanabata said.

"Which woman—Fas-Sang?" Okamoto asked.

"Yes."

"She is a good woman, I think. She seems to behave well."

"I have known her for only a short time. Do you think she will behave as well always?" Tanabata asked earnestly.

Okamoto was hesitant and would not explicate. "I cannot tell. But look at my wife. She is a peaceful woman," he answered simply.

"There, my good friend," reminded his neighbor; "you forget that your wife is Benguet, while Fas-Sang is Bontoc."

"Yes, they are good friends, as much as we are," came Okamoto's bright rejoinder. And they both laughed.

IV

Two days later, Tanabata proposed to Fas-Sang. He had frequently teased her before. But now, he was gravely concerned about what he had to tell. He had a great respect for this sturdy, native woman.

He called Fas-Sang into the big room where she had heretofore seldom entered except to clean. It was dimly lighted. Fas-Sang went in unafraid. It seemed she had anticipated this. She sat close beside him on a trunk. Tanabata talked carefully, convincingly, and long. He explained to her, as best as he could, his intentions. At last, she yielded. Without ceremony and without the law, they were wedded by a tacitly sworn agreement between themselves.

As has been said, Fas-Sang did not find it difficult to tend the truck garden. To be sure, it was sometimes dull. Now and then she would get exasperated with the routine work. But only for a short time. Ordinarily, she was patient, bending over the plants as she rid them of their worms, or gathered them for the sale in the market. Even her hands had been taught to handle with care the tender seedlings, which almost had to be prodded to grow luxuriantly.

When the sunbeam filled the valley, and the dewy leaves were glistening, it was a joy to watch the fluttering white butterflies that flitted all over the gardens. They were pests, for their chrysalis mercilessly devoured the green vegetables. Still, their advent in the bright morning would stir the laborers to be up and doing before they themselves were outdone by the insects.

In time, Fas-Sang was introduced to Japanese customs. Thus, she learned to use chopsticks after being prevailed by Tanabata; they had a zinc tub outside their hut wherein they heated water and took a bath in the evening; Fas-Sang picked radish after the Japanese fashion, salting them in a barrel; she began to use wooden shoes, though of the Philippine variety, and left them outside their bedroom before she retired; she became used to drinking tea and pouring much toyo sauce into their viands; matresses too and no longer a plain mat formed her beddings.

A year after they were married, they had a child, a boy. The baby was a darling. Tanabata decided to celebrate the coming of this new being. He gave a baptismal party to which were invited his Japanese friends. They drank saki; ate Japanese seaweeds, pickles, canned fish, and others.

But Fas-Sang, amidst this revelry, could not understand the chattering of her guests. So, she was very quiet, holding the baby in her arms.

The men (there were no women visitors) had brought gifts for the baby and the mother. Fas-Sang was very much delighted. She repeatedly muttered gracias to all as the gifts were piled before her.

Then the men consulted the Japanese calendar. Ultimately the child was given the name of Kato. And the guests shouted banzai many times, tossing glassfuls of saki to the ceiling. They wished the mother and child good luck.

Tanabata was most solicitous towards Fas-Sang as she began to recover from the emaciation caused by her strenuous child birth. He would not allow her to go out. She must stay indoors for a month. It was another Japanese custom.

At length, when August had passed, Fas-Sang once more stepped out into the sunshine, warm and free. The pallor of her cheeks had gone. She was alive and young again. Her odd springy steps came back and she walked briskly, full of strength and passion, it seemed.

V

But what news of home? Fas-Sang yearned to learn from her folks back in Bisao, Bontoc. Had the kaingin been planted with camote and corn? Her kinsman had heard of her delivering a child, and they sent a boy cousin to inquire about her. He was told to see if Fas-Sang lived happily, and if her Japanese husband really treated her well. If not, they

would do him harm. The Bontoc or busol were fierce.

The cousin came. Tanabata entertained him well. He bought short pants for the Igorot boy and told him to do away with his G-string. The boy was much pleased. After a week, the boy said he would go back. And Tanabata bought some more clothes for him.

Fas-Sang saw her cousin off. (Tanabata was in the shed house, cultivating the seedlings.) She instructed him well: "Tell Ama and Ina I am happy here. They must not worry about me. My husband is kind, and I'm never in want. Give this little money that I have saved for them. You see, I have a child, so I shall live here a long, long time yet. But I do wish I could go home sometime and see Ama and Ina. Often I feel homesick."

She wept. And when her cousin saw her tears, he wept also. Then they parted.

VI

It was no hidden truth that Tanabata loved his wife dearly. In every way, he tried to show his affection. Once, he had not allowed her to go to the city to see the movies. But he repented afterwards and sent her there without her asking.

Fas-Sang soon became a cine addict. She went to the show with one of the garden boys. Sometimes, she took her baby along. She carried the baby on her back. They had to bring a kerosene lamp with them to light their way coming home. They would return near midnight.

Tanabata alone would stay at home. He sat up reading his books, Japanese novels. When Fas-Sang arrived she would be garrulous with what she had seen. Tanabata would tuck her under the thick blankets to warm her cold feet. She would easily fall asleep. Then, after she had dozed off, he would retire himself.

More and more, Fas-Sang liked to attend the shows. The city was two miles away. But that did not matter. The theater was fascinating. Moreover, Fas-Sang admitted she often met several of her relatives and townmates in the theater. They, too, had learned to frequent the cine. Together, they had a good time.

Tanabata asked Okamoto what he thought of Fas-Sang's frequenting the shows. Okamoto, being less prosperous and more conservative, did not favor it. He advised Tanabata to stop her. But Tanabata was too indulgent with Fas-Sang to even intimate such a thing to her. Though inclined to be cautious, he loved her too much to deny her any pleasure she desired.

Thus, Fas-Sang, after the day's toil, would run off to the show. Tanabata had grown even more lenient. He could never muster courage to restrain her—much less scold her. She never missed a single change of program in the theater. Tanabata did not know what to do with her. He could not understand what drew her to the cine. For his part, he was wholly disinterested in screen shows, which he had attended but once long ago, and with which he had been disgusted.

Still Fas-Sang continued to attend them as devotedly as ever. One night, she did not come home. She only returned in the morning. Tanabata asked where she had slept, and she said, with her cousin at Camp Filipino. She had felt too lazy to walk all the way down to the valley, she said.

That whole day, she remained at home. Tanabata went out to the garden. Fas-Sang rummaged among her things. She tied them into a bundle which she hid in the corner. She dressed her child.

Then, at midnight, when Tanabata was sound asleep, she escaped. She carried her child and ran down the road where her lover was waiting. They would return to Bontoc, their native place. The man had been dismissed from the military post at Camp John Hay.

Fas-Sang left a note on the table before she left. It had been written by the man who had seduced her. It read: "Do not follow us. We are returning home to Bontoc. If you follow us, you will be killed on the way."

When Tanabata had learned everything, he dared not pursue the truant lovers. The note was too positive to mean anything but death if disobeyed. He was grieved. And for three days, he could hardly eat. He felt bitterly being betrayed and deserted. Helpless, he was full of hatred for the man who had lured his wife away.

Okamoto, faithful indeed, came to comfort his friend. He offered to come with his wife and live with Tanabata. But Tanabata would not consider the proposition. Nor could he be comforted. He politely begged his friend to leave him alone. He had suddenly become gloomy. He sat in his hut all day and drank much liquor. He shut himself in. The truck garden was neglected.

Months passed. The rows of cabbages were rotting. Tanabata was thought to be crazy. He cared not what happened to the plants. He had dismissed the few helpers that were left him. Weed outgrew the seedlings. The rainy season set in, and the field was devastated by the storm. Tanabata lived on his savings.

The rainy months passed. Sunny, cold November came. In a month, Tanabata would perhaps go home and die in Japan. His despondency had not been lessened. When he thought of his lost boy, he cried all the more.

VII

But one evening, Fas-Sang came back. She stood behind the house, scanning the wreck left of what was formerly a blooming garden. She had heard back home, from wayfarers who had returned, of Tanabata. The man who had alienated the affection of Fas-Sang had left her.

"Your Japanese husband is said to be ruining himself," some reported.

"He pines for you and his boy," others brought back.

"It is said he is thinking of going home across the sea, but he must see his little son first," still others informed her.

Fas-Sang at once decided. "Then I must return to him before it is too late." And so she came.

In the twilight, she stood, uncertain, hesitant. She heard the low mournful tune arising from the bamboo flute that Tanabata was playing. What loneliness! Fas-Sang wondered if that now seemingly forbidden house was still open to her. Could she disperse the gloom that had settled over it? There was a woman's yearning in her. But she wavered in her resolve, feeling ashamed.

The music had ceased. She almost turned away when the child, holding her hand, cried aloud. Tanabata looked out of the window. He saw the mother and child. He rushed outside, exultant. Gently, he took them by their hands and led them slowly into the house. Then he lighted the big lamp that had long hung from the ceiling, unused.

Edilberto K. Tiempo

THE GRAVE DIGGERS

With a hard knobby finger Nicolas drew a rectangle between the two mounds.

"That's too big for a small girl, don't you think?" said Agustin.

"I know, I know. The fat Ho Ya can lie in it comfortably also." He drove a bamboo peg in one corner of the rectangle with the base of his palm. Moving to the opposite corner he said, "I wonder what the Chinese bury with a man." He looked around, at the two men building a tomb sixty meters away, near the cemetery chapel. He cut a line in the middle of the rectangle. "We put her on this side, and the cement will be poured on the other side."

"Won't they know?"

"No, not exactly on this side, *chico*—but nearer this side than that. They won't know the exact spot when she's all covered, will they?"

Nicolas bent down for his pick mattock. "This," he indicated the left side of the dividing line, "is where we dig tonight. That's why the big hole—makes quicker work tonight."

He began hewing on the line of the rectangle. "Start in the middle, 'Gustin."

Their picks chopped steadily on the hard earth.

"Nobody'll know," said Nicolas. "Nobody'll ever know."

"You sure of that?"

"Sure's the quarter moon tonight." He added. "We'll work by the light of the moon."

"S'ppose we are seen."

"Only the ghosts will see us, and they don't talk. Stay watch at the gate if you want. I'll do the digging."

"You don't believe in ghosts, 'Gustin, do you?"

"Well—I don't know, I haven't seen one."

"Don't you believe what you don't see. When a man dies, he's dead. I've been digging graves seventeen years, and I've never met a ghost yet."

"Don't you believe in life after death, 'No Kulas?"

"I'm not sure. If there is such a place—you can't drink tuba out there, can you? I like my tuba now. After you've dug so many graves, you wonder what really happens."

They were quiet again.

"You don't have to feel guilty," said Nicolas. "What's buried with the girl—now tell me, where did Ho Ya get all his money? When I was a boy he had only a small candle business. He had it in a little room, dark and very dirty. D'you suppose he believes in the candles? The fat heathen makes the candles for money. Look at him now. Ho Ya makes the soap for the town—and other towns. He owns the biggest bakery. And where do you buy your petroleum? Go to him for a ganta of rice. Pay it on

Monday—or you sweat it out in his candle shop for one and a half days instead of one. And what does he do but sit on his fat tail and smoke his trombone of a pipe."

"But the dead, 'No Kulas. What's buried with the girl is hers."

"What use has the dead for a pearl necklace, can you tell me? Maybe it looks pretty around a vertebra. Your wife doesn't have to wear it. I know how to get the money for *them!*"

Nicolas drove his pick mattock hard into the ground, wrenched a block of earth, then looked at his companion. "Now listen to me, 'Gustin. I didn't have to tell you about this, you know that. I could get all—all for myself. But your wife is my niece, her mother's dead, and she's the only kinfolk I care about. I want her to eat good."

"With your share," Nicolas went on, "you can open a barber shop down town and stop digging graves. You can handle scissors better than that mattock. As for me, I'll go to Cebu City and see what it's like out there."

"You have done this before, 'No Kulas?"

"I wish I had the chance, *chico.* I know someone who had, and a nice digging he had. You wouldn't know he ever was a grave digger. Nobody in Cebu City would know I was a grave digger."

Nicolas spat into his hands, raised his mattock high and drove a mighty arc into the ground. "I won't be very unhappy if another rich Chinese girl's buried next week."

After some time Nicolas threw down the mattock. He took off his torn buri hat and fanned his sweating body. His splendid torso shone like wet bronze, his breasts like cymbals. His bulging muscles were rough and uneven, prominent around the shoulders and neck and arms from hauling lumber, bales of hemp, and sacks of rice and copra when he was not digging graves.

He turned to his companion who was throwing up earth out of the pit. "Take off your shirt, 'Gustin. By knee-deep you'll be wet all over. Besides, the sun's good for you."

Agustin was a pale, undernourished young man, about twenty-one, who took odd jobs that came his way. "It's all right. Sebia will wash my clothes when I get home." His real reason was that he did not want the penetrating earthy odor of the grave to stick to his skin. He stepped over to the next grave and picked two leaves of *carabo* growing lushly at the head of the mound. He crushed the downy leaves and the sap was cold in his hands. It had a tangy, secret, fertile smell. Why should people plant *carabo* on the grave when it was used to spice mashed mongo beans? The *carabo* didn't bear flowers. Perhaps the leaves, oval-shaped and thick with sap, absorbed the heat of the sun and kept the head part of the grave cool.

"Why do you suppose they plant *carabo* here?" he asked Nicholas.

"The maggots also need appetizers, *chico.*"

Nicolas picked up his mattock again and chopped at the ground. About an hour later they were joined by the two men who were cementing a tomb near the cemetery chapel.

Ingoy, one of the men, squatted on the edge of the grave. He was chewing buyo and betel nut. "When is the burial, Kulas?"

Nicolas turned to Ingoy. "Ho Ya said between four and five this afternoon. Maybe later because the girl's brother is coming on the *San Marcelino.* The boat comes late sometimes."

Julian, Ingoy's companion, pulled out a folded tobacco leaf from his left trouser pocket and moistened it with breath. "Want a smoke, Kulas?"

"Can't smoke now, but you may give me a little for *mascada.* I want the part near the stem."

Julian handed Nicolas a part of the tobacco which the grave digger popped into his mouth and masticated with relish.

Julian rolled the rest of the tobacco leaf into a thin cigar. "Ho Ya wanted us to begin work after the burial. We told him we couldn't do it because we're still busy with Lupo's tomb. We may not finish till late this afternoon. Ingoy's going home and can't help me."

"My wife," explained Ingoy, "is expecting the baby any time now."

"That makes it eleven now—or is it twelve? And you're still strong. Ingoy—strong as a two-year-old Bombai goat." Nicolas poked him in the rib.

"Only ten because one died last year. The one coming will be the last."

"If you can help it, but you can't," said Julian quietly.

Nicolas guffawed. And then becoming sober he asked. "Who'll make the tomb then, if you won't?"

"Ompong-Miguela," said Julian. "His brother-in-law will help."

"Are they coming for the funeral?"

"They should, but I don't know. But you'll be here, and you can talk it over."

"Yes, we will be here. In fact 'Gustin and I will be here all night."

The cement workers looked at Nicolas and Augustin.

"We're staying here all night," said Nicolas. "It's foolish to throw away four pesos for just keeping watch. Anyway, why should we be afraid?"

"The Chinese are very queer," observed Ingoy, squirting yellow-brown juice of the buyo and betel he was chewing at the mound of earth to his right. "I remember—after the burial of Bun Ting's wife two years ago, we had to cement the grave at once. We had to work until about nine at night. Perhaps it's part of their religion."

"Maybe," said Julian, fumbling for a match in his pocket. He lighted the tobacco roll. "I heard the Chinese bury trinkets and that sort with the dead. That may account for their cementing the grave in a hurry."

The group became quiet.

"If what I said is true," Julian went on, "much jewelry will be buried with Si Ya. She's Ho Ya's youngest and his only girl."

"I don't see how that could be possible," spoke Nicolas. "Most of the Chinese I know are thin as their chopsticks because even if they have money they don't eat enough. Ho Ya is one exception. A more tight-fisted people you'll never know."

Pushing his mattock to a corner of the pit,

Nicolas searched a pocket for some coins and gave twenty centavos to Ingoy. "I'm very thirsty," he said. "Run to Talya's and bring us one *dama* of tuba. If she has roasted fish, get twenty centavos' worth. I'll pay her when Ho Ya gives me money."

Ingoy hurried away.

Turning to his companion Nicolas said, "Now 'Gustin, let's get to work. Stay a while, Julian."

The two men dug steadily while Julian sat on his heels, smoking his tobacco contentedly. At waist-deep they struck bones. They shortly uncovered a skeleton, each bone to the smallest toe still in place. Nicolas picked up the skull and held it before him for some time. "I know this fellow," he said. "This is dear old Pantaleon. I chased him once for beating my dig. And now look at him." He tossed the skull to Julian.

"How do you know it's Pantaleon?"

"See the big scratch above the left ear hole? That's a scar from the bolo of Juan'g Libat. That was a fight I'd have paid to see. Besides," Nicolas added, "I dug his grave six years ago. I remember now this is the place."

While Julian was examining the skull, Agustin started throwing up the bones to one side of the grave. He was about to scoop up the hand bones with his spade, when he paused to look at them, fascinated. He picked up the middle finger. The bone was light and cold, and immaculately white. You will pull golden rings from cold fingers tonight. Rings from cold dead fingers. By night the hand will have bloated, the rings will be tight around the fingers. You will have to pull hard. Some flesh may come off with them. You may have to break the fingers.

Agustin stared at the finger bone in his hand and flung it away.

"I think the *gobierno* should expand the cemetery," Julian said, putting down the skull beside him. "You don't want to be evicted from your last resting place, do you, Kulas?"

"Come to think of it—no. Though how should I know I was evicted, like Pantaleon there? Would you know, Julian?"

"My soul wouldn't be around, but I certainly would like privacy. How did you happen to pick this place?"

"The mound had almost disappeared. Nobody to take care of it. The wife, you remember, had lung sickness like Pantaleon. Her grave's near that acacia."

Nicolas and Agustin were still throwing up the rest of the bones when Ingoy came back, with a tall-necked jar and four small mullets run through the body, from the caudal fin to the mouth, with the pointed bamboo sticks on which they had been roasted.

"Six centavos each," Ingoy told Nicolas. "Talya wants the money tomorrow."

"Your ears have the color of boiled lobster, Ingoy. You couldn't wait for us, could you. Bring the *dama* here, let's see what's left."

On the edge of the pit Nicolas tipped the jar and guzzled noisily like a very thirsty bull. His Adam's apple moved up and down, up and down.

"Are you trying to drown yourself, Kulas?" Julian looked apprehensively at the jar.

Nicolas paused for a long breath and again wrapped his mouth around the jar's opening. When he finally released the jar, sweat rolled down his face and armpits and along the narrow valley between his breasts. He wiped the foam around his mouth with a hairy paw and heaved himself out of the pit. The left foot barely touched the edge, and he toppled back. Agustin had to push him as he clambered up.

"You should have taken it easy," Julian said.

"I was thirsty. Very thirsty. But there's enough for all." He gave out one stick of the roasted fish to each of the three men. "Come up, 'Gustin. We'll finish the work later."

"I'm not hungry yet," Agustin said. "I had a late breakfast. I'll have some tuba, though."

" 'Gustin's not yet used to eat with bones around," Nicolas said. "But he'll get used to it in time—unless he'd rather have another job." He bit off a big chunk of the fish and drank another long draught.

Ingoy and Julian took turns drinking from the jar.

"You should have borrowed a cup from Talya," Julian said. He had difficulty drinking from the jar, and drops of the red wine had spilled on his gray cotton shirt and stained it.

"She couldn't spare a cup, not even a coconut shell," Ingoy said. "There are several men drinking in her store now."

"You could have stopped at Amalio's on the way—or Akay's. We can't be drinking like this, like animals."

"You want a cup in a cemetery, Julian?" Nicolas spoke with sudden brusqueness; in the grave digger's sensitive half-drunken state, Julian's complaint was a quick slight. "Then you will have one." He picked up Pantaleon's skull, wiped the smooth surface on the thigh of his rolled-up denim trousers, beat the cranium's top with his palm to knock off the dirt inside. He poured some tuba into it, shook the skull for a moment, and threw away its contents. Then he poured wine into it again and offered it to Julian. "Drink," Nicolas commanded.

Julian was too amazed to move or make any reply.

"I see you don't like my cup, but I'll show you."

Agustin, still in the pit, had watched every movement of Nicolas with growing horror. *Will he really do it? Can he really do it?*

Placing the base of the skull to his lips, Nicolas drank all of its contents, refilled it, and offered it again to Julian. "Now drink of it," there was sharpness in his command.

Knowing the temper of the grave digger, Julian received the skull gingerly, and then closing his eyes placed his mouth where the spinal column had joined the cranium.

Agustin saw the red wine oozing out like blood from the hollow eyes and ears and nose of the skull. He looked at Nicolas almost with fear. Was this the final evil gesture before despoiling the grave tonight, or was this only the beginning? He felt butterfly wings fluttering inside his stomach, but he couldn't turn away from the skull now oozing red into Julian's mouth. The nose was hollow. The eyes were hollow, and yet they seemed to glare protest. The ears weren't there...

But there will be ears tonight. You will be feeling for the ears in the dark for the earrings. Diamonds embedded in gold sockets clasped through tiny ear holes. You'll have to hurry, you won't unclasp them, you'll snatch off the earrings, tear the bloodless ears.

"Drink all of it!" Nicolas barked.

When Julian had emptied the skull and returned it to Nicolas, the digger said triumphantly, "Dear old Pantaleon's still serving us. Viva Pantaleon!" Refilling the skull, he gave it to Ingoy. "Ingoy," Nicolas spoke pompously, "drink, drink to the soul of dear old Pantaleon!"

Ingoy, himself now tipsy, got the skull, raised it high, facing him, and exclaimed, "To you, Pantaleon. I drink to your soul, Pantaleon. May you rest in peace!" Closing his eyes in ecstasy, he emptied the skull, and held it before him. "Poor Pantaleon. From the candles burned for you by your wife you should now be out of Purgatory." He refilled the skull to the brim and said, "Now it's 'Gustin's turn." He turned to the grave.

Agustin had run away.

T. D. Agcaoili

THE FIGHT

The heat of summer simmered over the flat sands as the sun rose to its zenith, dazzling and white like a mirror, and, like a mirror breaking, its pieces fell shining and brilliant on the river.

The source of the river was high up in the blue Cordilleras and never at any time of the year was the river bed dry. When the rains came in July the river would rise, noisy at its mouth like the sea, filling the whole breadth of its bed, overflowing the banks, and sweeping away the bamboo bridges. In an earlier summer such bridges were built to span the narrow but deep strip of water between the town-side of the river bank and the sandy island where the summer houses stood in which the townsmen stored their belongings against the threat of rampant summer fires.

It was still May and the heat was white. It clung to the leaves of the trees, seeped into the fine dry sand, and lay like colorless fire on the surface of the inert stones and pebbles. It clung to the bodies of the women washing clothes at the river's edge, making darker their dark hair and browner their brown bodies.

Only Nena Judalena, distinct in her red swimming suit as she sat by the river edge soaping her arms, her feet dipped in the water, was white. Young Pepe Dalloran, idling in the water nearby, his body laved shoulder-high, followed with his eyes the tractile swelling and contractions of Nena's bosom under the glistening fabric of her arms with virgin grace. She was fair, and her heavy hair, like fine skeins of spun copper, was a light brown, as was the hair of her Spanish mother, the fabulous Doña Elena, who lived in the town's biggest house and who seldom went out except to church on Sundays, riding in the only Cadillac in the province.

Pepe had seen Doña Elena on several occasions, and although he was always awed at the sight or thought of her, he hoped that Nena would never grow up to be like her mother, cold and distant. He hoped that she would have something of her father's warmth and amiability. Don Andres, whose admonitions against being called a Don by his drivers and conductors, did not keep them from addressing him deferentially as such just the same, was liked by everybody in town. His prosperity did not seem to affect his attitude toward the people among whom he had grown up from childhood as a traveling salesman's son. . . .

Nena, now through soaping her arms, threw her perfumed soap into the *batya* of Sela, her family's laundry-woman, and straightening up, eased herself into the shallow water. The sight of her white limbs as she stood erect a moment in the knee-deep water constricted Pepe's throat.

Nena was feeling the bottom of the river gingerly with her feet as she waded in his direction. When the water reached her waist, she paused and looked for the first time at him.

A smile formed on her lips.

"Hello," she said. "Is it very deep over there?"

"Not really," he said, getting up from his kneeling position.

Seeing that the water barely reached up to his chest, she continued moving toward him. When she was near enough, she extended her hand to him. It was something he had not expected and he felt deliciously thrilled as he hastily reached out with his own hand and felt the petal softness of her fingers.

"Your name is Pepe, is it not?" she said.

"Yes," he said. "Our house is next to yours."

"I know," she said. "I saw you yesterday shooting at a bird in your yard."

"I hit the bird, I saw it fall," he said. "But I could not climb over the wall into your yard to retrieve it."

"I know, those pieces of broken glass on top of the wall are sharp," she said. Suddenly, she dipped her head into the river. When she emerged, her hair clung all over her face. She combed the strands of hair away from her face with her free hand and then turned to him again. "I picked up the bird and buried it."

"You could have roasted it on a spit and eaten it. Bird meat is nice, all tender and sweet," he said, remembering how fat the bird had looked in the sights of his air rifle.

"Mama would have scolded me if I had," she said. "Besides, the idea of eating bird meat!"

He kept still, silent; but she did not seem to notice that she had hurt him. She was laughing gaily, her body slightly buoyed up by the current, but holding on to him firmly with both hands while she kicked in the water, creating a white foam around her feet.

"Teach me to swim, please teach me how to swim," she was saying. Accidentally swallowing, she frantically sprang to her feet, gasping.

He laughed at her while he gently patted her back to help her regain her breath. "There now," he said, his own hurt gone.

She laughed again. "How do you breathe while swimming?" she asked.

"I'll show you," he said, and kicked the bottom of the river while he dipped his head under the surface. For a moment, before he rose for air, he saw her young clean limbs, white through the clear water.

He came to the surface and with easy strokes struck out for a deeper part of the river where he knew there was an eddy. He had never been more conscious of his swimming, knowing he was being watched; and as he reached the fringe of the eddy he cleaved it with powerful strokes, fighting the current that swirled around his shoulders, and noting by the shoreline that he was progressing quite well. Another boy of his own age jumped into the swirling water, and a contest was tacitly on between them as they swam side by side toward the upper end of the eddy. He hoped that Nena would understand that though he was swimming against a fresher adversary, he was still winning. He was tired and his chest aching when he reached the slower water. He tried to touch bottom, but could not, and swam on easily, with his legs moving under the surface, buoying him up. His adversary, whom he now recognized as a boy who lived in the block next to his and who was called Bastian, was coming up.

"I will race you again downstream under water," Bastian said.

"Some other time," Pepe said, not looking at him.

Bastian followed Pepe's glance and smiled sneeringly. "Oh, you don't want the mestiza to see you beaten," he said.

"I can beat you any time," Pepe said, moving downstream to rejoin Nena.

Bastian quickly grabbed his arm and said, "Try it now."

"Let go off me," Pepe said.

"Try and get away," Bastian said.

"I don't want any trouble," Pepe said, still swimming downstream toward Nena.

"You're afraid," Bastian shouted.

And perhaps he was really afraid. Bastian had never been in his circle of neighborhood playmates or school acquaintances. The fellow played with a rougher group of boys—boys who hung around the lobby of the lone movie-house in the town, or worked sporadically as pinboys in the bowling alley near the the market, or lingered on the street corner adjacent to the Modern Hotel that offered a bold and inviting front before the garage where the buses from other provinces and from Manila stopped.... Pepe was vaguely aware of Bastian's reputation as a bully and fighter. And he was afraid.

He reached Nena's side.

"He's coming after you," she said.

He looked back but saw no sign of Bastian.

"He's swimming under water," Nena said. "I saw you beat him. He did not like it. He will make trouble. Let us go away."

Pepe quailed at the thought of fighting. Five years before, when he was only seven, he had fought another boy who had with one kick destroyed the house of sticks that he was building in his front yard. The boy was taller than he by a head; and when he complained, the boy's companion, a boy of high-school age, goaded them into fighting, and before he knew it, Pepe was exchanging blows. The fight had been brief. The wind was knocked out of him, and he was soon crying in anger and helplessness as more blows landed on him and the leering face of his enemy was everywhere, taunting, elusive, hateful. He was grateful when the high-school boy finally ended the fight by telling his companion to stop. "He's beaten," the fellow had said, "his nose is bleeding."

Since then Pepe had always been afraid of getting into a fight, and he had gone far to avoid getting into one.... But now, with Nena, he was not sure of what he feared more: to flee and show his cowardice, or to fight and risk being beaten up again.

They both saw the figure of Bastian approach under water.

"Let us get out of the water," Nena said, reaching for his hand.

"No," Pepe said, pulling back his hand.

He saw Bastian circle around them, his half-naked body graceful and golden under the water.

Then Bastian came up and faced Pepe.

"You are afraid," he said, laughing. He looked at Nena, leering. Then he suddenly dipped his head into the water. Pepe could feel the heat of the sun on his own skin, and scooping up water with both his hands, he laved his sunburned neck and shoulders. His eyes followed Bastian under the water and suddenly understood, before the action was accomplished, that Bastian intended to touch Nena's legs. He promptly plunged into the water and pulled Bastian up by the hair.

They both came to the surface holding their breaths, measuring each other quietly awhile.

Then Bastian laughed. "You're afraid," he said.

"I'm not afraid," Pepe said.

Before Pepe expected it, Bastian's fist descended on his head, glancing from his ear. For a moment he was gripped with terror. Then he remembered Nena, and the initial feeling was replaced by a maddening anger. The blow was foul. All right, he would show him. From his previous swimming contest, he had seen that Bastian was not as good in the water as he. He would use this knowledge, this advantage. He feinted for Bastian's face, taking a deep breath, but dived under and, reaching with both hands for Bastian's ankles, dragged him down. Then, releasing his hold on the ankles, he put an arm around Bastian's waist. He tried to deliver a blow on the dark flat belly, but felt his fist held back by the resistant current, and even when it landed he knew the blow was without power. He rose to the surface for air and then dived under again just as Bastian, gasping, also rose for air. From behind he caught Bastian's head in the crook of his arm, his forearm pressing hard and tight against the other's chin. It was a hold he had seen in a movie. He was aware of many voices, now, including Nena's cries, mixing with the gurgling noise that Bastian made, and a wild throbbing in his own head. Pepe was no longer afraid. In fact he felt new power surge in him, tensing and coiling as he wished it in the arm that held Bastian as helpless as in a vise.

"Give up?" he asked, but when he saw the dark scowl of defiance on Bastian's brow, he became insensate, wanting more than anything else at this moment to have his power recognized. He leaned back, then abruptly leaned to one side, forcing Bastian's face into the water, holding it down, pressing the chin harder with his forearm. Bastian's legs were beating wildly. For a moment Pepe thought that he was drowning him. He lifted the face from the water, turning it toward him. He saw the blinking, bloodshot eyes, and a discharge streaming like a pale thread from his nose.

"Give up?" Pepe said. Seeing Bastian nod, he relaxed his hold and let him go. Bastian closed his eyes gratefully and then suddenly went limp and fell face down into the water. Pepe leaned forward to reach him, but other hands were ahead of him; and for the first time Pepe was aware that people had gathered around to watch the fight. He even recognized a couple of Bastian's friends, and he stared at them coldly, looking for a sign of belligerence; but he noticed none. He wondered why they had not ganged up on him, but when he saw his uncle Fred in the water with all his clothes on, he understood why. Realizing how hastily his uncle must have stepped into the river when he saw it was he who was fighting, he wanted to laugh with relief.

But all he did was say: "He started it," addressing his Uncle Fred but wanting everybody to hear.

Nena was still there, and now he turned to look at her as she said: "Yes. That fellow tried to annoy me."

Sela, the laundrywoman of Nena's family, was also there and in turn she spoke, addressing Nena: "You finish your bath now and go home. If the Señora should hear about this, oh!"

Nena laughed at her and shook her coppery hair. She reached for Pepe's hand, and in front of everybody asked him to stay with her. Pepe was embarrassed and would have walked away, but he caught his Uncle Fred's eyes

which were smiling at him good-naturedly and advising him to go ahead and keep Nena company. Turning their backs on the crowd, they moved away in the water, Nena pulling him after her. Then she dipped her head under once, and in the summer sun he saw, as he, wading, planted his feet firmly in the bottom of the river so that the two would not be dragged downstream, her hair shining like burnished gold.

Pepe was in the middle of his supper, relishing the tasty warm broth of *marungay* leaves boiled with slices of roasted dried meat, when somebody called at the foot of the stairs. Rita, Pepe's younger sister, left the table to see who it was. His mother paused from eating, her eyes turned toward the door. Pepe continued eating as he listened to Rita talking with a woman whose voice he could not place.

Rita returned to the table, her eyes filled with wonder, and Pepe could not help but stop from eating in order to listen.

"Come on. Who is it?" their mother asked.

"It's. . . ." Rita looked over her shoulder.

And Pepe, following her glance, saw who it was. His mother stood up from the table and went to meet the woman who had halted at the threshhold.

It was Doña Elena, Nena's mother.

Seeing the way she looked around the room, briefly and coldly, and then toward their repast laid out on the table, Pepe felt suddenly ashamed, as if he were being scrutinized in his nakedness. For the first time he wished that they were not living in this small old house of nipa walls and bamboo flooring; he wished. . . .

In defiance he went back to his food, scooping up a handful of rice and stuffing it into his mouth. He picked up the bowl of *marungay* broth, and raising it to his lips, drank. He could sense the eyes of Doña Elena watching him.

He brought down the bowl resoundingly on the table. Then he cocked his ear to listen, for Doña Elena had stepped into the room and started talking.

"It's about your son."

"Pepe? Has he done anything wrong? Broken a window, perhaps? I always warn him against shooting that air rifle his father sent him from Hawaii."

"It's not about his air rifle at all."

"Ho," Pepe heard his mother sigh with relief. She was now becoming more composed, Pepe knew. Very soon she would be asking Doña Elena to supper. Unless she was stopped in time, she would be telling the Spanish lady about Pepe's father who was in Hawaii, working on a sugar plantation and sending money to them monthly, without fail, for his children's schooling, especially for Pepe, who would some day become a doctor. To his mother, being a doctor was the highest profession for any man, certainly the most honorable, for was it not a doctor who had snatched him from the jaws of death at the time he was sick with pneumonia when he was only three?

Pepe stood up and faced the room.

His mother was speaking. "I always tell Pepe to play his violin while he's on summer vacation. But he prefers his rifle. I understand it's your daughter Nena who plays the piano that I hear every afternoon. She plays beautifully. When is she going back to Manila to study?"

"That's what I came here for," Doña Elena said, her words queerly accented. "I don't want to send her back to Manila until her classes open in June. But if she continues...." She hesitated a moment, looking in Pepe's direction. Then she proceeded, her voice firmer: "If your son Pepe persists in going around with her, I'll have to send her back to college as quickly as possible."

Pepe looked at his mother, trying to read her mind because he suddenly realized that it was her reaction which was important. But his mother's face did not give away whatever she might be feeling. She was almost as cool and, it seemed, as tall as Doña Elena.

"Pepe, come here," his mother said. She had forgotten even to offer a chair to Doña Elena, and anyway the latter perhaps preferred to stand. Rita was leaning against the old study table in the center of the room, listening but holding herself apart.

Pepe approached his mother fighting down a desperate urge to run out of the house. He could not yet fully understand the purpose of Doña Elena's visit, but he could sense it; and he knew it was no good, that it was an insult, and that he did not want to have any part in it.

But at the same time he knew that running off was impossible because this thing concerned him more than anybody else, more than even his mother, who was facing the situation when it should be he instead.

"Here is Pepe," his mother said, turning to him. "What have you been doing with Nena? Tell me."

"We met at the river this morning, *Nanang*. And this afternoon, when the sand became cool, we played hide-and-seek in the summer huts with the other kids."

And he smiled inwardly, remembering how ingenious Nena had been in hiding. She was also so agile that the others had had a hard time catching her and making her "it." She had enjoyed playing with them so much that on the way home, when it was getting late, she had asked him if she could not join in some of their evening games, too. And he had told her she could because he found it very difficult to deny her. She was as friendly and unassuming as her father, Don Andres.

"You did nothing else? You did not hurt her?"

"No, *Nanang*. Why should I? In fact, this morning I fought another boy who annoyed her."

"It seems that you should be grateful to my son," Pepe's mother said.

"Because your son played with my daughter, the other boy annoyed her," Doña Elena said.

Feeling betrayed, Pepe looked at the Spanish lady, searching for some expression in her face that might belie her words. But he saw only her belief in her own words.

I hate you, I hate you ... he found himself thinking.

Turning to his mother, he was surprised to see a weary look come into her eyes. "So what do you want done now, Señora?" his mother asked.

"Tell your son not to play with my daughter again."

"Pepe. You hear the Señora?"

He nodded.

"He promises. You can be sure he will keep his word, Señora. And now, please go."

Pepe saw Doña Elena take a step forward, her hand raised in a conciliatory gesture toward his mother; but he did not wait to see how his mother would take it. For suddenly he could feel a hard lump choking him, and he knew that at any moment now he would either cry out in anger or burst into tears. He rushed for the door, brushing past Doña Elena's billowing lace skirt.

Coming down the stairs, he met Don Andres, who tried to hold him back smiling.

"Hey, where're you rushing to, *hijo?*"

Pepe stared at the face of Don Andres for a moment before he pulled away his hand.

"Have you seen my wife?" Don Andres asked.

Not trusting his voice, Pepe nodded toward the house. He went out into the yard, the summer night heavy with heat and trembling with stars. He walked between the rows of lime trees and *macopa*, and the fireflies darted away to let him pass. He reached the high wall separating his house from Nena's, and looking up, saw that the lights in her room were already on. He waited for some sign of her moving in the room; then the lights blurred as tears, stinging, finally came.

D. Paulo Dizon

THE BEAUTIFUL HORSE

One day my father brought home a beautiful horse. She was the most beautiful white horse anyone in our barrio of Pulong-Masle had ever laid eyes on. She had long and slender legs, a silky mane, and a flowing tail. She was, however, not the kind of horse anyone in our barrio would have any use for. She did not seem fit for pulling a rig. She was good only for the track, or for riding; but races were held only during the town festival, and even the rich bachelors in town did not ride horses any more. They preferred the bicycle. What good was such a beautiful white horse in Pulong-Masle?

My father did not exactly bring the beautiful white horse home. She followed him. When my father would stop to pull a thorn out of his foot or to scratch a bite on his leg, the horse would stop, too, and swish her tail from side to side. When father continued on his way, the horse, too, would come along. She had a grand way of walking, proud, and confident.

"Why, Estong," the people at the roadside or in the windows would say, "how did you come by such a beautiful horse?" But my father only smiled and stared straight ahead; he was as proud as the horse that was following him. He did not even notice my sister Victa and me. Victa and I walked behind among the other children.

The people we passed also wondered how my father had come by such a beautiful horse. He couldn't have bought her because he did not have that much money; everybody knew he earned no more than what we needed, and sometimes less.

I overheard some of the people say that my father might have stolen the horse, and I felt angry with my father and with the people and at the horse, and I knew my sister Victa also felt the same way. When I looked at her, I saw tears in her eyes.

Father was suddenly a stranger to us. He did not seem to be our father at all, and for the moment we hated him. In the past when we met him on the road on his way home, he would hug us or lift Victa or me way up in the air. We used to be very happy when Father came home.

When we reached the house, Father led the horse through the yard into the field. He sat down on a fallen bamboo and watched the horse beginning to graze. So absorbed was he in the sight of the beautiful horse, he didn't notice Victa and me sitting beside him. For a long time we sat there watching the horse cropping the wild grass. We did not say anything to one another. It was getting dark.

"What a beauty!" Father said, sighing dreamily and gazing at the horse. "What beautiful legs!"

"They are not beautiful," Victa said, curling her lower lip. "They are thin and weak."

That was when Father perhaps first took notice of our presence. He turned his face toward Victa, and all of a sudden there was anger in his dark eyes.

"Don't say that," Father said. "You know they are not thin and weak. They are slender and beautiful, are they not? Yes, they are. She is a beautiful horse."

"Doesn't she belong to us, Father?" I asked.

"She is such a beauty," Father sighed again, staring admiringly at the horse. She kept on swishing her tail, which was long and flowing and silky, as if she were enjoying herself immensely.

I was beginning to suspect the people were right after all. I trembled at the thought of my father stealing a horse. He used to tell us how good it was to be honest and truthful and obedient, and now, I thought, he wasn't any of those things he had told us to be.

Presently I heard my mother calling Victa and me, and then the chapel bells rang out the Angelus.

"Come up now, Victa, Marcos," Mother shouted from the window.

Victa crossed the yard and climbed up the stairs. I sat, silent, beside Father, who seemed to be immersed in thought. Then, suddenly, my mother was with us.

"Where did you get that horse, Estong?" she asked.

"She's beautiful, isn't she?" Father asked, as though he were talking to nobody in particular. He didn't even bother to turn his eyes away from the horse.

"Whose horse is that?" Mother asked again.

Without turning his face, father said, unconcerned, "I don't know."

"How come she is here in our own backyard?" Mother asked.

"She's a beautiful horse," Father said.

"Let us go in now," Mother said. "Supper is ready."

Father did not make the slightest move. He sat silent, his chin cupped in the hollow of his hand, his elbows resting on his thighs. He continued staring dreamily at the horse.

"Let us go, Marcos," Mother said, pulling me along.

We ate silently, for Mother was angry. We, Victa and I, knew better than to talk when Mother was in that mood. Finally she started mumbling, at first to herself, and then to us.

"I wonder where he got that horse," she said.

"Ask him, Mother," Victa said.

"The people on the road said he might have stolen it," I put in.

"Just who was it said that?" Mother asked, suddenly florid with anger. "Tell me, who was it said that?"

"I do not know," I said. "I just heard some people say it."

"Let us go right now. Point them out to me and I will show them how to judge your father better. Let us go, Marcos. Right now. Come." She took me by the arm, tugging me toward the stairs.

But just as we were about to leave the house, we met father coming up.

"You and your beautiful white horse, with her long, slender legs!" Mother cried at Father.

"Now don't say anything harsh against that horse, woman," Father said. "Don't say bad words about your cousin Barang."

"Why, what has my dead cousin to do with that beast, Estong? Don't you start invoking the dead, you . . . you impious. . . ."

"That horse is the reincarnation of your cousin Barang," Father declared solemnly. Father was a good jester; he loved to laugh, but this time he was dead serious, and his voice sounded sincere and stern.

Mother crossed himself three times her eyes almost popping out. "What is the matter with you, Estong?"

"I knew it the first time I saw her, that horse," Father said, walking past us, and then seating himself at the table. "The first time I saw her following me I knew she was somebody I used to know. Only, I couldn't remember who. Now look at the eyes. Just look at those eyes tomorrow when the sun comes up. They are the eyes of your cousin Barang."

Mother crossed herself again. "May she rest in peace," she prayed, clasping her hands across her breast. "Please, Lord, forgive my erring husband. And may the soul of cousin Barang forgive these utterances!"

Father continued: "When I turned around and saw that horse's face, I asked myself, 'Where did I see this face before?' It was very familiar. And then in the backyard while she was feeding, she wiggled her rump, and I remembered the way Barang used to wiggle her buttocks when she was feeling funny."

"Ohhh! . . ." Mother cried. "Heaven forgive him, for he does not know what he is saying. He is touched in the head, my husband. Ohhh . . . What have we done to deserve this?"

"She is such a very beautiful horse, your cousin Barang is," Father sighed.

"Where did you get that horse, Estong?" Mother wanted to know. "Tell me!" she pleaded. "How is it she is here in our own yard?"

"She followed me; don't know from where. But she just followed me. I told her to go her way, but she followed me just the same," Father said.

"You did not sell this house and buy yourself that horse, Estong? Please tell us the truth."

"I told you that she is your cousin Barang come to visit you," Father said. "Now please let us eat. I am hungry."

The next morning Victa awoke me. She was very excited. "Come, quick!" she said. "Quick!"

"What happened?" I asked.

"Look at our Aunt Barang," she said. "She is still there."

"Where?"

"In the backyard. Under the tamarind tree."

I remembered what my father had said about the souls of the dead coming back to life in another form. Father had been very fond of Aunt Barang. Many times he and my mother had quarreled on her account. My mother did not like Aunt Barang very much,

and when she died she cried only during the funeral, but one could see how relieved she was afterward. And now here she was again. Only, she was in the form of a beautiful white horse, come back to life to torment my mother again. Why can't the dead stay dead? I asked myself.

"Come, quick, Marcos," Victa shouted. She had gone down the stairs again, so excited was she. "Look at the eyes. They are the eyes of our Aunt Barang."

Mother was in the kitchen, silently doing her chores. She was beginning to take it all with resignation. Poor old Mother. She must have felt very miserable.

I went downstairs into the yard and joined my sister. Father was sitting there on the fallen bamboo, watching the reincarnation of our Aunt Barang feed on the grass, swishing her long tail from side to side.

"Look at her eyes," Victa said to me.

True enough, they were the eyes of our Aunt Barang. Indeed, she couldn't have been other than our Aunt Barang.

The men came to take Aunt Barang sometime before noon that day. They were a couple of strange-looking men in city clothes, a constabulary man, and some men from the barrio. One of the strange-looking men was short and had a mustache and long hair. The other was tall and carried a walking stick with a copper knob. The constabulary man said they were the owners of the circus which had been set up in the town.

When they saw the horse browsing peacefully on the sward beyond our backyard, the circus men rushed to her, stumbling over the bamboo trunk on which my father was sitting. They hugged the horse and kissed her on the face as if she were their sister.

"Oh, my Minda Mora, my beautiful Minda Mora," the taller of the two strange-looking men said. "I missed you terribly. Terribly so. Oh, my beautiful Minda Mora.

My father stood up. So bewildered was he by all this show of affection he could not utter a word.

The shorter one with the mustache and the funny nest of long hair was talking to the constabulary man. He was also very excited and very happy. Then the tall man took something out of his trousers pocket and handed it to my Father. A couple of silver coins.

"Thank you very much for keeping our dear Minda in your yard," the short funny man said to my father. "We hope she did not give you too much trouble. Come to the circus in the town tonight, and don't forget to bring the children along. It is the best show there is. And thanks again."

For a long time after they left, we stood in the yard silently, sadly.

"I did not know Barang would turn out to be a circus lady," Father said.

N.V.M. Gonzalez

A WARM HAND

Holding on to the rigging, Elay leaned over. The dinghy was being readied. The wind tore her hair into wiry strands that fell across her face, heightening her awareness of the dipping and rising of the deck. But for the bite of the *noreste,* she would have begun to feel faint and empty in her belly. Now she clutched at the rigging with more courage.

At last the dinghy shoved away, with its first load of passengers—seven boys from Bongabon, Mindoro, on their way to Manila to study. The deck seemed less hostile than before, for the boys had made a boisterous group then; now that they were gone, her mistress Ana could leave the crowded deckhouse for once.

"Oh, Elay! My powder puff!"

It was Ana, indeed. Elay was familiar with that excitement which her mistress wore about her person like a silk kerchief—now on her head to keep her hair in place, now like a scarf round her neck. How eager Ana had been to go ashore when the old skipper of the batel said that the "Ligaya" was too small a boat to brave the coming storm. She must return to the deckhouse, Elay thought, if she must fetch her mistress' handbag.

With both hands upon the edge of the deckhouse roof, then holding on to the wooden water barrel to the left of the main mast, she staggered back to the deckhouse entrance. As she bent her head low lest with the lurching of the boat her brow should hit the door, she saw her mistress on all fours clambering out of the deckhouse. She let her have the right-of-way, entering only after Ana was safe upon the open deck.

Elay found the handbag—she was certain that the powder puff would be there—though not without difficulty, inside the canvas satchel that she meant to take ashore. She came dragging the heavy satchel, and in a flurry Ana dug into it for the bag. The deck continued to sway, yet presently Ana was powdering her face; and this done, she applied lipstick to that full round mouth of hers.

The wind began to press Elay's blouse against her breasts while she waited on her mistress patiently. She laced Ana's shoes and also bestirred herself to see that Ana's earrings were not askew. For Ana must appear every inch the dressmaker that she was. Let everyone know that she was traveling to Manila—not just to the provincial capital; and, of course, there was the old spinster aunt, too, for company—to set up a shop in the big city. It occurred to Elay that, judging from the care her mistress was taking to look well, it might well be that they were not on board a one-masted Tingloy batel with a cargo of lumber, copra, pigs, and chickens, but were still at home in the dress shop that they were leaving behind in the lumber town of Sumagui.

"How miserable I'd be without you, Elay," Ana giggled, as though somewhere she was meeting a secret lover who for certain would hold her in his arms in one wild passionate caress.

And thinking so of her mistress made Elay more proud of her. She did not mind the dark world into which they were going. Five miles to the south was Pinamalayan town; its lights blinked faintly at her. Then along the rim of the Bay, dense groves of coconuts and underbush stood, occasional fires marking where the few share-croppers of the district lived. The batel had anchored at the northernmost end of the cove and apparently five hundred yards from the boat was the palm-leaf-covered hut the old skipper of the "Ligaya" had spoken about.

"Do you see it? That's Obregano's hut." And Obregano, the old skipper explained, was a fisherman. The men who sailed up and down the eastern coast of Mindoro knew him well. There was not a seaman who lived in these parts but had gone to Obregano for food or shelter and to this anchorage behind the northern tip of Pinamalayan Bay for the protection it offered sailing vessels against the unpredictable *noreste.*

The old skipper had explained all this to Ana, and Elay had listened, little knowing that in a short while it would all be there before her. Now in the dark she saw the fisherman's hut readily. A broad shoulder of a hill rose beyond, and farther yet the black sky looked like a silent wall.

Other women joined them on the deck to see the view for themselves. A discussion started; some members of the party did not think that it would be proper for them to spend the night in Obregano's hut. Besides the students, there were four middle-aged merchants on this voyage; since Bongabon they had plagued the women with their coarse talk and their yet coarser laughter. Although the deckhouse was the unchallenged domain of the women, the four middle-aged merchants had often slipped in, and once inside had exchanged lewd jokes among themselves, to the embarrassment of

their audience. Small wonder, Elay thought, that the prospect of spending the night in a small fisherman's hut and with these men for company did not appear attractive to the other women passengers. Her mistress Ana had made up her mind, however. She had a sense of independence that Elay admired.

Already the old aunt had joined them on deck; and Elay said to herself, "Of course, it's for this old auntie's sake, too. She has been terribly seasick."

In the dark she saw the dinghy and silently watched it being sculled back to the batel. It drew nearer and nearer, a dark mass moving eagerly, the bow pointing in her direction. Elay heard Ana's little shrill cries of excitement. Soon two members of the crew were vying for the honor of helping her mistress safely into the dinghy.

Oh, that Ana should allow herself to be thus honored, with the seamen taking such pleasure from it all, and the old aunt, watching, pouting her lips in disapproval! "What shall I do?" Elay asked herself, anticipating that soon she herself would be the object of this chivalrous byplay. And what could the old aunt be saying now to herself? "Ah, women these days are no longer decorous. In no time they will make a virtue of being unchaste."

Elay pouted, too. And then it was her turn. She must get into that dinghy, and it so pitched and rocked. If only she could manage to have no one help her at all. But she'd fall into the water. Santa Maria. I'm safe . . .

———

They were off. The waves broke against the sides of the dinghy, threatening to capsize it, and continually the black depths glared at her. Her hands trembling, Elay clung tenaciously to the gunwale. Spray bathed her cheeks. A boy began to bail, for after clearing each wave the dinghy took in more water. So earnest was the boy at this chore that Elay thought the tiny boat had sprung a leak and would sink any moment.

The sailors, one at the prow and the other busy with the oar at the stern, engaged themselves in senseless banter. Were they trying to make light of the danger? She said her prayers as the boat swung from side to side, to a rhythm set by the sailor with the oar.

Fortunately, panic did not seize her. It was the old aunt who cried "Susmariosep!" For with each crash of waves, the dinghy lurched precipitously. "God spare us all!" the old aunt prayed frantically.

And Ana was laughing. "Auntie! Why, Auntie, it's nothing! It's nothing at all!" For, really, they were safe. The dinghy had struck sand.

Elay's dread of the water suddenly vanished and she said to herself: "Ah, the old aunt is only making things more difficult for herself." Why, she wouldn't let the sailor with the oar lift her clear of the dinghy and carry her to the beach!

"Age before beauty," the sailor was saying to his companion. The other fellow, not to be outdone, had jumped waist-deep into the water, saying: "No, beauty above all!" Then there was Ana stepping straight, as it were, into the sailor's arms.

"Where are you?" the old aunt was calling from the shore. "Are you safe? Are you all right?"

Elay wanted to say that in so far as she was concerned she was safe, she was all right. She couldn't speak for her mistress, of course! But the same seaman who had lifted the old aunt and carried her to the shore in his arms had returned. Now he stood before Elay and caught her two legs and let them rest on his forearm and then held her body up, with the other arm. Now she was clear of the dinghy, and she had to hold on to his neck. Then the sailor made three quick steps toward dry sand and then let her slide easily off his arms, and she said: "I am all right. Thank you."

Instead of saying something to her the sailor hurried away, joining the group of students that had gathered up the rise of sand. Ana's cheerful laughter rang in their midst. Then a youth's voice, clear in the wind: "Let's hurry to the fisherman's hut!"

A drizzle began to fall. Elay took a few tentative steps toward the palm-leaf hut, but her knees were unsteady. The world seemed to turn and turn, and the glowing light at the fisherman's door swung as from a boat's mast. Elay hurried as best she could after Ana and her old aunt, both of whom had already reached the hut. It was only on hearing her name that that weak, unsteady feeling in her knees disappeared.

"Elay—" It was her mistress, of course. Ana was standing outside the door, waiting. "My lipstick, Elay!"

An old man stood at the door of the hut. "I am Obregano, at your service," he said in welcome. "This is my home."

He spoke in a sing-song that rather matched his wizened face. Pointing at a little woman puttering about the stove box at one end of the one-room hut, he said: "And she? Well, the guardian of my home—in other words, my wife!"

The woman got up and welcomed them, beaming a big smile. "Feel at home. Make yourselves comfortable—everyone."

She helped Elay with the canvas bag, choosing a special corner for it. "It will rain harder yet tonight, but here your bag will be safe," the woman said.

The storm had come. The thatched wall shook, producing a weird skittering sound at each gust of wind. The sough of the palms in back of the hut—which was hardly the size of the deckhouse of the batel, and had the bare sand for floor—sounded like the moan of a lost child. A palm leaf that served to cover an entrance to the left of the stove box began to dance a mad, rhythmless dance. The fire in the stove leaped intermittently, rising beyond the lid of the kettle that Obregano the old fisherman had placed there.

And yet the hut was homelike. It was warm and clean. There was a cheerful look all over the place. Elay caught the old fisherman's smile as his wife cleared the floor of blankets, nets, and coil after coil of hempen rope so that their guests could have more room. She sensed an affinity with her present surroundings, with the smell of the fish nets, with the dancing fire in the stove box. It was as though she had lived in this hut before. She remembered what Obregano's wife had said to her. The old woman's words were by far the kindest she had heard in a long time.

The students from Bongabon had appropriated a corner for themselves and begun to discuss supper. It appeared that a prankster had relieved one of the chicken coops of a fat pullet and a boy asked the fisherman for permission to prepare a stew.

"I've some ginger tea in the kettle," Obregano said, "Something worth drinking in weather like this." He asked his wife for an old enameled tin cup for their guests to drink from.

As the cup was being passed around, Obregano's wife expressed profuse apologies for her not preparing supper. "We have no food," she said with uncommon frankness. "We have sons, you know, two of them, both working in town. But they come home only on week ends. It is only then that we have rice."

Elay understood that in lieu of wages the two Obregano boys received rice. Last week end the boys had failed to return home, however. This fact brought a sad note to Elay's new world of warm fire and familiar smells. She got out some food which they had brought along from the boat—adobo and bread that the old aunt had put in a tin container and tucked into the canvas satchel—and offered her mistress these, going through the motions so absent-mindedly that Ana chided her.

"Do offer the old man and his wife some of that, too."

Obregano shook his head. He explained that he would not think of partaking of the food—so hungry his guests must be. They needed all the food themselves, to say nothing about that which his house should offer but which in his naked poverty he could not provide. But at least they would be safe here for the night, Obregano assured them. "The wind is rising, and the rain, too . . . Listen . . ." He pointed at the roof, which seemed to sag.

The drone of the rain set Elay's spirits aright. She began to imagine how sad and worried over her sons the old fisherman's wife must be, and how lonely—but oh how lovely!—it would be to live in this God-forsaken spot. She watched the students devour their supper, and she smiled thanks, sharing their thoughtfulness, when they offered most generously some chicken to Ana and, in sheer politeness, to the old spinster aunt also.

Yet more people from the batel arrived, and the four merchants burst into the hut discussing some problem in Bongabon municipal politics. It was as though the foul weather suited their purposes, and Elay listened with genuine interest, with compassion, even, for the small-town politicians who were being reviled and cursed.

It was Obregano who suggested that they all retire. There was hardly room for everyone, and in bringing out a rough-woven palm-leaf mat for Ana and her companions to use, Obregano picked his way in order not to step on a sprawling leg or an out-stretched arm. The offer of the mat touched Elay's heart, so much so that pondering the goodness of the old fisherman and his wife took her mind away from the riddles which the students at this time were exchanging among themselves. They were funny riddles and there was much laughter. Once she caught them throwing glances in Ana's direction.

Even the sailors who were with them on the dinghy had returned to the hut to stay and were laughing heartily at their own stories. Elay watched Obregano produce a bottle of kerosene for the lantern, and then hang the lantern with a string from the center beam of the hut. She felt a new dreamlike joy. Watching the old fisherman's wife extinguish the fire in the stove made Elay's heart throb.

Would the wind and the rain worsen? The walls of the hut shook—like a man in the throes of malaria chills. The sea kept up a wild roar, and the waves, it seemed, continually clawed at the land with strong, greedy fingers.

She wondered whether Obregano and his wife would ever sleep. The couple would be thinking: "Are our guests comfortable enough as they are?" As for herself, Elay resolved, she would stay awake. From the corner where the students slept she could hear the whine of a chronic asthma sufferer. One of the merchants snorted periodically, like a horse being plagued by a fly. A young boy, apparently dreaming, called out in a strange, frightened voice: "No, no! I can't do that! I wouldn't do that!"

She saw Obregano get up and pick his way again among the sleeping bodies to where the lantern hung. The flame was sputtering. Elay watched him adjust the wick of the lantern and give the oil container a gentle shake. Then the figure of the old fisherman began to blur and she could hardly keep her eyes open. A soothing tiredness possessed her. As she yielded easily to sleep, with Ana to her left and the old spinster aunt at the far edge of the mat to her right, the floor seemed to sink and the walls of the hut to vanish, as though the world were one vast dark valley.

When later she awoke she was trembling with fright. She had only a faint notion that she had screamed. What blur there had been in her consciousness before falling asleep was as nothing compared with that which followed her waking, although she was aware of much to-do and the lantern light was gone.

"Who was it?" It was reassuring to hear Obregano's voice.

"The lantern, please!" That was Ana, her voice shrill and wiry.

Elay heard as if in reply the crash of the sea rising in a crescendo. The blur lifted a little: "Had I fallen asleep after all? Then it must be past midnight by now." Time and place became realities again; and she saw Obregano, with a lighted matchstick in his hand. He was standing in the middle of the hut.

"What happened?"

Elay thought that it was she whom Obregano was speaking to. She was on the point of answering, although she had no idea of what to say, when Ana, sitting up on the mat beside her, blurted out: "Someone was here. Please hold up the light."

"Someone was here," Elay repeated to herself and hid her face behind Ana's shoul-

der. She must not let the four merchants nor the students either, stare at her so. Caught by the lantern light, the men hardly seven steps away had turned their gazes upon her in various attitudes of amazement.

Everyone seemed eager to say something all at once. One of the students spoke in a quavering voice, declaring that he had not moved where he lay. Another said he had been so sound asleep—"Didn't you hear me snoring?" he asked a companion, slapping him on the back—he had not even heard the shout. One of the merchants hemmed and suggested that perhaps cool minds should look into the case, carefully and without preconceived ideas. To begin with, one must know exactly what happened. He looked in Ana's direction and said: "Now please tell us."

Elay clutched her mistress' arm. Before Ana could speak, Obregano's wife said: "This thing ought not to have happened. If only our two sons were home, they'd avenge the honor of our house." She spoke with a rare eloquence for an angry woman. "No one would then dare think of so base an act. Now, our good guests," she added, addressing her husband, bitterly, "why, they know you to be an aged, simple-hearted fisherman—nothing more. The good name of your home, of our family, is no concern of theirs."

"Evil was coming. I knew it!" said the old spinster aunt; and piping out like a bird: "Let us return to the boat. Don't be so bitter, old one," she told Obregano's wife. "We are going back to the boat."

"It was like this," Ana said, not minding her aunt. Elay lowered her head more, lest she should see those man-faces before her, loosely trapped now by the lantern's glow. Indeed, she closed her eyes, as though she were a little child afraid of the dark.

"It was like this," her mistress began again. "I was sleeping, and then my maid, Elay—" she put an arm around Elay's shoulder—"she uttered that wild scream. I am surprised you did not hear it."

In a matter-of-fact tone, one of the merchants countered: "Suppose it was a nightmare?"

But Ana did not listen to him. "Then my maid," she continued, "this girl here—she's hardly twenty, mind you, and an innocent and illiterate girl, if you must all know...She turned round, trembling, and clung to me..."

"Couldn't she possibly have shouted in her sleep?" the merchant insisted.

Obregano had held his peace all this time, but now he spoke: "Let us hear what the girl says."

And so kind were those words! How fatherly of him to have spoken so, in such a gentle and understanding way! Elay's heart went to him. She felt she could almost run to him and, crying over his shoulder, tell him what no one, not even Ana herself, would ever know.

She turned her head a little to one side and saw that now they were all looking at her. She hugged her mistress tighter, in a childlike embrace, hiding her face as best she could.

"Tell them," Ana said, drawing herself away. "Now, go on—speak!"

But Elay would not leave her side. She clung to her, and began to cry softly.

"Nonsense!" the old aunt chided her.

"Well, she must have had a nightmare, that's all," the merchant said, chuckling. "I'm sure of it!"

At this remark Elay cried even more. "I felt a warm hand caressing my—my—my cheeks," she said, sobbing. "A warm hand, I swear," she said again, remembering how it had reached out for her in the dark, searchingly, burning with a need to find some precious treasure which, she was certain of it now, she alone possessed. For how could it be that they should force her to tell them? "Someone"— the word was like a lamp in her heart— "someone wanted me," she said to herself.

She felt Ana's hand stroking her back ungently and then heard her saying, "I brought this on," then nervously fumbling about the mat. "This is all my fault... My compact, please..."

But Elay was inconsolable. She was sorry she could be of no help to her mistress now. She hung her head, unable to stop her tears from cleansing those cheeks that a warm hand had loved.

Francisco Arcellana

THE WING OF MADNESS (II)
THE YELLOW SHAWL

I have received a singular warning,
I have felt the wind of the wing of
madness pass over me. . . .
                CHARLES BAUDELAIRE, *Journal Intimé*

I. THE MAN'S STORY

Pepe has a new place; but it wasn't hard to find. It is only a block away from Taft Avenue and about a hundred yards off San Andres corner. The street is not a first class street, it is practically a dirt road, but it is very quiet. You wouldn't believe it is within a stone's throw of the city's great south national highway.

The place is impressive. It is an apartment building that doesn't look like one at all. It looks more like a mansion. That is probably what it was, a rich man's home, before it was converted into a hostelry.

A wall almost a man's height surrounds it. The gate, two panels of very heavy wood with inlaid beaten brass filigree work, this afternoon was ajar—open only wide enough to admit one person at a time.

In the courtyard was a eucalyptus with liana vines, a fountain, a lot of ferns and flowering plants in huge pots, and a square lawn of thick Bermuda grass that has begun to bulge in places.

A concrete driveway leads beneath a porte-cochere, up beside the building, and disappears into the back.

I saw two entrances, a wider side entrance and a front one. I used the front entrance.

A flight of three concrete steps leads to an exposed square concrete landing. The door is tall, the lower third of stout oakwood, the upper two-thirds of Florentine glass and ironwork.

Inside, it was very cool. And it wasn't dim at all. Light came from the front door and the open side entrance. There was a central skylight above the system of stairs.

The panelling and the parquet flooring are all of strong rich brown oakwood. Against the wall near the foot of the first flight of steps are the letter boxes with the name cards and the black buttons with, above them, the cut-out brass letters from A to G.

The first stairs are wide and carpeted. Opening on to the first landing, also covered with a rug, are three doors—these are Apartments A, B and C.

Two narrow flights ascend from the first landing on either side of the first stairs. A long strip of rug covers all seven steps.

The second square landing ends in a tall window also of Florentine glass. Two narrow passageways, railed off from the stairwell, connect the landing with a long hall.

Four doors, two on either side, open onto this hall—Apartments D and E towards the rear and Apartments F and G forward. The hall is dominated by another window, again of Florentine glass.

Apartment F is Pepe's.

When I pushed the door in, I saw in the wall

facing me, even as the door swung open, another door opening, swinging outward, toward where I stood, out in the hall before the apartment. The doors came to a standstill simultaneously. I noticed the man before the farther side of the inner door, I stood and waited. It seemed the man could sustain silence and stillness longer than I could, so I decided to call out to him. Before I did so, I stepped over the threshold. When I saw him stride through the inner door the same time I crossed the threshold, I realized it was a mirror before me, a tall wall mirror.

The vestibule was bare.

The mirror was in the front room, set in a wall section directly facing the entranceway from the vestibule into the front room.

The front room was long and rectangular. There was a wide square back room. I went to the back room. I sat on Pepe's bed. I took off my shoes but left my feet socked. I stretched out on the bed to wait.

I hadn't had lunch and I was very tired but I wanted to be sure to be there when she arrived. I looked at my wrist watch. It was a quarter to two.

She didn't come until about three hours later. I waited, lying in Pepe's bed. The apartments were quiet. In the silence I could barely make out the hum of the traffic a block way. The afternoon was warm but it was cool in the apartment. There was a window in the front room, the only one in the apartment, but it was a tall massive window; it looked as if all of the front wall had been knocked out for it. The window was completely covered by drawn blinds. There were concealed ventilators. I could sense rather than hear them but I didn't bother to find out where they were.

A hoe drummed the earth in the public garden across the street. Water was run into pails and then after a while sprinkled on earth. Children laughed and shouted in the school-yard a block away in the direction of the church and the sea. Even the sighing of the surf in the sea, I imagined, came to me.

Every time I heard a car turning into the street I sat up in bed. As the car approached I would swing out of bed and run to the window. I would pull back the blinds and, through the gap between the side of the blinds and the window jamb, I would look into the street below. I did not leave the window until after each car left.

To and from the window, I passed the mirror every time. From the corner of my eye, I would catch a glimpse of my image as it entered, momentarily occupied, then left the silver frame.

Not many cars turned into Indiana Street that afternoon. But even so, some time during my vigil, I lost count. I decided she was probably not showing up at all. Every time I came away from the window I would tell myself that if she weren't in the next car I would leave. But I never did. I had borrowed the apartment for the afternoon and the afternoon was not over yet.

The children were not in the school grounds any more and I could hear the sea very clearly when she came.

I swung out of bed when I heard the car turning into the street. I was feeling weak and a little light-headed. I sat on the edge of the bed and held on to the thickness of the mattress to keep from keeling forward.

I rose to my feet unsteadily when I heard the car slowing down.

I was already in the front room when the sound of the tires gripping the gravel reached me.

I was striding past the mirror as the car screeched to a stop.

I reached the window, pulled back the blinds, and looked down into the street. The cab was drawn up before the gate, its engine running.

The cab door swung open.

I was leaning against the window jamb. Suddenly, above the purring of the idling engine, I could hear my rasping breath.

I saw her foot as it settled upon the car door sill. It was in a yellow sandal. I caught a glimpse of the swish of the hem of a yellow dress.

The late afternoon sun was sudden, caught

in her gleaming hair. Golden was the sunlight upon her yellow shawl. She was in a yellow dress but I didn't know which one.

I didn't notice when the cab drove away.

She stood on the sidewalk before the gate, hugging her hand bag—it was the square reed bag—to her body and I could see her plain and whole. It was like the first time I ever saw her and I could hear my booming heart.

Then she raised her face.

I stepped back, away from the window but only far enough not to be seen. Now I could see her face clearly: I saw her brow and her fine eyes and her fine nose and mouth; I saw her white throat: how flowerlike her face was, how like a flowerstalk her throat.

I moved to the window again when she dropped her eyes.

She slipped through the gate, her shawl barely touching either panel. She walked up the concrete driveway. She crossed the lawn and disappeared beneath the green and rust-colored canvas awning of the **porte-cochere.**

I let the blinds go: now she is going up the steps to the side entrance.

I noticed that I had fallen forward against the window sill and that the pale green slats of the blinds were almost against my face: now she is looking at the letter boxes and the name cards and the black buttons and the cut-out brass letters.

Then I felt my forehead hurting; I had leaned my head too heavily against the sharp concrete edge of the window jamb: now she has found the bell to the apartment.

I pushed myself away from the window, abstractedly I lifted my right hand and rubbed my brow where it hurt: now she is going to ring.

Something had come off my temple to my hand—gritty bits—and I was rolling the stuff absentmindedly between my thumb and fore and middle fingers; I had lifted my hand and was looking at what I was kneading there when the doorbell rang.

It wasn't really a bell: they were musical chimes. They were not meant to startle but I started at their sound. I looked at my thumb

and fingers and saw the bits of stucco there: now she is going up the first flight of steps.

I didn't know, as I stood, that I was swaying until I saw the stucco in my reeling hand: now she is on the first landing, looking at the cut-out brass letters on the doors; she will stop only long enough to know how the apartments are arranged and then she will not stop again.

I reeled away from the window and started weaving up the room: now she is going up one of the two second stairs.

Between the front room and the vestibule I caught at the door jamb and held myself there with my right hand: now she is on the second landing.

My hand held me trembling to the entrance-way: now she is walking up the passageway between the railing and the wall.

It was then I felt the eyes upon me, the eyes watching me; and I began to wheel around.

When I saw the seeking stricken eyes, I didn't know it was the mirror and I didn't recognize them for my own; I looked a long time at the long thin man with the wild wandering eyes and the drawn ruined face before I realized it was my own reflection.

Now she is in the hall outside the door. Now she is at the door.

I lurched into the vestibule and staggered to the apartment door. I broke my precipitate movement by left straight-arming the wall beside the door and catching at the brass door knob with my right hand.

When I pulled the door in she was there. Now I see you face to face; now I see your small white hands: how flowerlike your face is, how small and flowerlike your hands.

She was in the yellow dress with the square neckline and the short puffed sleeves. She was smiling; her eyes were bright and shining; and she was humming to herself.

II. THE GIRL'S STORY

He stood before me, holding the door open, his hand resting upon the door knob as if he held himself up that way. When I saw his soft hurt eyes and his pale thin face and his shock of hair, I thought that perhaps I shouldn't have come.

He looked at me a long time without saying anything as if he couldn't believe I was there. I said Hello. He didn't answer.

When he spoke, it was to say my name.

Then he stepped aside, away from the doorway. I walked into the small bare anteroom, I saw the tall wall mirror in the inner room facing the entranceway from the outer room and the apartment door.

I walked to the middle of the anteroom and stood there with my back towards him. In the mirror I saw how slowly he shut the door after me, leaned back upon it as if he was very tired, slowly lifted his right hand to rub his forehead with his palm and sweep back his uncombed hair with his fingers. I turned around and faced him when I saw his hurt unguarded hopeless eyes.

He pushed himself forward away from the door and walked towards me in the middle of the anteroom. As he passed me, he asked for my handbag and my yellow shawl. I fell in step beside him and, as we walked to the living room, I slipped the shawl off my shoulders and passed my bag and the shawl to him. We entered the living room. I saw in the looming mirror how he carried the shawl in one hand held stiffly up before him and the bag in the other which swung listless by his side.

He stopped as soon as we crossed the doorway. I walked on to the middle of the room and stood before the mirror with my back towards him. In the mirror I saw him place the bag on top of a wall table beside the doorway and then raise his arms and very carefully drape the shawl so it wouldn't rumple over the topmost arm of the coatstand to one side of the doorway beside the wall table.

I turned around and faced him as he walked towards me in the middle of the long room. He stood before me, his eyes upon me, as if he saw me for the first time, not saying anything. Then his eyes fell away. He looked around, swept up a chair by its back, set it right behind me where I stood before the mirror, and asked me to sit down.

I sat down and told him that I couldn't stay very long.

He stood before me, behind him loomed the mirror. In the mirror above him I could see the reflection of my yellow shawl.

"Yes, of course," he said.

Then he began to speak, he walked as he talked, his words sprang from his mouth like birds. He swung his arms; they beat like wings.

He paced up and down the long room from the window to the back room and I followed him with my eyes.

He stopped at the door into the back room and stood there; then he turned and, looking at me, said: "I can't get you out of my heart any more: I can't unlove you."

He walked down the long room and, as he crossed between me and the mirror and I saw in the mirror the reflection of the shawl spread like a wing above him, he said: "You are all the girls I have ever loved."

He stopped at the window and stood there. A breeze was blowing, the pale green blinds very near his face were beginning to stir. He walked up the long room and as he crossed between me and the mirror and I saw the shawl spread above him like a wing, he said: "Marriages are made in heaven. Marriages are made in hell. This is one marriage that shall never be, on earth, in heaven or in hell."

He stopped at the back room door and stood there; then he turned and, looking at me, said: "Love is dead: love doesn't hear. Love is dumb; love doesn't understand. It is exactly like talking to God."

He walked down the long room and as he crossed between me and the mirror and I saw the shawl like a wing spread above him, he said: "It is like knocking on a door that shall never open. It is like storming a wall that will never fall."

He stopped at the window and stood there. He lifted his face as if to smell the sea, as if to listen to the sea. The pale, green blinds almost against his eyes were rustling in the evening wind that was blowing from the sea laden with sea-scent and sea-sound. Then he turned and, looking at me, said: "I lost you even before I found you."

He was crossing between me and the mirror when he stopped and turned to me and stood before me, between me and the mirror.

I was looking up at him and I was looking at his reflection in the mirror too and I saw him as he was, as he stood rocking before me, and I saw him as his reflection also in the mirror that loomed large behind him when he said: "I might as well live as I might as well die."

Then he turned away from me.

I saw his face as he turned away, I saw in the mirror the reflection of his face as he turned towards the mirror, I saw his tortured twisted face.

It was not so much his face as it was the face of loss.

I saw in the mirror the yellow shawl hovering above him, I saw the yellow wing brooding over him.

Then the wing began to beat and to churn the air.

Then the wing lifted, leaving the air clear and shaken, filled with a yellow light.

Suddenly it wasn't early evening any more but deep night. It wasn't now but nine years back. It wasn't an apartment on Indiana Street but the Japanese garrison halfway between Valencia and Garcia Hernandez.

It wasn't he who stood rocking beneath the yellow shawl before me but my father.

And the yellow shawl that beat above him like a wing was not mine any more but my mother's.

I raised my hands and jammed the heels of my palms against my ears. But I heard again and couldn't shut off my mother's screams and my father's anguished cry.

He sat on his heels before me, wavering. His hands were on my shaking shoulders. His face, suffering and startled, was very near my eyes: it was clear and blurred by turns.

I didn't know that I was crying until I heard what he was saying over and over again.

"Please don't cry," he said. "How I love you! Don't—don't cry."

But I couldn't stop crying.

III. THE YELLOW SHAWL (1944)

The child woke up when her father lifted her from the bed. She knew it wasn't morning yet because the lights were on and they were very bright. She was already ten and she didn't like being carried any more, not even by her father. She tried to wriggle loose from her father's arms but found that she couldn't. She saw that she had been bundled up in bed-clothes. She was turning in her father's arms to ask him where they were going when she saw the many silent Japanese. She couldn't ask any more. Then she saw her mother: how pale she was, and distraught. her father told her to go to sleep right in his arms. She tried to but couldn't. The Japanese said: Come. At the door, her mother saw the lovely vivid yellow shawl and her mother asked the Japanese if she might not take it along with her. The Japanese said: All right. Her mother wrapped the shawl about her; the night was cold, the air struck at her face where it was exposed. It became even harder to try to get to sleep. She watched the many silent Japanese from her father's shoulder. They walked a long time; they reached a big house. The Japanese took them to a large room and left them there. In the room it was very bright; it was also very bare. There was nothing in it except a cot which was set against the wall facing the door. Her mother took the shawl off her. Her father set her down in the cot and told her to go to sleep. She tried to but couldn't. She watched her mother walk around the enormous room. Her mother stopped beside the door and stood on tiptoe and reached up with her arms to hang the shawl from a peg high up on the wall. Then she tried looking without blinking at the big bulb hanging by a cord from the roof. Her eyes hurt. She tried to sleep but couldn't sleep. She told her father, then her mother, that she couldn't sleep. They sat on the cot beside her to lull her to sleep. The light was too bright; the room was big and strange. Then the Japanese returned. Her mother stood up, stooped and kissed her, told her to be a good girl and sleep; and left with the Japanese. She looked at the shawl on the peg high up on the wall beside the shut door. Then her father told her to go to sleep. She heard her mother scream. It was so loud she thought her mother was back in the room with them. Suddenly her father was no longer beside her but was pacing up and down the middle of the room from the window to the wall. Every time her father crossed the room she saw how the shawl beat like a wing in the garish light above his head. Her mother stopped screaming and her father stopped pacing and stood still and tense, waiting. Her mother screamed again and her father fell to pacing the floor once more and every time he crossed the room he walked beneath her mother's shawl that hovered like a wing above him; her mother stopped screaming and her father stopped pacing and stood transfixed and tense, waiting. Her mother screamed

again and her father, released, lurched up and down the enormous room again. The screams came and went, grew fainter and fainter, and then the child couldn't hear them any more. Her father stood beneath the shawl that brooded like a wing over him, still and tense and waiting, but the screams didn't come again. The child stared, sleepless, at her father petrified beneath the yellow shawl. She saw her father sway and rock; she saw his incredibly coherent face break and crumble. The child didn't even start at the sound of the animal cry that tore savagely through her father's body and his throat. She watched her father fold and fall. She heard him whimper. Her eyes were wild and wide upon her father's body broken beneath the shadow of the yellow shawl when the Japanese came and carried her father's body away. She felt very wide awake. Her sleepless eyes hurt and felt very dry. She blinked her wakeful eyes long and hard many times trying to make the tears come but the tears wouldn't come no matter how hard and how long she tried.

Estrella D. Alfon

MAGNIFICENCE

There was nothing to fear, for the man was always so gentle, so kind. At night when the little girl and her brother were bathed in the light of the big shaded bulb that hung over the big study table in the downstairs hall, the man would knock gently on the door, and come in. He would stand for a while just beyond the pool of light, his feet in the circle of illumination, the rest of him in shadow. The little girl and her brother would look up at him where they sat at the big table, their eyes bright in the bright light, and watch him come fully into the light, a dark little man with protuberant lips, his eyes glinting in the light, but his voice soft, his manner slow. He would smell very faintly of sweat and pomade, but the children didn't mind although they did notice, for they waited for him every evening as they sat at their lessons like this. He'd throw his visored cap on the table, and it would fall down with a soft plop, then he'd nod his head to say one was right, or shake it to say one was wrong.

It was not always that he came. They could remember perhaps two weeks when he remarked to their mother that he had never seen two children looking so smart. The praise had made their mother look over them as they stood around listening to the goings-on at the meeting of the neighborhood association, of which their mother was presi-

dent. Two children, one a girl of seven, and a boy of eight. They were both very tall for their age, and their legs were the long gangly legs of fine spirited colts. Their mother saw them with eyes that held pride, and then to partly gloss over the maternal gloating she exhibited, she said to the man, in answer to his praise, But their homework. They're so lazy with them. And the man said, I have nothing to do in the evenings, let me help them. Mother nodded her head and said, If you want to bother yourself. And the thing rested there, and the man came in the evenings therefore, and he helped solve fractions for the boy, and write correct phrases in language for the little girl.

In those days, the rage was for pencils. School children always have rages going at one time or another. Sometimes it is for paper butterflies that are held on sticks, and whirr in the wind. The Japanese bazaars promoted a rage for those. Sometimes it is for little lead toys found in the folded waffles that Japanese confection-makers had such light hands with. At this particular time, it was for pencils. Pencils big but light in circumference not smaller than a man's thumb. They were unwieldly in a child's hands, but in all schools then, where Japanese bazaars clustered, there were all colors of these pencils selling for very low, but unattainable to a child budgeted at a *baon* of a centavo a day. They were all of five centavos each, and one pencil was not at all what one had ambitions for. In rages, one kept a collection. Four or five pencils, of different colors, to tie with strings near the eraser end, to dangle from one's book-basket, to arouse the envy of the other children who probably possessed less.

Add to the man's gentleness his kindness in knowing a child's desires, his promise that he would give each of them not one pencil, but two. And for the little girl, who he said was very bright and deserved more, he would get the biggest pencil he could find.

One evening he did bring them. The evenings of waiting had made them look forward to this final giving, and when they got the pencils they whooped with joy. The little boy had two pencils, one green, one blue. And the little girl had three pencils, two of the same circumference as the little boy's but colored red and yellow. And the third pencil, a jumbo size pencil really, was white, and had been sharpened, and the little girl jumped up and down, and shouted with glee. Until their mother called from down the stairs. What are you shouting about? And they told her, shouting gladly, Vicente, for that was his name. Vicente had brought the pencils he had promised them.

Thank him, their mother called. The little boy smiled and said, Thank you. And the little girl smiled, and said, Thank you, too. But the man said, Are you not going to kiss me for those pencils? They both came forward, the little girl and the little boy, and they both made to kiss him, but Vicente slapped the boy smartly on his lean hips, and said, Boys do not kiss boys. And the little boy laughed and scampered away, and then ran back and kissed him anyway.

The little girl went up to the man shyly, put her arms about his neck as he crouched to receive her embrace, and kissed him on the cheeks.

The man's arms tightened suddenly about the little girl, until the little girl squirmed out of his arms, and laughed a little breathlessly, disturbed but innocent, looking at the man with a smiling little question of puzzlement.

The next evening, he came around again. All through that day, they had been very proud in school, showing off their brand new pencils. All the little girls and boys had been envying them. And their mother had finally to tell them to stop talking about the pencils, pencils, for now that they had, the boy two, and the girl three, they were asking their mother to buy more, so that they could each have five, and three at least in the jumbo size that the little girl's third pencil was. Their mother said, Oh stop it, what will you do with so many pencils, you can only write with one at a time.

And the little girl muttered under her breath, I'll ask Vicente for some more.

Their mother replied, He's only a bus conductor, don't ask him for too many things. It's a pity. And this observation their mother said to their father, who was eating his evening meal between paragraphs of the book on masonry rites that he was reading. It is a pity, said their mother, People like those, they make friends with people like us, and they feel it is nice to give us gifts, or the children toys and things. You'd think they wouldn't be able to afford it.

The father grunted, and said, The man probably needed a new job, and was softening his way through to him by going at the children like that. And the mother said, No, I don't think so, he's a rather queer young man, I think he doesn't have many friends, but I have watched him with the children, and he seems to dote on them.

The father grunted again, and did not pay any further attention.

Vicente was earlier than usual that evening. The children immediately put their lessons down, telling him of the envy of their schoolmates, and would he buy them more please?

Vicente said to the little boy, Go and ask if you can let me have a glass of water. And the little boy ran away to comply, saying behind him, But buy us some more pencils, huh, buy us more pencils, and then went up the stairs to their mother.

Vicente held the little girl by the arm, and said gently, Of course I will buy you more pencils, as many as you want.

And the little girl giggled and said, Oh, then I will tell my friends, and they will envy me, for they don't have as many or as pretty.

Vicente took the girl up lightly in his arms, holding her under the armpits, and held her to sit down on his lap and he said, still gently, What are your lessons for tomorrow? And the little girl turned to the paper on the table where she had been writing with the jumbo pencil, and she told him that that was her lesson but it was easy.

Then go ahead and write, and I will watch you.

Don't hold me on your lap, said the little girl, I am very heavy, you will get very tired.

The man shook his head, and said nothing, but held her on his lap just the same.

The little girl kept squirming, for somehow she felt uncomfortable to be held thus, her mother and father always treated her like a big girl, she was always told never to act like a baby. She looked around at Vicente, interrupting her careful writing to twist around.

His face was all in sweat, and his eyes looked very strange, and indicated to her that she must turn around, attend to the homework she was writing.

But the little girl felt very queer, she didn't know why, all of a sudden she was immensely frightened, and she jumped up away from Vicente's lap.

She stood looking at him, feeling that queer frightened feeling, not knowing what to do. By and by, in a very short while her mother came down the stairs, holding in her hand a glass of zarzaparilla. The little boy followed her. The mother said, I brought you some zarzaparilla, Vicente.

But Vicente had jumped up too as soon as the little girl had jumped from his lap. He snatched at the papers that lay on the table and held them to his stomach, turning away from the mother's coming.

The mother looked at him, stopped in her tracks, and advanced into the light. She had been in the shadow. Her voice had been like a bell of safety to the little girl. But now she advanced into the glare of the light that held like a tableau the figures of Vicente holding the little girl's papers to him, and the little girl looking up at him frightenedly, in her eyes dark pools of wonder and fear and question.

The little girl looked at her mother, and saw the beloved face transfigured by some sort of glow. The mother kept coming into the light, and when Vicente made as if to move away into the shadow, she said, very low, but very heavily, Do not move.

She put the glass of soft drink down on the table, where in the light one could watch the little bubbles go up and down in the dark liquid. The mother said to the little boy, Oscar, finish your lessons. And then turning to the little girl, she said, Come here. The little girl went to her, and the mother knelt down, for she was a tall woman and she said, Turn around. Obediently the little girl turned around, and her mother passed her hands over the little girl's back.

Go upstairs, she said.

The mother's voice was of such a heavy quality and of such awful timbre that the girl could only nod her head, and without looking at Vicente again, she raced up the stairs. The little boy bent over his lessons.

The mother went to the cowering man, and marched him with a glance out of the circle of light that held the little boy. Once in the shadow, she extended her hand, and without any opposition took away the papers that Vicente was holding to himself. She stood there saying nothing as the man fumbled with his hands and with his fingers, and she waited until he had finished. She was going to open her mouth but she glanced at the boy and closed it, and with a look and an inclination of the head, she bade Vicente go up the stairs.

The man said nothing, for she said nothing either. Up the stairs went the man, and the mother followed him behind. When they had reached the upper landing, the woman called down to her son, Son, come up and go to your room.

The little boy did as he was told, asking no questions, for indeed he was feeling sleepy already.

As soon as the boy was gone, the mother turned on Vicente. There was a pause.

Finally, the woman raised her hand, and slapped him full hard in the face. He retreated down one tread of the stairs with the force of the blow, but the mother followed him. With her other hand she slapped him on the other side of the face again. And so down the stairs they went, the man backwards, his face continually open to the force of the woman's slapping. Alternately she lifted her right hand and made him retreat before her until they reached the bottom landing.

He made no resistance, offered no defense. Before the silence and the grimness of her attack he cowered, retreating, until out of his mouth issued something like a whimper.

The mother thus shut his mouth, and with those hard forceful slaps she escorted him right to the door. As soon as the cool air of the free night touched him, he recovered enough to turn away and run, into the shadows that ate him up. The woman looked after him, and closed the door. She turned off the blazing light over the study table, and went slowly up the stairs.

The little girl watched her mother come up the stairs. She had been witness, watching through the shutters of a window that overlooked the stairs, to the picture of magnificence her mother made as she slapped the man down the stairs and out into the dark night.

When her mother reached her, the woman held her hand out to the child. Always also, with the terrible indelibility that one associates with terror, the girl was to remember the touch of that hand on her shoulder, heavy, kneading at her flesh, the woman herself stricken almost dumb, but her eyes eloquent with that angered fire. She knelt. She felt the little girl's dress and took it off with haste that was almost frantic, tearing at the buttons and imparting a terror to the little girl that almost made her sob. Hush, the mother said. Take a bath quickly.

Her mother presided over the bath that the little girl took, scrubbed her, and soaped her, and then wiped her gently all over and changed her into new clothes that smelt with the clean fresh smell of clothes that had hung in the light of the sun. The clothes that she had taken off the little girl, she bundled into a tight wrenched bunch, which she threw into the kitchen range.

Take also the pencils, said the mother to the watching newly bathed, newly changed child. Take them and throw them into the fire. But when the girl turned to comply, the mother said, No, tomorrow will do. And taking the little girl by the hand, she led her to her little girl's bed, made her lie down and tucked the covers gently about her as the girl dropped off into quick slumber.

Nick Joaquin

THE SUMMER SOLSTICE

The Moretas were spending St. John's Day with the children's grandfather, whose feast day it was. Doña Lupeng awoke feeling faint with the heat, a sound of screaming in her ears. In the dining room the three boys, already attired in their holiday suits, were at breakfast, and came crowding around her, talking all at once.

"How long you have slept, Mama!"

"We thought you were never getting up!"

"Do we leave at once, huh? Are we going now?"

"Hush, hush, I implore you! Now look: your father has a headache, and so have I. So be quiet this instant—or no one goes to Grandfather."

Though it was only seven by the clock the house was already a furnace, the windows dilating with the harsh light and the .air already burning with the immense, intense fever of noon.

She found the children's nurse working in the kitchen. "And why is it you who are preparing breakfast? Where is Amada?" But without waiting for an answer she went to the backdoor and opened it, and the screaming in her ears became a wild screaming in the stables across the yard. "Oh, my God!" she groaned and, grasping her skirts, hurried across the yard.

In the stables Entoy, the driver, apparently deaf to the screams, was hitching the pair of piebald ponies to the coach.

"Not the closed coach, Entoy! The open carriage!" shouted Doña Lupeng as she came up.

"But the dust, señora—"

"I know, but better to be dirty than to be boiled alive. And what ails your wife, eh? Have you been beating her again?"

"Oh no, señora: I have not touched her."

"Then why is she screaming? Is she ill?"

"I do not think so. But how do I know? You can go and see for yourself, señora. She is up there."

When Doña Lupeng entered the room, the big half-naked woman sprawled across the bamboo bed stopped screaming. Doña Lupeng was shocked.

"What is this, Amanda? Why are you still in bed at this hour? And in such a posture! Come, get up at once. You should be ashamed!"

But the woman on the bed merely stared. Her sweat-beaded brows contracted, as if in an effort to understand. Then her face relaxed, her mouth sagged open humorously and, rolling over on her back and spreading out her big soft arms and legs, she began noiselessly quaking with laughter—the mute mirth jerking in her throat; the moist pile of her flesh quivering like brown jelly. Saliva dribbled from the corners of her mouth.

Doña Lupeng blushed, looking around helplessly; and seeing that Entoy had followed and was leaning in the doorway, watching stolidly, she blushed again. The room reeked hotly of intimate odors. She averted her eyes from the laughing woman on the bed, in whose nakedness she seemed so to participate that she was ashamed to look directly at the man in the doorway.

"Tell me, Entoy: has she been to the Tadtarin?"

"Yes, señora. Last night."

"But I forbade her to go! And I forbade you to let her go!"

"I could do nothing."

"Why, you beat her at the least pretext!"

"But now I dare not touch her."

"Oh, and why not?"

"It is the day of St. John: the spirit is in her."

"But, man—"

"It is true, señora. The spirit is in her. She is the Tadtarin. She must do as she pleases. Otherwise, the grain would not grow, the trees would bear no fruit, the rivers would give no fish, and the animals would die."

"*Naku,* I did not know your wife was so powerful, Entoy."

"At such times she is not my wife: she is the wife of the river, she is the wife of the crocodile, she is the wife of the moon."

═══

"But how can they still believe such things?" demanded Doña Lupeng of her husband as they drove in the open carriage through the pastoral countryside that was the *arrabal* of Paco in the 1850's.

Don Paeng, drowsily stroking his moustaches, his eyes closed against the hot light, merely shrugged.

"And you should have seen that Entoy," continued his wife. "You know how the brute treats her: she cannot say a word but he thrashes her. But this morning he stood as meek as a lamb while she screamed and screamed. He seemed actually in awe of her, do you know—actually *afraid* of her!"

Don Paeng darted a sidelong glance at his wife, by which he intimated that the subject was not a proper one for the children, who were sitting opposite, facing their parents.

"Oh, look, boys—here comes the St. John!" cried Doña Lupeng, and she sprang up in the swaying carriage, propping one hand on her husband's shoulder while with the other she held up her silk parasol.

And "Here come the men with their St. John!" cried voices up and down the countryside. People in wet clothes dripping with well-water, ditch-water and river-water came running across the hot woods and fields and meadows, brandishing cans of water, wetting each other uproariously, and shouting *San Juan! San Juan!* as they ran to meet the procession.

Up the road, stirring a cloud of dust, and gaily bedrenched by the crowds gathered along the wayside, a concourse of young men clad only in soggy trousers were carrying aloft an image of the Precursor. Their teeth flashed white in their laughing faces and their hot bodies glowed crimson as they pranced past, shrouded in fiery dust, singing and shouting and waving their arms: the St. John riding swiftly above the sea of dark heads and glittering in the noon sun—a fine, blonde, heroic St. John: very male, very arrogant: the Lord of Summer indeed; the Lord of Light and Heat—erect and goldly virile above the prone and female earth—while the worshippers danced and the dust thickened and the animals reared and roared and the merciless fires came raining down from the skies—the vast outpouring of light that marks this climax of the solar year—raining relentlessly upon field and river and town and winding road, and upon the joyous throng of young men against whose uproar a couple of seminarians in muddy cassocks vainly intoned the hymn of the noon god:

That we, thy servants, in chorus
May praise thee, our tongues restore us..."

But Doña Lupeng, standing in the stopped carriage, looking very young and elegant in her white frock, under the twirling parasol, stared down on the passing male horde with increasing annoyance. The insolent man-smell of their bodies rose all about her—wave upon wave of it—enveloping her, assaulting her senses, till she felt faint with it and pressed a handkerchief to her nose. And as she glanced at her husband and saw with what a smug smile he was watching the revellers, her annoyance deepened. When he bade her sit down because all eyes were turned on her, she pretended not to hear; stood up even straighter, as if to defy those rude creatures flaunting their manhood in the sun.

And she wondered peevishly what the braggarts were being so cocky about? For this arrogance, this pride, this bluff male health of theirs was (she told herself) founded on the impregnable virtue of generations of good women. The boobies were so sure of themselves because they had always been sure of their wives. "*All the sisters being virtuous, all the brothers are brave,*" thought Doña Lupeng, with a bitterness that rather surprised her. Women had built it up: this poise of the male. Ah, and women could destroy it, too! She recalled, vindictively, this morning's scene at the stables: Amada naked and screaming in bed while from the doorway her lord and master looked on in meek silence. And was it not the mystery of a woman in her flowers that had restored the tongue of that old Hebrew prophet?

"Look, Lupeng, they have all passed now," Don Paeng was saying, "Do you mean to stand all the way?"

She looked around in surprise and hastily sat down. The children tittered, and the carriage started.

"Has the heat gone to your head, woman?" asked Don Paeng, smiling. The children burst frankly into laughter.

Their mother coloured and hung her head. She was beginning to feel ashamed of the thoughts that had filled her mind. They seemed improper—almost obscene—and the discovery of such depths of wickedness in herself appalled her. She moved closer to her husband, to share the parasol with him.

"And did you see our young cousin Guido?" he asked.

"Oh, was he in that crowd?"

"A European education does not seem to have spoiled his taste for country pleasures."

"I did not see him."

"He waved and waved."

"The poor boy. He will feel hurt. But truly, Paeng, I did not see him."

"Well, that is always a woman's privilege."

―――――

But when that afternoon, at the grandfather's, the young Guido presented himself, properly attired and brushed and scented, Doña Lupeng was so charming and gracious with him that he was enchanted and gazed after her all afternoon with enamoured eyes.

This was the time when our young men were all going to Europe and bringing back with them, not the Age of Victoria, but the Age of Byron. The young Guido knew nothing of Darwin and evolution; he knew everything about Napoleon and the Revolution. When Doña Lupeng expressed surprise at his presence that morning in the St. John's crowd, he laughed in her face.

"But I *adore* these old fiestas of ours! They are so *romantic!* Last night, do you know, we walked all the way through the woods, I and some boys, to see the procession of the Tadtarin."

"And was that romantic too?" asked Doña Lupeng.

"It was *weird.* It made my flesh *crawl.* All those women in such a mystic frenzy! And she who was the Tadtarin last night—she was a figure right out of a flamenco!"

"I fear to disenchant you, Guido—but that woman happens to be our cook."

"She is beautiful."

"Our Amada beautiful? But she is old and fat!"

"She is beautiful—as that old tree you are leaning on is beautiful," calmly insisted the young man, mocking her with his eyes.

They were out in the buzzing orchard, among the ripe mangoes; Doña Lupeng seated on the grass, her legs tucked beneath her, and the young man sprawled flat on his belly, gazing up at her, his face moist with sweat. The children were chasing dragonflies. The sun stood still in the west. The long day refused to end. From the house came the sudden roaring laughter of the men playing cards.

"Beautiful! Romantic! Adorable! Are those the only words you learned in Europe?" cried Doña Lupeng, feeling very annoyed with this young man whose eyes adored her one moment and mocked her the next.

"Ah, I also learned to open my eyes over there—to see the holiness and the mystery of what is vulgar."

"And what is so holy and mysterious about—about the Tadtarin, for instance?"

"I do not know. I can only *feel* it. And it *frightens* me. Those rituals come to us from the earliest dawn of the world. And the dominant figure is not the male but the female."

"But they are in honor of St. John."

"What has your St. John to do with them? Those women worship a more ancient lord. Why, do you know that no man may join in those rites unless he first puts on some article of women's apparel and—"

"And what did *you* put on, Guido?"

"How *sharp* you are! Oh, I made such love to a toothless old hag there that she pulled off her stocking for me. And I pulled it on, over my arm, like a glove. How your husband would have *despised* me!"

"But what on earth does it mean?"

"I think it is to remind us men that once upon a time you women were supreme and we men were the slaves."

"But surely there have always been kings?"

"Oh, no. The queen came before the king, and the priestess before the priest, and the moon before the sun."

"The moon?"

"—who is the Lord of the women."

"Why?"

"Because the tides of women, like the tides of the sea, are tides of the moon. Because the

first blood—But what is the matter, Lupe? Oh, have I offended you?"

"Is this how they talk to decent women in Europe?"

"They do not talk to women, they pray to them—as men did in the dawn of the world."

"Oh, you are mad! mad!"

"Why are you so afraid, Lupe?"

"I, afraid? And of whom? My dear boy, you still have your mother's milk in your mouth. I only wish you to remember that I am a married woman."

"I remember that you are a woman, yes. A beautiful woman. And why not? Did you turn into some dreadful monster when you married? Did you stop being a woman? Did you stop being beautiful? Then why should my eyes not tell you what you are—just because you are married?"

"Ah, this is too much now!" cried Doña Lupeng, and she rose to her feet.

"Do not go, I implore you! Have pity on me!"

"No more of your comedy, Guido! And besides—where have those children gone to! I must go after them."

As she lifed her skirts to walk away, the young man, propping up his elbows, dragged himself forward on the ground and solemnly kissed the tips of her shoes. She stared down in sudden horror, transfixed—and he felt her violent shudder. She backed away slowly, still staring; then turned and fled toward the house.

———

On the way home that evening Don Paeng noticed that his wife was in a mood. They were alone in the carriage: the children were staying overnight at their grandfather's. The heat had not subsided. It was heat without gradations: that knew no twilights and no dawns; that was still there, after the sun had set; that would be there already, before the sun had risen.

"Has young Guido been annoying you?" asked Don Paeng.

"Yes! All afternoon."

"These young men today—what a disgrace

they are! I felt embarrassed as a man to see him following you about with those eyes of a whipped dog."

She glanced at him coldly. "And was that all you felt, Paeng? Embarrassed—as a man?"

"A good husband has constant confidence in the good sense of his wife," he pronounced grandly, and smiled at her.

But she drew away; huddled herself in the other corner. "He *kissed* my feet," she told him disdainfully, her eyes on his face.

He frowned and made a gesture of distaste. "Do you see? They have the instincts, the style of the canalla! To kiss a woman's feet, to follow her like a dog, to adore her like a slave—"

"Is it so shameful for a man to adore women?"

"A gentleman loves and respects Woman. The cads and lunatics—they 'adore' the women."

"But maybe we do not want to be loved and respected—but to be adored."

"Ah, he has converted you then?"

"Who knows? But must we talk about it? My head is bursting with the heat."

But when they reached home she did not lie down but wandered listlessly through the empty house. When Don Paeng, having bathed and changed, came down from the bedroom, he found her in the dark parlour seated at the harp and plucking out a tune, still in her white frock and shoes.

"How can you bear those hot clothes, Lupeng? And why the darkness? Order someone to bring a light in here."

"There is no one, they have all gone to see the Tadtarin."

"A pack of loafers we are feeding!"

She had risen and gone to the window. He approached and stood behind her, grasped her elbows and, stooping, kissed the nape of her neck. But she stood still, not responding, and he released her sulkily. She turned around to face him.

"Listen, Paeng. I want to see it, too. The Tadtarin, I mean. I have not seen it since I was a little girl. And tonight is the last night."

"You must be crazy! Only low people go there. And I thought you had a headache?" He was still sulking.

"But I want to go! My head aches worse in the house. For a favour, Paeng."

"I told you: No! Go and take those clothes off. But, woman, whatever has got into you!" He strode off to the table, opened the box of cigars, took one, banged the lid shut, bit off an end of the cigar, and glared about for a light.

She was still standing by the window and her chin was up.

"Very well, if you do not want to come, do not come—but I am going."

"I warn you, Lupe; do not provoke me!"

"I will go with Amada. Entoy can take us. You cannot forbid me, Paeng. There is nothing wrong with it. I am not a child."

But standing very straight in her white frock, her eyes shining in the dark and her chin thrust up, she looked so young, so fragile, that his heart was touched. He sighed, smiled ruefully, and shrugged his shoulders.

"Yes, the heat has touched you in the head, Lupeng. And since you are so set on it—very well, let us go. Come, have the coach ordered!"

———

The cult of the Tadtarin is celebrated on three days: the feast of St. John and the two preceding days. On the first night, a young girl heads the procession; on the second, a mature woman; and on the third, a very old woman who dies and comes to life again. In these processions, as in those of Pakil and Obando, everyone dances.

Around the tiny plaza in front of the barrio chapel, quite a stream of carriages was flowing leisurely. The Moretas were constantly being hailed from the other vehicles. The plaza itself and the sidewalks were filled with chattering, strolling, profusely sweating people. More people were crowded on the balconies and windows of the houses. The moon had not yet risen; the black night smoldered; in the windless sky the lightning's abruptly branching fire seemed the nerves of the tortured air made visible.

"Here they come now!" cried the people on the balconies.

And "Here come the women with their St. John!" cried the people on the sidewalks, surging forth on the street. The carriages halted and their occupants descended. The plaza rang with the shouts of people and the neighing of horses—and with another keener sound: a sound as of sea-waves steadily rolling nearer.

The crowd parted, and up the street came the prancing, screaming, writhing women, their eyes wild, black shawls flying around their shoulders, and their long hair streaming and covered with leaves and flowers. But the Tadtarin, a small old woman with white hair, walked with calm dignity in the midst of the female tumult, a wand in one hand, a bunch of seedlings in the other. Behind her, a group of girls bore aloft a little black image of the Baptist—a crude, primitive, grotesque image, its big-eyed head too big for its puny naked torso, bobbing and swaying above the hysterical female horde and looking at once so comical and so pathetic that Don Paeng, watching with his wife on the sidewalk, was outraged. The image seemed to be crying for help, to be struggling to escape—a St. John indeed in the hands of the Herodiads; a doomed captive these witches were subjecting first to their derision; a gross and brutal caricature of his sex.

Don Paeng flushed hotly: he felt that all those women had personally insulted him. He turned to his wife, to take her away—but she was watching greedily, taut and breathless, her head thrust forward and her eyes bulging, the teeth bared in the slack mouth, and the sweat gleaming on her face. Don Paeng was horrified. He grasped her arm—but just then a flash of lightning blazed and the screaming women fell silent: the Tadtarin was about to die.

The old woman closed her eyes and bowed her head and sank slowly to her knees. A pallet was brought and set on the ground and she was laid in it and her face covered with a shroud. Her hands still clutched the wand and the seedlings. The women drew away, leaving her

in a cleared space. They covered their heads with their black shawls and began wailing softly, unhumanly—a hushed, animal keening.

Overhead the sky was brightening; silver light defined the rooftops. When the moon rose and flooded with hot brilliance the moveless crowded square, the black-shawled women stopped wailing and a girl approached and unshrouded the Tadtarin, who opened her eyes and sat up, her face lifted to the moonlight. She rose to her feet and extended the wand and the seedlings and the women joined in a mighty shout. They pulled off and waved their shawls and whirled and began dancing again—laughing and dancing with such joyous exciting abandon that the people in the square and on the sidewalks, and even those on the balconies, were soon laughing and dancing, too. Girls broke away from their parents and wives from their husbands to join in the orgy.

"Come, let us go now," said Don Paeng to his wife. She was shaking with fascination; tears trembled on her lashes; but she nodded meekly and allowed herself to be led away. But suddenly she pulled free from his grasp, darted off, and ran into the crowd of dancing women.

She flung her hands to her hair and whirled and her hair came undone. Then, planting her arms akimbo, she began to trip a nimble measure, an instinctive folk-movement. She tossed her head back and her arched throat bloomed whitely. Her eyes brimmed with moonlight, and her mouth with laughter.

Don Paeng ran after her, shouting her name, but she laughed and shook her head and darted deeper into the dense maze of the procession, which was moving again, towards the chapel. He followed her, shouting; she eluded him, laughing—and through the thick of the female horde they lost and found and lost each other again—she, dancing and he pursuing—till, carried along by the tide, they were both swallowed up into the hot, packed, turbulent darkness of the chapel. Inside poured the entire procession, and Don Paeng, finding himself trapped tight among milling female bodies, struggled with sudden panic to fight his way out. Angry voices roses all about him in the stifling darkness.

"*Hoy,* you are crushing my feet!"

"And let go of my shawl, my shawl!"

"Stop pushing, shameless one, or I kick you!"

"Let me pass, let me pass, you harlots!" cried Don Paeng.

"*Abah,* it is a man!"

"How dare he come in here?"

"Break his head!"

"Throw the animal out!"

"Throw him out! Throw him out!" shrieked the voices, and Don Paeng found himself surrounded by a swarm of gleaming eyes.

Terror possessed him and he struck out savagely with both fists, with all his strength— but they closed in as savagely: solid walls of flesh that crushed upon him and pinned his arms helpless, while unseen hands struck and struck his face, and ravaged his hair and clothes, and clawed at his flesh, as—kicked and buffeted, his eyes blind and his torn mouth salty with blood—he was pushed down, down to his knees, and half-shoved, half-dragged to the doorway and rolled out to the street. He picked himself up at once and walked away with a dignity that forbade the crowd gathered outside to laugh or to pity. Entoy came running to meet him.

"But what has happened to you, Don Paeng?"

"Nothing. Where is the coach?"

"Just over there, sir. But you are wounded in the face!"

"No, these are only scratches. Go and get the señora. We are going home."

When she entered the coach and saw his bruised face and torn clothing, she smiled coolly.

"What a sight you are, man! What have you done with yourself?" And when he did not answer: "Why, have they pulled out his tongue too?" she wondered aloud.

═════

And when they were home and stood facing each other in the bedroom, she was still as light-hearted.

"What are you going to do, Rafael?"

"I am going to give you a whipping."

"But why?"

"Because you have behaved tonight like a lewd woman."

"How I behaved tonight is what I am. If you call that lewd, then I was always a lewd woman and a whipping will not change me— though you whipped me till I died."

"I want this madness to die in you."

"No, you want me to pay for your bruises."

He flushed darkly. "How can you say that, Lupe?"

"Because it is true. You have been whipped by the women and now you think to avenge yourself by whipping me."

His shoulders sagged and his face dulled. "If you can think that of me—"

"You could think me a lewd woman!"

"Oh, how do I know what to think of you? I was sure I knew you as I knew myself. But now you are as distant and strange to me as a female Turk in Africa!"

"Yet you would dare whip me—"

"Because I love you, because I respect you—"

"And because if you ceased to respect me you would cease to respect yourself?"

"Ah, I did not say that!"

"Then why not say it? It is true. And you want to say it, you want to say it!"

But he struggled against her power. "Why should I want to?" he demanded peevishly.

"Because, either you must say it—or you must whip me," she taunted.

Her eyes were upon him and the shameful fear that had unmanned him in the dark chapel possessed him again. His legs had turned to water; it was a monstrous agony to remain standing.

But she was waiting for him to speak, forcing him to speak.

"No, I cannot whip you!" he confessed miserably.

"Then say it! Say it!" she cried, pounding her clenched her fists together. "Why suffer and suffer? And in the end you would only submit."

But he still struggled stubbornly, "Is it not enough that you have me helpless? Is it not enough that I feel what you want me to feel?"

But she shook her head furiously. "Until you have said it to me, there can be no peace between us."

He was exhausted at last: he sank heavily to his knees, breathing hard and streaming with sweat, his fine body curiously diminished now in its ravaged apparel.

"I adore you, Lupe," he said tonelessly.

She strained forward avidly. *"What?* What did you say?" she screamed.

And he, in his dead voice: "That I adore you. That I adore you. That I worship you. That the air you breathe and the ground you tread is holy to me. That I am your dog, your slave..."

But it was still not enough. Her fists were still clenched, and she cried: *"Then come, crawl on the floor, and kiss my feet!"*

Without a moment's hesitation, he sprawled down flat and, working his arms and legs, gaspingly clawed his way across the floor, like a great agonized lizard, the woman steadily backing away as he approached, her eyes watching him avidly, her nostrils dilating, till behind her loomed the open window, the huge glittering moon, the rapid flashes of lightning. She stopped, panting, and leaned against the sill. He lay exhausted at her feet, his face flat on the floor.

She raised her skirts and contemptuously thrust out a naked foot. He lifted his dripping face and touched his bruised lips to her toes; lifted his hands and grasped the white foot and kissed it savagely—kissed the step, the sole, the frail ankle—while she bit her lips and clutched in pain at the windowsill, her body distended and wracked by horrible shivers, her head flung back and her loose hair streaming out the window—streaming fluid and black in the white night where the huge moon glowed like a sun and the dry air flamed into lightning and the pure heat burned with the immense intense fever of noon.

Ibrahim A. Jubaira

BLUE BLOOD OF THE BIG ASTANA

Although the heart may care no more, the mind can always recall. The mind can always recall, for there are always things to remember: languid days of depressed boyhood; shared happy days under the glare of the sun; concealed love and mocking fate; etc. So I suppose you remember too.

Remember? A little over a year after I was orphaned, my aunt decided to turn me over to your father, the Datu. In those days, datus were supposed to take charge of the poor and the helpless. Therefore, my aunt only did right in placing me under the wing of your father. Furthermore she was so poor, that by doing that, she not only relieved herself of the burden of poverty but also safe-guarded my well-being.

But I could not bear the thought of even a moment's separation from my aunt. She had been like a mother to me, and would always be.

"Please, Babo," I pleaded. "Try to feed me a little more. Let me grow big with you, and I will build you a house. I will repay you some day. Let me do something to help, but please, Babo, don't send me away..." I really cried.

Babo placed a soothing hand on my shoulder. Just like the hand of Mother. I felt a bit comforted, but presently I cried some more. The effect of her hand was so stirring.

"Listen to me. Stop crying—oh, now, do stop. You see, we can't go on like this," Babo said. "My matweaving can't clothe and feed both you and me. It's really hard, son, it's really hard. You have to go. But I will be seeing you every week. You can have everything you want in the Datu's house."

I tried to look at Babo through my tears. But soon, the thought of having everything I wanted took hold of my child's mind. I ceased crying.

"Say you will go," Babo coaxed me. I assented finally. I was only five then—very tractable.

Babo bathed me in the afternoon. I did not flinch and shiver, for the sea was comfortably warm and exhilarating. She cleaned my fingernails meticulously. Then she cupped a handful of sand, spread it over my back, and rubbed my grimy body, particularly the back of my ears. She poured fresh water over me afterwards. How clean I became! But my clothes were frayed....

Babo instructed me before we left for your big house: I must not forget to kiss your father's feet, and to withdraw when and as ordered without turning my back; I must not look at your father full in the eyes; I must not talk too much; I must always talk in the third person; I must not... Ah, Babo, those were too many to remember.

Babo tried to be patient with me. She tested me over and over again on those royal, traditional ways. And one thing more: I had to say "Pateyk" for yes, and "Teyk" for what, or for answering a call.

"Oh, Babo, why do I have to say all those things? Why really do I have . . ."

"Come along, son; come along."

We started that same afternoon. The breeze was cool as it blew against my face. We did not get tired because we talked on the way. She told me so many things. She said you of the big house had blue blood.

"Not red like ours, Babo?"

Babo said no, not red like ours.

"And the Datu has a daughter of my age, Babo?"

Babo said yes—you. And I might be allowed to play with you, the Datu's daughter, if I worked hard and behaved well.

I asked Babo, too, if I might be allowed to prick your skin to see if you had blue blood, in truth. But Babo did not answer me any more. She just told me to keep quiet. There, I became so talkative again.

Was that really our house? My, it was so big! Babo chided me. "We don't call it a house," she said. "We call it *astana*, the house of the Datu." So I just said oh, and kept quiet. Why did not Babo tell me that before?

Babo suddenly stopped in her tracks. Was I really very clean? Oh, oh, look at my hare-lip. She cleaned my hare-lip, wiping away with her *tapis* the sticky mucus of the faintest conceivable green flowing from my nose. Poi! Now it was better. Although I could not feel any sort of improvement in my deformity itself. I merely felt cleaner.

Was I truly the boy about whom Babo was talking? You were laughing, young pretty Blue Blood. Happy perhaps that I was. Or was it the amusement brought about by my hare-lip that had made you laugh? I dared not ask you. I feared that should you come to dislike me, you'd subject me to unpleasant treatment. Hence, I laughed with you, and you were pleased.

Babo told me to kiss your right hand. Why not your feet? Oh, you were a child yet. I could wait until you had grown up.

But you withdrew your hand at once. I think my hare-lip gave it a ticklish sensation. However, I was so intoxicated by the momentary sweetness the action brought me that I decided inwardly to kiss your hand every day. No, no, it was not love. It was only an impish sort of liking. Imagine the pride that was mine to be thus in close heady contact with one of the blue blood. . . .

"Welcome, little orphan!" Was it for me? Really for me? I looked at Babo. Of course it was for me! We were generously bidden in. Thanks to your father's kindness. And thanks to your laughing at me, too.

I kissed the feet of your *Appah,* your old, honorable resting-the-whole-day father. He was not tickled by my hare-lip as you were. He did not laugh at me. In fact, he evinced compassion towards me. And so did your *Amboh,* your kind mother. "Sit down, sit down; don't be ashamed."

But there you were plying Babo with your heartless questions: Why was I like that? What had happened to me?

To satisfy you, pretty Blue Blood, little inquisitive One, Babo had to explain: Well, Mother had slid in the vinta in her sixth month with the child that was me. Result: my hare-lip. "Poor Jaafar," your *Appah* said. I was about to cry, but seeing you looking at me, I felt so ashamed that I held back the tears. I could not help being sentimental, you see. I think my being bereft of parents in youth had much to do with it all.

"Do you think you will be happy to stay with us? Will you not yearn any more for your Babo?"

"Pateyk, I will be happy," I said. Then the thought of my not yearning any more for Babo made me wince. But Babo nodded at me reassuringly.

"Pateyk, I will not yearn any more for . . . for Babo."

And Babo went before the interview was through. She had to cover five miles before evening came. Still I did not cry, as you may have expected I would, for—have I not said it?—I was ashamed to weep in your presence.

That was how I came to stay with you, remember? Babo came to see me every week as she had promised. And you—all of you—had a lot of things to tell her. That I was a good worker—oh, beyond question, your *Appah* and *Amboh* told Babo. And you, outspoken little Blue Blood, joined the flattering chorus. But my place of sleep always reeked of urine, you added, laughing. That drew a rallying admonition from Babo, and a downright promise from me not to wet my mat again.

Yes, Babo came to see me, to advise me every week, for two consecutive years—that is, until death took her away, leaving no one in the world but a nephew with a hare-lip.

Remember? I was your favorite and you wanted to play with me always. I learned why after a time, it delighted you to gaze at my hare-lip. Sometimes, when we went out wading to the sea, you would pause and look at me. I would look at you, too, wondering. Finally, you would be seized by a fit of laughter. I would chime in, not realizing I was making fun of myself. Then you would pinch me painfully to make me cry. Oh, you wanted to experiment with me. You could not tell, you said, whether I cried or laughed: the working of my lips was just the same in either to your gleaming eyes. And I did not flush with shame even if you said so. For after all, had not my mother slid in the vinta?

That was your way. And I wanted to pay you back in my own way. I wanted to prick your skin and see if you really had blue blood. But there was something about you that warned against a deformed orphan's intrusion. All I could do, then, was to feel foolishly proud, cry and laugh with you—for you—just to gratify the teasing imperious blue blood in you. Yet, I had my way too.

Remember? I was apparently so willing to do anything for you. I would climb for young coconuts for you. You would be amazed by the ease and agility with which I made my way up the coconut tree, yet fear that I would fall. You would implore me to come down at once, quick. "No." You would throw pebbles

at me if I thus refused to come down. No, I still would not. Your pebbles could not reach me—you were not strong enough. You would then threaten to report me to your *Appah*. "Go ahead." How I liked being at the top! And sing there as I looked at you who were below. You were so helpless. In a spasm of anger, you would curse me, wishing my death. Well, let me die. I would climb the coconut trees in heaven. And my ghost would return to deliver . . . to deliver young celestial coconuts to you. Then you would run home, helpless. I would shout, "Dayang-Dayang, I am coming down!" Then you would come back. You see? A servant, an orphan, could also command the fair and proud Blue Blood to come or go.

Then we would pick up little shells, and search for sea-cucumbers; or dive for sea-urchins. Or run along the long stretch of white, glaring sand, I behind you—admiring your soft, nimble feet and your flying hair. Then we would stop, panting, laughing.

After resting for a while, we would run again to the sea and wage war against the crashing waves. I would rub your silky back after we had finished bathing in the sea. I would get fresh water in a clean coconut shell, and rinse your soft, ebon hair. Your hair flowed down smoothly, gleaming in the afternoon sun. Oh, it was beautiful. Then I would trim your fingernails carefully. Sometimes you would jerk with pain. Whereupon I would beg you to whip me. Just so you could differentiate between my crying and my laughing. And even the pain you gave me partook of sweetness.

That was my way. My only way to show how grateful I was for the things I had not tasted before: your companionship; shelter and food in your big *astana*. So your parents said I would make a good servant, indeed. And you, too, thought I would.

Your parents sent you to a Mohammedan school when you were seven. I was not sent to study with you, but it made no difference to me. For after all, was not my work carrying your red Koran on top of my head four times a day? And you were happy, because I could entertain you. Because someone could be a water-carrier for you. One of the requirements then was to carry water every time you showed up in your Mohammedan class. "Oh, why? Excuse the stammering of my hare-lip, but I really wished to know." Your Goro, your Mohammedan teacher, looked deep into me as if to search my whole system. Stupid. Did I not know our hearts could easily grasp the subject matter, like the soft, incessant flow of water? Hearts, hearts. Not brains. But I just kept silent. After all, I was not there to ask impertinent questions. Shame, shame on my hare-lip asking such a question, I chided myself silently.

That was how I played the part of an *Epang-Epang*, of a servant-escort, to you. And I became more spirited every day, trudging behind you. I was like a faithful, loving dog following its mistress with light steps and a singing heart. Because you, ahead of me, were something of an inspiration I could trail indefatigably, even to the ends of the world....

The dreary monotone of your Koran-chanting lasted three years. You were so slow, your Goro said. At times, she wanted to whip you. But did she not know you were the Datu's daughter? Why, she would be flogged herself. But whipping an orphaned servant and clipping his split lips with two pieces of wood were evidently permissible. So, your Goro found me a convenient substitute for you. How I groaned with pain under her lashings! But how your Goro laughed; the wooden clips failed to keep my hare-lip closed. They always slipped. And the class, too, roared with laughter—you leading.

But back there in your spacious *astana*, you were already being tutored for maidenhood. I was older than you by one Ramadan. I often wondered why you grew so fast, while I remained a lunatic dwarf. Maybe the poor care I received in early boyhood had much to do with my hampered growth. However, I was happy, in a way, that I did not catch up with you. For I had a hunch you would not continue to avail yourself of my help in certain intimate tasks—such as scrubbing your back when you took your bath—had I grown as fast as you.

There I was in my bed at night, alone, intoxicated with passion and emotions closely resembling those of a full-grown man's. I thought of you secretly, unashamedly, lustfully: a full-grown Dayang-Dayang reclining in her bed at the farthest end of her inner apartment; breasts heaving softly like breeze-kissed waters; cheeks of the faintest red brushing against a soft pillow; eyes gazing dreamily into immensity—warm, searching, expressive; supple buttocks and pliant arms; soft, ebon hair that rippled....

Dayang-Dayang, could you have forgiven a deformed orphan-servant had he gone mad, and lost respect and dread towards your *Appah?* Could you have pardoned his rabid temerity had he leaped out of his bed, rushed into your room, seized you in his arms, and tickled your face with his hare-lip? I should like to confess that for at least a moment, yearning, starved, athirst... no, no, I cannot say it. We were of such contrasting patterns. Even the lovely way you looked—the big *astana* you lived in—the blood you had.... Not even the fingers of Allah perhaps could weave our fabrics into equality. I had to content myself with the privilege of gazing frequently at your peerless loveliness. An ugly servant must not go beyond his little border.

But things did not remain as they were. A young Datu from Bonbon came back to ask for your hand. Your *Appah* was only too glad to welcome him. There was nothing better, he said, than marriage between two people of the same blue blood. Besides, he was growing old. He had no son to take his place some day. Well, the young Datu was certainly fit to take in due time the royal torch your *Appah* had been carrying for years. But I—I felt differently, of course. I wanted.... No, I could not have a hand in your marital arrangements. What was I, after all?

Certainly your *Appah* was right. The young Datu was handsome. And rich, too. He had a large tract of land planted with fruit trees, coconut trees, and abaca plants. And you were glad, too. Not because he was rich—for you were rich yourself. I thought I knew why: the young Datu could rub your soft back better than I whenever you took your bath. His hands were not as callous as mine. . . . However, I did not talk to you about it. Of course.

Your *Appah* ordered his subjects to build two additional wings to your *astana.* Your *astana* was already big, but it had to be enlarged as hundreds of people would be coming to witness your royal wedding.

The people sweated profusely. There was a great deal of hammering, cutting, and lifting as they set up posts. Plenty of eating and jabbering. And chewing of betel nuts and native seasoned tobacco. And emitting of red saliva afterwards. In just one day, the additional wings were finished.

Then came your big wedding. People had crowded your *astana* early in the day to help in the religious slaughtering of cows and goats. To aid, too, in the voracious consumption of your wedding feast. Some more people came as evening drew near. Those who could not be accommodated upstairs had to stay below.

Torches fashioned out of dried coconut leaves blazed in the night. Half-clad natives kindled them over the cooking fire. Some pounded rice for cakes. And their brown glossy bodies sweated profusely.

Out in the *astana* yard, the young Datu's subjects danced in great circles. Village swains danced with grace, now swaying sensuously their shapely hips, now twisting their pliant arms. Their feet moved deftly and almost imperceptibly.

Male dancers would crouch low, with a wooden spear, a *kris,* or a *barong* in one hand, and a wooden shield in the other. They simulated bloody warfare by dashing through the circle of other dancers and clashing against each other. Native flutes, drums, *gabangs, agongs,* and *kulintangs* contributed much to the musical gayety of the night. Dance. Sing in delight. Music. Noise. Laughter. Music swelled out into the world like a heart full of blood, vibrant, palpitating. But it was

my heart that swelled with pain. The people would cheer: "Long live the Dayang-Dayang and the Datu, MURAMURAAN!" at every intermission. And I would cheer, too—mechanically before I knew. I would be missing you so. . . .

People rushed and elbowed their way up into your *astana* as the young Datu was led to you. Being small, I succeeded in squeezing in near enough to catch a full view of you. You, Dayang-Dayang. Your moon-shaped face was meticulously powdered with pulverized rice. Your hair was skewered up toweringly at the center of your head, and studded with glittering gold hair-pins. Your tight, gleamingly black dress was covered with a flimsy mantle of the faintest conceivable pink. Gold buttons embellished your wedding garments. You sat rigidly on a mattress, with native embroidered pillows piled carefully at the back. Candle-light mellowed your face so beautifully you were like a goddess perceived in dreams. You looked steadily down.

The moment arrived. The turbaned *pandita,* talking in a voice of silk, led the young Datu to you, while maidens kept chanting songs from behind. The *pandita* grasped the Datu's forefinger, and made it touch thrice the space between your eyebrows. And every time that was done, my breast heaved and my lips worked.

Remember? You were about to cry, Dayang-Dayang. For, as the people said, you would soon be separated from your parents. Your husband would soon take you to Bonbon, and you would live there like a countrywoman. But as you unexpectedly caught a glimpse of me, you smiled at once, a little. And I knew why: my hare-lip amused you again. I smiled back at you, and withdrew at once. I withdrew at once because I could not bear further seeing you sitting beside the young Datu, and knowing fully well that I who had sweated, labored, and served you like a dog. . . . No, no, shame on me to think of all that at all. For was it not but a servant's duty?

But I escaped that night, pretty Blue Blood. Where to? Anywhere. That was exactly seven years ago. And those years did wonderful things for me. I am no longer a lunatic dwarf, although my hare-lip remains as it has always been.

Too, I had amassed a little fortune after years of sweating. I could have taken two or three wives, but I had not yet found anyone resembling you lovely Blue Blood. So single I remained.

And Allah's Wheel of Time kept on turning, kept on turning. And lo, one day your husband was transported to San Ramon Penal Farm, Zamboanga. He had raised his hand against the Christian government. He had wished to establish his own government. He wanted to show his petty power by refusing to pay land taxes, on the ground that the lands he had were by legitimate inheritance his own absolutely. He did not understand that the little amount he should give in the form of taxes would be utilized to protect him and his people from swindlers. He did not discern that he was in fact a part of the Christian government himself. Consequently his subjects lost their lives fighting for a wrong cause. Your *Appah,* too, was drawn into the mess, and perished with the others. His possessions were confiscated. And your *Amboh* died of a broken heart. Your husband, to save his life, had to surrender. His lands, too, were confiscated. Only a little portion was left for you to cultivate and live on.

And remember? I went one day to Bonbon on business. And I saw you on your bit of land with your children. At first, I could not believe it was you. Then you looked long deep into me. Soon the familiar eyes of Blue Blood of years ago arrested the faculties of the erstwhile servant. And you could not believe your eyes either. You could not recognize me at once. But when you saw my hare-lip smiling at you, rather hesitantly, you knew me at last. And I was so glad you did.

"Oh, Jaafar," you gasped, dropping your *janap,* your primitive trowel, instinctively. And you thought I was no longer living, you said. Curse, curse. It was still your frank, outspoken way. It was like you to be able to jest even when sorrow was on the verge of

removing the last vestiges of your loveliness. You could somehow conceal your pain and grief beneath banter and laughter. And I was glad of that, too.

Well, I was about to tell you that the Jaafar you saw now was a very different—a much improved—Jaafar. Indeed. But instead: "Oh, Dayang-Dayang," I mumbled, distressed to have seen you working. You who had been reared in ease and luxury. However, I tried very much not to show traces of understanding your deplorable situation.

One of your sons came running and asked who I was. Well, I was, I was. . . .

"Your old servant," I said promptly. Your son said oh, and kept quiet, returning at last to resume his work. Work, work, Eting. Work, son. Bundle the firewood and take it to the kitchen. Don't mind your old servant. He won't turn young again. Poor little Datu, working so hard. Poor pretty Blue Blood, also working hard.

We kept strangely silent for a long time. And then: By the way, where was I living now? In Kanagi. My business here in Bonbon today? To see Panglima Hussin about the cows he intended to sell, Dayang-Dayang. Cows? Was I a landsman already? Well, if the pretty Blue Blood could live like a countrywoman, why not a man like your old servant? You see, luck was against me in sea-roving activities, so I had to turn to buying and selling cattle. Oh, you said. And then you laughed. And I laughed with you. My laughter was dry. Or was it yours? However, you asked what was the matter. Oh, nothing. Really nothing serious. But you see. . . . And you seemed to understand as I stood there in front of you, leaning against a mango tree, doing nothing but stare and stare at you.

I observed that your present self was only the ragged reminder, the mere ghost, of the Blue Blood of the big *astana.* Your resources of vitality and loveliness and strength seemed to have been drained out of your old arresting self, poured into the little farm you were working in. Of course I did not expect you to be as lovely as you had been. But you should have retained at least a fair portion of it—of the old days. Not blurred eyes encircled by dark rings; not dull, dry hair; not a sunburned complexion; not wrinkled, callous hand; not. . . .

You seemed to understand more and more. Why was I looking at you like that? Was it because I had not seen you for so long? Or was it something else? Oh, Dayang-Dayang, was not the terrible change in you the old servant's concern? You suddenly turned your eyes away from me. You picked up your *janap* and began troubling the soft earth. It seemed you could not utter another word without breaking into tears. You turned your back toward me because you hated having me see you in tears.

And I tried to make out why: seeing me now revived old memories. Seeing me, talking with me, poking fun at me, was seeing, talking, and joking as in the old days at the vivacious *astana*. And you sobbed as I was thinking thus. I knew you sobbed, because your shoulders shook. But I tried to appear as though I was not aware of your controlled weeping. I hated myself for coming to you and making you cry. So . . .

"May I go now, Dayang-Dayang" I said softly, trying hard to hold back my own tears. You did not say yes. And you did not say no, either. But the nodding of your head was enough to make me understand and go. Go where? Was there a place to go to? Of course. There were many places to go to. Only, there was seldom a place to which one would like to return.

But something transfixed me in my tracks after walking a mile or so. There was something of an impulse that strove to drive me back to you, making me forget Panglima Hussin's cattle. Every instinct told me it was right for me to go back to you and do something—perhaps beg you to remember your old Jaafar's hare-lip, just so you could smile and be happy again. I wanted to rush back and wipe away the tears from your eyes with my headdress. I wanted to get fresh water and rinse your dry, ruffled hair, that it might be restored to flowing smoothness and glorious luster. I wanted to trim your fingernails, stroke your callous hand. I yearned to tell you that the land and the cattle I owned were all yours. And above all, I burned to whirl back to you and beg you and your children to come home with me. Although the simple house I lived in was not as big as your *astana* at Patikul, it would at least be a happy, temporary haven while you waited for your husband's release.

That urge to go back to you, Dayang-Dayang, was strong. But I did not go back for a sudden qualm seized me: I had no blue blood. I had only a hare-lip. Not even the fingers of Allah perhaps could weave us, even now, into equality.

F. Sionil José

TONG

Conrado Lopez fell deeply in love for the first time when he was thirty. It was one of those beautiful things destined to bleakness and from the very beginning, he had an inkling that this was how it would be. And all because Alice Tan was Chinese.

When he first saw her, it seemed as if she had blossomed straight out of a Chinese art book; she had a complexion as clear as it was fair. When he got to know her better, he used to trace the blue veins in her arms, the blood vessels in her cheeks. Her nose was perfect, and her Chinese eyes had a brightness that could dispel the gloom which came over him. Long afterwards, when he remembered her eyes, how she looked, how she smiled, an intense feeling akin to physical pain would lance him.

Alice Tan's parents used to run a small grocery store in Ongpin; both came from Fookien and Alice could trace her family back to Amoy. Conrado Lopez did not know his lineage beyond his great grandfather and was not interested in the Chinese traditional kinship system. But he got so interested afterwards, he started to delve into his own background. He lived with his spinster sister, Remedios, in a small house in Makata, a sidestreet parallel to Rizal Avenue in Santa Cruz. He had inherited the house with its pocket-size yard from his parents. The lower floor which had its own entrance was rented out to a lawyer who was adept at fixing things at City Hall. He and his sister lived in the second floor which had two bedrooms, a living-dining room and a toilet and kitchen with antique fixtures. His sister looked after the house, his clothes and his general well being. Conrado had finished accounting at one of the Azcarraga universities and would have amounted to something more than just being an accountant in Makati but he had let opportunities pass—opportunities which would have taken him away from Manila and his older sister whom he supported. It was because of such a responsibility that he had never really been serious with any girl.

He was unprepared for Alice Tan; in fact, in the beginning, he was not sure at all about his feelings for her. It started in March when brownouts were frequent so that when the lights went out that early evening, he thought it was another brownout. But he noticed that the lights in the other houses were on so he immediately concluded there must be something wrong with the fuse. He always kept an extra fuse so he threw the main switch off and changed it. But he had hardly thrown the switch on when the line in the ceiling started sputtering. Then a loud report and darkness.

By now, Meding was alarmed but Conrado assured her the house would not burn down as long as the switches were off. He dashed off to Bambang two blocks away to one of the electrical shops there.

He had passed the New Life Electrical Supply a few times but had rarely looked in; for one, he never bought electrical supplies in the neighborhood as he always bought them in the supermarket in Makati. It was then that he saw Alice Tan; she was in jeans and a *katsa* blouse with a high, lace collar and long sleeves that imparted to her an appearance at once regal and demure.

It was not a big shop. It carried hardware, nails, ropes, flashlights, but mostly electrical goods. She sat behind the glass counter and when he came in, she put down the weekly women's magazine she was reading.

"I don't think I will need an electrician," he said. "It is just a burned line, I think. I put the switch off."

"That is the first thing one should do," she said with a professional tone. "I think you will need rubberized tape, and a pair of new fuses."

"I am sure of that," he said. "But how do I go about fixing it?" He was not too sure now, having forgotten most of his physics classes in high school, the positive, the negative . . .

"Simple," she said, bringing out a roll of blue tape from the counter. "The lines should never get mixed up. When the covering is worn out and they cross each other, that's when the trouble starts."

"It is like a boy and a girl then," he said with a laugh. "If they really get mixed up, there's bound to be some result . . ."

She smiled at his little joke. "I hope you are not fooling me," she said.

"You can come to my house—it's close by, in Makata," he said. "It is dark."

"I believe you," she said. "Well then, first see to it that the main switch is off. Then look for the line that was burned. Sometimes rats gnaw the line. If you touch it and it is live . . ."

"I will not forget that," he said.

"Clean the wires, then tape them individually. See to it that they do not meet. That they do not touch."

"No touch, no fireworks," he said. "Thanks for the lesson."

In three months, Conrado Lopez learned a bit more about electricity and a lot about Alice Tan. She was studying in one of the Recto universities in the mornings and in the afternoons, immediately after school, she came to the shop where she had lunch, usually cooked by her aunt. At eight in the evening, she walked to Avenida for her ride to Ongpin and the apartment she shared with her brothers. She seldom went out even on the Sundays when the shop was closed. She looked at television or played Ping-Pong in one of the Chinese clubs in Binondo.

Conrado Lopez took to having a late *merienda* at the shabby Chinese restaurant across the street. The restaurant was never full— there was always an empty table dirty with noodle drippings and dried blobs of beer, the loud talk of jeepney drivers who frequented the place, and the juke box oozing Rico Puno and Nora Aunor songs. It was a good place to watch Alice Tan as she went about her chores.

Many a night, too, he would return to the restaurant for a cup of bad coffee and wait for her to leave and walk the short stretch to her jeepney stop, sometimes with him just a few steps behind.

In three months, too, Conrado could have opened a small shop for electrical supplies. He was buying yet another light bulb when Alice finally accosted him.

"I will not sell it to you," she said simply.

He was taken aback.

"I don't know what you are trying to do but I know you are not buying the goods to use. You don't need all those bulbs. I have been counting them. A light bulb lasts more than six months. You have bought more than a dozen in a month."

"I like changing them, you know, different watts."

"Mr. Lopez, tell me the truth."

"I also like collecting lengths of electric wire, sockets, rubber tapes. Have you heard of Thomas Alva Edison? Maybe, I am an inventor . . ."

"You are a liar," Alice Tan said, her eyes crinkling in a smile.

Conrado Lopez melted. "Yes, a terrible liar, am I not?"

"What really are you trying to do?"

Conrado Lopez stammered. "I . . . I wanted to talk with you. I want to see you. I enjoy talking with you. That's the simple truth. Believe me. And I don't mind buying all this useless stuff as long as I can see you . . ."

"But you can talk with me anytime as long as there are no customers. My uncle does not mind . . ."

He sighed. "That is good to know. But I was not sure. You are Chinese . . ."

"I am a human being," she said. "Will you stop buying things then?"

"No, I cannot come here without a reason. I must talk with you again even if I have to spend doing it . . ."

She appeared thoughtful. "All right, as long as it is not too often. And there are not customers . . ."

The door at the rear opened and Mary's uncle came in with a cup of coffee. He looked at Conrado without a flicker of recognition then sat before his table, impassive and still.

"Thank you, Miss Tan," Conrado said gratefully.

The following night, he finally found the courage to walk up to her. She thought, perhaps, he was one of those bag snatchers who had become so blantantly open, her first impulse was to hold her bag tightly and draw away when he moved closer to greet her.

"You frightened me, Mr. Lopez," she said.

Bambang was never brightly lit. They walked slowly. "I would like to take you home," he said. "But I don't have a car. We can take a taxi if you like."

"I prefer *calesas,*" she said, "but it is such a fine evening, can we walk?"

Indeed, an evening washed with rain, the street glistening. Home was quite a distance but it pleased him nonetheless for they would have a lot of time to talk.

He asked how long she had lived in Ongpin and she said, all her life, that she was familiar with its alleys, its shops, just as he knew Makata and Bambang and Misericordia— these were the names of the streets of his boyhood as he remembered them.

"We are Ongpin Chinese," she said. "Do you know what that means?"

He shook his head.

"That means we are not rich," she said. "The rich Chinese are in Greenhills. That's where they live anyway. Before the war, they said it was in Santa Mesa."

He did not realize there were social distinctions among the Chinese, too; he had always thought they were all of the same class, that they were all Fookienese, and that to a man, they looked down on the Filipinos, what with their Chinese *tong* associations, their schools.

He wondered if this was the time to bring out his cliché sentiments and he worried that if he did, he would be creating a barrier between them. He decided it was better to be frank, to be honest.

His difficulty was that he could not quite trust his feelings no matter how strong they were; he did not know enough about the Chinese really. "I must just as well admit, Alice," he said, "that I have some views on our Chinese problem. I am really glad that the Chinese schools have been taken over by the Department of Education, that we have relations with Peking now. But if I had my way, all those Chinese schools should have been closed a long time ago . . ."

"What don't you like in us?" she asked, looking at him briefly, a smile darting across her face, a smile so pretty that it disarmed him completely.

"Your clannishness, for one," he said.

"But you are clannish, too," she said. "Look at all the people in power, they are either Ilokanos or from Leyte."

"Chinese girls never marry Filipino boys. It is always the other way around."

"You call us *Intsik Baboy.*"

"Because it is true—you are filthy. No, not you personally."

"And the Filipinos are stupid. Not you personally," she mimicked him.

He checked himself. "Hey," he said, "on our first time together—and look, we are quarrelling."

"You started it," she said petulantly.

"I don't like quarrels. Can you imagine how it would be if we were married?"

"You are going too fast," she said. "Now, you are talking about us being married. We barely know each other."

"After all those things I bought from you? I could start another store..."

"I don't want your money wasted," she said. "Give them back to me and I will sell them for you."

They had reached Recto and had crossed over, the air around them now thick with the scent of rotting vegetables and chicken droppings as they passed the public market. They walked on through a dimly lit neighborhood, the street pocked with craters, the gutter slimy with refuse and mud. Beyond, the lights of Ongpin shone, Chinese characters in red and blue. Now, the sidewalk was red brick, the shops bright with red candles, gold leaf pictures. *Calesas* jostled each other on the street and the uneven sidewalk was crammed with fruit stalls. Around them, the smell of Chinese cooking, of incense and acrid oils, the wail of Chinese flutes. They went beyond a stone arch, bright green and red, and a creek which befouled the air, then turned right and after a few steps, she stopped. "This is as far as you go. I live over there," she said, pointing to an alley.

"But I want to see you to your door. I am not hiding. I am a bachelor. My intentions are honorable. I would like to visit your house, maybe not tonight, but someday, meet your parents..."

"I have no parents," she said. "I have three brothers and I am the youngest. My uncle— Mr. Tan, you have seen him in the store, he is our guardian; he took care of us when we were young..."

"I still would like to see where you live," he said.

"No," she was firm and there was an edge to her voice. "This is as far as you go, or you will not walk me home again."

He did not argue. "Is it because I am Filipino?" he asked dully, as she turned to go. She took three, four steps, then she turned, and shook her head.

He watched till she entered the alley and disappeared in its black maw. He stood there for a while, taking in the huddle of houses, the people talking in a language he could not understand, absorbing the feel of exotic distances. Then it started to drizzle.

———

The following evening, Conrado Lopez passed by the shop before proceeding to the Chinese restaurant across the street. Her uncle was not there but Alice was and as he passed, their eyes locked. He positioned himself in the restaurant, toying with his cup of coffee, and watched her reading a magazine. Soon it was time to close. Mr. Tan went out to pull the steel accordion door shut, and it was then that Conrado noticed the black Mercedes in front of the shop to which, as if she was in a hurry, Alice went. She sat in front with the driver and as they drove off, in the soft dark, he could see her turn and take a last look at him.

He now realized with some apprehension, of panic even, that she was being cordoned off, and he wondered if this was her doing, if she did not really want to talk with him again. He reproached himself for having talked so openly when what he should have done was to say the usual niceties. In his office that Saturday, he asked to be excused in the afternoon. He proceeded to Bambang at once; he must see her, apologize to her, anything to have her talk with him again, walk with him again.

She was at the store and he was vastly relieved when he saw that her uncle was not at his table. The moment Conrado went in, however, her eyes told him that this was not the time to talk. "I am sorry," he said, barely raising his voice above a whisper, "but I would like to see you again."

He could not continue for the door at the rear opened and Mr. Tan came in, a coil of electric wiring in his arms.

Without his telling her, Alice stood up, got a bulb from the shelf and tested it. "It is three pesos and eighty centavos," she said, wrapping it in a sheet of old newspaper. She took some time writing the receipt while Mr. Tan brought down another roll of wiring from the rack and started measuring a length.

"It is in the receipt," she told Conrado, handing him the receipt. "The receipt," she repeated with a smile.

That evening, as he and his sister sat down to dinner, he told her about Alice Tan. "I have been thinking about our life," he said. "I don't think we would need to spend much more if I got married . . ."

Meding looked at him; she was fifteen years older but she had taken good care of herself and really looked no older than forty or so. She could have easily got married—there was still that chance if she had a mind to—but she had been reclusive. It had often bothered Conrado to think that she had not got married so that she "could take care of him."

"And if I do get married, you will continue to live with us, of course, like it always has been. How does the idea look to you, *Ate?*"

He had expected her to sulk and was pleasantly surprised when she beamed. "I have often wondered when it would be," she said. "I am sure by now you know the right kind of girl . . ."

It was then that he told her she was Chinese, that he was interested in having them meet . . . He did not realize till then the depths of his ignorance about his sister's feelings, but from the expression on her face, he knew at once that Alice Tan—if and when the moment came—would have difficulty living in the same house with her.

Through the night, he could not sleep, wondering how he would be able to talk with her, to see her without that black Mercedes tailing them, without Mr. Tan eavesdropping on them. Sunday morning, he decided to go to Ongpin, to the maze of wooden houses and shops that made up Chinatown. He went up the alley where she had disappeared in the night; it was a dead-end, a dark and dispirited

place, flanked by decrepit apartment houses, with laundry in the windows and a pile of garbage at the end. Children were playing in the alley, and the houses were filled with people who did not once look at him as he passed. He peered briefly into open doorways, and soon reached the dead-end without seeing her. He walked back to the main street clogged with *calesas* and vehicles and entered the first movie house he passed. It was a Kung Fu movie in Chinese, without subtitles and he could not understand a word but with all that action, dialogue was hardly necessary. It was when he finally came out, long past noon, that he remembered how Alice gave him his receipt. She had repeated, "the receipt." Then, it struck him, what she was trying to say. He grabbed a taxi and hoped to God that his sister had not emptied the wastebasket where he had thrown the piece of paper. Breathless, he dashed to his room and was greatly relieved to find the receipt still there. Sure enough, in her legible penmanship: "Rizal Park Post Office, Sunday four p.m."

He looked at his watch; it was three fifty. By no miracle could he get there in ten minutes but just the same, he raced down to Avenida and told the taxi driver to hurry, in heaven's name. It had started to rain when they crossed the Pasig and it was really pouring when he reached the Park Post Office in front of the Manila Hotel. He was also fifteen minutes late. He dashed from the cab to the shade of the Post Office marquee. He cursed himself not so much for not bringing an umbrella but for being so stupid as not to have understood what Alice wanted him to know. She must have got tired waiting and had left. He sat, wet and forlorn, on the stone ledge. Maybe, if he went to her apartment—that was what his sister always said, that a man whose intentions are honorable should always visit the girl in her house.

The rain whipped the Park in gusty sheets. It was stormy weather and beyond the Park, the Walled City and all of Manila seemed enveloped with mist. But in half an hour, the rain diminished, then stopped altogether and in the direction of the Bay, the dark clouds were rimmed with silver.

It was Alice Tan who was late and it was good that he did not leave; he saw her get out of her taxi and his heart leaped and pounded so hard he could hear it. He ran to her and hardly heard her apologies, how she had difficulty leaving; he was aware of nothing else but this creature who had come bringing light to this dismal afternoon.

They walked to the sea and now, with the rain that still threatened the city, they had the whole sea-wall to themselves.

"I am stupid," he said, "for not having understood when you said, it is in the receipt."

"I was worried about that," she said, sitting close to him so that their arms touched. "Filipinos are like that, anyway. *Gong.*"

"What's that?"

"Stupid, like you said."

"Now," he said. "I hope we will not start an argument again. What don't you like in us, anyway?"

"First," she said, "you are lazy. You don't know what industry is—and this is why, no matter what your leaders say, you will never amount to anything."

"You don't know what you are saying. We work very hard." he said. "Our farmers work very hard."

"My father used to wake up at four in the morning," Alice Tan said with pride. "And we never went to sleep earlier than eleven o'clock at night."

"Many Filipinos are like that."

"Show me," she said. "And then, you are so corrupt. Why, almost every week, someone goes to the shop—policemen, revenue agents, all of them. All they want is money. My uncle always gives of course. And everytime, he increases the price of what we sell. In the end, it is the customer who suffers."

"He is just as guilty then," Conrado told her.

"My father had to pay a bribe of ten thousand pesos—way back in 1950—for his citizenship. It almost broke him."

"So you are a Filipino citizen then," he said.

"This is where you make your living, where the rich Chinese and your uncle make their money, exploiting the country, its resources, its people. If you don't like it here—why don't you go back to Peking or Taipei, whichever you choose?"

"Be careful now," she told him. "You misunderstand me completely. My oldest brother—he was very impressed with what the communists were doing in Peking. He went there and returned, disillusioned. It was not so much that the life there is harsh . . . it was that he did not feel at home. Can you not see, Conrado? Our home is here. China—it would be foreign to me, although I could get sentimental about it. I just want this country to have better things—less corruption, less enmity, less poverty . . ."

He realized then that he had spoken again in a way that wouldn't endear him to her. He was determined to salvage the afternoon. "It is just as well that we have our arguments now. For when we get married . . ."

The waves lapped on the rocks below them. She turned to him, wonder in her eyes. "Please don't talk about something impossible," she said. "Let us just be friends . . ."

"But I am serious," he said. "I am not making a lot. Just a thousand and a half a month. Plus that four hundred pesos rent from the house. I can support you, not in style. But I have a career still ahead of me. You can go on with your schooling if you want to. We may have some problems with my sister but she will adjust. Why don't we go and meet her? There's just the two of us . . ."

It was then that she told him. "It cannot be, Conrado. I have been promised in marriage to someone already. There is just a little time for us . . ."

———

For the rest of his life, Conrado Lopez would never really know why Alice Tan saw him again, and still again, every Sunday at four p.m. in the park. When he took her back to Ongpin that evening, she had extracted from him a promise that he should never go to the shop again, or sit like some corner thug in that restaurant across the street where it was obvious to her uncle even that he was watching her. He got her address in Ongpin and he promised too that he would never go there unless it was for some very, very serious reason. She would see him again that Sunday and the Sundays thereafter. Now, at least, Conrado Lopez had something to look forward to. He went eagerly back to his history books, to the references on the Chinese, Limahong, the Parian, the galleon trade which carried Chinese silks and other luxury goods to Mexico thence to Europe. He asked the Chinese embassy in Roxas for handouts and in the bookshops in Avenida, he searched for pocketbooks and other bargains that described China. He even fancied himself learning Mandarin and going to a Buddhist temple although Alice Tan had told him that she was Protestant.

On the next Sunday, the sun was out; a storm had just blown over and the grass was soggy. Alice Tan arrived in a blue print dress; it was the first time he saw her in a dress and her legs, as he had always suspected, were shapely. They went to the Manile Hotel for a cup of coffee—that was all that he could afford when he studied the menu and he warned her about it. This time, they did not argue. Instead, she told him about herself, that it was her dream—as it was the dream of most Chinese girls—to get married and raise a family. She had gone out with Chinese boys to discos in Makati and had exchanged confidences with her Chinese girlfriends who had dated Filipino boys and they were all agreed that their Filipino dates were more interesting, for their Chinese dates talked of nothing but business. And yes, she said with a slight laugh, they told her, too, that Filipino boys were quicker and that they made better lovers.

"And now," he said, "you would like to find out for yourself."

She unwrapped the special *hopia* that she had brought while an amused waitress looked on. A couple of Chinese boys passed; they stared at her so she whispered to him: "See?" They never like Chinese girls to date Filipino boys. They think Filipino boys are just making fools of us..."

"Am I?" he asked.

She reached across the table and almost spilled the goblet, held his hand and pressed it.

On the fifth Sunday, Conrado Lopez took Alice Tan to one of the motels on M. H. del Pilar. The August sky was threatened with rain clouds, it had become dark and they had embraced behind the palms near the sea-wall. He had told her simply that he wanted to hold her, make love to her and she had not replied but had, instead, kissed him with passion. They walked to the boulevard and hailed a taxi. She sat wordless beside him, and even when they had finally entered the motel garage, and the door had shut behind them, still, she did not speak.

Only when they were finally in the room, her face flushed, his hands eager and his whole being aflame, did she tell him that she had expected this to happen, but not too soon.

She was a virgin and the sheet was soiled. They lay together for a long time and he told her what he knew of the old days, how the Filipino groom would hang the blood-stained blanket by the window the following morning for all his relatives to see. And she said it was the same in Old China.

It was when they made ready to leave that she started to cry, the sobs torn out of her in pain and trembling. He embraced her, kissed her cheeks wet with tears, her hair.

"We will get married in the morning—if this is what worries you," he said. "Now—if you wish, we can walk to the Malate Church and ask. I did not do this to take advantage of you, to fool you..."

"I know," she said, pressing closer still to him.

"Then what are you crying about?"

"I cannot marry you," she said.

He drew away and looked at her tear-stained face.

"Is it because you are Chinese?"

She nooded.

"But you love me, you said so. I am not rich but you will not starve..."

"It is not the money."

"If it is not the money...?"

"Tradition, custom. Whatever you call it."

"Hell with it!" Conrado cursed in his breath.

Then it came out. "My uncle, Conrado. He took care of us when we were orphaned. I told you. And there is this rich Chinese who lives in Greenhills. He is a widower. He has helped my uncle. Given my brothers very good jobs..."

He drew farther from her, looked at her, beautiful and true and then he went to her, hugged her. "Don't, Alice," he said in a voice hoarse with entreaty. "Let us elope. Let us go to my house now. They cannot find you there..."

She looked at him and shook her head. "I am Chinese," she said simply.

═══

When he passed the shop that Monday, he was surprised to see she was not at the counter; he hurried around the block, and when he got to the shop again, she was still not there. He returned shortly before eight when Mr. Tan would bring the accordion iron shutter down but neither the black Mercedes nor Alice were there. Every day that week, he passed by the shop. Sunday, he went to the Park and stayed there till dark.

That Monday afternoon, straight from his office, he went to see Mr. Tan. There was no hint of recognition in the face of Alice's uncle—just this bland, expressionless mien, as Conrado introduced himself.

"Where is Alice, Mr. Tan?" he finally asked.

He replied in excellent Tagalog; Alice was no longer working in the shop.

"Where can I find her then?"

The Chinese shook his head and did not reply.

"Mr. Tan," he said in a voice which quavered. "I know you don't like a Filipino husband for your niece. But I love her and I want to marry her. You think I am interested

in her money—then don't give her any dowry. No dowry, is that clear?" He took his wallet out and drew a calling card, laid it on the counter, "I have a good job with a big firm. I am young and industrious. I can support her and I can even continue sending her to school. I know you took care of her and I am grateful."

The Chinese shook his head again and this time, he smiled, gold teeth flashing, and held Conrado Lopez' arm across the counter. "Don't misunderstand," he said. "But you are very, very late. You must leave and don't bother us anymore. There is nothing I can do for you..."

"What don't you like in me?" he asked tersely as he backed away into the noisy sidewalk.

He had memorized the address which she had given him. He took a taxi to Ongpin. It was very dark, the neon lights were on. He walked up the alley, and when he got to the door, 14-D, on it was posted a sign in Chinese. A young man was at the next door playing a guitar and he asked where the people next door were. "They have moved," he said, "to Greenhills." Did he know the street? The number? No. And what is this sign? "For rent," the young man said.

For many days, it was as if Conrado Lopez was in a daze, in a limbo without rim. After office hours, he would wander around the shops in Binondo in the hope that he would see her visiting the old neighborhood. He made a list of the best Chinese restaurants in the city and on occasion, visited them specially at night when there were parties attended by the wealthy Chinese. He would wait in their lobbies, watching, searching.

On Sundays and holidays, he frequented the supermarket in Greenhills knowing this was where the wealthy Chinese shopped and many a time, he would hurry after what seemed a familiar back, a turn of the head, only to find it was not her.

He took to compulsively reading on China until he was quite familiar with contemporary happenings there. On Sundays, he made a round of Ongpin and even got to visiting funeral parlors—"La Paz" particularly, where the Chinese held the wake for their dead. And twice, he went to Benavides, to the air-conditioned Protestant chapel there, hoping that Alice would attend a service.

He no longer went to the Park except one Sunday in mid-February; it was a cool, pleasant afternoon with a pure blue sky. He sat on the stone ledge as he had done in the past. It was four and for a time, he was lost in reverie, remembering how it was the first time, the splashing rain, the anxiety that he would miss her.

It was then that he noticed the black Mercedes parked at the edge of the green and beyond it, Alice walking to the car, her arm held by a fat, bald Chinese, old enough to be her father. She was big with child and as she looked at Conrado, there was this brief, anguished look on her face which told him not to move, not to speak. She got into the car, her husband after her, and as they drove away, he still stood there reeling with emotion, knowing clearly now what it was all about, the *tong* that must be paid, the life that must be warped because it had to be lived.

Aida L. Rivera

LOVE IN THE CORNHUSKS

Tinang stopped before the Señora's gate and adjusted the baby's cap. The dogs that came to bark at the gate were strange dogs, big-mouthed animals with a sense of superiority. They stuck their heads through the hogfence, lolling their tongues and straining. Suddenly, from the gumamela row, a little black mongrel emerged and slithered through the fence with ease. It came to her, head down and body quivering.

"Bantay. *Ay,* Bantay!" she exclaimed as the little dog laid its paws upon her shirt to sniff the baby on her arm. The baby was afraid and cried. The big animals barked with displeasure.

Tito, the young master, had seen her and was calling to his mother. "Ma, it's Tinang. Ma, Ma, it's Tinang." He came running down to open the gate.

"*Aba,* you are so tall now, Tito."

He smiled his girl's smile as he stood by, warding the dogs off. Tinang passed quickly up the veranda stairs lined with ferns and many-colored bougainville. On the landing, she paused to wipe her shoes carefully. About her, the Señora's white and lavender butterfly orchids fluttered delicately in the sunshine. She noticed though that the purple *waling-waling* that had once been her task to shade from the hot sun with banana leaves and to

water with a mixture of charcoal and eggs and water was not in bloom.

"Is no one covering the *waling-waling* now?" Tinang asked. "It will die."

"Oh, the maid will come to cover the orchids later."

The Señora called from inside. "*Ano,* Tinang, let me see your baby. Is it a boy?"

"Yes, Ma," Tito shouted from downstairs. "And the ears are huge!"

"What do you expect," replied his mother; "the father is a Bagobo. Even Tinang looks like a Bagobo now."

Tinang laughed and felt a warmness for her former mistress and the boy Tito. She sat self-consciously on the black narra sofa, for the first time a visitor. Her eyes clouded. The sight of the Señora's flaccidly plump figure, swathed in a loose waistless housedress that came down to her ankles, and the faint scent of *agua de colonia* blended with kitchen spice, seemed to her the essence of the comfortable world, and she sighed thinking of the long walk home through the mud, the baby's legs straddled to her waist, and Inggo, her husband, waiting for her, his body stinking of *tuba* and sweat, squatting on the floor, clad only in his foul undergarments.

"*Ano,* Tinang, is it not a good thing to be married?" the Señora asked, pitying Tinang because her dress gave way at the placket and pressed at her swollen breasts. It was, as a matter of fact, a dress she had given Tinang a long time ago.

"It is hard, Señora, very hard. Better that I were working here again."

"There!" the Señora said. "Didn't I tell you what it would be like, huh? . . . that you would be a slave to your husband and that you would work with a baby eternally strapped to you. Are you not pregnant again?"

Tinang squirmed at the Señora's directness but admitted she was.

"*Hala!* You will have a dozen before long." The Señora got up. "Come, I will give you some dresses and an old blanket that you can cut into things for the baby."

They went into a cluttered room which looked like a huge closet and as the Señora sorted out some clothes, Tinang asked, "How is Señor?"

"*Ay,* he is always losing his temper over the tractor drivers. It is not the way it was when Amado was here. You remember what a good driver he was. The tractors were always kept in working condition. But now . . . I wonder why he left all of a sudden. He said he would be gone for only two days . . . ."

"I don't know," Tinang said. The baby began to cry. Tinang shushed him with irritation.

"*Oy,* Tinang, come to the kitchen; your Bagobito is hungry."

For the next hour, Tinang sat in the kitchen with an odd feeling; she watched the girl who was now in possession of the kitchen work around with a handkerchief clutched in one hand. She had lipstick on too, Tinang noted. The girl looked at her briefly but did not smile. She set down a can of evaporated milk for the baby and served her coffee and cake. The Señora drank coffee with her and lectured about keeping the baby's stomach bound and training it to stay by itself so she could work. Finally, Tinang brought up, haltingly, with phrases like "if it will not offend you" and "if you are not too busy" the purpose of her visit—which was to ask the Señora to be a *madrina* in baptism. The Señora readily

assented and said she would provide the baptismal clothes and the fee for the priest. It was time to go.

"When are you coming again, Tinang?" the Señore asked as Tinang got the baby ready. "Don't forget the bundle of clothes and . . . oh, Tinang, you better stop by the drugstore. They asked me once whether you were still with us. You have a letter there and I was going to open it to see if there was bad news but I thought you would be coming."

A letter! Tinang's heart beat violently. Somebody is dead; I know somebody is dead, she thought. She crossed herself and after thanking the Señora profusely, she hurried down. The dogs came forward and Tito had to restrain them. "Bring me some young corn next time, Tinang," he called after her.

Tinang waited a while at the drugstore which was also the post office of the barrio. Finally, the man turned to her: "Mrs., do you want medicine for your baby or for yourself?"

"No, I came for my letter. I was told I have a letter."

"And what is your name, Mrs.?" he drawled.

"Constantina Tirol."

The man pulled a box and slowly went through the pile of envelopes most of which were scribbled in pencil, "Tirol, Tirol, Tirol. . . ." He finally pulled out a letter and handed it to her. She stared at the unfamiliar scrawl. It was not from her sister and she could think of no one else who would write to her.

Santa Maria, she thought; maybe something has happened to my sister.

"Do you want me to read it for you?"

"No, no." She hurried from the drugstore, crushed that he should think her illiterate. With the baby on one arm and the bundle of clothes on the other and the letter clutched in her hand she found herself walking toward home.

The rains had made a deep slough of the clay road and Tinang followed the prints left by the men and the carabaos that had gone before her to keep from sinking in mud up to her knees. She was deep in the road before she became conscious of her shoes. In horror, she saw that they were coated with thick, black clay. Gingerly, she pulled off one shoe after the other with the hand still clutching the letter. When she had tied the shoes together with the laces and had slung them on an arm, the baby, the bundle, and the letter were all smeared with mud.

There must be a place to put the baby down, she thought, desperate now about the letter. She walked on until she spotted a corner of a field where cornhusks were scattered under a *kamansi* tree. She shoved together a pile of husks with her foot and laid the baby down upon it. With a sigh, she drew the letter from the envelope. She stared at the letter which was written in English.

My dearest Tinay,

Hello, how is life getting along? Are you still in good condition? As for myself, the same as usual. But you're far from my side. It is not easy to be far from our lover.

Tinay, do you still love me? I hope your kind and generous heart will never fade. Someday or somehow I'll be there again to fulfill our promise.

Many weeks and months have elapsed. Still I remember our bygone days. Especially when I was suffering with the heat of the tractor under the heat of the sun. I was always in despair until I imagine your personal appearance coming forward bearing the sweetest smile that enabled me to view the distant horizon.

Tinay, I could not return because I found that my mother was very ill. That is why I was not able to take you as a partner of life. Please respond to my missive at once so that I know whether you still love me or not. I hope you did not love anybody except myself.

I think I am going beyond the limit of your leisure hour, so I close with best wishes to you, my friends Gonding, Serafin, Bondio, etc.

Yours forever,
Amado

P.S. My mother died last month.
Address your letter:
Mr. Amado Galauran
Binalunan, Cotabato

It was Tinang's first love letter. A flush spread over her face and crept into her body. She read the letter again. "It is not easy to be far from our lover. . . . I imagine your personal appearance coming forward. . . . Someday, somehow I'll be there to fulfill our promise. . . ." Tinang was intoxicated. She pressed herself against the *kamansi* tree.

My lover is true to me. He never meant to desert me. Amado, she thought. Amado.

And she cried, remembering the young girl she was less than two years ago when she would take food to the Señor in the field and the laborers would eye her furtively. She thought herself above them for she was always neat and clean and in her hometown, before she went away to work, she had gone to school and had reached the sixth grade. Her skin, too, was not as dark as those of the girls who worked in the fields weeding around the clumps of abaca. Her lower lip jutted out disdainfully when the farm hands spoke to her with many flattering words. She laughed when a Bagobo with two hectares of land asked her to marry him. It was only Amado, the tractor driver, who could look at her and make her lower her eyes. He was very dark and wore filthy and torn clothes on the farm but on Saturdays when he came up to the house for his week's salary, his hair was slicked down and he would be dressed as well as Mr. Jacinto, the schoolteacher. Once he told her that he would study in the city night-schools and take up mechanical engineering someday. He had not said much more to her but one afternoon when she was bidden to take some bolts and tools to him in the field, a great excitement came over her. The shadows moved fitfully in the bamboo groves she passed and the cool November air edged into her nostrils sharply. He stood unmoving beside the tractor with tools and parts scattered on the ground around him. His eyes were a black glow as he watched her draw near. When she held out the bolts, he seized her wrist and said: "Come," pulling her to the screen of trees beyond. She resisted but his arms were strong. He embraced her roughly and awkwardly, and she trembled and gasped and clung to him. . . .

A little green snake slithered languidly into the tall grass a few yards from the *kamansi* tree. Tinang started violently and remembered her child. It lay motionless on the mat of husk. With a shriek she grabbed it wildly and hugged it close. The baby awoke from its sleep and cried lustily. *Ave Maria Santisima.* Do not punish me, she prayed, searching the baby's skin for marks. Among the cornhusks, the letter fell unnoticed.

Anthony Morli

DADA

As he went up the stairs he felt the old fear return. There was a dryness in his throat and his hand sliding along the banister left wet imprints on the polished wood.

He had not wanted to come. There was that leaden weight within him when his mother had said he was well enough now to meet his uncle. He had thought up evasions, had put up various subterfuges, and when these did not avail him, had pitted a stolid stubborn front against his mother's nagging insistence. But she had been equally stubborn. Through the years, he did not remember a time when she had not had her way with him. However headstrong he might have been, she always won her point, always routed his resistance, so that in the end, his will broken, and the fortress of his desire battered down, a cold shuddering sensation would force him to say the one conciliatory word that stopped his torment. Such scenes with his mother left him shaken. That cold shuddering sensation would be the precursor to a strangling fit that turned him in one staggering moment into a mute. And when under such a fit the need to speak arose because his mother, unaware of his anguish, had spoken to him and he must needs answer her, the words would come limping out of his mouth in the gaspy stuttering whine of an imbecile. At such times his mother's eyes narrowed to a steely glare and with her strong thin arms akimbo, she would taunt him with her strident: "Idiot! Can't you talk straight?" And she would bring about his utter annihilation with her grotesque mimicry of his splintered speech: "Ah-ah-ah-ah . . . !" until hatred for her would so well up in him that the explosive desire to wreak violence would stir his hands to trembling.

"Don't be a baby," his mother whispered to him as she followed him up the stairs. "Speak up to him and tell him outright the things I told you to say. Make him listen to you. You're old enough now to demand his attention. Talk straight and don't be a baby."

At the top of the stairs he wiped his sweating hands, moistened his lips. Behind him he felt his mother's hand straighten his shirt collar, heard her emphatic whisper in his ear: "Do as I told you."

From where she was playing with her paper dolls on the Persian rug, his cousin Silawahnti looked up at them in calm wonder, her round eyes black buttons on the thin fabric of her face.

"Mummee-e-e, Mummee-e-e-e," the little girl rose and ran into the kitchen. "Luisa is here with Rama."

His aunt Jhamna came out of the kitchen wiping her floury hands on a towel. Among the Hindu women he had known, she was the most nearly Caucasian in color and features.

She was tall, slender, upright as a reed, had auburn hair which she wore in fat twin plaits behind her head; and she had hazel eyes and a spray of freckles on her face and arms which deepened her complexion to a most becoming beige. Draped around her shoulders and trailing to the floor was a large white cambric stole (which when the moment called for it became the characteristic veil, the symbol of reverence all Hindu women wore in the presence of their menfolk). One side of her beak-like nose was pierced. The tiny eyelet was at the moment bared of its diamond stud which, were she dressed up, would lie embedded there, small and glittering. On her wrists she wore a loose cluster of thin gold bangles.

She bade them be seated on the low capacious chairs grouped around the glass-topped table on the center of the huge red Persian carpet that covered the living room floor. When his aunt Jhamna sat down, she drew up a trousered leg, rested the ball of her foot on the edge of the chair, leaned an elbow on the apex of her drawn-up knee and in the course of their conversation, gently swung her sandal that hung by a thong on her big right toe.

He noticed that his aunt Jhamna drew up her veil over her head as she sat opposite him, and the full import of her action as it swiftly dawned on him caused a sharp flicker of shyness, inferiority, self-consciousness, to clutch at his already suffering ego so that he felt constrained to lower his eyes and fix his gaze vacantly on the folded newspaper at the glass-topped table. She had never before covered her head solely in his presence, had never before looked at him with this new intentness, this utterly confusing attention, this new respect as from one adult to another and she had never before addressed him by his full name Ramchand as she did now. So that there was that one second of stupefied awareness when his aunt Jhamna in her high hoarsey voice said: "*Aré*, Ramchand, how are you?"

He shifted his gaze from the table to his aunt's smiling face now framed like a madonna's in the thin white veil, swallowed and gave her a sly, lank smile. "Fine," he said.

His aunt Jhamna turned to his mother. There was a gently teasing humor in her cold-husky voice when she spoke, "*Aré*, Luisa, now you have a big boy. Soon he marry, then what you do? You like him marry Indian girl? Or you like him marry Filipino girl? What you like?"

His mother suggested that his aunt Jhamna ask him the question herself and determine his preference.

His aunt Jhamna turned to him again, and in the scant English she had learned from her husband, his uncle Vassanmal, she said, her gold bangles jingling thinly as she swept her arm out in a large gesture of admonition: "Filipino girl no good. Talk too much. Go out alone. Maybe fight with mother-in-law. Maybe fight with husband. But Indian girl good. She no talk too much. No fight mother-in-law. No fight husband. Can sew. Can cook. She bring you big dowry. Then you have money to open store. What you say?"

Both his aunt Jhamna and his mother turned on him the combined barrage of their appraisal, awaiting his answer; his aunt's, with that new attention and respect he found so disturbing; his mother's, with her possessive proprietary air that always made him squirm and which always loosed within him a hot swift tide of resentment against her.

"I don't know," he finally said, flushing under their probing stares.

His aunt Jhamna's freckles stood out clearly in the tiny mounds of her cheeks now raised in a smile of amusement suddenly widening and breaking into a gale of wheezy mirth. The little, girl, Silawahnti, barefoot and in red silk trousers and yellow tunic, leaned inside the parenthesis of his aunt Jhamna's thighs, looking at him with dark wondering eyes, her lips convolved about a dirty thumb. Amused tolerance softened his mother's eyes but there lingered about her firmly set mouth the taint of smug triumph.

Then his mother snapped her fan open and

while she employed it she launched, in broken English so his aunt would readily understand, into a spirited account of his recent, almost fatal bout with pneumonia. His mother was a large spare-boned woman with small restless eyes and a firmly set mouth sharp like an old knife grown thin with use. Her face had gone slack with the encroachment of age, and her neck was long and flabby like the pitiable obscene throat of an unfledged bird. She wore her hair bobbed, allowed herself the illusion of make-up which somehow was not incongruous with her thighs and legs which were well-preserved and had remained through the years firm and rounded and virginal.

His aunt Jhamna listened, asked questions, from time to time glanced at him. Meanwhile, he had opened the folded newspaper on the glass-topped table and had desperately tried to engross himself in its contents.

"You no more sick?" his aunt asked him, her hazel eyes soft like a doe's.

He was startled when his mother jarred with her fan the paper he was reading and in dialect snapped at him. "Pay attention when you're spoken to!"

He lowered his paper and hastily smoothed out the consternation from his face.

His aunt Jhamna's hazel eyes slanted, crinkled in their corners as she laughingly repeated her question.

"I'm all right now," he said, the words coming out low, depleted of their vocal force from squeezing past a parched, constricted throat. Catching the grim look in his mother's eyes, he lowered his gaze to the paper on his lap.

His mother snapped her fan in a weary, impatient gesture of disgust and said, her voice shrill with held-back anger: "He's very stubborn. Very hard-headed. Only likes reading. Always, always reading." Her face worked with exasperation and folding her fan with a snap, exclaimed: "I don't know what more to do with him."

His aunt Jhamna lowered her foot from the edge of her chair and discovering that Silawahnti was sucking her thumb, slapped the child's hand away and hoarsely chided her daughter: "How many times I told you no put finger in mouth? You also hard-headed like Ramchand? *Halá*, go! Go take bath now! Tell Felisa give you bath!"

Silawahnti wriggled her toes on the Persian rug and made no move to go.

"If you no take bath," his aunt continued, "Dada get angry and Dada no take you in auto to Luneta this afternoon."

Silawahnti considered this, then quickly turning on her heels, she scampered to the kitchen shouting as she ran: "Felisa, you give me bath now. I go Luneta this afternoon."

"Foolish child!" His aunt Jhamna told his mother. "Also very hard-headed. Even I beat her sometimes she still hard-headed."

"Beating is good for children." His mother's tone was firmly authoritative. "They never behave unless you beat them. Look at Rama. When he makes me very angry I still beat him."

"Yes?" a husky chuckle gurgled in his aunt Jhamna's throat. "Suppose he have wife, you still beat him?"

"Why not?" His mother's tone bristled with righteousness. "Even if he has wife, he's still my son."

"Oh yes." Then leaning toward him, her bangles again jingling thinly in her series of admonitory gestures, his aunt Jhamna said: "*Aré*, Ramchand! You always obey mother. You be good boy. Mother make sacrifice for you. Many sacrifice she make. When your father die she no marry again because she afraid maybe new husband no love you same like true son. She afraid maybe new husband beat you. Always happen. Even in India. So your mother make sacrifice ... no more marry ... always take good care of you ... make many sacrifice when you sick ..."

"That's true." His mother's voice went crumbly with tears. "He never will know all the suffering I've gone through bringing him up after his father died ... when he was barely six months old. I always tell him: Even if his body were cut into a thousand pieces he never will be able to repay what it cost me to bear him and raise him into a decent boy."

"So you must love mother. You always be good boy," his aunt Jhamna said. Then as an afterthought, she asked, "You love mother?"

He was acutely ill at ease. His stomach was hot, tight with embarrassment. It was all he could do to manage a soft "Of course" from a throat and mouth arid with shame.

As his mother further related the details of his illness, her voice became by turns whining with self-pity, petulant with grief, somber with martyrdom.

Try as he would he could not avoid hearing all that was said, and what he heard brought a faint roaring in his ears, hot flushes racing through his body. He was sick with shame at his mother's volubly remembered instances of his obstinacy and her consequent distress on their account. He raised the newspaper he was reading so that it hid him from the two women in the room.

"Now, he's well." His mother's voice contained a contrary note of hopeless resignation as if his being well were not at all what she had wished. "Doctor said give him special kind of food. To make him strong. He is thin, you see. And still he takes injections. And that cost money. We have not as yet paid the doctor. And the hospital." Over the rim of his paper, he saw his mother; the turned-down corners of her sharp mouth gave her care-worn face a tragic cast.

His aunt Jhamna became bothered with her sniffles and searching for a corner of her cambric stole, blew her nose on it.

"What time will Dada come?"

"Maybe twelve. Maybe one o'clock. Today Sunday. They fixing store, putting new *estante.* Maybe new goods come this afternoon."

His aunt Jhamna rose from her chair, adjusted the cambric stole about her shoulders, hunted for one sandal that had somehow wedged itself under her chair. She pulled it out with her foot, slipped it on, and turning to his mother said, "Better I finish making *pan* now. By and by Dada come. If *pan* not yet make, he angry." Her hazel eyes took on a glint of mischief. "Maybe he beat me also, no, Ramchand?" She arched her neck back, snuffling out her rustling laughter at him. "Come, Luisa. I have buttermilk in ice box. I give you for Ramchand." She approached him at the same time pulling the veil over her head so that when, feeling her close presence, he looked up at her, he saw her head entirely covered with that symbol of reverence as if he were a man fully grown and in accordance with strict dictates of her caste she must needs defer to his superior position. "You like buttermilk, Ramchand?"

Slightly flushing, he met her gaze, softly said, "Yes, Jhamna."

She turned and while she walked to the kitchen she said, "You wait and Luisa bring you buttermilk. You be big boy now. You be good. No make mother angry. She make many sacrifice for you," she added, her voice coming to him, remote, from the kitchen.

=====

He had drunk his buttermilk, eaten *pakhorra* and drunk ice water copiously to relieve his mouth of its peppery sting, read and yawned many times through the one newspaper on the glass-topped table when at precisely a quarter of two o'clock he heard the car arrive, heard the metallic slam of its door, the noisy babel in Sindhi floating up the stairwell, the leathery scrape of shoes on the stair treads.

He had a moment of quick terror until he remembered to hold the newspaper before his panic-stricken face and spare himself the cold impact of greeting any of the arrivals. He felt them enter the room, felt their actual bodily nearness slap at his senses, felt the room saturated with their oily pungent foreign talk.

Over the top of his newspaper he discerned his uncle Vassanmal's swarthy round head pass by, and, remembering his mother's stern injunctions, he manfully surmounted his panic and threw in his uncle's direction what he intended to be a casually affectionate "Hello, Dada," but what instead came out as an inaudible, abortive croak-like mumble. Almost at once he saw himself impaled on the spear of his terror, felt his stomach contract in a series of shuddery tremors.

"*Aré, Mr.* Ramchand, how are you?"

The voice was deep, throaty, bland with the spurious geniality of the subtly obsequious Indian salesman who comes to a customer with a silky smile and a "What can I do for you, Miss? Is there anything I can show you in the way of rayon, silk, satin?" The boy looked up into the droll beaming face of Mr. Krishinchand Lalchand seated beside Mr. Schwani Bhagwani on the sofa opposite him, the two of them accompanied by their wives, having come with his uncle Vassanmal obviously for Sunday dinner. They were large, portly men with paunchy middles; dark-visaged, thick-necked, and their wives, big handsome women swathed in yards and yards of silk *sari,* were likewise sleek and fat. The two men visitors owned the two Indian bazars adjoining his Uncle's "Taj Mahal Silk Emporium" on the Escolta. The arrivals, aside from the two couples who were guests, included the three Indian salesmen apprenticed to his uncle's store, his cousin Shewakram who was a young man of twenty, and Arjhani, his uncle Vassanmal's only son, age five.

He knew them all and they in turn remembered him from the small chubby boy they had seen through the years lagging behind the heels of a large spare-boned dour-faced woman who jerked him out front whenever he had the tendency in the presence of strangers to disappear behind her skirt. They had twitted the small boy with the round dark eyes that looked at you as if he might at any moment burst into tears, had tweaked his nose, waggled his cheeks, balanced bits of a broken toothpick on his long upcurving lashes, swung him up in the air by his armpits until he fairly shrieked with terror, stuffed him with candies, a bit of money, and mechanical toys during Christmas, inveigled him to stay with them (*Aré, Rami! Better you stay with us. No more go home to Luisa. You stay and we take you to India. You like go India?*), teased his mother by hiding him behind show cases, behind bales of goods inside empty crates,

until he gave himself away by bawling out loud, "Mama! Mama!"

He could feel them all looking at him, seeing a pale thin slat of a boy, his dark eyes rounder than ever but no longer seeming at any moment to burst into tears, now inscrutable rather and deep with only a trace of his boyhood chubbiness remaining on his lean hard cheeks now blotched with the eruptions of adolescent acne.

"What you do? You big boy now. You open store or you study more? Maybe you have sweetheart now, ha? When you marry?" Mr. Krishinchand Lalchand enjoyed his joke hugely, and the fat smirk across his shiny face gave him the aspect of a coarse billiken. The others in the room snickered deliciously like a pack of dark horses whinnying.

At dinner the two men visitors continued to discuss him with his uncle Vassanmal. As was customary, the men sat down to dinner first, his uncle at the head of the table, the two men visitors next, then the three Indian salesmen, his uncle's nephew Shewakram, himself, and at the foot of the table, the little boy Arjhani (perched on his high chair) whom his mother was trying to feed. His aunt Jhamna with the maid Felisa in her wake shuttled back and forth between the kitchen and the table, ladling out platters of the spice-fragrant thick-gravied foods, passing around bottles of ice water, replenishing the rapidly emptied bread platters with stacks of piping-hot *pan* wet with lard.

He watched the diners tear small chunks of *pan,* shape these into tiny cornucopias, dip these into the gravy saucers before them, scoop up gravy and pieces of meat and chuck the succulent morsels into their mouths; and the moist tongue-lapping sounds of their eating—*ptak-ptchak, ptak-ptchak, ptak-ptchak*—were, he thought, kin to the splashy gustatory sounds in a sty.

He did not understand Sindhi very well but occasionally he was able to grasp the gist of a sentence, the essence of their talk about him, and what he heard turned the food in his mouth into wads of thick fuzzy wool. It was a pity, the two men visitors said, clucking their tongues, that his uncle Vassanmal had sadly neglected the boy's upbringing. With the proper coaching in Sindhi reading and writing and a bit of fattening up, he would undoubtedly turn into as fine a specimen of young Hindu manhood as any young buck born and raised in India, and would command no less a handsome dowry in the Indian marriage mart.

He became aware of the three Indian salesmen teasing him with their eyes like black velvet swatches in the thin pasteboard of their faces. Across the table from him, his cousin Shewakram sniggered salaciously and ground a shoe on his foot under the table. He swung his leg in a vicious kick, stubbing his toe on the hard edge of the other's chair, and as he chafed at his futile retaliation, he saw Shewakram lifting the corners of his grease-coated lips in a grin of triumph.

The diners gorged themselves, and he saw a beatific expression like a brooding Buddha's spread over his uncle's face as he hoisted his mammoth pot-belly, shifted his weight on one buttock, and slowly, casually, matter-of-factly, broke wind. The others exhaled fat zestful belches and rose from the table.

At the lavatory he waited until everybody had finished washing their hands, rinsed their mouths, before he moved toward it. As he did so, he saw Shewa deliberately taking his own sweet time about soaping his hands. He stood to one side of Shewa, prepared to wait patiently for his turn and was indeed startled when Shewa, by inserting a finger in the tap nozzle, directed a taut squirt of water at him, catching him pointblank on the belly. Facing him, Shewa smiled wickedly, and hurrying past him, flicked the drops of water from his still wet hands into the boy's astonished face. As Rama washed his hands clean of their goaty smell, his thwarted anger stirred them to trembling, twitched his jaws in a quivery spasm.

"*Now!*" his mother said over his shoulder as he dried his hands on a towel hung on a nail above the washbowl. "There he goes into his room. Follow him, plant yourself squarely before him so he'll have no reason to ignore you. Tell him outright the things I told you to say. Catch his attention for he'll soon be sitting down at the card table and you know that once he's there, not even cannon shot can dislodge him. Make him understand, talk straight, and don't be a baby. Get results or you'd better take care when we return home. Better take care!" She left him then, for his aunt Jhamna was calling her to come to dinner.

He walked into the living room, saw that Krishinchand Lalchand and Sehwani Bhagwani were setting up the card table. Lhadu, the eldest of the three Indian salesmen, was mixing brandy and soda at the cellarette beside the cabinet radio, while the others were sprawled on chairs, leisurely picking their teeth. Shewakram, with one leg flung over the arm of his chair, was intent on the movie page of the newspaper, now and then rooting into the inner corner of his thigh where apparently the soft plump worm of his sex was snagged upon the crotch of his tight trousers. The boy waited until he was sure no one was paying him the least attention and then, swiftly crossing the living room, entered his uncle Vassanmal's room.

———

As he paused on the threshold, he felt his stomach tighten. His uncle Vassanmal, like a gross idol, was sitting on his bed, one leg bent and raised upon a knee. Slowly, his uncle leaned forward and unlaced a shoe which dropped on the floor. He raised his other foot and in the same laborious manner unlaced and shucked the shoe off, thumping it on the floor. He then emitted a faint belch after which he rested his hands on his hammy thighs as he worked his toes up and down inside their brown silk socks. It was then his uncle noticed him leaning there by the doorjamb and his uncle spoke across the room to him in a neutral perfunctory tone: "*Aré*, Rama, how're you?"

With marked diffidence, the boy walked into the room, stopped by a chair beside the round table with the crocheted lace tablecloth, watched his uncle wheeze as his enormous pot-belly pressed on the edge of the bed while he leaned over to peel off his socks, then tenderly rub his bunions. He was of middle height but enormously fat so that his bloated torso and mammoth pot-belly were in grotesque contrast to his rather small-calved spindly legs. Still discernible on his swarthy face were the ravages of smallpox he once had many years ago, the pockmarks no longer distinct but shallow and blurred by time. His black slick hair, austerely brushed down, hugged his head in the round clasp of a skullcap and fringed the edge of his narrow brow with a tiny fluted curl. His face was broad, his mouth wide, and the high ridge of his nose dominated the landscape of his face like a mountain peak.

As he watched his uncle wipe his toes with his socks, he felt the desire to speak erupt within him like a shooting geyser. He must have sputtered an involuntary mumble, for his uncle looked up at him and said, still quite perfunctorily: "You go to school?"

The boy's tenseness, like boiling liquid when the heat is lessened, ebbed a little and he was glad for this release of tension, for this brief respite from the fear that his uncle, as he had habitually done in the past, would leave to him the sole burden of their conversation while maintaining, as he struggled and suffered the damnation of the chronic stutterer, a cold stoic silence. His fear of meeting his uncle had stemmed from those excruciating moments in the past when he had stood before him mute and tongue-tied, a welter of words stillborn on the threshold of his lips, while the other regarded him with an impassive stare and did not by so much as a gesture, a look, a word, ease the torment that clotted in his belly like tangled twine. *Now* his uncle had spoken to him *first*, wanted to know if he went to school, was kind, was generous, was altogether not the hard, mean, avaricious bogeyman of his childhood fancy; oh, he'd been wrong, now all that would be *past*, his uncle would speak to him, would have sympa-

thy, would above all understand how it was, how it is with a chronic stutterer who every waking moment of his day must strain and struggle and try to break away from the crippling tenacious strands of shyness, inferiority, self-consciousness that hamstrung him and made of him a suffering prisoner.

He managed a clumsy smile and when he replied, his voice, at first unsteady and quavering, became more natural, normal, even warm towards the end of his little speech. "No, Dada, we have no school. We are on vacation since March. School will open in June, next month. Then I'll . . . I'll be fourth year. I got 92 average. That is second highest. The first is 94. She's a girl. Teacher said maybe if I study more I can be first in class."

He watched his uncle wheeze again as he leaned over and tried to hunt for his slippers under the bed. "You find slippers, Rama, I think they go there . . . in corner, there!"

The boy was glad for this preoccupation. He had long wanted to move; standing there by the chair was making him feel absurd, only he didn't quite know how to manage any movement without attracting attention, without appearing awkward. He always felt glad whenever he could be of use to anybody even if it were only in doing the least little thing. If only people kept asking him to do something for them instead of, as often happened, staring at him and what was most intolerable, trying to make fun of him and speaking to him as if he were a dimwit or a child! He walked over to the bed, crouched on his hands and knees, and thrusting an arm under the bed, reached for the slippers that lay there against the wall. He dropped the sandals before his uncle's feet and shyly sat himself on the edge of the bed. Now that he was closer to his uncle, his fear was no longer as potent as before; in fact it had almost completely disappeared, and he was only hoping that their relation could stay forever thus, without terror, closer, more congenial.

His uncle rose from the bed and the sudden release of his enormous weight shot the bedsprings upward into position bouncing the boy on his back. He laughed, scrambling to his feet, and quickly looked at his uncle to see if he had noticed his momentary discomfiture. Apparently he hadn't for he was at the moment standing before his clothes bureau rummaging in its drawers. His uncle pulled out pyjama trousers and a house shirt, slung these over one shoulder, started unbuckling his belt. He dropped his trousers to the floor, shook loose the silk pyjamas and stooped over to step into these. His uncle wore no underwear and the sight of his swollen half-nudity made the boy turn away and study the linear pattern on the chenille bedspread. When he looked up again his uncle was clad in wide loose silk pyjamas over which his pin stripe silk house shirt hung to his knees. He watched his uncle grunt and stoop over to pick up his trousers and empty the pockets of balled dirty handkerchiefs, keys, loose bills, coins, receipts, swatches of men's suiting, a button, string, a checkbook which he tossed on the lace-covered round table.

The boy remained seated on the bed with his knees crossed, swinging one foot in an attempt at nonchalance while deep down, tiny licking tongues of panic swept inward from the outer fringes of his well-being. Between his uncle and himself there had been silence perhaps for the better part of five minutes, and the thought that if he didn't quickly think of something to say next, this silence would rise like a flood and submerge him completely into a vortex of speechlessness, tormented him because he now knew as well as if the other had explicitly told him that his uncle had nothing more to say to him, would not attempt anything else to say to him, was in fact, as was his habit in the past, ignoring him, snubbing him, as a Brahmin a pariah. The simmer of anger in him clove his tongue to the roof of his parched mouth. Words started seething inside him, clamoring for release, for utterance, for spitting out against an injustice he felt was being done him. He started taking deep breaths to still his violently agitated heart and retain a measure of calm with which to speak out his mind

clearly, lay out his plea coherently, manfully. He was no longer a child. His aunt Jhamna had covered her head in his presence, the Messrs. Krishinchand Lalchand and Sehwani Bhagwani, including their wives, thought him mature enough to warrant marriage speculations, his mother was now even more hysterically careful about his making acquaintances with girls; no, he was no longer a child. His uncle had better realize the fact here, now, at once.

He watched his uncle seated at the lace-covered round table appearing to balance the stubs in his checkbook. After several false starts in his mind, he managed to blurt out: "Dada, I . . . I . . . I've been sick. I've been sick with pneumonia. I stayed in hospital for three weeks. Doctor said my illness serious." He paused to lick his dry lips, and suddenly frightened at the lengthening silence, hurtled on, impelled with the notion to let the momentum of his excitement push out everything he had to say. "D-d-doctor said if I not careful I'll have p-p-pleurisy. I'm all right now but I take injections. We have n-n-not yet paid the doctor and the hospital. Mama already paid part but there's still a balance of ninety pesos. Mama said you please give me the money including the thirty pesos for tuition and books I need next month. So next month I no bother you again. That makes a total of one hundred twenty pesos in all. Mama said you please give me because doctor is waiting and she is ashamed."

Halfway in his speech his uncle looked up, turned to him, hitching his armpit over the back of his chair. "*Aré, Rama*," his uncle said in a voice only a little less loud than a shout. The tone made the boy wince for he did not wish the people in the living room to know the nature of his talk with his uncle. "I have idea for you . . . Nice idea I have for you. What grade you now, ha?"

"I just finished third year. Next month in June, I'll start the fourth year."

"No use going back school. I have better idea for you. You stop school. You work for me. I send you Zamboanga with Lhadu. I open branch there. You have nice house, nice food, nice clothes. You no more sick. I tell Lhadu give you small money for cinema, for ice cream. Luisa stay here. She can go here every month, get small money. What you say?"

All the food he had eaten turned into a grey blubbery lump that weighted him down, inclined him on the brink of nausea. He sat dumbfounded staring at his uncle who stared back at him, his mammoth pot-belly resting between his thighs, looking now more than ever like a toad. When he was a child, he had regarded his uncle's belly with awe, remembering a remark heard from his mother that if you pierced his uncle's stomach and slashed a hole therein, the money his uncle had seized from his father when the latter died would come tumbling out like pennies from a slot machine.

"B-b-but I can't stop now. This is my last year. I have to finish high school to go to college."

"Study? Study? Why you always study? What you like? Become governor-general of Philippines?"

"I must go to college to study medicine. I-I-I want to be a doctor."

"Why you want to be doctor? That crazy idea. Always doctor, always lawyer. No attend to business. What I do with doctor? Many doctors poor people, no make money. Why you want be like that?"

The boy squirmed on the bed, cast his eyes down, toyed with his fingers, cracking them one by one.

"*I* no study," his uncle continued. "*I* finish only third grade in India. *I* make good business. *I* work hard. Why you no do the same? In Zamboanga you learn little Sindhi. Then later you go India. Learn some more reading, writing. Then you marry. I arrange for you. Maybe you get ten thousand, fifteen thousand rupees dowry. *I* keep money for you. Maybe *I* make you partner in business. What more you like? You own half store, half mine. You have money, you live nice. What more you want?"

He was sick, miserable, and it was a struggle to say this: "D-d-doctors also get to make a lot of money."

His uncle looked at him sharply. "Where you get money for study?" His uncle's tone was low, packed with muffled thunder.

Inside the boy's head, his thoughts ran like frightened mice. He had a desperate time of it trying to collect them, to align them in one convincing rebuttal. "I-I-I get money from you. Bef-bef-fore, you promised you send me through school."

"*I* no have money." His uncle rose from the chair, lumbered toward the clothes bureau where he tossed the checkbook into a drawer. "What you think I am, millionaire?"

"But—but Dada, I need one hundred twenty pesos now for doctor and school——"

"I no have money. I give you twenty pesos, that enough. When you go home, you get from Jhamna. I tell her give you twenty pesos. *I* no millionaire."

From the living room the bland throaty voice of Mr. Krishinchand Lalchand rose in a shout for his uncle, "*Aré,* Vassu,"—the boy caught the gist of the Sindhi words—"You hurry up if we are going to play. Also bring a new deck of cards, will you?"

Now panic gripped him. In a moment his uncle would waddle out of the room, leaving him and his plea for money washed dry like wreckage in the tide of their argument. He had to think fast, speak fast, try to hold his uncle's attention a little longer. Words hurled themselves against the gates of his mind, and he became frantic with worry, fear, panic, that he would never be able to use them, unleash them to assist him, avenge him. But his throat and mouth were again dry, and speech became an effort, strenuous and tiring.

"But—but—but Dada, I need the money b-b-badly. This is my last—last—last year in school. I have to finish that."

"You hard-headed," his uncle said, rummaging in his bureau drawers for a pack of cards. "Luisa spoil you. She teach you wrong things. *I* give you nice idea but you hard-headed. I no have money to give you. *I* have many expense.

I pay house rent, store rent, *I* pay salary. Why *I* give you money? Why *I* always give you?"

"Be—beb—because—because——" His heart was thumping faster. He wondered whether he had the nerve to say what his mother had coached him to say if his uncle proved difficult. "Be—beb—because it's much more mine than it is yours. It's my father's money!"

His uncle slowly turned and fixed him across the room with a black flashing glare.

His audacity surprised him, and curiously enough, it gave him a pervading sense of calm. As from afar he heard his voice say, slowly, distinctly, with dreamy languor, "It's my . . . father's . . . money . . . you . . . stole . . . it . . . when . . . he . . . died." An impulse cranked him to say it, like a record needle caught in a groove, softly, dreamily—"s-s-stole it . . . s-s-stole it . . . s-s-stole it . . ."

The slap jarred his head back. His cheeks burned and his head rang with the force of the blow.

His mind screamed: *You hog! You toad! You thief! It's true! You took over Papa's store when he died, took his money, that's why you promised the lawyer you'd support us . . . send me through school . . .* But his mouth said: "Mh . . . mh . . . mh . . . mh . . . ," the whimpery syllables borne on shuddery gusts of breath that escaped through locked teeth.

His uncle towered over him, hunched there on the bed, one hand raised to his cheek now radiating heat like a flat iron. For a minute his uncle looked at him with scorn, then turned and walked away. Halfway across the room his uncle whirled, spat an Indian obscenity at him, thrust a beefy hand toward him, its fingers stretched apart, the thumb pointed downward—the whole brown hand seemingly a fat obscene spider dangling in the air. His uncle regarded him once more, then picking up a deck of cards from the drawer, walked slowly out of the room.

Hunched there on the bed, he felt cold perspiration break out on his brow, felt his blood roar and recede and scamper innerwards to a cold leaden core somewhere in his belly. The sensation was like a foot going to sleep, only this time, magnified to the height and breadth of his whole body. The palms of his hands itched and he felt a bowel movement coming on.

When his mother entered the room and confronted him with her "Well, what did he say? What did he say?" he swung his stricken face to her and, as his bleary senses made out her sharp features thrust before him like a blade, there dropped out of his mouth, like the whir of an unraveled spring in a snapped mechanical toy, the dry gaspy splintered whine of idiot syllables.

Andres Cristobal Cruz

SO

One nice thing about all this is that they were neighbors—he living in the house on the other side of the *estero* spanned by a small wooden bridge that had its one end lying firmly on the wide cement edge of the *estero* on his side, and she living, with her mother and aunt and brothers and elder sisters, who were all married and had had their own secret affairs with the men they were going to marry and had married and were now having their own children, in the house with the backstairs that went down directly on the other end of the wooden bridge under which flowed *estero*-water with its daily load of scum and waterlogged floating refuse—their houses with their backs to each other but connected to each other's lot by the bridge which she would soon cross on her way to the street several blocks away from the place.

The twin-tone will indicate exactly nine-fifteen a.m. Manila time, the radio announcer in the *sala* announced. She paused to listen. Ding-dong meant she had fifteen minutes more and she wished her elder sister Ka Puring would stop looking now and then at her outside the door of her room so she could look out of the window and see if he had gone ahead of her. She felt uneasy as Ka Puring watched her combing her long thick, dark-brown hair. Your hair makes such a soft pillow, Pin, she remembered him saying.

A nicer thing about all this is that they have never considered themselves as friends although they knew each other when they happened to meet, smile, greet, pass each other several years ago when she was still studying in the high school, where he was also studying in the same year as she was but in a higher section. The only time we got to see each other more often was since we moved to the vacant lot on the other side, at the back of your house. She knew him then the way she had always thought he knew her—a cousin, third or fourth. And as such she would come to him to their house and help him type his research papers in the afternoons he would come home very early from the university, and it was during those times she got to know him more and enjoyed being with him not because he was teaching her now and then the things he had learned from his professors and also not because she was feeling she was learning higher college things but ... I really didn't know why, Cris, I just had the desire to see you, hear you, I always wanted to be with you often, and now I know why ... because you were feeling the same way too.

And the nicest thing about all this is that she was going out with him again after almost three weeks now since the last time they spent a whole day together when she was supposed to be out with her best friend Tessie, and her mother always let her go out as long as it was with Tessie she was going, but it was always with him that she spent the day each time she told her mother she was going out with Tessie.

Tessie is sick, am going to visit her, she answered her elder sister. She wished Ka Puring would go out so she could look out of the window to see if the window of his room was closed. He closed the window every time he was going out with her.

In the *sala* the smooth-voiced man in the radio said: And finally the same song is dedicated to Marica, Ellen, and Joan for their listening pleasure from Carmen, here now is the song Always, Always. She listened to the song. The last three nights she had sung the song with him, she washing plates in the kitchen and he taking his nightly bath. The song in her mind. Ka Puring went out of the room and turned off the radio. She looked at herself in the mirror. By the time I get there it'll be nine-thirty, she thought. She looked out of the door. Ka Puring was putting her baby to sleep. She went out of the room to the backdoor. She made the sign of the cross as she went down the rungs of the backstair. Am going, Inay, she told her mother who was washing clothes under the stair. Her legs felt a little shaky. She steadied herself on the end of the bridge. She looked up behind her. Ka Puring was coming down the stair.

She looked at his window as she crossed the bridge. His window was closed, she knew that in two minutes and a half she would be out on the sidewalk of the street, where a bus would stop for her without her giving any sign for the driver to stop, she would get into the bus to a backseat where he would be sitting.

Her Ka Puring followed behind her. She passed through the small passage at one side of his house. She crossed the small street in front of his house and hurried out of the corner of the small chapel, out of Ka Puring's now suspicious eyes. She gave herself a pat on the cheek, she walked fast. He liked punctuality. She was anxious all over to be with him. She crossed the central street where a bus would stop for her with him in it. Two buses passed her. When the street cleared itself of passing jeeps and cars and other vehicles she saw him crossing the street.

Ka Puring will get angry, she said when he stood beside her on the sidewalk, your window was closed. She stopped a passenger jeep.

He helped her into the front seat. There is Ka Puring, he said pointing in the direction of their place which could be seen from the street. She looked to where he was pointing. Ka Puring was standing akimbo on the sidewalk across the Canlapan house. Am sure she'll follow, but I don't care any more, let her, let your elders know about us, he said. The jeep was running away from the place.

Am going to see Tessie, she said leaning back on the seat to rest herself on his arm across her shoulders. Ben said she's sick although I know Tessie just don't want to see Ben. She's fed up with him.

And you, are you fed up with me too? he asked.

She answered, no! no! grasping and pressing his hand between their thighs pressing against each other.

Don't go to Tes then, he said, let's spend the day together.

She didn't answer, but moved closer to his side . . .

They sat beside each other in a private curtained booth of a snack bar looking across the boulevard to the sea. She drank her glass of milk. She loved the way he always reminded her of her health, the way he always patted her cheek saying, be a good girl, or I want you to be strong and enduring forever, or, that's my girl, when she said something nice or witty extemporaneously, or when she reminded him to finish his studies, get a job, save . . . then we'll settle, nothing can stop me from doing what I like . . .

'What do you want? he said, when they were resting, locked in a small world so big enough to contain all of themselves without fear, unseparate, without time, undying. And she answered: You.

It was already raining hard outside. They sky above her poured its wild song through the ceiling. She felt her pores opening to the spasms and gusts outside, her softness in a sweet ache as it welled with the rhythm of the hard long song sinking into her. She closed her eyes to the scattering song, to its crashing and bursting of her tenderness. It said, Pin, Pin. And she released her Cris, Cris, as the adagio of the rain came deeply drawn out.

If they should find out about us, she said after a long while, about this, never mind, it's you and I. On her side, a little below her waist, was a wet gash of rain that had seeped through the line of crevice between two boards of the wall on her side. He reached across her and slowly wiped the purplish gash of wetness with his three middle fingers making the sign of the cross on it. She took up his wet fingers and rubbed each of them with her fingers in the goldish light of the bulb hanging down the ceiling.

It was already mid-afternoon when they went down to the boulevard along the sea. The wide street smelled fresh and clean and it lay shining under a full sun. The boulevard trees were still wet and dripping, and from their branches buds and leaves fell spiralling to the grass and the asphalt.

Do not walk fast now, he told her as they went across the street, we still have three hours, walk normally, can't you?

She nodded, murmuring: I'll try, I'll try. She walked slowly, keeping herself from dragging her feet, leaning on his shoulder and smiling at her successful effort. She felt his hand on her waist pressing encouragements.

They found a seat on the breakwater. There were a few couples away from them. You're heavy, he told her as she leaned on his shoulder.

You were heavy, she answered, and I'll be heavier some day.

She watched him crinkling the skin on the bridge of his nose and under his eyes as he made her favorite funny-face. She imitated him. They laughed together, the waves rolling and dashing against the large boulders a little below them on the foot of the breakwater. She watched the sea with him. The waves repeatedly formed, rolled, closed in and under each other on the bouldered margin of the sea. The deep blue sea would gather itself far out into long curved shutters, then each shutter would open foaming on its emerged end as another shutter would close under it. The endless sound and force and wind was a nude view of perfection in opening and closing in each other in the creation of another like themselves. She watched and listened and felt the sea with him whose hands she held, a long dark husk of her hair blowing against his cheek, a deep crevice between two leg-shaped boulders in front of her releasing a steady flowage with sticky-looking foam. She released his hands and pressed herself down on her front. She felt tired. She felt like vomiting and she told him. He placed a rubbing hand on her back as she leaned out beyond her legs. She opened her mouth. Nothing came out. In her throat was a line of sour and bitter liquid which she tried to gurgle out. Her eyes smarted, the sharp tears hazed her eyes as she shook her head to take out the liquid in her throat. She heard him say: Tickle it out with a finger. She crooked her left index finger in her mouth and her fingertip tickled her throat, her tongue pulled itself up on its sides and jerked back deep into her throat, she drew out her finger quickly. Still no mess came out. She swallowed hard. His hand on her back kept rubbing and patting. She straightened up from her waist and said: Let's go, Cris. He helped her down the breakwater, saying: Nothing can really part us now. And she answered: Forever . . .

It was beginning to dark when she arrived on the wooden bridge across the *estero*. Ka Puring was at the backdoor. The black scummy water of the *estero* was beginning to rise in, she walked up fast on the backstair. Ka Puring pulled her up viciously into the kitchen and said: So! Ka Puring left her in her room to call up their mother.

So. It contained all the things she knew would soon be said to her harshly without her having a chance to be understood. Even before she was left alone in her room where she had put on and was now taking off the rust-brown dress she had worn the first time she secretly spent a day with him, she knew that it would take a long time, weeks, months, a year or two, before she would wear it again for him, before she could be able to go out with him again. Nothing can really part us now. And she knew that what she had taken into herself out of his being would outlast all the painful things that would be done, said, thought of her by those who would not understand her much less him to whom she had given all of herself as he had given all of himself to her who was now in her house-clothes she had worn that afternoon she, for the first time in her life, gave her answer: Yes, forever, Cris . . . to him to whose allness her allness responded in suffering and joy, to whom she was related even before they found themselves, the one and the other like lock and key to a door that held in its room their one identity before a holy knowledge of a fountainhead to perfection—Life, out of their sowing into each other, perfect into and out of each other like the waves.

Cris, Cris she called him in her being as she tried to press back in her closed eyes the sudden teasing that had rushed up from her breast to her face and now out of her opened eyes that saw the dim outline of her mother's old but big bulk blocking the light of the living room outside her silently waiting bedroom where she was caught full by her mother's shadow. She bent over the edge of her bed, pulled up the hem of her dress and wiped her eyes with it. She heard the sharp, tearing *traidores* of her mother's voice that was now hating and hateful. She raised her face bravely to her mother who blocked the light of the living room where she heard her elder sister Puring's I suspected, and went to Tessie, and your angel of a sister was not

there, to her eldest brother Nayong, and her brother's I'll talk to him, with as much hate in his voice as in her sister's.

I forbid you ever to see him again, her mother said, don't you people know you're cousins, you were both blinded by your youth. You deceived me, Tessie, Tessie, all the time it was really with him you were going out, the foulness of a rot could never be hidden. What will people say, I am a *consentidora*. No! no! you must part from each other.

She stayed in her room while her brothers and sisters and their husbands and the children ate silently. They were suddenly strangers to each other. I will kill myself, she repeated what she had told her mother, she repeated the words to herself in her mind. She lay in bed. Her mother had closed and locked the only window of her room.

It was late in the night when she heard him singing in his room on the other side of the *estero*. She could not sing now the way she used to.

His song caught her. His voice came through the darkness, came over the mud and flowing filth of the *estero*. She remembered the afternoon, the long lovely hours when she was most alone with him; she saw him again sitting beside her and watching and feeling the sun with him; she saw themselves in the full light of the sun, heard themselves; she felt him now as he sang song after song of promise and love and yearning, of remembering.

She heard the mating sounds of lizards somewhere on the ceiling. She heard Ka Puring's baby Lita crying in the room next to hers. She hard her brother-in-law Tony saying, my child. She heard her Ka Tony and Ka Puring teasing each other about having another child.

She breathed quietly. The darkness in her room seemed to be breathing a song into her. And the song seemed to heave with her body. She imagined the stars outside. Her wakefulness in the darkness as she recalled him eased into her body. She pressed herself below her bosom throbbing. He was still singing in his room on the other side of the *estero.* She was still listening in her room on the other side. And between them she saw in her mind the black water flowing in the *estero.* She smiled as she imagined him coming on the bridge, bravely coming into her room. She felt him now singing into her.

Her hands on her bosom she counted months on her fingers. She was now a woman. Forever. So.

Gilda Cordero-Fernando

PEOPLE IN THE WAR

Our front door opened right into the sidewalk, and the street sloped down to a lily-dappled river, in our house in the city. Across the river a soap opera was always taking place: a man with two wives lived in an unpainted house beside the lumber mill. When the sun went down the wives began to quarrel, clouting each other with wooden clogs, and a bundle of clean wash came flying out of the window into the silt below. We watched them chase each other down the stairs, clawing each other's clothes off and rolling down the embankment, and the dogs of the neighborhood surrounded them, barking and snarling—till from the lumber mill the husband emerged—a shirtless apparition with a lumber saw in his hand.

At least once a month they held a wake on the river bank. They rented a corpse, strung up colored lights and gambled till the wee hours of the morning. Sometimes a policeman wandered in—having heard some rumor, and poked around with his night stick. But there would be the corpse, and it was truly dead, there would be the card games, but no suspicion of betting (the chips having been scooped away together with the basket of money) and the policeman would saunter away, wiping a tear, leaving the poor relatives to their grief and their gambling.

We must move to another neighborhood, my father said every day. We planted trees to screen them from sight, we planted trees to preserve our respectability. A truck unloaded two acacia trees on our doorstep, saplings no bigger than I. The houseboy made a bamboo fence around their trunks and every afternoon the maids hauled out pails to water them.

Soon the trees grew tall and lush with yellow-green leaves and the crickets sang in them. Then the street boys shook them down for bugs and crickets, or stripped off the bark with penknives or swung on the branches till they snapped. My father waged an indefatigable battle with the street boys for why should they want to destroy beautiful things? He was terribly good with a slingshot and seldom missed his target—for ammunition he used a round clay pellet instead of a stone and it made a painful red mark. In time my father just had to lean out the window and the boys scampered down the trees, and after a while they learned to leave the trees alone.

The soft dappled shade served many purposes. The branches sheltered a group of nursery school children with sausage curls whose playground had been turned during the Occupation into a garrison. In the afternoons a Japanese girl named Sato-san came to air a nephew and a niece and lay out rice cakes under the spreading trees. She was a masseuse in the Japanese barbershop at the corner which was always brilliant with neons and sweet with the odor of Bay Rum. Occasionally, a dispossessed family of tattered jugglers did their act in the shade of the acacias. They laid a dirty tarpaulin on the ground and tumbled on it, juggling wooden balls and bottles. Then the father stood on a barrel and balanced his two daughters on his shoulders and it was the most daring, most brilliant finale I had ever seen. As they made their bows, an indifferent crowd dropped a coin or two into the man's soiled hat, and once I saw someone drop in a rotten mango.

Our driver now turned houseboy (our Plymouth had been commandeered) hailed from a pot-making region and he would come from vacation with a tobacco box full of hard clay pellets baked in the sun, for my father's slingshot—a year's supply till the next vacation. My father had a low opinion of the Imperial Army. When I showed him my report card, he thundered, What do you mean 75 in Algebra, 95 in Nippongo! Am I raising a little geisha?

Oh yes, one night he almost got into real trouble with the slingshot. A drunken Japanese officer was kicking noisily on the door of the family living downstairs, calling the young girl's name amorously and growling like a jungle ape. Annoyed, my father flung back the bed sheets and charged to the window with his slingshot. Mother tried to pull him back, but already father had aimed and hit—right in the seat of the olive drab pants. It was blackout and the Jap was at a disadvantage— flattened behind the window, his treacherous opponent let loose another hail of pellets. With horrible war cry, the soldier unsheathed his sword, a grim Samurai brandishing reprisal in the air. Mother and I cowered in our nightgowns and embraced each other. Whenever the officer's drink-clouded eyes looked up at our direction, my father shot at him from another window. Finally, the Jap stumbled away, his hobnailed boots echoing in the deserted midnight street. We half-expected the Imperial Army to storm our door the next

morning, but they never came, I guess the Jap was too drunk to remember it.

After a while our curtain of trees became useless. The people on the other side of the river raised a contribution to build a bamboo bridge across it and the bad elements started coming into town. It was a narrow, split-bamboo bridge that swayed, and the Japanese soldiers loved to walk on it.

As the beggars with coconut shells in their palms increased in number, it became a usual thing to find a bloated corpse under a newspaper. Everyone was suddenly interested in food production: twin curly-haired young men from acoss the river began to cultivate the ground surrounding the acacias. From two o'clock until sundown they puttered among the neat plots, loosening the soil around the flourishing yams and *talinum* buds, fetching water in cans, collecting fertilizer from under the *dokars* parked in the street. Aquilino was the leaner, handsomer twin, he was my brown god in an undershirt, reeking of sweat and fertilizer; but when Santos knocked on our door with a basket of *talinum* tops for Mother, I couldn't decide whom I liked better. When the jasmine climbing from our window box was replaced with the more practical *ampalaya,* I carved their names on the fruit, and the letters grew as the fruit grew: Santos and Aquilino.

II

The Spanish family renting the downstairs portion of our house opened a small laundry but retained their fierce pride. The women sat behind the unpainted counter in their bedraggled *kimonas,* like soiled aristocracy, handling the starched pants drying on the wire hangers with pale finicky fingers. They pretended to understand nothing but Spanish and a customer's every Tagalog word sent them huddling together in consultation. If you were overtaken there by lunchtime, in the kitchen, Señora Bandana placed a wet rag on her hot frying pan. The daughter then came out and said wheedlingly, *Cena tu ya aqui,* having made you believe, by the fabulous sizzle that there was a chicken or at least a milkfish in the pan. Since it was unthinkable to stay over for a meal during those hard times, you left with thanks and profuse apologies. The family then commenced on its meal of rice and *bagoong*, smugly sitting on their reputations.

They had been paying P 15 a month before the war and insisted on paying the same rent in Japanese money. My father continually begged them to leave so we could take in boarders, but whenever he brought up the subject, Señora Bandana had one of her heart attacks. Finally, they compromised by giving us back two rooms which we needed for Mr. Solomon and Boni.

Boni was a fourth cousin from Batangas on my mother's side. He had gotten stranded in Manila when the schools closed and came to live with us because he found it easier to make money in the city, on buy-and-sell. He always had some business or another: he had converted an old German bicycle into a commercial tricycle and rented it to a man every morning. He also dealt in wooden shoes, *muscovado,* agar-agar from the sea and cotton batting for auto seats. On father's birthday, Boni presented him a skeletal radio he had tinkered with, that could catch the Voice of Freedom and it pleased my father no end. Once Boni bought three truckfuls of bananas wholesale—our garage was so full of them there was hardly any space to walk. That venture had been a fiasco—before he could resell the lot, half of them rotted away while he was at a dance in Parañaque.

Boni was an expert *balisong* wielder..He could hit a coin four feet away, the knife making a clean hole in the center of it. He also had a bad habit of throwing the knife at cockroaches and lizards and cutting them to ribbons. Once he threw it at a stray cat that was annoying him below his window and my mother almost had a fit. Send him away, my mother told my father over the *tulia* broth. Make him go home to the province. My father took the knife away and told Boni to behave. Boni's father was an unbeliever, and when he died, which was three years before the war, he

asked the family to erect a devil on his gravestone. And there it still stands in the cemetery in Batangas, regal and black, its tail long and sharp as an arrow, its eyeballs and armpits a fiery red, lording it over all the weeping angels and white crosses. On All Souls' Day Boni alone came to visit the grave, to cut away the weeds and repaint the devil a deep, glossy black.

Mr. Solomon occupied what had been Señora Bandana's sala. He hung up his crucifix and his hat and locked the door and never opened it again. Mr. Solomon owned vast salt beds in Bulacan and his dream was to control the salt market in Manila. Just before the war he was competing even with the Chinese merchants and whatever price he dictated the merchants had to follow. In the great salt war there was a time when salt was selling for ten centavos a sack.

His four sons joined Marking's Guerrillas after the fall of Bataan, and Mr. Solomon became its heaviest contributor. The Japanese had seized his salt beds and when he became the *kempeitai*'s most hunted man, he begged my papa, who was his old friend, to hide him and that was why he was boarding with us.

Mr. Solomon stayed all day in Señora Bandana's sala, gazing out the window saying nothing. He listened to the nursery school children singing; he watched Sato-san air her nephews and nieces; he dropped coins into the juggler's hat. But we had to pass his food down a wobbly dumbwaiter. My brother Raul and I complained whenever we were assigned to deliver the food, especially if there was hot soup, but Mother said to be patient with Mr. Solomon as he was a man who had "gone through the fire of suffering." The only time Mr. Solomon ever went out of his room was when he offered to show Papa how to make ham. After rubbing the fresh pig's thigh with salt, he brought out a syringe and shot the red meat full of salt-peter and other preservatives. Then he wrapped it in a cloth and told Mama to keep it in the ice box for three months. Mama said Mr. Solomon was probably getting tired of eating fish.

When Eden and Lina came to stay with us, I gave up my room to sleep with Mother. They were home-loving sisters who made my room look nice with printed curtains and put crocheted covers on the beds. Under the bed they had many boxes of canned goods, mostly milk for Eden's baby. A basket lined with diapers was hung from the rafters and the baby slept in it.

Eden and Lina's father was Papa's brother and they used to live in Cabanatuan where they had a rice mill. As children, we used to play baseball on the area of cement beside the granary where the palay was spread out to dry during our vacations in the province before the war. Their mother ran a restaurant called "Eden's Refreshment" where she served a thick special *dinuguan* smoking right from an earthen pot. Tia Candeng had a fault—she played favorites. It was always "Eden is pretty, Eden is valedictorian, My child Eden..." Never Lina. Lina ran around in ragged slacks and played *cara y cruz* with the mill hands. On Eden's eighteenth birthday they rented the roof garden of the *municipio* and held a big dance. Her dress was ordered from Manila and cost three hundred fifty pesos. The town beautician worked all day putting a lot of pomade and padded hair in her pompadour. They sent us an 8 × 10 photograph of Eden on her debut with a painted waterfall in the background.

After that, a rich widower used to motor all the way from Tarlac to visit Eden. An engineer also fell in love with her and lavished the family with *bangus* from their fishpond. When the charcoal-fed Hudson and Ford stopped by their gate, Tia Candeng, all aflutter brought out from her stock of pre-war canned goods precious hot dogs to fry and serve to the rivals. But one day a small squat soldier without a job blew into town and Eden ran away with him. He was a mere lieutenant and a second one at that, and Tia Candeng never forgave them. They came to the city to live, in a muddy crooked street. Minggoy and Eden had violent quarrels. Whenever they did, Eden bundled her cake pans and pillows and

mats and photo albums and the week-old baby and stayed with us for a few days. In the latter part of the Occupation, her husband joined the guerrillas and Eden came to live with us permanently.

Lina came later. Her stringiness had blossomed into a willowy kind of slenderness and she had her mother's knack for housekeeping. But she was of a nervous temperament. Continually, she wove "Macrame" bags of abaca twine in readiness for the day when we would be fleeing the bombs. She had also fashioned a wide inner garment belt of unbleached cotton, with numerous secret pockets.

III

My brother's room was the largest in the house, it was the size of the sala and the dining room together because in the good old days it had been a billiard room. It led out to an *azotea* and had a piano in it. His friends, Celso, Paquito and Nonong were always in Raul's room for they were trying to put out an ambitious book of poems. Celso's father had an old printing press, rusty from disuse, and they lugged it up to the room and were always tinkering with it, trying to make it work. Boni offered them a price for the scrap metal, and they threw an avalanche of books at him.

The piano had been won by an uncle of Nonong who was timbre-deaf from a raffle. This uncle was so timbre-deaf in fact that the only tune he could tell from another was the National Anthem because everyone stood up when it was played. All he had to spend for was the ticket and the transportation, and on Nonong's birthday the beautiful second-hand Steinway was presented to him instead of the books he wanted. Nonong's room was too small for the piano, and so of course it ended up in Raul's room. Mother never objected to the boys lugging things into the house just as long as they never lugged things out.

Sometimes they stuck a candle in a bottle and my brother Raul read the Bible deep into the night. They called me their Muse and allowed me to listen to their poems for I had read Dickinson and Marlowe and of course that made me an authority, and besides I was always good for a plateful of cookies or to fetch an extra chair. Paquito could play "Stardust" on the Steinway and Celso could do a rib-splitting pantomime, but best of all I liked Nonong although he couldn't do anything. Nonong gave me a Ticonderoga pencil he had saved all the way from before the war—it was stuck on a painted card where you could read your fortune. On Christmas I gave him a handkerchief embroidered with his initials in blue thread.

Nonong was always trying to make an intellectual out of me. The few books I read— *Les Miserables*, *Rashomon*, *Graustark* and *Inside Africa*—were all from him. I ransacked by father's trunk of books for something to present him in return and came up with the fourth volume of the *Encyclopaedia Britannica*, from *John the Baptist* to *Leghorn*.

I have read a lot of authors, Nonong used to say teasing me, but best of anything I've read I like the *Encyclopaedia Britannica*, from *John the Baptist* to *Leghorn*.

Once, after a visit to a friend's house, Raul couldn't fetch me and my mother telephoned, Don't go home alone, Nonong is here, I will send him over to fetch you. We walked down the avenue laughing under the unlighted street lamps, the carretelas and tricycles zigzagging past us.

Let's drop by your office, Nonong, I said, so you can get the book you promised to lend me.

All right, Nonong said, although there's not much print left to read any more—the Bureau has inked out all the nice pages and covered the pictures.

That's all right, I said, flinging my arms in a bored gesture the way I had seen movie stars do. It's better than dying slowly of boredom.

Are you lonely, Victoria?

No I said defiantly, deep in my heart, lying, We walked.

We turned into the stairs of his office in R. Hidalgo over which was a sign in Japanese characters. The back of the building had been bombed out and no one had bothered to clear up the rubble. There was a blackout notice again that night and it was pitch dark in the building. We groped our way to the head of the stairs and into the room. There were five desks and Nonong's was the farthermost, under the electric fan. Kneeling, Nonong opened each drawer and ransacked its contents. It's here somewhere, he said.

I went out to the little balcony and stood looking down at the gradually emptying street. It was four days before Christmas. There were paper lanterns hanging at the windows of the houses but none of them was lighted, and they swayed, rustling drily in the cold wind. I was tired of the war. I wished Nonong would put his arms around me and kiss my mouth and always love me, but I knew that if he even as much as touched my hand I would slap him hard on the mouth and kick him on the shin and never speak to him again. He stood silently beside me and put his lean arms on the window sill, I could see the veins taut on them. Behind us, the darkness was absolute and complete.

What are your going to be after the war, Nonong?

Oh . . . a writer, I guess, or a bum or something.

Me, I'm going to buy a house on top of a hill and live there all my life alone.

Suppose someone falls in love with you?

Who's going to fall in love with me, silly?

I looked up at the stern profile etched in the dark, thin and beautiful and ascetic, like the face of Christ. Heavens, Nonong, I exclaimed. You look like God!

Don't be blasphemous, Victoria, where's your convent school breeding. He smiled. I've got the book now, let's go if you're ready.

We felt our way through the pitch-dark corridor to the stairs at the foot of which was the door in a well of smoky light.

We were the lost generation: My brother Raul and his friends were neither men nor boys, they were displaced persons without jobs and they roamed the streets restlessly in search of something useful to do. My father had started a business making oil lamps and the boys helped him in the mornings, cutting the glass and hammering open the tin cans and shaping them in the vise to fit the pattern. But their afternoons were empty. Nonong and I learned to lag behind after church and walk, nibbling roasted coconuts that tasted like chestnuts when we were together. Sometimes I went with the gang to the Farmacia de la Rosa where we could order real fresh milk ice cream. Mrs. de la Rosa told us her fresh milk came all the way from Pampanga every day and had to pass four sentries and that was why it was so expensive. Sometimes we went into a Tugo and Pugo stageshow to buy an hour's laughter, at other times we rented bicycles and rode to the very end of town where nobody knew us, peeping over the fences of Japanese garrisons with the flag of the Rising Sun fluttering over it.

One day I told my mother that Nonong was coming that afternoon and if I could ask him for supper. I slaved over a plateful of cassava cookies in front of a hot tin charcoal oven. Lina was the good cook but I disdained her help and advices. For supper we had fresh *tawilis* from Batangas, and a good piece of the ham that Mr. Solomon had made. We waited for an hour past suppertime and still Nonong had not come. When we finally did sit down for supper, nobody said anything except for Boni who, having arrived late, looked at the extra plate quizzically, opened his mouth and closed it again like a fish gasping for air.

It was raining when Nonong came, smelling of beer, three hours late and sorry. I had already put away the supper dishes and the cassava cookies I had sweated over all afternoon, and I was still angry. He sat on the large *kamagong* chair and I sat on the other *kamagong* chair opposite him with the vase of santan flowers between us. And then we looked at each other and stopped dead still. For we could feel each other's hearts and knew what was there, what had been growing for months without our knowledge and consent. And heavy with grief I said simply, I dreamt of you last night. You were sitting on a chair and I was on the floor hugging your

knees and I said I love you, and you said, That's all right you'll get over it.

He put out his fingers tentatively and stroked the back of my hand and I pulled it away. But in a minute we were touching again and I was crying into his palm and he said, Help me, I'm so unhappy. But after a while we heard Eden's slippers slapping on the floor of the dining room where she had gone to open a can of milk for the baby, and I told him to go away and never see me again.

On February 17, Nonong telephoned me. We talked a long time about this and that and many useless things. Then just before the Japanese cut off our line, I heard his voice at the other end say soft but clearly, Listen to this, Victoria, and remember: I-love-you. And that was the only time he ever said it.

IV

We had run to the church rotonda and even there the dug-outs were every place, you were lucky if you could find a place to dig. The house had burned down and Boni had gotten himself burned trying to save Mr. Solomon who had panicked and couldn't get himself out of his locked room. Father and Raul were carrying Boni in a blanket fashioned into a hammock. Lina and I walked together—she had on her belt in which were all her treasures, and the six string bags with clothes in them. I was carrying my favorite dress, a pillow and a bottle of precious water. Immediately behind us Eden walked, the two-month-old baby in her arms. Mother walked last of all, pale and tight-lipped, carrying the kettleful of rice she had boiled for the noonday meal, and the slices of roasted pork. From Taft you could see clear through to the seashore for all the buildings were charred and rutted. The Japanese had barricaded themselves in the Rizal Coliseum and you could hear the mortar shells go boom from there and boom again a mile away.

A trio of planes roared dangerously low. Shakily, Lina and I dived into a shelter where a Chinese consul and his family crouched, and bitterly, they reproached us for crowding them in the already cramped space. Mother had run into another hole and ran out screaming for there was in it a man with half his face shot off. Outside the shelter, we could hear Boni begging, Please don't leave me . . . We were scattered in all directions.

Somehow we found each other again. Papa's plan was to go south to Pasig to escape the mortar shells that were coming from the north. He and Raul took up Boni again and started to walk. Somewhere in the running, I had lost my shoes and was proceeding barefoot; I had also forgotten my favorite dress in the last dugout. Whenever the mortar shells dropped around us, we threw ourselves flat on the ground and covered our ears, but still we could hear the whistling and the unearthly screams of the people who had been hit. After one of the raids which lasted longer than usual, we burrowed out of the shelters to find Boni gone. Someone told us later that he had been seen crawling to Taft Avenue.

On our way to Pasig we scampered for safety into the old Avellana home, the only one standing in Malate. A Japanese sniper in a battered car was shooting at us and we went into the enclosed ruins, picking our way hurriedly over the wounded and the dead. Raul was the calmest of all. He had taken the kettle of rice from Mother and whenever he dived to the ground, a little of the rice spilled but he gathered it again, brushing the earth from the pork with invincible good humor. He had his rosary with him and never parted with it, he vowed that if nobody got hurt he would become a priest.

We entered the damaged cellar and found there a group of hysterical mestizas. One of them, Señora Bandana's daughter, a friend of Lina's, persuaded her that the place had been continuously machine-gunned and that they should transfer to a concrete garage nearby where the rest of the family were. Lina left with her. We were willing to take our chances and remained behind. We settled ourselves comfortably, taking small swallows of water from our bottle, but not one of us could eat.

The baby sucking at Eden's breast was drawing blood and Eden's tears were falling on its face. In a few moments Lina was back, alone. She was hysterical. The garage she and her friend had gone into had been hit by a grenade, and she had seen the whole Bandana family and her friend perish in it.

We ran without any sense of direction. Finally, we found a high concrete wall against which several galvanized iron sheets had fallen, forming a safe shelter, but everytime someone moved, the sheets clattered noisily, betraying our presence. The few remaining Japanese soldiers were desperate: with bayonets bared, they stalked the ruins, thirsting to run through anything that moved. Raul pillowed his head in his arms and snored like a baby. We heard a Japanese soldier patrolling nearby, his hobnailed boots crunching heavily on the rubble. Eden's baby began to whimper. Eden offered her breast but the baby refused it, for it could no longer give any nourishment. Keep him quiet, my mother hissed. The footsteps were growing fainter and then they stopped all together. We heard a revolver cock. Then the footsteps started again, tracing the same path outside our shelter. The baby was now whimpering in earnest. Beat its head with a bottle, somebody suggested. The bottle was thrust into Papa's hand. He raised his hands for the blow and brought them down limply, he had a weak stomach. He next tried to strangle the tiny neck but his fingers turned weak and rubbery. The soldier was almost upon us. Luckily, the baby quieted for a moment.

Only when the footsteps receded could we talk. Papa said, Eden, go away with your child and save us, and maybe you too can be saved elsewhere. Eden crept out slowly, making an infernal racket with the sheets. In a moment she was crawling back. Wordlessly, she turned over the baby to Papa like an offering. The Japanese was returning. Lina cursed, restlessly she paced back and forth, standing up and sitting down. I've got it! she cried, Let me . . . She took the pillow I had been carrying all this time and put it on the baby's face. Then she sat on it, hard. The mother stared dumbly at the earth, her hands dangling between her legs. There was a struggle under the pillow and a smothered whimper. Slowly, Lina got up, biting her nails. She became hysterical and Papa had to hit her across the mouth. Eden took the dead baby and began rocking it to sleep.

We slept from exhaustion. The crunching footsteps had disappeared. The moon rose bright and clear, like the promise of another time, and we could find our way out. A group pushing a wooden cart full of pots and pans and mats and bundles was coming towards us. The Americans are here, the father of the group we met said. They have gone over Santa Cruz bridge. Papa counted the heads. Boni was gone, Mr. Solomon was gone. We couldn't find Eden. We looked back to where we had come from and through the twisted steel buttresses of the ravished homes, we could see a lonely figure poking amid the debris.

She has probably gone back to bury the child, Mother said.

Let's go ahead then, Father said. She'll catch up with us.

Gregorio C. Brillantes

FAITH, LOVE, TIME, AND DR. LAZARO

From the upstairs veranda, Dr. Lazaro had a view of stars, the country darkness, the lights on the distant highway at the edge of town. The phonograph in the *sala* played Chopin—like a vast arrow controlled, made familiar, he had been wont to think. But as he sat there, his lean frame in the habitual slack repose he took after supper, and stared at the plains of night that had evoked gentle images and even a kind of peace (in the end, sweet and invincible oblivion), Dr. Lazaro remembered nothing, his mind lay untouched by any conscious thought, he was scarcely aware of the April heat; the patterns of music fell around him and dissolved swiftly, uncomprehended. It was as though indifference were an infection that had entered his blood; it was everywhere in his body. In the scattered light from the *sala* his angular face had a dusty, wasted quality; only his eyes contained life. He could have remained there all evening, unmoving, and buried, as it were, in a strange half-sleep, had his wife not come to tell him he was wanted on the phone.

Gradually his mind stirred, focused; as he rose from the chair he recognized the somber passage in the sonata that, curiously, made him think of ancient monuments, faded stone walls, a greyness. The brain filed away an image; an arrangement of sounds released it ... He switched off the phonograph, sup-pressed an impatient quiver in his throat as he reached for the phone: everyone had a claim on his time. He thought: why not the younger ones for a change? He had spent a long day at the provincial hospital.

The man was calling from a service station outside the town—the station after the agricultural high school, and before the San Miguel bridge, the man added rather need-lessly, in a voice at once frantic yet oddly subdued and courteous. Dr. Lazaro had heard it countless times, in the corridors of the hospital, in waiting rooms: the perpetual awkward misery. He was Pedro Esteban, the brother of the doctor's tenant in Nambalan, said the voice, trying to make itself less sudden and remote.

But the connection was faulty, there was a humming in the the wires, as though darkness had added to the distance between the house in the town and the station beyond the summer fields. Dr. Lazaro could barely catch the severed phrases. The man's week-old child had a high fever, a bluish skin; its mouth would not open to suckle. They could not take the baby to the *poblacion*, they would not dare move it; its body turned rigid when touched. If the doctor would consent to come at so late an hour, Esteban would wait for him at the station. If the doctor would be so kind. . . .

Tetanus of the new-born: that was elementary, and most likely it was also hopeless, a waste of time. Dr. Lazaro said yes, he would be there; he had committed himself to that answer, long ago; duty had taken the place of an exhausted compassion. The carelessness of the poor, the infected blankets, the toxin moving toward the heart; they were casual scribbled items of a clinical report. But outside the grilled windows, the night suddenly seemed alive and waiting. He had no choice left now but action: It was the only certitude—he sometimes reminded himself—even if it should prove futile, before the descent into nothingness.

His wife looked up from her needles and twine, under the shaded lamp of the bedroom; she had finished the pullover for the grandchild in Baguio and had begun work, he noted, on another of those altar vestments for the parish church. Religion and her grandchild certainly kept her busy. . . . She looked at him, not so much to inquire as to be spoken to: a large and placid woman.

"Shouldn't have let the driver go home so early," Dr. Lazaro said. "They had to wait till now to call . . . Child's probably dead. . . ."

"Ben can drive for you."

"Hardly see that boy around the house. Seems to be taking his vacation both from home and school."

"He's downstairs," his wife said.

Dr. Lazaro put on a fresh shirt, buttoned it with tense abrupt motions. "I thought he'd gone out again . . . Who's that girl he's been seeing? . . . It's not just warm, it's hot. You should've stayed on in Baguio . . . There's disease, suffering, because Adam ate the apple. They must have an answer to everything . . ." He paused at the door, as though for the echo of his words.

Mrs. Lazaro had resumed her knitting; in the circle of yellow light, her head bowed, she seemed absorbed in some contemplative prayer. But her silences had ceased to disturb him, like the plaster saints she kept in the room, in their cases of glass, or that air she wore of conspiracy, when she left with Ben for Mass in the mornings. Dr. Lazaro would ramble about miracle drugs, politics, music, the common sense of his unbelief, unrelated things strung together in a monologue; he posed questions, supplied his own answers; and she would merely nod, with an occasional "Yes?" and "Is that so?" and something like a shadow of anxiety in her gaze.

He hurried down the curving stairs, under the votive lamps of the Sacred Heart. Ben lay sprawled on the sofa, in the front parlor, engrossed in a book, one leg propped against the back cushions. "Come along, we're going somewhere," Dr. Lazaro said, and went into the clinic for his medical bag. He added a vial of penstrep, an ampule of caffeine to the satchel's contents; rechecked the bag before closing it; the catgut would last just one more patient. One can only cure, and know nothing beyond one's work . . . There had been the man, today, in the hospital: the cancer pain no longer helped by the doses of morphine; the patient's eyes flickering their despair in the eroded face. Dr. Lazaro brushed aside the stray vision as he strode out of the whitewashed room; he was back in his element among syringes, steel instruments, quick decisions, and it gave him a sort of blunt energy.

"I'll drive, Pa?" Ben followed him through the kitchen, where the maids were ironing the week's wash, gossiping, and out to the yard, the dimness of the single bulb under the eaves. The boy pushed back the folding doors of the garage and slid behind the wheel.

"Somebody's waiting at the gas station near San Miguel. You know the place?"

"Sure," Ben said.

The engine sputtered briefly and stopped. "Battery's weak," Dr. Lazaro said. "Try it without the lights," and he smelled the gasoline overflow as the old Pontiac finally lurched around the house and through the trellised gate, its front beams sweeping over the dry dusty street.

―――――

But he's all right. Dr. Lazaro thought as they swung smoothly into the main avenue of the town, past the church and the plaza, the kiosko bare for once in a season of fiestas, the lamp posts shining on the quiet square. They did not speak; he could sense his son's concentration on the road, and he noted, with a tentative amusement, the intense way the boy sat behind the wheel, his eagerness to be of help. They passed the drab frame-houses behind the market place, and the capitol building on its landscaped hill, the gears shifting easily as they went over the rail tracks that crossed the last asphalted section of the main street.

Then the road was pebbled and uneven, the car bucking slightly; and they were speeding between open fields, a succession of narrow wooden bridges breaking the crunching drive of the wheels. Dr. Lazaro gazed at the wide darkness around them, the shapes of trees and bushes hurling toward them and sliding away, and he saw the stars, nearer now, they seemed, moving with the car. He thought of light years, black space, infinite distances; in the unmeasured universe, man's life flared briefly and was gone, traceless in the void. He turned away from the emptiness. He said: "You seem to have had a lot of practice, Ben."

"A lot of what, Pa?"

"The way you drive. Very professional."

In the glow of the dashboard lights, the boy's face relaxed, smiled. "*Tio* Cesar let me use his car in Manila. Special occasions."

"No reckless speeding now," Dr. Lazaro said. "Some fellows think it's smart. Gives them a thrill. Don't be like that."

"No, I won't, Pa. I just like to drive and go places, that's all."

Dr. Lazaro watched the young face intent on the road, a cowlick over the forehead, the small curve of the nose, his own face before he left to study in another country, a young student full of illusions, a lifetime ago; long before the loss of faith, God turning abstract, unknowable, and everywhere, it seemed to him, those senseless accidents of pain. He felt a need to define unspoken things, to come closer somehow to the last of his sons; one of these days, before the boy's vacation was over,

they might go on a picnic together, a trip to the farm; a special day for the two of them— father and son, as well as friends. In the two years Ben had been away in college, they had written a few brief, almost formal letters to each other: your money is on the way, study hard, these are the best years. . . .

Time was moving toward them, was swirling around and rushing away, and it seemed Dr. Lazaro could almost hear its hollow receding roar; and discovering his son's profile against the flowing darkness, he had a thirst to speak. He could not find what it was he meant to say.

═══

The agricultural school buildings came up in the headlights and glided back into blurred shapes behind a fence.

"What was that book you were reading, Ben?"

"Biography," the boy said.

"Statesman? Scientist maybe?"

"It's about a guy who became a monk."

"That your summer reading?" Dr. Lazaro asked with a small laugh, half mockery, half affection. "You're getting to be a regular saint like your mother."

"It's an interesting book," Ben said.

"I can imagine . . ." He dropped the bantering tone. "I suppose you'll go on to medicine after your A.B.?"

"I don't know yet, Pa."

Tiny moths like blown bits of paper flew toward the windshield and funneled away above them. "You don't have to be a country doctor like me, Ben. You could build up a good practice in the city. Specialize in cancer, maybe, or neuro-surgery, and join a good hospital." It was like trying to recall some rare happiness, in the car, in the shifting darkness.

"I've been thinking about it," Ben said. "It's a vocation, a great one. Being able to really help people, I mean."

"You've done well in math, haven't you?"

"Well enough, I guess," Ben said.

"Engineering is a fine course too," Dr. Lazaro said. "There'll be lots of room for engineers. Far too many lawyers and sales- men. Now if your brother—" He closed his eyes, erasing the slashed wrists, part of the future dead in a boarding-house room, the landlady whimpering. "He was such a nice boy, doctor, your son..." Sorrow lay in ambush among the years.

"I have all summer to think about it." Ben said.

"There's no hurry," Dr. Lazaro said. What was it he had wanted to say? Something about knowing each other, about sharing; no, it was not that at all....

The station appeared as they coasted down the incline of a low hill, its flourescent lights the only brightness on the plain before them, on the road that led farther into deeper darkness. A freight truck was taking on a load of gasoline as they drove up the concrete apron and stopped beside the station shed.

A short barefoot man in a patchwork shirt shuffled forward to meet them. "I am Esteban, doctor," the man said, his voice faint and hoarse, almost inaudible, and he bowed slightly with a careful politeness. He stood blinking, looking up at the doctor, who had taken his bag and flashlight from the car. In the windless space, Dr. Lazaro could hear Esteban's labored breathing, the clank of the metal nozzle as the attendant replaced it in the pump; the men in the truck stared at them curiously.

Esteban said, pointing at the darkness beyond the road: "We will have to go through those fields, doctor, then cross the river." The apology for yet one more imposi- tion was a wounded look in his eyes. He added, in his subdued voice: "It's not very far..." Ben had spoken to the attendants and was locking the car.

The truck rumbled and moved ponderously onto the road, its throb strong and then fading into the warm night stillness.

"Lead the way," Dr. Lazaro said, handling Esteban the flashlight.

They crossed the road, to a cleft in the embankment that bordered the fields. Dr. Lazaro was sweating now in the dry heat; following the swinging ball of the flashlight beam, surrounded by the stifling night, he felt he was being dragged, helplessly, toward some vast and complicated error; a meaning- less ceremony. Somewhere to his left rose a flapping of wings, a bird cried among unseen leaves; they walked swiftly, and there was only the sound of silence, the constant whir of crickets, and the whisper of their feet on the path between the stubble fields.

With the boy close behind him, Dr. Lazaro followed Esteban down a clay slope to the slap and ripple of water in the darkness. The flashlight showed a *bangka'* drawn up at the river's edge; Esteban waded waist-deep into the water, holding the boat steady as Dr. Lazaro and Ben stepped on board. In the darkness, with the opposite bank like the far rise of an island, Dr. Lazaro had a moment's tremor of fear as the boat slid out over the black waters; below prowled the deadly currents; to drown here in the depths of night... But it took less than a minute to cross the river; "We're here, doctor," Esteban said, and they padded up a stretch of sand to a clump of trees; a dog started to bark, the shadows of a kerosene lamp wavered at a window.

Unsteady on the steep ladder, Dr. Lazaro entered the cave of Esteban's hut. The single room containted the odors he often encoun- tered but had remained alien to, stirring an impersonal disgust: the sourish decay, the smells of the unaired sick. An old man greeted him, lisping incoherently; a woman, the grand- mother, sat crouched in a corner, beneath a framed print of the Mother of Perpetual Help; a boy, about ten, slept on, sprawled on a mat. Esteban's wife, pale and thin, lay on the floor with the sick child beside her. Motionless, its tiny blue-tinged face drawn away from its chest in a fixed wrinkled grimace, the infant seemed to be straining to express some terrible ancient wisdom.

Dr. Lazaro made a cursory check—skin dry, turning cold; breathing shallow; heartbeat fast and irregular. And in that moment, only the child existed before him; only the child and his own mind probing now like a hard gleaning instrument; how strange that it should still live, his mind said, as it considered the spark that persisted within the rigid and tortured body. He was alone with the child, his whole being focused on it, in those intense minutes shaped into a habit now by so many similar instances: his physican's knowledge trying to keep the heart beating, life rising again.

Dr. Lazaro removed the blankets that bundled the child and injected a whole ampule to check the tonic spasms, the needle piercing neatly into the sparse flesh; he broke another ampule, with deft precise movements, and emptied the syringe, while the infant lay stiff as wood beneath his hands. He wiped off the sweat running into his eyes, then holding the rigid body with one hand, he tried to draw air into the faltering lungs, pressing and releasing the chest; but even as he worked to rescue the child, the bluish color of its face began to turn grey.

Dr. Lazaro rose from his crouch on the floor, a cramped ache in his shoulders, his mouth dry. The lamplight glistened on his pale hollow face as he confronted the room again, the stale heat, the poverty. Esteban met his gaze; all their eyes were upon him, Ben at the door, the old man, the woman in the corner, and Esteban's wife, in the trembling shadows.

Esteban said: "Doctor...."

He shook his head, and replaced the syringe case in his bag, slowly and deliberately, and fastened the clasp. There was a murmuring behind him, a rustle across the bamboo floor, and when he turned, Ben was kneeling beside the child. And he watched, with a tired detached surprise, the boy pour a trickle of water from a coconut shell on the infant's brow. He caught the words half-whispered in the quietness: "...in the name of the Father...Son...the Holy Ghost...."

The shadows flapped on the walls, the lamplight quivering before it settled into a slender flame. By the river, dogs were barking. Dr. Lazaro glanced at his watch; it was close to midnight. Ben stood over the child, the coconut shell in his hands, as though wondering what next to do with it, until he saw his father nod for them to go.

"Doctor, tell us—" Esteban clutched at his arm.

"I did everything," Dr. Lazaro said. "It's too late—" He gestured vaguely, with a dull resentment; by some implicit relationship, he was also responsible, for the misery in the room, the hopelessness. "There's nothing more I can do, Esteban," he said. He thought with a flick of anger: Soon the child will be out of it, you ought to be grateful. Esteban's wife began to cry, a weak smothered gasping, and the old woman was comforting her—"It is the will of God, my daughter...."

In the yard, Esteban pressed carefully folded bills into the doctor's hands; the limp, tattered feel of the money was part of the futile journey. "I know this is not enough, doctor," Esteban said. "As you can see we are very poor...I shall bring you fruit, chicken, someday...."

A late moon had risen, edging over the tops of the trees, and in the faint wash of its light, Esteban guided them back to the boat. A glimmering rippled on the surface of the water as they paddled across; the white moonlight spread in the sky, and a sudden wind sprang rain-like and was lost in the trees massed on the river bank.

"I cannot thank you enough, doctor," Esteban said. "You have been very kind to come this far, at this hour."

They stood on the clay bank, in the moon-shadows beside the gleaming water. Dr. Lazaro said: "You better go back now, Esteban. We can find the way back to the road. The trail is just over there, isn't it?" He wanted to be rid of the man, to be away from the shy humble voice, the prolonged wretchedness.

"I shall be grateful always, doctor," Esteban said. "And to your son, too. God go with you." He was a faceless voice withdrawing in the shadows, a cipher in the shabby crowds that came to town on market days.

"Let's go, Ben," Dr. Lazaro said.

They took the path back across the field;

around them the moonlight had transformed the landscape, revealing a gentle, more familiar dimension, a luminous haze upon the trees stirring with a growing wind; and the heat of the night had passed, a coolness was falling from the deep sky. Unhurried, his pace no more than a casual stroll, Dr. Lazaro felt the oppression of the night begin to lift from him; an emotionless calm returned to his mind. The sparrow does not fall without the Father's leave, he mused at the sky, but it falls just the same. But to what end are the sufferings of a child? The crickets chirped peacefully in the moon-pale darkness beneath the trees.

"You baptized the child, didn't you, Ben?"

"Yes, Pa." The boy kept in step beside him.

He used to believe in it, too, the power of the Holy Spirit washing away original sin, the purified soul made heir of heaven. He could still remember fragments of his boyhood faith, as one might remember an improbable and long-discarded dream.

"Lay baptism, isn't that the name for it?"

"Yes," Ben said. "I asked the father. The baby hadn't been baptized." He added as they came to the embankment that separated the field from the road: "They were waiting for it to get well."

A fine gesture; it proved the boy had presence of mind, convictions, but what else? The world will teach him his greatest lessons.

=====

The station had closed, with only the canopy light and the globed neon sign left burning. A steady wind was blowing now across the fields, the moonlit plains.

He saw Ben stifle a yawn. "I'll do the driving," Dr. Lazaro said.

His eyes were not what they used to be, and he drove leaning forward, his hands tight on the wheel. He began to sweat again, and the empty road and the lateness and the memory of Esteban and of the child dying before morning in the cramped lamplit room fused into a tired melancholy. He started to think of his other son, the one whom he had lost.

He said, seeking conversation, "If other people carried on like you, Ben, the priests would be run out of business."

The boy sat beside him, his face averted, not answering.

"Now, you'll have an angel praying for you in heaven," Dr. Lazaro said, teasing, trying to create an easy mood between them. "What if you hadn't baptized the baby and it died? What would happen to it then?"

"It won't see God," Ben said.

"But isn't that unfair?" It was like a riddle, trivial but diverting. "Just because—"

"Maybe God has another remedy," Ben said. "I don't know. But the Church says—"

He could sense the boy groping for the tremendous answers. "The Church teaches, the Church says..." God: Christ: the communion of saints: Dr. Lazaro found himself wondering again at the world of novenas and candles, where bread and wine became the flesh and blood of the Lord, and a woman bathed in light appeared before children, and mortal men spoke of eternal life, the vision of God, the body's resurrection at the end of time. It was like a country from which he was barred; no matter—the customs, the geography didn't appeal to him. But in the car suddenly, driving through the night, he was aware of an obscure disappointment, a subtle pressure around his heart, as though he had been deprived of a certain joy....

A bus roared around a hill toward them, its lights blinding him, and he pulled to the side of the road, braking involuntarily as a billow of dust swept over the car. He had not closed the window on his side, and the flung dust poured in, the thick brittle powder almost choking him, making him cough, his eyes smarting, before he could shield his face with his hands. In the headlights the dust sifted down and when the air was clear again, Dr. Lazaro, swallowing a taste of earth, of darkness, maneuvered the car back onto the road, his arms numb and exhausted. He drove the last half mile to town in silence, his mind registering nothing but the grit of dust in his mouth and the empty road unwinding swiftly before him.

They reached the sleeping town, the desolate streets, the plaza empty in the moonlight, and the huddled shapes of houses, the old houses that Dr. Lazaro had always known. How many nights had he driven home like this through the quiet town, with a man's life ended behind him, or a child crying newly risen from the womb; and a sense of constant motion, of change, of the days moving swiftly toward an immense revelation touched him once more, briefly, and still he could not find the words. He turned the last corner, then steered the car down the graveled driveway to the garage, while Ben closed the gate. Dr. Lazaro sat there a moment, in the stillness, resting his eyes, conscious of the measured beating of his heart, and breathing a scent of dust that lingered on his clothes, his skin, before he finally went around the tower of the water-tank to the front yard where Ben stood waiting.

With unaccustomed tenderness he placed a hand on Ben's shoulder as they turned toward the cement-walled house. They had gone on a trip; they had come home safely together. He felt closer to the boy than he had ever been in years.

"Sorry for keeping you up this late," Dr. Lazaro said.

"It's all right, Pa."

"Some night, huh, Ben? What you did back in that barrio—" there was just the slightest patronage in his tone—"Your mother will love to hear about it."

He shook the boy beside him gently. "Reverend Father Ben Lazaro." The impulse of uncertain humor—it was part of the comradeship. He chuckled drowsily: "Father Lazaro, what must I do to gain eternal life?"

As he slid the door open on the vault of darkness, the familiar depths of the house, it came to Dr. Lazaro faintly in the late night that for certain things, like love, there was only so much time. But the glimmer was lost instantly, buried in the mist of indifference and sleep rising now in his brain.

Rony V. Diaz

DEATH IN A SAWMILL

You can cleave a rock with it. It is the iron truth. That was not an accident. That was a murder. Yes, a murder. That impotent bastard, Rustico, murdered Rey.

You have seen the chain that holds logs on a carriage in place. Well, that chain is controlled by a lever which is out of the way and unless that lever is released, the chain cannot whip out like a crocodile's and hurl a man to the wheeling circular saw.

I was down at our sawmill last summer to hunt. As soon as school was out, I took a bus for Lemery where I boarded a sailboat for Abra de Ilog. Inong met me at the pier with one of the trucks of the sawmill and took me down. The brazen heat of summer writhed on the yard of the sawmill which was packed hard with red sawdust.

My father met me at the door of the canteen. He took my bags and led me in. I shouldered my sheathed carbine and followed. The canteen was a large framehouse made of unplaned planks. My father's room was behind the big, barred store where the laborers of the sawmill bought their supplies. The rought walls of the small room looked like stiffened pelts.

My father deposited my bags on a cot and then turned to me. "I've asked the assistant sawyer, Rey Olbes, to guide you."

The machines of the sawmill were dead. Only the slow, ruthless grinding of the cables of the winches could be heard.

"No work today?" I asked my father.

"A new batch of logs arrived from the interior and the men are arranging them for sawing."

Then a steam whistle blew.

"They are ready to saw," my father explained.

The steam machine started and built solid walls of sound that crashed against the framehouse. Then I heard the saw bite into one of the logs. Its locust-like trill spangled the air.

"You'll get used to the noise," my father said. "I've some things to attend to. I'll see you at lunch time." He turned about and walked out of the room, shutting the door after him.

I lay on the cot with my clothes on and listened to the pounding of the steam engine and the taut trill of the circular saw. After a while I dozed off.

After lunch, I walked out of the canteen and crossed the yard to the engine house. It was nothing more than a roof over an aghast collection of soot-blackened, mud-plastered balky engines. Every inch of ground was covered with sour-smelling sawdust. The steam engine had stopped but two naked men were still stoking the furnace of the boilers with kerts and cracked slabs. Their bodies shone with sweat. I skirted the boiler and went past the cranes, tractors, and trucks to the south end of the sawmill. A deep lateral pit, filled with kerts, flitches, and rejects, isolated like a moat the sawmill from the jungle. Near the pit, I saw Rey. He was sitting on a log deck. When he saw me, he got up and walked straight to me.

"Are you Rustico?" I asked.

"No, I'm Rey Olbes," he answered.

"I'm Eddie," I said; "my father sent me."

He was tall, a sunblackened young man. He had an unusually long neck and his head was pushed forward like a horse's. His skin was as grainy as moist whetstone. He stooped and picked up a canter and stuck it on the ground and leaned on it. Then he switched his head like a stallion to shake back into place a damp lock of hair that had fallen over his left eye. His manner was easy and deliberate.

"Your father told me you wanted to go hunting," he said slowly, his chin resting in the groove of his hands folded on the butt end of the canter. "Tomorrow is Sunday. Would you like to hunt tomorrow?"

"Yes, we can hunt tomorrow."

Inside the engine shed the heat curled like live steam. It swathed my body like a skirt. "It's hot here," I said. "Do you always stay here after work?"

"No, not always."

Then I saw a woman emerge from behind one of the cranes. She was wearing gray silk dress. She walked toward us rapidly.

"Rey!" she bugled.

Rey dropped the canter and turned swiftly about. The woman's dress clung damply to her body. She was fair; her lips were feverish and she had a shock of black electric hair.

She faced Rey. "Have you seen Rustico?"

"No." Rey answered. There was a small fang of frenzy in his voice.

"Tonight?" the woman asked.

Rey glanced at me and then looked at the woman. He reverted to his slow, deliberate manner as he said: "Dida, this is Eddie. The son of the boss."

Dida stared at me with frantic eyes. She said nothing.

"He's a hunter too," Rey continued.

Then I saw a man striding toward us. He walked hunched, his arms working like the claws of a crab. Tiny wings of sawdust formed around his heels. He was a small squat man, muscle-bound and graceless. He came to us and looked around angrily. He faced the woman and barked: "Go home, Dida."

"I was looking for you, Rustico," Dida remonstrated.

"Go home!" he commanded hoarsely.

Dida turned around, sulking, and walked away. She disappeared behind the boilers and the furnace that rose in the shed like enormous black tumors. Rustico set himself squarely like a boxer before Rey and demanded almost in a whisper. "Why don't you keep away from her?"

Rey looked at him coldly and answered mockingly: "You have found a fertile *kaingin.* Why don't you start planting?"

"Why you insolent son of the mother of whores!" Rustico screamed. He reached down to the ground for the canter and poised it before Rey like a harpoon. I bounded forward and grappled with Rustico. He pushed me. I sank to the sawdust; Rustico leapt forward to hit me on the jaw. Rey held him.

"Keep calm," Rey shouted. "This is the son of Mang Pepe."

Rey released him and Rustico dropped his arms to his side. He looked suddenly very tired. He continued to stare at me with eyes that reflected yellow flecks of light. I got up slowly. What a bastard, I thought. Rustico wheeled about and strode to the whistle box. He opened it and tugged at the cord. The steam whistle screamed like a stuck pig.

"All right, men," he yelled. "It's time. Load the skids and let us start working."

Rey picked up his canter and walked toward the log carriage. Rustico was supervising the loading of the log deck. He was as precise and stiff as a derrick as he switched levers and pulled clamps. He sparked like a starter and the monstrous conglomeration of boilers, furnaces, steam machines, cranes, and winches came alive. I walked away.

When I reached the door of the canteen, I

heard the teeth of the circular saw swarm into a log like a flight of locusts.

The next day Rey, carrying a light rifle, came to the canteen. He pushed open the door with his foot and entered the barred room. He stood near my father's table. His eyes shifted warily. Then he looked at me and said: "Get ready."

"I did not bring birdshot," I said.

"I thought you wanted to go after deer?" he asked.

I was surprised because I knew that here deer was hunted only at night, with headlamps and buckshot. The shaft of the lamps always impaled a deer on the black wall of night and the hunter could pick it off easily.

"Now? This morning?" I asked.

"Why not? We are not going after spirits."

"All right. You are the guide." I dragged the gun bag from under the cot and unsheathed my carbine. I rammed the magazine full with shells, pushed it in, and got up. "Let's go."

We entered the forest from the west end of the sawmill and followed a wide tractor path to a long station about four kilometres from the sawmill. The forest was alive with the palaver of monkeys, the call of the birds and the whack of the wind. Then we struck left uphill and climbed steadily for about an hour. The trail clambered up the brush. At the top of the rise, the trail turned at an angle and we moved across the shoulder of an ipilipil ridge.

Rey walked rapidly and evenly, his head pushed forward, until we reached the drop of the trail. I looked down into a valley walled in on sides by cliffs that showed red and bluegray gashes. Streaks of brown and green were planed across the valley. Islands of dark-green shrubs rose above the level rush of yellow-green grass. On the left side of the valley, a small river fed clay-red water to a grove of trees. At the north end, the valley flattened and the sky dropped low, filling the valley with white light and making it look like the open mouth of the jungle, sucking at one of the hot, white, impalpable breasts of the sun. We descended into the valley.

Rey's manner changed. He became tense.

He walked slowly, half-crouched, his eyes searching the ground. He examined every mound, bush, and rock. Once he stopped; he bent and picked up a small rock. The rock had been recently displaced. He raised his hand to feel the wind and then he backtracked for several yards and crept diagonally to a small clump of brush. I followed behind him.

"Urine," he said. The ground near his feet was wet. "Work in a cartridge," he told me, "and follow as noiselessly as possible." I pulled back the bolt of my rifle.

We crept on half-bent knees toward a grove of trees. Rey, carrying his rifle in the crook of his arm, was swaying gently like a weather vane. I looked around. I saw nothing save the trees that rose to the sky like smoke and the tall grass that swirled with the breeze. Rey was intent.

Then he stopped and stiffened.

"Remove the safety," he whispered. I heard the safety of Rey's rifle click off. I pushed mine off.

"There is your deer," he said in a low voice. We were still crouched. "Near the base of that tree with a dead branch. Only its head was visible but it should be somewhere near that dry patch of leaves. Shoot through that. Do not move until I tell you to do so."

I did not see the deer until it moved. It turned its head toward us. Its antlers were as brown as the dead branch of the tree. The deer regarded us for a long time. Then it dropped its head and quickly raised it again. We did not move. The deer, reassured, stepped, diffidently out of the shadows.

"Now!" Rey said, falling to his knees. The deer stopped, looked at us, its antlers scuffling against the leaves. I raised my rifle and fired. The deer went high in the air. Then, dripping his head, it crashed through the trees and vanished.

"Your aim was too high," he told me quietly. He was still on his knees. "Too high," he said softly. "But you got him."

He stood up slowly, pushed down the safety of his rifle and walked toward the grove of low trees.

We found the deer. It was stretched out on the ground. Its neck was arched upward as though it had tried to raise its body with its head after the bullet had ripped a hump of flesh off its back. Blood had spread like a fan around its head. Rey sat down on the ground and dug out of his pocket a small knife. He cut an incision at the base of the deer's neck. He stood and picked the deer up by its hind legs. Blood spurted out of the cut vein.

"You got your deer," he said. "Let's turn back."

Rey hauled the deer up and carried it around his neck like a yoke.

I felt my nerves tingle with triumph. The earth was soaking up the blood slowly. I had a crazy urge to wash my body with the blood. I felt that it would seep into my body and temper my spirit now forging hot with victory. I looked at Rey. He was smiling at me. In a strained voice I said: I"ll try to do this alone."

"You'll learn," he said. "The forest will surely outlive you."

We walked out the valley.

After about an hour's walk, we came to a *kaingin*. Rey was sweating. We crossed the charred ground. At the end of the *kaingin*, Rey stopped. He turned around. The deer had stiffened on his shoulders.

"This used to be deer country," he said. We surveyed the black stumps and half-burned branches that lay strewn on the ground. The bare soil looked rusty.

"You know these parts very well, don't you?" I asked.

"I grew up here. I was a logger for your father before I became a sawyer."

His rifle slipped from his arm. I picked it up and carried it for him.

"It is the sawmill," Rey continued. "It is the sawmill that opened the forest. The sawmill has thinned the jungle miles around." I stared at him. He continued meditatively, veins showing on his long, powerful neck. "But I do not think they can tame the forest. Unless they can discover the seed of the wilderness and destroy it, this place is not yet done for."

"Don't you like your job in the sawmill?" I asked.

He shot a glance at me and grimaced. "I do not complain. You do not have to tell this to your father but Rustico is making my stay very trying. You saw what happened yesterday."

"Yes," I said. "What made him so mad?"

Rey did not answer. We crossed a gully and worked our way to the end of a dry river bed before he answered. The shale crumbled under our feet. The trees that grew along the bank of the river were caught by a net of vines. Rey, yoked by the deer, was now panting. Under a *kalumpit* tree he threw his burden down and sank to the ground.

"You know why?" he asked. "Because his wife is pregnant."

"Dida? So?"

"He's impotent."

The revelation struck me like a slap.

"And he suspects you," I asked tentatively, unsure now of my footing.

"He knows. Dida told him."

"Why doesn't he leave her then?" I said, trying to direct the talk away from Rey.

"He wouldn't! He'd chain Dida to keep her!" Rey flared.

I shut my mouth. It was noon when we reached the sawmill.

Late that afternoon we left to shoot fruit bats. Rey knew a place where we could shoot them as they flew off their roost. He had several tubes of birdshot and a shotgun.

It was almost eight o'clock when we returned. We followed the road to the saw-mill. The shacks of the laborers were built along the road. Near the motor pool, a low grass hut stood. We passed very close to this hut and we heard suppressed, angry voices. "That is Rustico's hut," Rey said.

I heard Rustico's voice. He sounded strangled. "I want you to drop that baby!" The words were spewed out like sand. "Let me go!" Dida screamed. I heard a table or a chair go, it crashed to the floor. "I'll kill you," Rustico threatened. "Do it then!" the yellow wings of light that had spouted from a kerosene lamp shook violently.

Rey quickened his steps. He was carrying a bunch of dead bats. One of the bats had dropped, its wings spread. It looked like a black ghoul on Rey's side.

The next morning, I heard from the men who were huddled near the door of the canteen that Dida ran away. She had hitched a ride to town on one of the trucks.

I was eating breakfast in the store with my father when Rustico entered. He approached my father carefully as though his feet hurt. Then he stood before us and looked meekly at my father. He was gray.

"Mang Pepe," he began very slowly, "I want to go to the town. I will be back this afternoon or early tomorrow morning."

"Sure," my father said. "Inong is driving a load of lumber to the pier. You go with him."

"Thank you," he said and left at once.

After breakfast my father called in Lino, the foreman. "Tell Rey to take charge of the sawing today. Rustico is going to town. We've to finish this batch. A new load is arriving this afternoon."

"Rey left early this morning," Lino said. "He said he will be back tomorrow morning."

"Devil's lightning!" my father fumed. "Why didn't he tell me! Why is everybody so anxious to go to town?"

"You were still asleep when he left, Mang Pepe," Lino said.

"These beggars are going to hold up our shipment this week!" my father flared. "Eddie," my father whirled to face me, "look for Rustico and tell him that he cannot leave until Rey returns. We've to finish all the devil's logs before all these lightning-struck beggars pack up and leave!"

I walked out of the canteen to look for Rustico, I searched all the trucks first and then the engine house. I found him sitting on the log carriage. He was shredding an unlighted cigarette.

"My father said he is sorry but you cannot leave until Rey comes back from the town. We have a lot of work to do here. A new load of logs is expected this afternoon," I spoke rapidly.

He got up on the carriage and leaned on the chain that held the log clamps. He acted tired.

"It is all right," he said. "I've plenty of time." He spat out a ragged stalk of spittle. "Plenty of time." I turned about to go but he called me back.

He looked at me for a long time and then asked: "You are Rey's friend. What has he been saying about?"

"Nothing much," I lied.

"Why?"

"Nothing much!" he screamed, jumping off the carriage. His dun face had become very red. "He told you about my wife, didn't he? He delights in telling that story to everybody." He seized a lever near the brake of the carriage and yanked it down. The chain lashed out and fell rattling to the floor.

Rustico tensed. He stared at the chain as though it were a dead snake. "Now look at that chain," he said very slowly.

He mounted the carriage again, kicked the clamps into place and pulled at the chain. The chain tightened. He cranked the lever up and locked it.

He was trembling as he unlocked the lever and pulled it down with both hands. The chain lashed out again like a crocodile tail.

"Just look at that chain," he mused.

Wilfrido D. Nolledo

RICE WINE

When Santiago saw her in the mirror, comb in hand, he knew it was time for him. It was time to leave the hut. For it was the time of the crescent moon, and if there were people he knew in the corner store, it was time for a cup.

Though his limbs were still numb, Santiago rose. He went to the basin with the fresh water and washed his face. His remaining life was measured: the uniform in the trunk; the medal under his pillow; the kiss of his daughter on the cheek. The day was made for waiting, and the night, for wine. Nothing was missing.

When he looked at her once more, she had put on her beige skirt, a sheath.

"Are you going out?" he asked, as was his wont.

"Yes, father," she replied automatically. There was a ribbon in her hair.

He went back to his cot near the window. The moon was out. The street shimmering below like a lake drifted evenly toward the mountains in the east while mad traffic droned into the dolorous hum of the beggars, kinsmen all, stretched in a column on the sidewalk, banging their pails, sleeping resignedly on the cold cement, yelling at God. From a distance, in a yard, the smell of rice fermenting in earthen jars oozed from the depths of the earth. Earlier, the sun had aged it into essence and at the rising of the moon, the

wind carried it, sweet, sourish, the dead aroma of beans—the wine of rice that the shriveled people on the sidewalk, drunk with its flavor, inhaled and swallowed greedily in their slumber.

Now Santiago leaned on the wall, trying not to look at her, trying not to ask her again.

"Where are you going after the piano lesson, Elena?" he asked.

"To my mother's grave," she said.

He turned to the moon, and sighed. In the old days, they had attended the *misa de gallo* under the sweet *dama de noche,* the scent sending them frolicking to the church in the *barrio* where already gathered the last flirtations of the fiesta. It was their own Binondo, though their prayers pleaded crosswise to the altar and to all the womenfolk that ever swayed in their *camisa.*

"How is the pupil doing in his lessons?"

"Father, he is only seven. He cannot even put sugar in his milk."

"That is a strange child—learning to play the piano at night."

"He plays in the sun all morning."

He sighed.

"What are they raising now?"

She took out a tube of lipstick and began to work on her lips.

"They are quiet tonight," she said, indicating the window where outside lay the world.

"If they are quiet, they are dead."

She was now pulling out her hair-pins.

"Is it not time for the corner store? I pressed your other *barò* this afternoon."

"In a moment."

"Perhaps De Palma will sing again," she said cheerfully.

Santiago grinned.

"It is a truth. He sings every night. There he will come, coughing, epileptic, climbing out of a fit, holding *sampaguitas* he has not sold, a guitar slung across his shoulder as though it were a hump on his back—a birthright. The songs he sings are straight out of the *kaingin,* like arrows from the vows of our beloved. Nobody understands us, we two. We are the irredeemable fragments of the veranda, reuniting on the pass, swimming in the ravine where the star apples fell from the siege and where only memory can hurt us. Sing, De Palma, old goat! There is new grass in every song."

"Is he still in good voice?"

"Cracking, but still there."

"And still ill."

"Ill? The man is dying, even as I am. Do you not know? He was the lamplighter of the Old Manila and he still cannot believe the new city has no more need of him."

"Poor old De Palma. Poor old warrior . . ."

Santiago wiped his forehead with the back of his arm.

"And Ruben?" This, her back to him.

"Ah, that one. He is a sponge. What are you doing to him, daughter? He works hard in the daytime and has school in the evening, but he comes to the corner store and reminisces with us. What has happened between you two?"

She stood up from the mirror.

"I have my pride," she snapped, combing her hair.

"Of course. That is what Ruben is trying to reach at the bottom of the cup. But I suppose the well runs deep."

She turned to him, eyes flashing.

"It is my life, father."

She made ready to leave, her things neatly arranged on the rattan table as they had been every night for a year now. On her ears, hung her only pair of earrings, ornaments of blue, none the less bluer than her way with them, for she wore everything elegantly, even the cheap leather belt, the high-heeled shoes, the purse she had bought in a fire sale. Once more arrayed for her evening, she loomed before him, erect, radiant, a product from the solicitude of the cracked mirror in the room—a jewel cast in nerve and mulatto. As Santiago studied her, wondering where the year had deposited itself, he realized that she was altered. When she spoke, she was not as passive as she had been before her change of clothes.

"Tell De Palma to sing a little louder that I may hear him, where I will be."

Santiago grimaced. "Do not worry. The wine will do that."

"The wine is a good guitar. Better than that wood he strums on."

"The wine understands."

"Yes. Well, I have to go."

"And is this why Ruben is so sad?"

"Please. Let us not speak of him. He is just a boy."

"He is drinking himself old before he is twenty."

"That is not my doing."

"How brave we all are."

"The wine is braver. Go to it, father. I am no comfort to you."

She lingered by his side, fidgeting, uncertain.

"Fetch your mother's umbrella," he commanded. "It might rain tonight."

"Yes. It always rains at night."

"I will light a candle while you are gone," he said, going to the cabinet where she kept their things.

She unhooked the red umbrella from its post.

"Father . . ."

"Yes, daughter?"

"Please. Don't lose The Revolution tonight."

Before he could answer, she had hurried down the stairway and he heard her footfalls on the gravel road. He settled back in the cot, listening to the injury of rice on the pavements, thinking of wine.

——————

De Palma was deep in his cups when Santiago, a medal conspicuous on his breast, arrived in the store. The old *sampaguita* vender was heavy with drink and oratory, aging with every sip. He cut a ridiculous figure on the bamboo bench as he imposed upon his wine-mates a visage of whiskers and a rambling, ranting talk of another century. The minor drunkards avoided him passionately, this ragged creature who lavished the small change he earned from his garlands on a morose old veteran who received the wine and returned the wildness. Illustrious, dazzling in their era, the twin patricians maintained, among the stevedores, a stern, traditional front.

"How now, my courier of Malolos? Still compiling the evils of the 10,000 pieces of silver from the battle?" De Palma taunted.

Santiago sneered. "I see the vintage is on your tongue already."

"Why not? It is my legacy."

"Speak with caution then. I am not well disposed."

"You have no spirit."

"Leave that to the wine."

"With edge, as always, my courier, my Malolos—lost to a congress in the bushes."

Santiago took the tin cup Fermin the proprietor offered him, gulping down the liquid hungrily, feeling it warm the pit of his stomach. He exhaled and licked the drops on his lips.

"They do not make wine like they used to, in my home town."

De Palma gurgled noisily. "They do not know how to age these days. These distilleries ... they are a crime."

They sat there, ("*los grandes*"), the *aficionados* of the Lost Republic, both flaming in their piety, burning the marble epitaphs, correcting history, fumbling, precise, rigid, restless, whole, divided: the future of the past.

"Remember how we used to read Carlyle?" sighed De Palma.

"Remember the Mayorca?" chorused Santiago.

"The *ayuntamiento?*"

"The Fort?"

"The mauser hidden in the mind?"

"The Treaty?"

"The Domecq?"

"The Zorilla?"

"The Pasig?"

"The Yanqui?"

"The carriages?"

"The Binondo?"

"The theater?"

"The opera?"

"The assignations?"

"The Cause?"

"The secret literature?"

"The parks?"

"The *puñal?*"

"The rogues?"

"The women of salt?"

"The fandango?"

De Palma sniffed, spanning his arms at the swelling sidewalk.

"Now watch the calamity spread like an epidemic over the rice terraces."

Now Santiago saw the mothers and their children filling the sidewalk, swaying in rhythm, swinging their baskets in the dust, their moan, one call only: rice! It was the talk and terror of the town; a topic boiled and fried or taken raw with a grain of salt. And even at the weddings, nobody ever threw it any more.

Santiago saw the embankment bear the weight of the line stretching from the fire hydrant to the granary and he heard the pedestrians talk about The Bomb.

"There was no bomb in our time, eh, *caballero?*" he said to his friend.

The flower man smiled patiently.

"But there has always been a bomb, Santiago. There will always be a bomb."

"Where is that Ruben?" Santiago protested, searching for an ally.

"You cannot change progress. That is the will of Our Father and the scientists."

"Someday, I shall free the people."

"Sit down, *caballero*. Drink your wine and let it happen. The Bomb will fall whatever you do. Ask the people there, living for their *ganta*. Ask the mothers. Ask the children. The Bomb is in their bellies. The Bomb is in the market. The Bomb is in the pawn shop."

"No!"

"Yes! The Bomb is God Who will not come."

"Have you abandoned the faith, too, *viejo?*"

"I am two months younger than you," complained De Palma.

"Do not change the subject, old man!"

"Faith?"

"That is what we fought for!"

"The Man was what we fought for."

"And is that not faith—was he not, is he not—religion?"

De Palma spat. "He whistles in the dark, incumbent in a hospital, mended by young doctors who exhaust their scholarships reviving the loneliness of the past. There he reigns in a wheelchair, waiting for *the day*, longing for the night. You and I, we have forfeited him. He is nothing but the weakness in my limbs and the whiteness of my hair."

"The greatness!"

"And the failure. They embalm him there; The Promise, sheltered, shuttered, analyzed, anesthetized; a relic in a museum that has forsaken its heritage. This"—and he pointed to the line on the asphalt—"is our heritage. This is what we fought for in the mountains: a retailer's bin that has squeezed the rice out of our land to bleed our people. Are you blind? Do you not see the hunger? Are you deaf? Do you not hear the thunder? And you sit there moaning about The Man whose blunder has led to this! Is this your grandeur?"

Santiago threw his cup away.

"Traitor!" he bellowed. "If The Man goes, every flower withers. Do you hear me, spawn of the *sampaguita?*"

De Palma glared at him.

"Man, why do we always quarrel?" boomed Santiago.

"Because that is all we have left, brother. We keep the dates accurate, the facts intact, though we destroy their meaning. The Man must suffer his mistake over and over and over, lest he vanish from our affection. Build him again, Santiago. Build him again. I thirst for *our day* once more when you drank from the brook where his gray mare stood like a dragon as he surveyed the forest range and traced a vision of the enemy in every acacia. Build him for me, *caballero*. He is my life too. They do not know him *there*; no one will ever know. But we do, we, the last chips of the monument; we know him. And it is a knowledge that is my breath."

A young man, lean and disheveled, suddenly clambered on the bamboo bench, scraping his shoes, flinging his books disdainfully on the dirty counter.

"You are late, Ruben," Santiago greeted gladly, delighted at this intrusion in the debate.

Ruben motioned cryptically to the proprietor who immediately poured wine in a large glass and gave it to the new arrival. The glass was full to the brim.

"Yesterday," the young man began hoarsely, "I presented my fraternity pin to Elena, and she would not accept it. I asked her why and she said she loved me like a brother."

De Palma howled. Santiago colored.

"I just hate everybody," Ruben said, sulking over his wine.

"Do you not love anyone?" Santiago asked irritably.

The young man guffawed.

"Look around you and see the inequality of love. Love your wife and she runs away with another man. Love your best friend and he was that *other man*. Love your industry and it retires you to the gutter. Love your dog and it bites you. Love your God and there is a flood."

Bristling, Santiago wagged an imperious finger.

"Love your son, and he grows up."

"Don't feel like Job. The prophets deserted the Bible long ago."

"Just because you are an underpaid clerk in the backroom of some terminal, does that give you the gall to dislocate the anatomy of this government?"

"The government?" Ruben hissed. "The government is a brat that cannot even feed the malnourished child outside the door. The government is blind when it cannot see the blind dying like flies in front of the Quiapo church. The government is lame when it cannot walk to the cripple on Avenida and lead him away. Not that I care for the masses, personally. But they must be removed from the wound."

"But do you not see, Ruben, that the wound is you?"

"Poetry! Three hundred years of losing our corn to The West and we celebrate a man and his two novels written in Europe. You cannot liberate the slave with a metaphor! So dance the *zarzuela*; I will take my rice in a mug, not in the harvest!"

"I do not know what you are talking about," Santiago mocked. "But in my time, there was Spain, there was The Treaty, there was The Man. And that was enough. In my heart, there is a statue of him so tall only my love can reach it; so soft only the guitar can speak to it. *Por Dios*, young man of today, you with your present that has no future, only journalism, you are trampling on the last petal of the garden. You are adding to the water when you should be turning the sea into the bridge of the armada! Oh, country that never was, that was to me, my name, my sword, my armor, my pendant and my memory, I am surrounded by absence! By a worship that has descended into a whore! By the voice, not of my *harana*, but of the jukebox! *Adiós . . .*"

De Palma applauded.

Santiago ignored him and continued addressing the sullen young man.

"I look at you and I drown in Candaba; I look at you and I see a crack in the mirror at Malolos where I held the reins of his horse and touched the tip of his saber. All this, desecrated in your face forever, a face I would never have fought for had the gypsies told me it was such I was fighting for."

A toothless wheeze issued from the flower man.

"Another cup, *patrón*," he rasped.

Still, Santiago raved, and the bench rattled with his wrath.

"When they captured him in Palanan, it was as though my own identity had stopped; reason stopped. There was no longer any island without The Man; without him, there was no longer anything, only turncoats who bartered their allegiances for a puff of occidental tobacco. We were not beaten; we were betrayed."

"*Arriba!*" De Palma hooted.

Santiago was undaunted. "Nowadays, all you see is the tattoo in everybody's eyes."

Ruben, piqued, toasted his glass.

"That is in effigy of all the things that could have been—the synthesis of illusion."

"Is that your poetry on the walls? The charcoal scrawlings that say BEWARE OF MAN?"

"Put on your spectacles, old man. That's nothing but a detour. The sign actually says BEWARE OF VICIOUS GOD."

The proprietor flung up his hands helplessly. "This could go on forever," he moaned.

"And it will!" snarled Santiago. "For such a race as you! For such a disgrace as you!"

The young man picked up his books.

"I think I'll attend Political Science after all."

But De Palma pulled him back.

"Stay," he mumbled drunkenly. "I want to sing to you."

"Lunatics!"

Both of them studied Santiago contemptuously. Unable to stand the sting, De Palma sprang up, confronting his friend toe to toe. Retaliating fiercely, his words were clear and they did not pronounce the wine.

"The Bomb is in that house where your Elena—she that your shrunken hag of a wife danced into life one summer—lies naked waiting for the possession of the world!"

"Hold your tongue, old man!" Santiago blurted.

"Naked in that tall house with a balcony, I tell you, and I should have told you but you are so stupid!"

Santiago slapped him across the mouth.

"My Elena teaches the son of a rich man to play the piano!"

"Your Elena teaches the son of lightning to play on her body!"

Santiago slapped him again. "You have no honor!"

"Ask the boy here why he drinks!" De Palma whined.

Santiago whirled at the boy.

"I have my pride," Ruben whispered.

"Ask the store here where she passes every night," said De Palma. "Ask the beasts on the corner who whistle at her. It seems the earth knew the fragrance of your daughter before she ever touched the keys of a piano. She is no ivory, Santiago." With this, purged and remorseful, the old *sampaguita* man fell back limply on the bench. Santiago was running now, and behind, De Palma was beginning to pluck on his guitar.

Santiago moved among the brief lives in the tenements, inspecting the other insects big enough to leave a mark on the gravel as they moaned their rice; moved among the flow in the garbage cans and among the ardors in the alleys releasing their anguish. He stumbled among the hollow men and women on their rags and newspapers, breathing an apology, swearing to lead them out of the famine.

He inched his way into the avenue, picking up a trail through the city, boring a hole into the inlets shrieking its commerce in his ears. His pulse was beating as it had on the eve of The Battle when they heard the cannon as it blasted a tunnel through the lumber in the swamps and the bugles echoed and the horses neighed. He had blazed an escape route into the thicket, though he was only a courier, for his tender years had responded to the speeches of The Man on his mount as he preached a decade of reforms when he returned to rule.

Cannon and hoof in his ear, Santiago wended his way street after street, looking for a tall house with an *azotea* where his daughter played the piano to a child not old enough to sweeten his milk. The darkness chilled his sight, weed caked about his ankles, the sweet chant of De Palma caressed him with hymns that always spoke of the mountains and the

stars and the stream that guarded the plateau where their leader stood, dreaming on his mount, looking to the east while The West advanced with Arkansas farm boys who washed their cotton socks in the ponds of Bacolor.

In half an hour, as though peering into hedges rich with Americans, Santiago had thrust his head into swinging doors where purple lights beckoned and the eyelashes of hostesses flapped like miniature bat-wings, as though, as he stood there, they were asleep and were having nightmares about a man of the revolution, glistening with a medal. In this half hour, frantic with a labor that thumped furiously in his chest, he collided into their figures, coiled and scented, a weary old man upon whose face hung a tear. Seeing this, they would giggle, rock, shake their heads knowingly, disappear into their florid spaces—an island so terrible to behold the old man eluded it as if a bullet had nicked his temples. There was no way of knowing where the tall house with the *azotea* might be, and he wished they would play their lesson louder, Elena and the retarded boy, that he might hear everything was well. But there was no sound of music, only the wind with the message of wine that transported him, head thrust in doorways, women laughing, not believing, then calling to him, a customer, to come, break bread with them before the hour of twelve when perforce he must retire the bones of his body. Finally, exhausted, he rested on the pavement under an awning, gasping sweat and tears washing his medal. As he stroked his face, burning with his heart, he saw it: the house, like a monastery, rising majestically out of a hill, the tallest tree of all, a castle winking its neon in the north. Slowly, his mind dancing in the rice wine, his cheeks flushed, he bolted from his resting place, heading directly toward this eagle of a house that leaned on a passage of leaves, a phantom, a windmill glowing ugly in the moon. When he knocked on the massive iron door, something like a thunder rumbled inside. No one answered. He knocked again. Still no one. Then he saw it, the balcony. Up there, in one of the rooms—for it was a big house—he felt the presence of people; heard a woman's quick tread; a man's thick voice, and what Santiago knew to be the creaking of a bed.

"Open this door!" he screamed.

Upstairs, someone lighted a cigarette.

Santiago gazed up, not so much at the window but at Whatever Man watched this spectacle from above. He leaped, caught hold of a vine, but his hand slipped and he felt the earth mothering his face. Rising, he leaped again, this time not even catching the vine, and slipping again.

He could not climb the balcony.

Looking around, he saw this house, which, a decade ago, was used as a chapel, was interlaced by a park. Fronting it was untended shrubbery with a stone bench. A fountain lay at the far right, facing the main street. A hero's stone monument held up its arms in salute of the dawn, though in the morning the sun normally rose on its back.

Santiago dragged himself to the bench, nursing his wounded fists. By now, the upstairs window had remained serene, untouched by his fury, a sinister chamber clinging to the silence of the city. Santiago looked up, seeing nothing but his pain, and he pushed himself down to the ground where he bit at pebble and scratched at rock and his loins ached and tore out at him in their own mute rebellion. The wine washed every part of him, every sense that could remember his story, stabbing at the coil of years curled like a snake in his throat. He was pounding on the earth with all his age, but not a sound came from him, for he was striking all the citizens now asleep in the city while he endured—ever loyal to the silence—the agony in the park.

He lay as he had lain in the green fields of the wild young country in the days of The Dream, looking into the eyes of The Man who told them about the coming of The Time. Lying in the sweet air, eating nothing but praise in the sudden doubling of a fist in the heart that now lived only in the memory of the loveliness, the bread was not stale, nor the water salty . . .

(Aguinaldo!) Like the terrible strength of all beginnings; the wine of his dream dancing wildly in his eyes, now a dried old man, a wraith in a rocking chair, sick, convalescent, a trophy honored once a year, a patriarch of the tomb, alone with revolution, transfixed in the twilight, a poet whose poetry rushed like pearls in the landscape.

Prostrate on the ground, twisting, writhing, he saw the moon, a circle in the heavens, repeating its aura, revering its own beauty, at random in the atmosphere: a destiny. Then a cloud, like a swift and ominous wing, touched it and the cloud sparkled and the moon darkened and he who lay on his back struggled up and went to the door, hammering with his knuckles at the silence.

The door opened. An old couple holding out a lamp, holding each other, questioned the dark together.

"What do you want?" asked the two.

Santiago's lips quivered.

"I want a woman."

The old man stared at his woman; held the lamp closer upon this shivering white man who would be a lover.

"Enter," the old man said.

Santiago followed the lamp and when it illuminated the interior, he found that the house was indeed a castle and must have been the home a governor-general once bequeathed to his *querida.*

"Is this a harem?" Santiago snickered, though he shook so.

"Follow, old one," the old man ordered harshly. The old woman had not spoken.

The couple and the lamp led Santiago into a maze of rooms, one dungeon succeeding another, each one unlocked ceremoniously by a key that swung from a chain the old woman encouraged to dangle by her side. As the old man introduced the caves, the old woman opened them, exposing women and children of all ages undoing packages and bundles, some sleeping, others disrobing, many just staring vacantly, and Santiago asked where the others were, for he was told that there were the new ones, just off the interisland ships.

The old man with the lamp studied his customer maliciously and began scratching his bald head.

"We don't have your age right now, if you can wait..."

Santiago was going to answer when he tripped over some obstruction. "Pardon me," he said sincerely, and then he saw them. They were all lying on what appeared to be a huge mat, each covered with respective blankets; a tarpaulin here, a canvas there, a coat, even a towel. The women were strewn about like cattle.

"They are not prepared," the old man explained politely. "But go ahead. Choose one."

Santiago went around, lifting their covers, blinking in the oil lamp that followed, pulling out a leg, brushing aside a concealing arm, a lock of hair. A woman with pimples bit his hand and Santiago withdrew, pale. Out of nowhere, the old woman who had hovered perfectly still by the doorway, lunged with the agility of a cat, and with what looked like an animal's dried tail converted into a whip, struck the pimpled one twice in the face and thigh. A sob was stifled. The pimpled one cowered, covering herself with her end of the tarpaulin. The old woman, baring gold teeth in the lamp's glow, smiled apologetically at Santiago.

"They get listless sometimes," she said.

The guided tour was finished. The old woman restored her keys; the turnkey had done her duty. The master of the manor now mentioned a roster and a price. Going over their names, Santiago noticed there were thirty in all.

"Are they all here?"

"All present and accounted for," the old man announced, sweeping back a curtain with a flourish. "Sorry, they are still resting. We didn't expect business... the late hour. But since you are a rare case..."

Santiago smiled happily. "Then I must be ——"

"There's that one upstairs," the old woman said naughtily, biting at a strand of her whip. "Special."

The wine stirred in Santiago. And without speaking, seeing the stairway, he ran up quietly, the old man stepping lightly behind him.

"If you can wait," he was saying.

But Santiago did not hear him. There, outside the middle door by a landing, stood a piano, a weird box with a mantle; and leaning on one of its legs, was a red umbrella. Santiago snatched it, and running downstairs, fell on top of the woman with the whip, sending her careening to the floor. Santiago slipped out of the curtain, ran out of the caves, still unlocked, fled out of the castle, chased by the couple; the old woman, just temporarily halted, lashing out blindly with her whip. And into the night Santiago fled, carrying a heart and its beating and a red umbrella clasped to his chest.

———

Half of the candle had melted when she returned. She was shivering, breathless.

"Was there wine tonight, father?"

He nodded. "There is always wine."

"Did De Palma speak of his bomb?"

"He has nothing else."

"Yes. He loves his misery. It is his only luxury. But tomorrow, we shall have rice and you can invite him for a change. There will be shrimps too."

"And will you fish the canals of the Pasig?"

She smiled indulgently, rubbing her hair with a towel. "No, father. Just the market by the way. I shall have money."

And then they were quiet.

When it seemed they would not speak at all, when there would always be this silence between them, he reached out, his hand full, and when she stooped to accept it, whatever it was, she found that this was a small wreath, a crown that he was giving her: flowers for the dead.

"I saw you in the graveyard," he said, his voice not rising.

Wet from the rain, she shuddered. She gripped the crown, still trembling, and now, she saw the red umbrella, dripping, as though drying its grief. At last, she understood and she flung herself at him.

"Father!"

". . . Forgive them!" he cried. "For she knows not what she is doing!"

Together, they sobbed out the sin of the house on the boulevard, their pain mingling, young and old, veil and uniform, sword and sheath.

"She danced for you, Elena, child," he stammered, "danced her soles worn, her lungs torn. I saw her thin every day that she was childless; thinner while she danced, clapping her tiny palms, cursing the barrenness and chanting the glory in the *barrios* where we went with the Virgin's image in her missal . . ."

"Father . . ."

"I would pray too, for I could not father a child and your mother was bent from the old love of an old man ancient with revolution. And then one day, burning a taper in front of San Pascual, she danced in Obando, for some relative had told her of the miracle and there we went, carrying her wooden shoes and the rosaries and my guitar whose fifth string was the necklace of my mother; a string heavy with the music of her country. So one night in Obando, I played for my wife; I played in the crook of my arm, the splendor of your face while she danced her bounty, danced you into her belly. In that night wild with omens, she danced you, Elena, on the earth that summoned the substances of providence. That body you now sell every night and that you cut for my meal each day—she danced every morsel of it in that rain in Obando when I played to her the songs of my father. Obando bore you, my daughter, on the heels of your mother's love!"

And Elena, weeping, dropped on her knees to clutch at his feet.

"No more! No more!" she begged.

"I have been a monster, eating the nights of my daughter. The visitations of my child to the grave were nothing but license. And I thought it was rice, rice! Oh, I was feeding on you, my daughter! Eating your flesh day and night, your body, piece by piece, on the table while you surrendered it on the bed! Daughter!"

She shook violently.

He looked at the room, wincing at its every object. Her limbs made the steps of the hut strong; the cot, the stools, the spoons—her beauty. Perhaps the lantern shone because her mouth had loved sufficiently. Even the trunk she bought him could be a part of her, a mortgage to the men in her life. Everything in the house belonged to her body, everything. He was only a shadow in the womb burning out his candles, aging his wine.

Santiago buckled on his belt. Armed with his mission, he paced the floor; austere, elegiac, a Don Quixote in his cups.

Alarmed, she cried: "Where are you going?"

"I must free the people!" he said.

"No!"

And pulling out his sword from the sheath. "You are a prisoner in my belly while I eat!"

"I won't let you go!"

"I must perform the operation!"

"You cannot do anything!"

She blocked his way.

"Do you think you can hold back my conscience?"

And he swept her aside with a strength he had not known since the last hierarchy. Elena sank into a swoon.

He was rushing down the stairway, into the street, around the corner, still hearing the plaintive cry of De Palma, and was gone in the direction of the rice store, rousing the rice beggars, inciting them to the victory.

A truck loaded with cereal sped by, but Santiago, like a warrior, speared the point of his sword, once, twice, and a burst of rice flowed down the dirt and a burst of people swooped down, scooped up grain and ground, screeching grotesquely, drunkenly, like cannibals. The truck bumped on a garbage can, swerved and smashed on its side, rice spilling out like white blood, exploding from the seams, inundating the sidewalk where haggard mothers suckled their infants still groaning from cockroaches, lice and vaccination. An old woman broke from the throng, a sack of rice twice her size saddled on her back. Santiago roared with sword and wine, charging, rallying the people to the compound.

Before the guard could see him, Santiago had hurled himself into the barbed wire, and with a length of it sticking to his temples, he ran to the sacks in the nook where the dogs of the owner were fed with fish in the morning. And then, sword held tightly in his fist, cutting, slashing, crying, grabbing, he had clawed one sack open with his fingernails, and still clawing, he bled the rice out even as his fingers stained the grains and his people swarmed the fence. He crushed a handful of rice in his palm, scratching, moaning, swearing at the loot that ran like wine down his veins. When the guard called to him, who was obviously their leader, Santiago was running, leaving the butchered sack, running with rice in his hands. When the guard called again imploring and the old man fleeing did not answer, would not answer, the wind howling in the land—when calling again, the guard did not reach the thief running away, something like wind blew at Santiago, for the guard who was only a boy who had never held a gun before, had fired his rifle, dispersing the storm, leaving an old man resplendent with his medal.

And when Santiago fell—falling like a tear from a man's grief—he fell not on a pile of jute sacks in a sawdust yard above the *estero,* but on a cool moonscape of grass in a long ago September, in the hollow of belief, in the pool of all their blood, in the mountains. Like a sigh, like an old coin, gleaming, that would soon roll, lost, in a hole, he fell, as fallen he was part of the city's mountains whose loneliness became his fall; whose loveliness became his absence. So still he died, the bullet that took him almost seemed a gift, once given seemed absolute, seemed somehow a god of peace, a feast to God. Then alone, in a quiver of rice, he lay there with no one, save a sword and the sequins in the sky.

Leoncio Deriada

PIGPEN

The girl Inocencia emptied into the huge wooden trough the kerosene can full of feed. The pigs, their appetites sharpened by the delicious mixture of rice bran and green papayas boiled into a pastelike mush, rushed to the feeding place from one corner of the pen. Grunting and bumping into one another in awkward haste, they were soon positioned along the elongated trough, which was actually a hollowed-out trunk of a *lawaan* tree, their gluttonous mouths chomping noisily. A piglet crowded out of the trough blindly squeezed itself between Inocencia's legs. Annoyed, she hit its fat flank with the empty can. The piglet squeaked shrilly and wobbled to the end of the hollow wood where now it gobbled up its share of the daily staple.

Inocencia straightened her body and surveyed the pigpen with satisfaction. She was a short girl, squat-featured and stoutish, but among these grunting animals, she was a mistress that towered over them with authority and a strange affection.

One, two, three, four, five ... She counted the animals again. This habit of counting the pigs she developed sometime back, and later she counted not only the pigs but also the chickens when she fed them early in the morning. She could not remember how many fowls there were in the yard for the chicks and the young roosters scattered in all directions every time she had counted fifty or fifty-one. Which was just as well, for she could not count beyond one hundred.

But she knew exactly how many pigs there were in the pen. Three were big ones, two sows and a boar. The boar was huge and looked like a monster. The older sow had a brood of eight brownish piglets. The other sow had a litter of six born a week after the brown ones. Mixing freely in the enclosure, all the little pigs seemed to look alike especially now that the brownish pigment of the older ones was beginning to turn black.

All in all there were seventeen pigs—three big ones and fourteen little ones. Now watching them lined along the *lawaan* trough—eight piglets with their fat rears pointed towards her, their little tails curling beautifully—Inocencia felt a subtle kinship with the animals. To her they were lovelier than pets, and the thought of selling most of them and slaughtering one or two during the harvest season saddened her.

Soon the animals made noises, a signal that their appetites had not yet dulled. Inocencia stepped to the door of the pigpen for the other can of mush. She poured the feed into the trough and before the pigs licked it clean, she returned to the house to finish the last chores of the day. It was late afternoon and before long her father Purok and her brother

Turo would be home from the fields. They would come promptly with the dark—tired and dirty and hungry like the pigs in the pen.

Inocencia paused at the top of the stairs. She almost slipped and she cursed under her breath. The stairs were made of crudely hewn hardwood and the steps had become shiny, slippery in fact, but she could never remember to be more careful every time she went up or down the house.

She heard a whimpering sound from inside. She frowned and hurried into the house.

Inocencia had a baby.

In the little room that was cluttered with various rags, the baby lay on a buri mat on the floor. Inocencia stopped at the door and stared at the baby. Among stained pillows of various sizes, it kicked the air vigorously and cried harder, but the sound from its mouth remained muffled, almost unhuman. Inocencia looked at the baby with a mixture of repulsion and pity. In a split moment she thought how beautiful and more lovable were those baby pigs in the pen....

For Inocencia's baby was a freak.

Inocencia stared harder at the baby on the floor. It was pale like a Chinese child and like a Chinese, too, its eyes slanted into slits. Its head was huge and almost hairless. When it was awake and not crying, its eyes crossed grotesquely as the baby focused them against the light. Otherwise, they glowed like a snake's.

The baby was almost choking now, its expression of hunger purely animal. Inocencia picked the baby up; her finer instincts had finally won over her. Gently rocking the baby in her arms, she pressed it close to her breast and opened her dress. The baby blindly found the swollen nipple and sucked noisily. Inocencia remembered the piglets making the same sounds over their food in the pigpen. She smiled. Then she frowned.

Soon the baby was asleep. Inocencia put it down on the mat on the floor and hurried to the kitchen. It was time to cook supper.

The kitchen overlooked the pigpen. From the window, Inocencia could see the pigs huddled together in one corner of the enclosure. They were no longer eating. The wooden trough must have been licked clean and dry. Now contented and noiseless, they seemed to have bloated to twice their sizes.

The sun was low in the west. It momentarily stood above a jagged mountaintop and sent down a cool glare over the swampy geography of the settlement. As the fire crackled under the pot of rice, Inocencia leaned out of the window. Her eyes swept the area beyond the pigpen, beyond the tall kapok trees laden with mature fruit that hung like dark, elongated bottles. The wide riceland below was lush green, and in the late afternoon sun, the soft sheen of the palay blades blended with the cool air to produce a certain peace. The house was perched on a low hill—like most homes in the settlement—and, from the kitchen window, Inocencia could see practically all the world she had ever known.

This world was the most elemental world of settlers who sailed all the way from the northern provinces to carve barrios out of the forests and swamps of this new land. Inocencia's parents came from an arid *sitio* in central Capiz. With a dozen other families—four from Iloilo, two from Cebu, two from Bohol, two from the Ilocos, one from Antique, and one (an old bachelor) from Leyte—Inocencia's parents and the young Turo cut down trees, and with bare hands and improvised tools, turned the swamps into the riceland it was today. The native Mansakas called the place Bawani. The neighboring settlements, whose features were almost the same, were Gisok, Tabon-Tabon, and Nuevo Iloco. Sawsaw, to the east, was all flat land. There the Ilongos celebrated their fiesta in May and the Boholanos theirs in October.

Inocencia was born after Purok's second harvest. There was no doctor, not even a native midwife. Before Turo could bring Tia Julia, the housewife from Antique, panting to the door, the baby was already born. Purok was bending over the mat on the floor, his loam-stained hands trembling and streaked with warm blood. His wife Reynalda smiled wanly, her body exhausted from the pains of giving life. The baby's cry sounded strange in the dark valleys and tall trees of this unknown frontier.

Inocencia was baptized by the American missionary priest of Mawab during the Boholano fiesta in Sawsaw.

Reynalda died of snail fever when Inocencia was three years old. Her belly had gradually become big. Purok at first thought his wife was pregnant again.

Turo married one of the Ilongo girls when Inocencia was seven. Her name was Amparo. She was pale and had periodic attacks of asthma. Like Reynalda, she, too, died of snail fever. She bore Turo no child.

Inocencia never went to school. The nearest public school was in Mawab, eight muddy kilometers away. When school opened, children from Bawani, Sawsaw, Gisok, Tabon-Tabon, and Nuevo Loco enrolled, but most of them dropped out the moment the planting season and the rains came.

Neither had Turo been to school back in Capiz. Purok himself had not learned to read and write. His real name was Fructuoso but the nickname Purok was good enough for him. He could not spell it anyway and he never knew the difference between a *p* and an *f*. His wife, however, had studied the *cartilla* as a young girl and she could sign her name on her residence certificate and she could read the *Hiligaynon* and the novena to Sant Antonio de Padua. She had voted once— when Manuel Roxas ran for president and Capiz seemed to be the capital of the country.

Purok and Turo built this house on the hill after Amparo had died. Earlier, the two had planted fruit trees around the base of the roundish hill. They also planted a row of kapok trees that soon grew taller than any orange or caimito or jackfruit tree.

The slightly rolling land between the trees and the house was well tended for crops like cassava and camote and an assortment of vegetables and ornamental plants. A choice patch to the east had been alternately planted to corn and mongo beans.

Inocencia grew up in this simple world of hill and trees and swamps. She seldom went farther than the ricefields below or the creek on the eastern side of the hill.

At fourteen she was a full-bodied woman though she was quite short and plumpish. She was dark brown but her skin was clear and smooth. The youngest son of the Cebuano family once carried Inocencia's basin of wash from the creek. Purok met them under the rattan clothesline, and in a funny mixture of Kinaray-a and Cebuano, said that his daughter was strong enough to carry anything, even a sack of rice, so she did not need anybody's help. The young man opened his mouth to explain, but the sight of Turo sharpening a long-handled blade and eyeing him sharply from the first step of the stairs rendered him speechless. No Cebuano ever ventured within the vicinity after that. In fact no other young man dared visit Inocencia in that house on the hill.

Until something happened to Inocencia when she was sixteen. She became pregnant.

The man was a lumberjack from the Valderrama logging camp in Compostela. He was twenty-one and built like a *lawaan* tree. He was a distant relative of the old bachelor from Leyte. During one of his rare visits, he surprised Inocencia among the ferns. Rather, it was Inocencia who surprised him as he bathed naked in a shadowed bend of the creek.

After washing a few pieces of working clothes and bathing, Inocencia decided to gather young *pako* fronds. This species of fern made a delicious salad when boiled and soaked in vinegar or dressed in halved tomatoes. Draped in her red patadiong, Inocencia rose from the water, her hair faintly fragrant with lemon rinds. The ferns grew abundantly along the banks of the creek, their young, powdery fronds gracefully coiled or opened into an array of tender leaflets. Inocencia stepped onto the bank to her right and plucked the choicest fronds. Farther ahead, overlooking the bend of the creek where the water was deeper, grew taller ferns. Almost soundlessly, she forced herself through the bushes and tall grass and reached for the fronds.

Then she saw that below the bank a man was bathing. His back was turned to her. The water was down to his waist and now he was rinsing his hair and arms vigorously.

She stopped plucking the fern fronds and looked. Then suddenly, the man arched his body backwards, towards her, and splashed flat on the water. Nimbly, his arms and legs spread and closed like wings, rendering him beautifully afloat. He stayed like that on the water, almost motionless but for the soft paddling of his hands and the kicking of his legs.

Inocencia stared. She had never seen a man completely naked. Every day she saw her father and her brother without their shirts on or stripped to their soiled shorts. She never noticed anything. But now, watching a stranger swimming naked below her, she trembled in a mixture of fear and curiosity.

The fern fronds dropped from her hands. Her hands instantly covered her breasts, which seemed to have swelled altogether and she felt a sudden tightness of the wet patadiong around her.

She must have made a sound, for the man instantly rolled on his back and stood up. He looked around him, then fixed his eyes on the thick clumps of vegetation in front of him. Inocencia froze. She knew she was well-hidden behind the green leaves but a slight movement would betray her.

The man smiled, it seemed. Did he know she was there—all eyes, all ears, all desire for something fearful and beautiful and forbidden? Now he emerged completely out of the water and stood on the sand. Inocencia held her breath. The man executed a few steps forward then stopped, arrested, by the mossy bank. Now she could see the whole of him: his body was pure bronze and his muscles tensed and throbbed and rippled like lovely snakes. He was so close that she thought she could smell the whole of him.

Then, like a wild animal, he leaped into the

ferns. Inocencia stifled a scream and stepped back, but the thick greenery held her, like a hundred tendrils. And now he was there at her feet, his eyes blazing, his naked body pulsating and glistening under the dappled mid-morning sun. Now she could truly smell him!

The man grabbed the hem of the red patadiong and pulled it down with a lovable violence. Inocencia shouted soundlessly as his two steel arms encircled her quivering naked-ness and bore her down to the ground among the soft moss and the scattered blades of fern. . . .

A week later, Turo complained during lunch that he was getting tired of Inocencia's *pako* salad. Young fern fronds were very good once in a while, but to eat them every day could be terrible. Besides, wasn't it a bother to go down to the creek just to gather wild leaves when the vegetables in the backyard bloomed unharvested?

Purok said Inocencia was getting pale. Was there something wrong with her?

Nothing, Inocencia said and ate all the *pako* salad on the table.

When at last Purok and Turo discovered the mystery behind the abundance of the fern salad, it was five months later and Inocencia was getting as bloated as one stricken with snail fever. She had altogether stopped going down the hill. It took the two men one whole morning—cursing her, slapping her, kicking her—to learn who the man was. Inocencia told when she could no longer bear the pain in various parts of her body. With a jungle bolo on his side, Purok trotted to the Waray's house on the other side of the next hill to the east and demanded to see the lumberjack. The old bachelor, his voice as falsetto as a transvestite's, explained that his cousin (of the fourth degree) had left weeks ago to cut down more trees in a new Valderrama concession in Monkayo. *"Ay linti!"* Purok hissed and presented his daughter's case with appropriate parental anger. He should marry Inocencia right away. But Boy Ponciano was married last week, the Waray said. *"Ay linti!"* Purok thundered, whereupon the Waray gallantly offered to marry Inocencia himself. Purok did not say *ay linti* but to show his disapproval and utter contempt, he unsheathed his jungle bolo and hacked to pieces the first step of the bamboo stairs as the Waray fled screaming into the house.

Nobody in the whole settlement knew anything about Inocencia's disgrace. The Waray had taken an oath of silence. During the sixth month of Inocencia's pregnancy, Purok brought her to Esperanza, in Agusan, where his only relatives in Mindanao lived. One foggy dawn, they walked to Mawab to catch a bus to the north before the sun rose. Between Nabunturan and Monkayo, the bus met some dozen Valderrama logging trucks. Inocencia stuck her head out of the bus window, tearfully hoping to see Boy Ponciano standing on one of those gigantic *lawaan* trunks, waving to her, his eyes blazing, his muscles rippling like snakes in the sun.

Months later, Inocencia returned to Bawani. She looked pale but nobody would ever suspect that she had left behind her in Esperanza a baby six weeks old.

Life in the house on the hill resumed its dull routine. Though she was not forbidden to go anywhere, Inocencia did not go to the creek to wash the men's clothes. Instead, she washed them at the well Turo had dug under the kapok trees on the western side of the hill. The three never talked about the child. In fact they seldom talked about anything at all except their necessities.

———

A lusty, hoarse cry surprised Inocencia. At the same time, she smelled the acrid odor of burned rice. She left the window and discovered that her arms had become numb leaning on the bamboo sill. She opened the pot of rice and dropped the lid noisily. It was burning hot and the unpleasant smoke from the pot filled her nostrils.

The baby in the room howled in earnest. Inocencia stood at the door and looked at the disfigured child. The old repulsion gripped

her and for a moment she wondered if things would have been different had she kept the first child. It was a pretty boy. How easy it was to leave him to relatives in Esperanza. She tried to picture how the boy looked now, two years later. Did he have flashing eyes like Boy Ponciano?

The baby on the floor had slit eyes emphasized by a large mouth. The big head and little limbs made the baby extremely ugly. This child was certainly God's punishment, Inocencia thought—her punishment for being such a sinful girl. But was it all her fault?

She had never stopped desiring Boy Ponciano. No father, no brother in the world could stop her. Even if they killed her. Even if Boy Ponciano had married another girl. The pain of giving birth to his son in secrecy and shame had not stopped her thoughts from stealing away from her work and reliving those rapturous hours under the ferns.

These last three years, Purok and Turo had been raising pigs for sale. It had become Inocencia's assignment to feed the animals morning and afternoon though it was Turo who gathered, chopped, and boiled the green papayas mixed with rice bran. Father and son had constructed an enclosure just below the vegetable patch a few meters from the well under the kapok trees. They started with two native sows and a hybrid boar Purok had bought from an agriculturist in Tagum. The boar was so aggressive that he could sire hundreds of brownish, short-snouted piglets. Soon the farmers of the settlement brought their sows to mate with Purok's famous boar. For every six of the litter born, Purok got one as payment for his boar's generous services.

One particularly hot morning a year ago, Mariano, the Ilocano who lived on the hill next to the Waray's, dragged a seemingly disinterested sow to Purok's pigpen. It was a big sow, one of the hundreds fathered by Purok's boar many months before. Turo had left early for Mawab to buy some sugar and dried fish. Inocencia was washing clothes at the well. The noise made by the protesting sow aroused Inocencia's attention and curiosity. She had never seen the mating of pigs this close. She had just finished washing clothes and before she started pouring water on her head for a cool bath, she stood up and watched the two men and the pigs in the pen. The boar was grunting hotly, impatiently nudging the cold female. Mariano and Purok held the sow still but the pig refused to cooperate. It seemed so long, until at last the sow stood still and the boar hungrily steadied its mount and the two animals groaned amorously.

A hot sensation rose to Inocencia's cheeks. She closed her eyes tight as a flash of fern fronds and the softness of damp moss stirred her memory. She felt the tightness of her patadiong under the frenzied heat of the mid-morning sun. But she quickly checked herself. She saw her father coming and she felt ashamed of her own thoughts. She scooped a coconut shellful of water collected in an aluminum basin beside her and poured it on her head.

Her father came to wash his hands. He was stripped to the waist and sweating profusely. Flushed by the sun, he did not look old at all. His farmer's chest and arms glowed and Inocencia could see something inexhaustible in the body of this man her father . . .

Purok proffered his hands and Inocencia poured water on them. For the first time she noticed how old and ugly his hands were: they were stained with loam and the veins showed like tiny, wriggling snakes. Her father's hands trembled.

Suddenly, she became acutely aware that her father was staring at her. She looked at his face and she saw his eyes blazing. He was staring at her body revealed by the wet patadiong.

Inocencia dropped the coconut shell. She picked up her basin of washed clothes and ran away.

After hanging her wash on the rattan clothesline, she started for her room to change. Her heart beat fast. She was expecting something terrible. And there it was. Her father was at the door. She could smell him.

His body loomed, huge and terrible, and she trembled, but she was not afraid. She did not want to run anymore. When she entered the room, she brushed her body against him. He grabbed the patadiong and pushed her inside. She reeled into a pile of kapok pillows in a corner. No sound came from her throat though she opened her mouth and screamed and screamed. At last she closed her eyes and saw a flash of young ferns strewn over a mat of moss. She saw Boy Ponciano's eyes blazing in the frenzied heat of the mid-morning sun . . .

When it was all over, she screeched and spat and vomited through the cracks of the bamboo floor. She felt dirty and damned and she hated herself and her father and Boy Ponciano and everything in the world. But she did not cry.

Her father said nothing. If he had felt anything at all, any sense of remorse, Inocencia did not care to know. He went down the house and walked to the pigpen where now his magnificent boar was assaulting another sow.

For days, neither father nor daughter spoke. Turo did not notice anything strange. It was Inocencia who was becoming vaguely aware of something in her brother's eyes. They seemed to blaze, too, and she felt a queasy excitement every time Turo looked at her.

Inocencia realized, not entirely with shame, that she was beginning to desire a man, any man.

And when it was her brother who ripped her clothes and pinned her down among the kapok pillows in the little room, she did not struggle anymore. She closed her eyes and forgot all sense of shame and damnation. But now, no fern fronds flashed in her inner eye. Neither did she see Boy Ponciano's eyes and his muscles rippling in the dappled sun. Instead, she saw her father's prize boar grunting and frothing in the mouth as the animal madly mounted Mariano's sow.

———

The baby on the floor cried louder. Inocencia's thoughts returned to the room, and just as fast, went back to the pigpen, among the piglets with beautiful, curly tails. Her thoughts back to the room again, she at last faced squarely the reality in front of her. Crying like that, this monstrosity on the floor no more stirred her instincts to cuddle and to feed. She could feel the primeval repulsion gripping her womb, her guts, the whole of her—and, not surprised at all, she felt a terrible cruelty stiffening her fingers.

She bent over the child, her fingers flexed like claws. But sensing her presence, the baby stopped crying. Inocencia stepped back. Her heart failed her.

Then the baby cried again. With a final resolution, Inocencia picked up a pillow on the floor. Nothing could stop her now.

And with a violence never expressed before, she laid the kapok pillow on the baby's face and pressed it hard, putting all her weight on her hands. The pillow covered not only the freak's face but also its chest. Inocencia felt a weak, whimpering sensation under her hands and she pressed harder. The exposed legs kicked jerkily and stopped.

Sweating and perversely jubilant, she lifted the pillow from the baby. She looked at the still, frail body—without emotion, without guilt. Now silent and dead, the baby did not look monstrous anymore. Its narrow, slanting eyes were closed. The ugly gash that was its mouth was closed, too, and traces of saliva and undigested milk streaked its sides.

Inocencia heard voices in the yard. Her father and her brother had come home and she could picture them now climbing the stairs.

The smell of burned rice was all over the house. They must have smelled that acrid odor for she heard them hurrying to the kitchen. Purok was calling her.

She did not answer. She just stood there in the little room, her hands holding the pillow, her eyes staring at the dead child on the mat on the floor.

Suddenly they were in the room, demanding to know what had happened. Inocencia fixed her eyes on them, and for the first time saw how alike they looked. Stripped to their waists, they were the same height and chest and arms and though the other's face was old, both wore the same undefinable animal expression. Even their smell was alike. They reeked of mud and decayed forest leaves.

"I killed it!" Inocencia announced.

"No!" Turo screamed and grabbed her and shook her and pushed her hard against the wall. "No! That is my child! You killed my child!"

Inocencia faced him and with all the contempt her tongue could articulate, lashed back: "No, that is not your child! That child is his! His! His!"

She raised her trembling hand and pointed at her father.

Purok just stood there, dumbfounded.

"That child is his!" she repeated. "His! His! He raped me before you did!"

She spat out the words, her body shaking in anger and hate.

His eyes flashing, Turo faced his father and raised his arms to strike him. But his arms froze in the air. The two men stood there, their eyes flashing, their animal smell mixing with the odor of burned rice.

Inocencia fled, darting between the incongruous twins, her body brushing against both of them. Again, she forgot the slippery steps, and in her blind flight she slid down from the second step, landing on her rump on the ground. But she was not hurt. She picked herself up from the ridiculous fall, not knowing where to go.

Then she heard the grunting of the pigs in the pen.

She reached for Turo's long-handled blade hung on the wall. Carrying the large blade above her head, she hurried to the pigpen. The sun had set and the shadows of the trees had now become one with the coming dark.

The pigs were milling around inside the enclosure. The boar stood tall among them, like a king.

Inocencia opened the door of the pen wide. Seeing the unexpected freedom, the animals rushed out in one movement and spilled out into the vegetable patch.

But the boar defiantly stayed inside the pen. He lifted his head and faced Inocencia, his brute face uglier than it ever was before. Inocencia recoiled. She saw something human in the animal.

Tightly holding the blade with both hands, Inocencia entered the pen. The boar grunted and held his ground fast. Then he growled and lunged forward, all the fat in his body shaking in awkward attack. Inocencia raised the blade and struck with all her might.

The blade found its way clean and deep into the animal's thick neck. With a horrible groan that was not a pig's but a monster's, the boar drew back, pulling the blade and her. The blade held fast and the blood flowed and the boar growled. Inocencia released her hands as the animal retreated into a corner deep in swine dung.

Inocencia sank to the ground, exhausted but watchful. Her eyes glinting in savage joy, she watched the animal fiercely shaking off the blade stuck into its nape. She laughed.

Then she put her hands in her face and cried. It was a loud, convulsive crying. Her mind was blank.

When she looked up, she saw her father and her brother. They held her arms to lift her up from the ground, but she squirmed away from their touch and shrieked for all the trees and the twilight to hear: "Don't touch me! Pigs! Pigs! Pigs!"

Renato Madrid

THE DEATH OF ANACLETO

It was during the last Saturday's spying that Cleto first felt himself rewarded.

For perhaps the first time that he could remember, he was late. He came in upon them rigid in their chairs. He caught his father in the act of rising from his seat in the center of the room, the base of the imperfect oval they made.

Cleto raised himself above the balustrade to catch his father's irritated progress toward the window, flinging at the others one word, spoken in his peculiar manner, which accused them all.

"Stories!" his father said with contempt.

There was silence. His father turned round to squint at them. The boy noted how they seemed to shrink in their seats while his father took his annoyance out on the floor.

"Stories!" his father repeated, with less vehemence. From their edge of the oval the women looked as one at Uncle Blas, who felt authorized to speak.

"I say very readily again, Celestino," said Uncle Blas, "I *saw* this man myself. There's nothing false about him."

His father grunted. Beside his vacated chair a dark-clad tiny figure stirred—his mother.

"Blas," she said, "this man, this Cyrus—" she groped inwardly to shield her sentences from her husband's intense gaze, and stopped altogether.

Cyrus. The name sounded like something the boy had heard mentioned at school when he had not been listening. Cyrus, Cyrus . . . But of course! He'd heard them, the small boys at the close of school yesterday, repeat the name—with awe! Hearing it now, in these surroundings, made the unfamiliar syllables suddenly settle beneath a cloud of authority; there were words, he knew, which you could not repeat at home—which nevertheless kept on vibrating in the mind like the dusty picture-book in the library you could not reach, or the mysterious portion of a roast's anatomy you were not permitted to touch.

"It is too soon," the little woman spoke again after her husband's crippling look had lifted. "It is too soon to say that. The circus opened only this morning."

"Last night," Uncle Blas corrected.

"Oh?" Micaela, his spirited aunt, dropped her knitting and raised her voice, certain that Uncle Blas had made a mistake.

"But they have been here a week now. Or almost."

"Why, last Thursday I did not see a single tent. A week . . . Are you sure about that, Blasito?"

"Anyway, it must seem all of a week to you," Cleto's father snorted in the direction of Uncle Blas. "You have all the time to spend in the park."

Uncle Blas studied the floor.

"They say he dresses rather oddly," said Aunt Micaela as her hands fluttered excitedly with her needles. "Why, if I met him on the street, I certainly wouldn't know where to look!"

"Then you must try fainting sometime, dear sister," a disembodied, starched voice issued from the aunt who sat, rigid as a mummy, beside Uncle Blas. "Sometimes it is most convenient. In fact, no known remedy works better for a starved..."

Their looks disengaged as Cleto's father stirred.

"Blasito..." someone spoke.

"What?"

"Is it true, he wears a dress?"

"A *robe*," Uncle Blas, quite recovered, corrected.

"Well! I didn't know when a robe was not a dress."

"Well, I can tell you that it is not. There's nothing... nothing *feminine* about the man, anyone can see that."

"You forget that *we* have not seen him. When you dress like a woman there must be something the matter with you."

"There's absolutely nothing wrong with him. And he doesn't look like a woman, *por Dios!*"

"*Unfortunately,*" said Cleto's father, who had been silent, listening. "You'll all be running after him, the next thing I know."

"Why, Celestino Villaflor!"

"And," his father pursued, "he's got something that works wonders for the ladies, I hear."

Cleto ducked quickly into hiding as his father moved to the library door directly beneath him.

"It will be all the poor policeman in the park can do to keep your hands off the man," he heard his father say before he disappeared, and a vast silence gripped the room.

"Well, I never...!" Aunt Micaela said later.

"Something must be wrong with you, Micaela. You don't even know anymore when you're being a bit too lively."

Aunt Micaela laughed out loud. "Really!" she said, with sudden candor. "Well! Who would have thought to hear that from one who had to be literally *dragged* home from the convent, to keep her from further scandalizing the poor nuns."

Uncle Blas spoke without vehemence: "Be still, Micaela."

Aunt Micaela turned to him and laughed. "The king is dead," she said. "Long live the king!" Really, the boy said to himself, Aunt Micaela is being impossible tonight! And yet he found himself warming to her, and to Uncle Blas. For a moment they seemed to him the only persons alive in the whole house. Uncle Blas who sometimes drank and who thinly disguised the fact whenever the memories of his dissipated business pressed heavily on him. Aunt Micaela who once picked him up at the gate and hid him in the attic until he sobered up, unaware of Cleto who was playing there.

Presently he heard another voice speaking, timidly: "I wonder what charm Father could be talking of. They say *he limps.*"

"He's really grotesque. I think I ought to see him."

"*Oye,* Blas, this man—does he limp, truly?"

She's mocking me, Uncle Blas's eyes seemed to say when he glanced around before answering. With the air of one trying vainly to defend a dear and absent friend, he said, "He has his defects, this Cyrus. But he redeems them—which is more than any of us here can say for himself."

"Really!" said one.

"Heavens," said Aunt Micaela. "Heavens, hear our brother rave! One would think he was actually in this man's pay. Are you in this man's pay, Blasito?"

"Micaela—" one of the silent brothers reproved.

"Every man..." Uncle Blas broke off and surveyed his family with eyes sparking hate, "every man commits himself to something or other in his life. Perhaps it is my added defect to believe in this man. And to believe strongly. You cannot mock me out of it." They were silent.

"Is it true, Blas, he has only one foot?"

"Maybe he lost it in the war."

"Maybe this man is chicken at heart... *cobarde!*"

"Or maybe he lost it trying to save a friend."

"That's certainly an improvement on what *I* hear."

"Why, what did you hear, brother?"

"You would be shocked out of your seats."

"*Como*—let us decide that."

"He sold it to the devil! Bargained it for his magical powers."

"*Santa Maria!*"

"There. I told you."

"Still, these are all rumors. For all we know, he might walk into this room right now, a complete man."

"Yes. A complete man."

"No important part missing."

"So?"

"Blasito dear, you have seen him. Tell us. Do."

"In the interest of truth," Uncle Blas let himself be persuaded, "let me tell you that he not only limps. He actually *creaks* when he walks. No, no, I'm not joking. But there was that sound, last Friday, when I stood on the curb of Colon and he passed by me."

"And that creak, it convinced you that he must be real."

Uncle Blas chose not to mind this. He said, "Let me tell you what happened on Friday."

The women fell into a hush and put away their needles, which made the boy afraid that Uncle Blas would stop, thinking they were mocking him again. But his fears were unwarranted. Uncle Blas was deep in his story even before he began it, setting for them the mood of that day (it was drizzling, the sun shone full, and a strip of rainbow bridged Mactan and the mainland's hills) when Cyrus had brushed past him on Calle Colon.

The wonderful thing about it (his Uncle Blas said) was not that the man was bearded, or dressed like that; or even that he, Uncle Blas, was there at all at that precise moment. There was a huge crowd trailing after Cyrus that afternoon, and children running from all directions. Cyrus' face was red, as if he might

be very angry. Uncle Blas had followed the crowd, which soon grew even thicker. He had been puzzled outright when Cyrus stopped right where the beggars and other useless folk made a haven on Juan Luna.

As Uncle Blas closely described the magician, Cleto wondered if he might not have been adding the details from some loved and long-forgotten book. Several women actually emitted shocked cries, as at a blasphemy, when Uncle Blas added a detail that scratched their consciences. For then, Uncle Blas dipped into the heart of his story, how Cyrus had marshaled *them* together: the cripples on the sidewalk, who could only crawl on their hands. The crowd cleared the street for them. Then Cyrus challenged the congregated freaks to stand up and walk. The crowd began to cheer, as at a race, when the beggars, hardly able to understand the power of the man, stood up at Cyrus' repeated urgings. And all of them had stood up. And walked! 'On to San Nicolas,' the crowd chanted after the struggling beggars, so that these soon knew nothing except that they must keep steady and walk on, on to San Nicolas.

Uncle Blas' voice rose and fell with passion, with a glowing pride, as though it had been he who had made the cripples stand up and walk. His gestures drew for them a vivid picture of men walking like blighted trees, the enormity of their defect clearer upon their faces than it had ever been. But they did walk to San Nicolas, swore Uncle Blas. He had followed behind the freaks among the cheering crowds. And behind them all walked Cyrus, throwing one foot past the other with a creak that made Uncle Blas shiver; looking displeased, or ill at ease (said Uncle Blas), looking as if he would feel no differently if he had turned them all into cripples.

Uncle Blas gave a shy laugh to crown this conceit and all at once a shy babble rose among his listeners.

Cleto's father entered the room again, looking deep in thought, and he did not seem to notice, or to mind, how unruly his family had become—which made the boy glad, and made him marvel at this man he did not love. So there was room for some hope.... Ah, but he might be feigning, the boy thought—which accepted, promptly became for him a certainty.

For his father, smiling abstractedly at his cigar, reentered the broken oval, and said, "I forbid any of you to go to the circus."

=======

When Cleto decided to go to the circus he did not count on being recognized. A lot of people do not even know I exist, he thought.

But as he stood outside the tent of Cyrus, waiting for his ticket to be given out by a large, pretty lady who stood at the mouth of the tent, he felt a hand on his shoulder and wondered if he should run.

He spun round, taking in first the blue vest, then the gold chain across the breast.

The man laughed aloud, and suddenly he found he could look at the face.

"And what is our young man doing here?" asked Uncle Blas, who seemed not really to object.

"So you want to see the magician's show, eh?" he said when Cleto did not answer. The boy nodded. The water in his mouth flooded his throat. "I'll even do better than that," said Uncle Blas, smiling.

Uncle Blas took his hand. Cleto did not want any sugared peanuts; he did not even know what popped corn was. It seemed all new to him, and he wanted nothing of this.

He seems to know the place rather well, thought Cleto when Uncle Blas pulled him past a crowd that had congregated at the tent door flanking the magician's. They skirted a cart vending iced sweets. Then, suddenly, they were at the deserted door of a huge tent—I get lost so quickly, he said to himself when he realized that it was the back entrance to the magician's tent.

"Hullo," said Uncle Blas, rapping on an empty crate. "Anybody inside?"

The tent-door flapped open and Cyrus' head appeared. He smiled at Uncle Blas and held the canvas flap open for them. He was wearing a shabby robe that looked like one of his own colored nightdresses. Cleto looked at the man's face, and away.

Cyrus pointed puckered lips at the boy. "One of yours?" he asked Uncle Blas.

"Oh no," said Uncle Blas. "I'm not married."

"No?"

"I'm just taking him around."

Which is not true, thought Cleto, wavering between his dislike for his uncle's meeting him and being brought so close to Cyrus. "But if you really want to know," Uncle Blas went on, "I caught this boy buying a ticket to your show. How he came here, I really don't know, but his father would certainly throw a fit if he found out he had been here. He's my brother's boy."

Cyrus looked at him closely. (I'm glad I dressed up before I came. He might not want a dirty kid messing up his room.)

Oh, but the "room" was a mess. Trunks were piled one on top of each other. Bright strips of cloth hung from wires over their heads in gaudy disarray. At the room's end there was a large grey-colored coffin.

They had not been there half an hour when he heard his Uncle Blas say, "I guess he'll be safe here," motioning to him, and Cyrus answered, "It's perfectly all right." And he was left alone, for his Uncle Blas went out the back door, and Cyrus, with a muttered excuse, went into some inner partition humming a tune that blended queerly with his creaking walk.

When Cyrus came out again he had tied a crude sash about his waist. His costume was a dark red robe, somewhat faded, his manner one of utmost gentleness.

"Don't be afraid," he said. "Your uncle and I are friends. I guess you and I are friends, too. Here's a token." He pulled out a piece of candy from the recesses of his robe. Perhaps he pulled the candy *out of the air,* thought Cleto as he accepted the gift.

After a little silence Cyrus caught the boy looking, fascinated, at the coffin. "You must be wondering about that," he said. "But I am sure your uncle must have told you. He was at the show last night. It's got holes. Here—look," he took the boy by the hand and led him to the coffin. "They push the swords through here while I lie in the coffin. I called in some men from the crowd last night, but normally Clara does it for me. Your uncle was one of them last night."

"Clara?" Cleto asked; and as at a signal the outer curtain parted and the woman who sold tickets outside walked in.

"Look, we have a visitor," Cyrus told her.

She came nearer. He could smell the perfume of her hair when she bent close to him and asked him his name.

"Anacleto," he said shyly.

"And I am Clara, your friend's sister."

"A friend of mine brought him," said Cyrus. "He's gone out for something."

Cyrus' sister. How alike you look, he wanted to say, holding out his love to them. He did not know why; but they suddenly filled him with all the ease that he had long learned to dissociate from the company of adults. She touched him on the head, rumpled his hair, and gave him more sweets (now he was certain the candy came from one of the tins lined over her dresser), and he did not feel any of the distaste that used to send his skin crawling. Cyrus had disappeared through the outer curtain, and the thought that the magician's act was about to begin (so it seemed) made him a trifle breathless.

Like one very wise she sensed this in him.

"Don't worry," she said, "about him. We won't be performing for an hour yet. It's too early."

His heart sank. He hadn't counted on that: noontime coming, his missing his meal, sweat all over his clothes, being found out.

"What's wrong?" she asked.

"I must be home soon."

She touched him on the chin and her sympathy gladdened him. She called out to Cyrus.

He came in limping somewhat markedly.

"There's something wrong with my foot," he said. "It's paining me."

She went to her brother, who sat down on a trunk, and lifted his robe, revealing a black leather boot bound tight with thongs. She unlaced these.

"What was that you said," Cyrus beckoned him nearer, "you have to go?"

He takes me so seriously, he thought. He said, "Yes," drawing nearer the man who reclined over the trunk.

"And your uncle?"

"Oh, we did not come here together," he answered, and his glancing over the roomful of queer things told Cyrus his true sorrow. The woman unwound the boot and Cyrus steadied himself when she began pulling.

"It's my leg," he told the boy, pointing at the shin, rounding off abruptly where a foot should have been. "Fix it better, Clara. I do think I'll be making myself another one soon."

The woman smiled and held out the boot to Cleto. He drew back. "Hold it," she coaxed. He took the boot from her. It felt horribly light. "Look inside," she invited. There's nothing inside, he said to himself, except—a tin foot!

She laughed at his consternation and took the boot away. "It's always the good men that keep losing a part of themselves all the time," she said. "You want to know how he lost his foot?"

He nodded and Cyrus laughed, reaching for his head and rumpling his hair.

"Well," she said, tying the leather strap back with infinite care, "we used to have an act— The Burial—everybody called it. How they loved that one! More so since it was free of charge, sort of an advertisement. We'd set a day and an hour and spread the news, and every man with a curious bone in his body came to watch. We'd have a grave dug for my brother. But deep. Then we'd bury him. Everybody was asked to throw a handful of earth on him, who had meanwhile gone to sleep. The hole would be filled in, and they would be asked to stamp on the mound. Then the long watch would begin. Three hours, can you imagine!"

She pulled a strap too tight and Cyrus winced in pain.

"But once' she said, "when they dug him up (I had been telling my brother over and over again that it was dangerous, but he can be a perfect ass sometimes!) a shovel blade dug too deep." She patted the well-tied boot playfully. "And there you have my brother." She pulled the boy close and whispered conspiratorially in his face: "He has his faults, but I love him!"

They laughed together at this, Cyrus bending over them, a hand on the shoulder of each and laughing too—and the boy perilously close to tears.

======

No one saw him enter the front gate at home and linger beside the fountain that had stopped playing long ago. He felt immensely happy, a happiness that curled at the edges when he thought about being found out.

But no one found him out. Impulsively he ran beneath a tree whose branches hung low; picked a fruit and sat there eating, looking for all the world as if he had been nowhere else all morning. He thought about Uncle Blas. He wouldn't tell on me. No, not him. Still, it was terrible, meeting him there, at the circus. At Cyrus' very door!

Then deliberately, he chose to remember, with great affection, Cyrus and his sister. Something dawned on his boy's mind that nullified his pressing fears. He took off his shoes and rolled them beneath a hollow near the garden wall. He ran up the back stairs, by-passed the turning to his room, and smoothly disappeared into the trapdoor guarding the attic of the great house.

He felt the gloom about him lighten as his feet skirted the familiar obstacles. Here in this attic room the traps were plentiful. You might wedge a foot between two loose boards, and the noise would proclaim your truancy to the whole house. Or you stubbed a toe against a chest that lay in wait, and that too drew a cry from you.

But Cleto had quickly learned the surfaces of this room. Here he had discovered himself capable of thrill; here he found all the motley interests of his ancestors celebrated, each given a niche complete with label and dates, which without fail combined to give the boy a feeling that he had wandered into a graveyard full of friends.

From the time he first stepped into the room he had been aware that here a whole series of lifetimes had been gathered in orderly fashion like the chapters in a childish saga, gathered by a kindly hand. And had he been granted his wish, he could have made a playground of this. But the adult hand had descended upon him with inexorable severity and, as he was later to understand it, quite a measure of blight: no garden or yard could be more pleasant to him afterwards. Cleto had been taken bodily from his haven while an unsmiling uncle preceded him, carrying a pillow and soiled blankets down the steep stairs, to be deposited in his room, screaming as if fires had been lighted under his feet. . . . The air of neglect that summed up the whole attic in one square foot did not succeed in driving the boy away. You might even say that what he loved about it was precisely its untended look. You moved near a gable and disturbed a whole galaxy of spiders circling around in their mysterious ballet.

Cleto was apt to do all these; and in these acts today he brought the full force of his idea to bear. He blew across the curving surface of a great chest. For a while it looked to him like the curve of the classroom globe. He lifted the lid, opened the chest fully.

This was grandmother Vita's; and her spirit, so much at one with the past, seemed to rush over him at this moment of exposure to the present, the creak becoming her gentle voice protesting, the pungence of the Spanish perfume, the memory of her graciousness enveloping all in the room and lighting caressingly upon the head of the offending boy.

This was how you smelt. And: *how I wish you were here, my old friend, my old, old friend.*

The boy detached a thick pile of what seemed to him dresses, laid them on the dusty floor, and returned his touch to something silken and tasseled that had grazed his fingertips.

Your shawl. The one in which, aeons ago, you wrapped the peanuts for the munching boy beside you, and the chestnuts roasted in the park. A handful for a tiny silver coin.

He took the shawl out reverently, and as he did a hand mirror fell among the clothes, its handle looking like the eye of a huge needle. He took the mirror out, propped it against the chest lid, and crept nearer to examine the dim room that lay within the mirror beside his huge cow eyes. *It's my world all right,* he thought. *It's my world. There is the sleeping man behind me, folded on his bed, sleeping the years away. The thorns like jewels on a crown resting upon a damask handkerchief. His face, bearded—like Cyrus's!*

Framed by a badly hung gable window, the sleeping man's profile leapt out of the dark. He would touch it, see how closely the face resembled the one in his mind. *Or I, Cyrus, might make you rise and walk!*

He had never touched the thing before. Something in his pulsing brain told him he must not. Yet now, having lingered, playing with his grandmother's dress, which swept the floor when he walked, he went nearer the carved pallet of the sleeping man.

The dress, caught on a broken sliver of floor, gave way with a soft tearing sound. But he was intent on the sleeping head, from which the rats had distended the wide floor-length drape. He did not notice the hand that hung stiffly beneath the feathery cloth, almost touching the floor. As he moved closer, his own knee jolted the hand out of place, flinging it to the floor.

A rusty wire vibrated at the pit of the arm like a pulled vein. For the first time in the attic, fear gripped him, softly, with a tender hand.

He knelt on the floor. The dress made it awkward, but he managed. He sat half under the shadow of the sleeping man; took the broken arm in his hands, and shook it. *It's not heavy, not at all!*

He stood up quickly, gripped by an insane idea. He hesitated (*he* might wake) and placed both hands against the man's side. A tentative motion, lest he feel the man breathe. No. No movement. *But is he as heavy as he looks?*

Cleto began shaking the sleeping figure. *I would have liked him solid, and true.* He shook some more, unaware of the strength which his idea had given him. And at last he gave a quick shove that sent the sleeping man rolling to the side of the pallet down to the floor!

He stood very still. *What have I done? What have I done?* The noise—horrible, like pans falling off a kitchen ledge. Worse. *What have I done?*

He crept under the pallet, observing how the drape had fallen over the sleeping figure. As if the man had pulled it after him!

Feel him. Broken. Body parted in two at the waist. He felt some more, hands darting here and there, making little slapping sounds on the floor as if he'd been grasshopper-hunting.

He pulled away the heavy cloth. The pieces. *What's this? Hollow! A hollow Christ they've been hiding up here all the time!*

He forced himself to imagine a hoarse grandfather (third chest by the window) shockedly commenting on the discovery: *"Scooped the whole damned stuffing out— that's what they've done. Can't trust these local artisans. Pass a hollow Christ on you first chance they get. Damnation . . . !"*

But *they* were on the corridor below him now. Steps heavy with indignation. He rose, hit his shoulder against the pallet, grimacing in pain—*they've got me. They've got me.* He looked about him, desperate. *Hide. Tread softly. They're on the ladder now.*

Grateful for the total dark of the farthest corner he settled himself in a nest of dust. But they had come up, prepared. His father, at first a disembodied wraith, a light illumining his despot's face. Wrath burned in his eye redder than the glow of the electric torch he carried.

Where are you—beast of a boy!

The torchlight zoomed up and down, shaped from pear to moon. The erratic motion of the torch brought the boy a keen sense of his father's anger. *He'll kill me if he finds me. But he's going to find me. He knows the attic, too. Like the palm of his hand...* Duck! The light shot past him, lit up for the briefest second his wide, hunted eyes.

Sensations crowded upon him with oppressive speed. He lay flat on the floor, felt his heart pound mercilessly, whereupon, suffocating, dust thick in his throat, a flash seemed to explode behind his eye, and floating off into a dead faint, he knew that he was found.

=======

It was completely dark in his prison— darkness that began in the mind. It was to this moment that others, not the man himself (for the boy would grow into a man, Anacleto, the incident forgotten as though it had never taken place), would trace the opaque, inaccessible dark that was to be the quality of his life-in-death. Anacleto would be the man you meant when you wanted to speak of someone the child had fathered: a sparse, spare individual without roots—but certainly not without the desire for any: a listless, lethargic, loveless cynic who sometimes went out in search of his beginnings and who chancing upon them, would find in himself no virtue to stoop and recognize them. It was him you meant, but not for the above facts alone which, to the coldly analytical, would seem so transparent and untranscendental. You had to go farther; trace, for instance, what the darkness in his child's soul dictated him to do: what made him run away, to form, in the end, his home with an old childless couple who were reassured by his lost air that he had never been anywhere but in the streets, on the wharves, or jumping boats and being generally friendless.

For on this evening there was a wind about, and the chill curled up in the boy's stomach, which turned each time he saw the white blur of his food uneaten on the floor.

Cleto lay very still in bed, listening to the sounds they made eating downstairs. He could hear the soft accents of his sister reading to the company, and his mind threw

up a wall against this. The sounds were suddenly hateful to him, rushing up in waves like the numberless little pains that exuded from the welts on his small body.

The rebellion coursing through his spirit took a selective turn, and in a flash he knew at once that this room could never be his again; the company he wanted was not that of any in this huge, musty prison. He knew at once where he must go.

He rose. The windows were open and he trembled from the cold as he lifted himself to the ledge and looked down into the darkness, the sheer drop that a sweep of vines made deceptive. The leaves burned his feet. There was an instant of recoil as he clutched at protruding bricks that had formed some kind of intelligible design once, long ago, before the vines began their searching climb. His foot touched a downstairs window. In the instant of suspension he heard the thin rattle it made, and he jumped onto the soft grass. Once on the lawn, he ran, lights burgeoning in every spot he glanced at. The wind bit at his flesh, which had been opened in several places.

He broke into a cautious trot, hands clasped before his breast, cupping like a bird what fluttered loudly there—deathly afraid that it would spill out into the street, that they would hear the noise it made.

The lamps lit up in spots a clear stretch of road, and again and again the sound of a rig, always on another street, gave him a sense of his rejection, and speeded him all the more toward Cyrus, to whom he was turning now clearly with a look of love.

The road sped past him, shutters beside it uniformly drawn. Once he reached the stone bridge he knew that his rebellion was complete, for this was forbidden ground. He was remembering: he had been thrashed once, for venturing out into a place hereabouts with a company of boys he had never really taken to. That had been an act of rebellion, too. Watching them slosh in the muddy water in unembarrassed nakedness had given him a fleeting glimpse of their true place in the garden story that, read to him repeatedly, had taunted his innocence.

Now here he merely contented himself with a glance at the bridge and sped past it. And after an infinity of running, he was there. He found the correct turn. His feet padded lightly on the cold turf: the park, at whose far end the lights played feebly with exhausted mirth.

There were still people about: couples returning home, pictures of an illusive city evening that had been finally run to earth and found flat. None of them minded the fear-eyed boy hurrying through the emptying park nursing a private grief.

He reached the side shows. The gigantic colored wheel was still. A barker slept in his box, his color and attitude making him resemble a broken toy. Slower now, Cleto searched for the doorway tied askew, which a single visit had made familiar. Once, twice, he stopped—that doorway there, the faded Arabian carpet for a curtain. . . . No, Cyrus' would have his name in huge letters on a bunting. And where was that now?

Briefly he felt terror. Had they gone? It did not seem possible. He searched on. A woman hanging clothes on a line beside her tent glanced at him and went on with her work, clamping a huge cigar between her teeth. I might ask her, he thought, and decided against it. *It's not a big place, I could find it if I made another round.*

He spotted it at the second turn. He ran toward the doorway, over which Cyrus' name gleamed redly in the light coming from within. His heart sank. *They're asleep. They have left me alone.* The canvas doorway was tied tight from within.

Cleto stood thinking for a moment, ran swiftly to the side of the tent. He felt the ground for spaces beneath the drawn canvas. *Cyrus, Cyrus . . .*

Cleto found it. An opening he could creep into. His head went in first, and he lay there listening to the sounds, confused by the music that he still heard from somewhere. Then he heard it: a soft slithering sound. A man's voice.

He's there, he thought. *And I have only to call out . . .*

But a woman's laugh interrupted him. It was a breathless, undulating laugh, oddly restrained, as against a pillow.

He wondered for a moment, and heard Cyrus' voice again, whispering. Other sounds crept in from outside, and the thin rasp he made pulling his body inside was scarcely audible. He stood up. *I'll call out. Let him know I'm here.* He moved and ran into a chair, dashing a bruise, and he winced in pain.

There was a soft light. He looked around: an empty program hall filled with tumbled seats. The light and the voices came from the same direction. Treading on damp sawdust, he made it slowly to the curtained doorway beside the tiny stage, and once more he heard the woman's laughter. He touched a hand to a welt on his thigh which began to bother him, and after deliberating he opened the curtain.

Cyrus was bent low over the bed, his arms around the woman who lay there. Cleto looked up, away from the unknowing figures on the bed, to the lamp that shone from its perch on a tall trunk. *What to do,* he thought, *what to do,* not able to understand this passionate vision, yet feeling it touch some queer, unfamiliar nerve in him.

"O my God," he said softly, as he returned his gaze upon the struggling figures on the bed. He felt his body suddenly twang with all the open wounds on it, begin to throb, pain him beyond endurance. He turned on his heels and ran, unknowingly catching the curtain in the crook of his arm as he fled.

The whole spread of curtain came down, and then the lamp atop the trunk, which smashed on the ground and went out. The terrifying dark swallowed him, while all about, as he ran, soared the voices of Cyrus and his woman, searching for him, the two of them separately.

He felt someone rush nearby, instinctively shot out a fist, and struck tender flesh, which burned at the touch. He heard the rhythmic creak of Cyrus' tin foot somewhere not far from him.

"He's here!" the woman screamed to Cyrus, who in the same instant drove into a pile of chairs.

Then she closed in on the boy. He felt her nakedness sear him.

The sound Cyrus made struggling to get up, and his desperation to free himself were the same. He was caught in a vise-like grip which, at the edges, was sharp claw. *There must be blood on her hands.* He kicked at her and she cursed. And before the boy knew it *he* was there, beside him, listening to the woman scream unintelligible words in a strange dialect.

Arms gripped the boy.

"Who are you?" Cyrus demanded.

When he did not answer, Cyrus felt his face with a moist hand, and the boy bit hard into the man's finger. Then he found the tin foot and jumped on it, hearing Cyrus howl in pain.

"It's that boy!" he said to the woman angrily, and in that moment Cleto forced himself out of the man's grip. He ran to the other end of the aisle, felt the canvas graze his head, and he threw himself on the ground, clawing at the canvas' fringe until he found an opening that led him out. He squirmed free, all his wounds hurting simultaneously with maddening pain. He picked himself up and started to run.

He fled past the stalls, past the pillar that grew ferns. He did not look back. *Run,* his only thought, *run or they'll catch you. Their laughter will drown you till you become as mad as they.*

Run. But where? They were at his heels— he fancied as a road sign caught his elbow, spinning him round and throwing him spread-eagled to the ground. He picked himself up, neglecting to examine the knee that instantly throbbed as if it had been a drum.

No one looked at the boy as he streaked past the last sideshow shack, whose walls advertised a serpent with a woman's head. His fear seemed to cover him up, inure him to the eyes of people who had gone there, to the park, seeking something else, not someone else's pain.

He did not know for how long he had been running, and as he fell utterly exhausted on soft grass, miles from the park, and felt his eyes closing, heavy with experience, he hardly felt his arms as they lifted, opening what would be a horizontal door, reaching out to keep it open, as he would, later in life, at a much happier date, reach out to touch a cottage door, unlatch it hurriedly (rain rioted over his head) to find behind it a woman smiling her weird smile at his approach, holding a wormy blanket to her lips as though it had been the dregs of some merciful draught or the hem of Cyrus' garment. By which she would mean to celebrate the happy moment in her life, when she walked, joining the astonished crowd of cripples on that sullen afternoon (she was twenty-two). "Ah, but I walked!" she would cackle, the edge of her voice eaten away by disease. "The memory is enough—one single hour in my life, when I walked!" She would repeat this, with a private laugh that he would also hear at his own deathbed, transformed into one of pious mockery. The laugh (hers) would end in a fit of coughing; he would try to touch her, becalm her out of her memory's frenzy, exorcise her of the magician's ghost. But she would die, in the lap of that laugh, and with the pain of remembered sin he would see himself in her, all alone in her cottage as he was all alone in the world: without father, without mother, and rather like the man Melchisedech, without genealogy.

Resil B. Mojares

ARK

There is a dead body in one of the rooms. I could hear them whispering excitedly as they filed past my door. In my mind, I followed them down the narrow, dimly-lit corridor, down the sagging stairway, into the lobby.

Pinned in bed, I tried to shape the sounds, invading, into some compelling meaning. Failing, I relaxed into darkness.

Once, twice, that night, I straggled into involuntary awareness where, from the strangely wakeful house, the message was repeated: Someone is dead.

I did not rise. I knew I was not far from waking. I was conscious—within the sluggish pelagic sense of a vastly unexciting flood—of a body alive, mine. But I did not rise.

———

Over breakfast the following morning they talked about the dead. Meal was the unappetizing usual: fish, spiceless, lard-wet eggs on greasy plates.

... The man's been dead for two, three days, they were saying at the Parlor last night.

And to think I'd been passing that door all that time ...

No, no foul play. Must have been the heart ...

I did not bother to look up from my plate as the talk went back and forth. To blunt any expectation of a reaction from me, I tackled my food with grim, exaggerated relish. A common table with strangers had never ceased to be an ordeal with me. There were many boarders in the house—permanents and transients—all steeped in a common stale smell, and I had never been able, through the years, to pin down a single name with a single face. Socializing to me was such a needless tax on the spirit, such a task.

... They said it was someone in the next room who finally got suspicious over the lights that never went out.

The poor man must have worked himself to death. He sold encyclopedias, I heard ...

There were no relatives in the Parlor. Cruz said there was no one to notify ...

I indolently watched a cockroach madly scurry across the table. I waited until it was gone. Noisily pushing my chair back from the table, I stood up and left.

———

It was near midnight when I returned. A group of boarders had collected in the lobby.

They were curiously impassive as if they had been returned from frustratingly unimportant errands. Before this motley gathering someone was talking of the death.

I watched the man because he was different from all the rest. It was not only the enormous white polo that drowned his frame. He was clearly agitated, distractedly doing things as he talked: fingering buttons, smoothing creases in his shirt, crackling his knuckles. Though acutely clerk-faced—his face peaked and undernourished—he was pointedly immaculate.

Something should be done, I heard him saying. He was crackling his knuckles nervously. The sweat stood out on his upper lip.

Sipping at a paper cup of Coke I had brought in from a vending machine, I watched the man. It was a hot night and I was edgy and wakeful.

...We're in this together, you see. And the man's our responsibility.

His manner tight and breathless, he trembled slightly when he talked as though words in him did not simply issue from the mouth, they rolled in the blood, collected in the heart.

The others, slumped on the sofa or standing, lulled by heat, appeared to be listening.

The man's our responsibility, he repeated. This house killed him, you see. The rooms are so small, we're packed so tight, there's simply no air to breathe. The walls so grimy, we must have new paint to brighten them up. And, yes, more frequent cleaning... Everything is falling apart and no one bothers.

This house killed him, you see... He repeated the statement for what must have seemed, to him, the urgency of what he secretly felt.

The man seemed easily exhausted. His silences were long, and he cracked his knuckles. In the spell of midnight heat the others were silent. Sticky with sweat, I scoured my head for laughter. The man's nervousness was beginning to irritate me.

Some of the ground floor rooms must be broken down, the man continued. For games, recreation. That's necessary, you see, the owner must be told.

A fat cockroach flew whirring across the room. The men watched it pass.

Cruz is a lackey, the owner's not here. Someone, sitting up on the lumpy sofa, was

saying, I've been here years, I tell you, I've never seen the man, not once.

The owner must be told, the nervous man persisted.

There was a near-fire once, the rheumy-eyed man on the sofa was saying. This house is a damned firetrap. But even that didn't bring the owner down, wherever he was. He's waiting to collect insurance, that's what they say.

There was a round of indifferent titters among those gathered but the nervous man did not seem to hear.

This is our house. And the man who died... he's one of us, too.

Perhaps it was the burgeoning headache I had from the heat, the senseless drift of talk, that made me snap.

You don't like it here. Why, go... I found myself speaking. Go, I said, suddenly regretting my having allowed myself to be drawn into the pettiness of it all.

Go? he said. Go where? he said, turning around hesitantly to face me.

When I saw his face, I was rather sorry for the man. He looked incongruously meek with some secret suffering, the sweat wet on his forehead, it seemed like he was running a fever. But it appeared like the others, lethargic in the heat, did not notice.

There was something I found strangely obscene in his pain. I looked at him fully with what I felt was a fair distaste. I crushed the paper cup in my hand, tossed it carelessly to a corner, and went up to my room.

===

It was extraordinarily hot that night. I woke up, spat out of a dream's diluvial darkness, to find my sheets soaking with sweat, my senses strangely sharp to my skin's familiar stink. I sat up on my pallet, thirsty and dizzy.

Moments later, as I lumbered down the corridor on my way to the washroom, still drunk with sleep, I almost bumped into the man. It was dark. He was still dressed in his clownish shirt and he was smiling at me when I looked up. I hurried past him, shuddering involuntarily because, at that instant, the thought that the man was queer had crossed my head.

In front of the washroom, at the end of the corridor, I turned in time to see him reach the other end and turn, slowly walking back towards where I stood. I rushed into the toilet before he caught me looking. I did not want him to get the idea I was interested in his business, whatever it was.

Although later, back in my room, I had to admit I was indeed struck by the strangeness of his walking the corridor so late in the night.

I could still hear him walking as I fell asleep.

———

The following morning, going through the dusty lobby, I saw some boarders huddled before the bulletin board, talking animatedly, breaking into occasional laughter.

Tacked to the board was a note written in an ornate, feminine hand. FIRST PETITION FOR THE AMELIORATION OF LIVING CONDITIONS, it read. TO WHOM IT MAY CONCERN.

And there followed, among others, the plans for improvement which the nervous man had outlined in the lobby the previous night. The sad little theatrics of the protest note amused me. Touched by a stranger's death, the man's obviously playing out his misplaced fears in a kind of game: I thought to myself.

I have never been able to successfully sympathize with the small, sad passions of men. They all tire me to death—activists with syphilis, small souls choking with claptrap and superstition. I have always thought of the matter as such a sorry waste. Men whose eyes stretch white with looking for the living points of their drowned earth excite in me nothing but pity, a feeling I have long discovered hopelessly futile and messy.

———

I met him walking the corridor again when I returned late that night. I did not bother to smile when I passed him. And when I entered my room I locked the door behind me.

I went to work on my journal that night. I am, you see, what you would call a miscellaneous writer: I write term papers, speeches, releases, love letters, anything, all for a fee. It's a killing business but I'm in my element, the feel of life's invisible wilderness, the hard thin joy of stalking, skirmishes. An office in my head, I hang around in campuses, newspaper offices and printing shops, talking with the men; in beer parlors, looking at the waitresses. In short, I'm around a lot.

But nights I spend on my journal. People buy memorial park lots, I write my journal. I leave people to believe in history, I collect moments. I shan't bet a tin crown on kingdoms, public destinations, the messiah's a very dead horse. There's nothing but moments the mind creates out of whipped air and sticks and on these the soul miraculously feeds before it finally, slowly, chokes to death. And that's why I don't believe in poets and writers, either, straddled as they are on their wooden horses of presumptions. I'm talking now of the living ones, I reverence the dead.

I go whoring, yes, but never anything serious. Somewhere, I don't know where, I have two children, perhaps three, but it's nothing serious. Perhaps I shall soon be able to write after my name: H.C.E. But that's an irrelevant private joke. The point, I always say, is to compose yourself for the grave. And that's the secret of serenity.

Making love to a girl, I would say, after Baudelaire: I'm wooing my grave. And that would be enough to kill all silliness of the heart in me. Peace replaces the tiring small-nesses of love and friendship: there is then in me some universal, dying tenderness that encloses her and me, then finally only me then finally nothing. The mind creaks to a stop. And that's what I have long resigned myself to calling just. I take this journey forward in the mind and I end up with nothing but this indeterminacy of deed, this drowning in thought. The mental journey leaves me so tired I'm completely emptied of the desire and the strength for the physical repetition. And so I declare cease, I stop. The breathless girl is bewildered, hurt. How can I tell her of the root of my weariness. Tell her that I'm dewinded, empty, stopped.

I wrote this down on my journal.

Feeling prelatic, I closed my notebook. I went to bed. A plump roach whirred across the room and was gone. As I descended into darkness, the only sound remaining in the house was his walking.

=====

The following morning I saw a Second Petition tacked to the board in the lobby. I did not bother to read it.

Coming home late that night I met him walking the corridor. I nodded vaguely when he greeted me with a wide smile. I went directly to my room and closed the door behind me.

I wanted to get back to my writing but nothing came. I was feeling dull, impatient. I dallied with the thought of constructing a brightness machine to squeeze out, at the pull of a lever, the juice of genius in me but I simply could not concentrate.

An ache curled livid in my head and, compounding it, I was bothered by the sound of his walking outside my room.

For such a small man he had such a heavy tread. I went to the door with the mind to yell at him but when I let myself out, all wrought up, he was so close by me—I was looking into his eyes—that it was all I could do to stare at him harshly, pointing heavily down at his heavy shoes.

For a moment, he just stood there smiling at me stupidly. And then finally looking down at his shoes, he must have realized what I wanted for he hurriedly mumbled his apologies, his mouth breaking into an even wider, sillier smile. There was something feverish about the way his thin hands fluttered as he bent to untie his laces, something comic about the passion with which he unshod himself right then and there at my feet. When he straightened up I almost expected him to execute a bow. But he just smiled and turned away. I watched him disappear down the corridor, his shoes now dangling on their laces from his hands. And I withdrew to my room.

The silent encounter momentarily unnerved me. I went to my window and faced the blank concrete wall of the next building. Furiously dragging on my cigarette, I held down my irritation at the almost theatrical stupidity of the man.

Later, my calm returned. And when I finally heard him shuffling past my door in what now sounded like soft slippers, I had to smile to myself.

I went to sleep that night with the sound of his walking, memory of childhood rain impinging on the brain.

=====

The third Petition was on the board when I went out the next morning. A few boarders were gathered at the lobby. It was the morning of the funeral. I did not linger to listen or inquire.

That night when I met him in the corridor I was feeling sufficiently high, I gave him a jaunty salute when he greeted me.

But my exhilaration slowly died down when I was inside the room. The stale smell of things stirred in an almost liquid heat. The lightness I felt was floating, sourceless. It readily perished.

The rats were busy at work. I heard them gnawing on wood and paper under the pallet. When I moved about they paused; when I stood stockstill they began again. I repeated the motions, taunting, testing the little creatures. I finally tired of the game and composed myself to write.

There were so many things in my head, each rushing forward into darkness whenever I strained to grasp them, momently flaring, leaving behind bright tracks, dying. To sleep in that astral quiet...

Life is a mad, bright congenital sickness inducing delusions, hyperesthesia. Between life and non-life, the essential conflict, is not one breath, one simple gasp of fitful air, but a vast mental wilderness of diseased tissues and nerves. In this rotting forest there are no swift magical transformations: Io a cow, Cygnus a swan, the daughters of Minyas bats. Dostoevsky's sufferer does not become the mouse in the hole, Harry Haller does not become the wolf of the steppes. Yes, Samsa became the vermin in the mind's grim game but that was no magic. It was K., seeing things, stretched out on his own greasy, creaky rack.

The field of tension is this persistent, loveless desire to coagulate the creature, soulbound, heliotropic, helical. The field stinks with malodorous sweat. We have become such passionate reasoners, such passionate sufferers . . .

I was tired. I saw myself getting in and out of boxes, clean square boxes that got smaller and smaller. It is this obsessive desire for predication, uroboric, self-eating. My mind played with the thought; and expanding, filled out with irrelevancies:

To purge the organism of bright fatal helios. Is futile. S + P = CONCEPT. The futile urge to purge. Is real. S + P = C. The real futile urge. Is sick. The real sick futile urge . . .

I was growing lightheaded, a deep strange laughter was squirming to life within me. As I paused in thought two sounds returned to me with unusual clarity: the rats gnawing on wood, and him walking the corridor. I shunted the sounds from my mind, I was thinking.

To trace the passage of an old story: the temptress on a raft, I see her in a cave in the mountains; watch her seduce the monk child, the stone child, to man replete with eyes and skin and sin. Speak, speak: she whispers with mouth imparting warmth, with hands kneading warm. The crops are withered now, carcasses litter the dry, hard fields. She traces the veins of rock to veins of tensile pain, she wraps him in the odor of her nearness, diuretic and sheer. Now I see her bearing him down the river. They bear him through the dying village. I see him in the bridal bed now smelling thickly of his seed. That night, the rains fell and, as myth foretold, life began again.

The tale throbbed in my head for the ritual was senseless to me.

The room was oppressively warm. I was tired, subdued. And thirsty, I made for the door. On my way back from the washroom, I met the man.

Go and sleep, I said.

No, he simply stated. He made to go but I held him by the shoulder, surprised at once by his frailness.

Sleep, I said.

I must keep watch, he said.

For what? I almost laughed in his face. My nerves were frayed in the lateness of the hour and I was tired.

I must watch while you sleep, he said. And then he looked at me, leaned towards me. He tensed to speak but no word came. And then, finally, stuttering, he said:

The man who died . . . no one was there. Don't you see . . . if someone cries out in his sleep then someone shall hear.

I should not have laughed but I did. And the man should not have smiled. It was then that the lurking thought rose sharply in my head. The man was mad. I withdrew my hand from his shoulder. I saw then how his eyes glittered with fever, felt that the skin I had brushed was hot.

I could not exactly recall what happened next. I found myself back in the room, the door locked behind me.

I had a fitful, dream-wracked sleep that night. Lying in darkness there filtered down to me the sound of someone carelessly walking over my grave.

———

The morning after the funeral, I found the lobby deserted. The board was empty except for the usual List of Letters I never bothered to read.

Returning late that night I did not meet him in the corridor. Thinking he must have been somewhere in the lower floor when I came up, I waited for the sound of his walking. But it did not come.

The suddenly unnatural silence of the

house bothered me. But I quickly banished it from my thoughts as I composed myself to write. I stared at the bleak concrete wall fronting the window, listened to the sounds of night outside, below, astride my senses, like a dull flood, indeterminate, mechanic.

I could not explain it but I was suddenly gripped by a deep irrational fear—the house carried away in dark waters, the sounding death.

I cursed my weakness. I returned to the table. Seated, I began to order my thoughts.

The struggle between the mineral and spiritual in us is such an unexciting contest. It takes place in a murk. What intoxicated Kurtz was the smell of death, heady and thick. And he, being the passionate, spiritual man, tensed himself tautly against it even as it ate slowly at his brain. And that is why, tensing, his senses metalbright, corroded, he was almost unrecognizable in death. To give up the ghost is not so easy, the damned thing so inextricably sticky, it is not so easily released, does not easily levitate into nothingness as free, configured smoke such as that we see in medieval picture books.

I paused. As my mind went blank, the dull mechanic flood coursed in my ears like water over a crumbling spillway. It seemed always like the multiple, disorganized sounds of roiling, splintering, falling were dammed only by my thinking. I brought my mind to attention once more, but even as I waited no comets laid bright tracks on blackness.

In the room the trapped heat had a sourish human taste. I went out for a drink from the washroom tap. It was when I returned to the room that I realized I must have half-expected to meet the man for I could not explain, there, the vague disappointment, loneliness, I felt.

Without thought, weariness in the body was liquid, liberated, Casting for a center, I pinned my tiredness on a cockroach stain on the smeary wall.

I went to sleep that night heavy with many things: a dull humming mesh of sleeping bodies; strange, silent, almost animal souls rubbing their hides against walls; the clamorous gray and unsubsiding flood.

Once, a rat scuttled across my genitals and I bolted up in horror. The house was silent. My mouth was dry. Alive to the stench of my own sweat, I cocked my ear for a familiar sound but there was nothing.

====

I forgot all about the man the next morning. I was in haste to collect from a guy for whom I had written a paper.

I returned late that night, frustrated in my business. I found the corridor empty. I went straight to the room. I was feeling faint and sick.

A film of dust covered the table, the pile of books. It was strange that I should notice distinctly the feel of fine, grainy dust as I passed my hand over things. I judged I was running a fever because I was edgy and sweating, my senses honed to a vague, debilitating excitement.

I laid myself on bed, itchy with dust and heat. I spent time staring at a gaping hole in the ceiling, the peeling paint. I listened to the dark whirring, the tiny scampering feet. Unable to collect, must get up early, walk tomorrow; I must rest now, conserve my strength—a jumble of petty thoughts crowded my head as I listened patiently to my shallow breathing.

But I was soon up. Lighting my cigarette, my last, I walked about the room, putting books, things, into place. I was caught up in a slow indefinite burning and I was trying to organize. But the aimless excitement was eating me.

Finally, opening the door, I looked out into the corridor and there, near the head of the stairway where the bulb was dead, I saw him standing. I thought he smiled, but he did not move. An excitement so thick it felt like sickness surged through me, I looked again, feeling all the while a sudden rush of shame, relief. But he was not there.

I pressed a cold hand over my face because my eyeballs were sticky and warm. And I looked again. He was not there. The corridor was empty. Withdrawing, sick, I closed the door and locked it. I found myself leaning heavily against it, sweating cold. And turning back towards the bed, I was struck by the stupidity of my blindness, my shame, that, throwing my head up, I laughed.

I fell laughing on the bed.

And the house came sharply alive at my laughter. There was an answering rattle of sticks and bottles and walls from the many rooms of the house, and I shrieked louder. The rattle grew louder in answer. I stopped so suddenly I choked on my laughter.

In the sudden silence that followed I said to myself: They are listening, mistrustful, afraid, choking on the faint sad odor of their own semen on the grimy walls; soon they will return to sleep and drown in their own bad dreams. A wave of oppressive darkness swept over me. Breathing thickly, I began once more to collect my thoughts.

It's simply this fever, a sheer trick of heat. He was not there. Watch that simple fact. I must get up, spend myself on something. Organize.

I pushed myself from the bed and headed for the table. Seated, I started, methodic, to think. I closed my eyes but before me there was only black swimming space. I caught my head in a vise to keep the throbbing down, the swimming still. In that interior blackness I thought I caught the reflected sheen of vague angelic bodies but then it was only the dim pained white of my eyelids pressing.

No, he was not there. It's just that I haven't eaten, my seeing him a pure trick of hunger. A simple fact. Now to have water. To steady the head . . . But wait! suppose he had gone down the stairway to the lower floor when I had that second look. And he's coming up now on the other end. I'll catch him if I go, open the door, now. He's barefoot, he has cast off his slippers, yes. And that's why I can't hear him. And he's there now, yes, walking past the door.

I stifled a laugh. My eyes were smarting with heat. I must get hold of myself, I said.

Organize, I said. To effect balance when the ground is moving, I said.

But soon I was at the door. I thought I heard steps down the stairs. But when I rushed out, the corridor was empty. I went down the defective dark of the stairway, listening for a sound. I walked the deserted lower corridor and when I finally turned up the other sagging staircase, there was no one. For a very long time I went up and down, walking the corridors. I was feeling so faint and sick I thought my knees would give way if I stopped, that they would hold if I just kept on walking. And I walked.

It was a long time. My brain in wires, a sour feathery feel, rising, tickled my throat as I walked. I rushed towards the washroom. I bent over the rank-smelling bowl but nothing came. I doused my head in water. In the bodied odor of the toilet I was all ghostly, atmospheric head. Light, like the singing air was rising through a hole in my head, I returned to the room.

Organize, I said. Need for ballast in a rising murk, I said. Hold still, I said.

Inside the room I fixed my mind on the cockroach stain. My body burned with attention until, lifted up in a strange lightness, my mind cleared.

In the middle of my sleep that night I dreamed I clambered up the heights of fever, and he came, bending over me, whispering away the storm, passing over my face his hand, lonely memory, the feel of the gentle heaviness of my father's hand.

———

The following day I saw them carry his body down the dingy stairway.

They found him in his room. He must have died in his sleep, someone said.

I did not go out that day. I stayed in the room. I waited for the darkness to come because I felt there were many things I had to do, and I wanted to begin.

Ninotchka Rosca

GENERATIONS

Mumbling calmed the soul. To Selo, this was knowledge that came with old age. He would sit outside on the front ladder, his bare feet resting on the last rung, and mumble. Words would push up from between his lungs, past his tonsils, and work their way between his toothless gums. His lips spat them out in small explosions. There were any number of things to mumble about: sometimes he told a story, sometimes he just followed the movement of the sun from east to west, sometimes he grumbled about the house, the road, the harvest. Today he made sounds. It was summer, but enough water remained in the irrigation canal to feed the seedbeds. Viewed from the house, the canal was a shimmering distortion in a brown palm of land distorted by heat waves.

The two boys playing in the yard had grown used to Selo's mumbling. The older, nine years of age, drew a circle on the ground with his dirty forefinger. He was not quick enough, and two drops of sweat fell from his brow into the circle. Against the soil's glitter, the sweatdrops were black, shallow holes. He studied them for a moment; then, carefully, he covered the holes with two chipped marbles—one orange, one blue. Just outside the line he had drawn, his brother's toes dug into the powdery earth. The older boy ignored his brother just as he ignored old Selo.

Grandfather's bad humour, their grandmother used to say, had started with the withering of his right hand. The bird-claw that resulted had not been her fault. As a matter of fact, she had saved his life. The claw was nothing more than an extraneous addition to the whole affair—regrettable but unimportant. She had saved his life. Because of the debt, the boys' memories of the old woman were rimmed with guilt. No one had been able to help her when her turn to die came.

It took place at the height of the monsoon season. The house was so waterlogged the bamboo posts had split their brown skins and were mottled green. A translucent pair of leaves even sprouted from the middle node of the bamboo holding the kitchen wall up. Grandmother, who had complained of chest pains for weeks, had a coughing attack so fierce she sounded like a joyous frog. The fit lasted for hours. It would take her by the throat and snap her small head back and forth, while bits of matter—red, flecked with foam—ejected from her mouth and darted around like tiny bats. Mother, a Lysol-soaked rag in her hand, chased the steaming bats and shouted for the rest of the family to keep away. It was hard work, but she would not allow anyone to help. Finally, grandmother gave a terrible series of yelps. Her eyes disappeared into her head. She fell, cutting her brow on the pallet's edge and overturning the chamber pot.

Since that time, the boys had known that a man's interior was dark-red and grey, spongy and foamy. This was wisdom uncovered by death: a man's interior was uninteresting, made up of tissue so dark-red it turned black in the gaslight. A man was neither good nor bad inside, only uninteresting.

Old Selo, on the other hand, could not remember that evening. One day his wife was there; the next, she wasn't. After thinking about it, old Selo decided that death was a sin of omission where the dead forgot to live. It was all as simple as that. The dead didn't do anything. The living mumbled like him, shouted like his daughter-in-law, cursed like his son, cried like his grandsons, or turned into beauties like his granddaughter. She was fifteen years old and had dark brown skin and straight black hair reaching down to the small of her back. With her large eyes, her nice mouth, she could have a future. Selo glanced at the sacks piled near the shed—brown jute sacks fat with rice grains. It had been a good harvest.

His claw itched. His left hand caressed it. Like all the men in the village, he had indulged in man-talk in his youth. He and the other men had been members of a supposedly national society of peasants. They had gathered in the empty schoolhouse during evenings and had made plans for the future. It had been exciting to think of cramming the landlord's genitals down his throat. It had been exciting to talk of snaring and roasting his dogs grown vicious on a diet of meat. The dogs had chased old Selo once, when he had tried to deliver the landlord's share of the harvest himself.

In high hopes, Selo had had the society's insignia tattooed on the skin web between his thumb and forefinger. Other men in the village carried the blue sickle on their bodies—on the chest, above the heart; on the thigh; on the skin web between thumb and forefinger. It betrayed them when the landlord's goon squads started kicking house doors down. The massacre went on for

months, with the odor of putrid flesh mingling with the harvest fragrance. The rivers seemed full of crocodiles then, with all the bodies floating in the water.

The landlord's men hadn't reached their village yet, but old Selo's wife was already screaming that he was a dead man. Taking his courage in hand, he whetted his fan-knife and prepared to excise the tattoo. At the last moment, however, he remembered his friends' bodies fertilizing the fields. He dropped the knife. His wife cursed him for three hours and finally lost her patience. She heated a silver coin in the charcoal stove and with her blackened firethongs dropped it on Selo's tattoo. The house posts shook with the old man's bellows, and disconsolate screams answered him from a cloud of ricebirds hovering over the field. The trick worked. When the metal cooled, his wife ripped the coin off Selo's hand, deftly stripping the flesh underneath. Selo, angered by his wife's triumph, wrapped his hand in a rag. He refused to let anyone look at the wound.

———

The boys waited for the vehicle to come into sight before rising to their feet. It was a jeep with a trailer and a dust cloud streaking behind it. When the jeep stopped before the bamboo gate, the dust cloud blew towards the house, forcing the boys to avert their faces. Old Selo remained as he was and tasted gritty soil on his lips. Four men jumped off the jeep. All had tooled leather gunbelts around their waists. One wore a *buri* hat.

"Your father home?" the man with the hat asked.

The boys looked at each other. Finally, the older one shook his head.

"That's all right," one of the men called out. "The rice's here, anyway."

The hatted man scratched his nape and frowned.

"Listen now," he said to the boys. "Tell your father he left only thirty sacks of rice for the *propietario*. He should have left fifty. Then, he owes me ten more for the seeds and five more for the weeder. So, we're taking thirty-five sacks now. Can you remember that?"

The boy felt he should say something but could not find the words for what he wanted to say. He gave a shrug and nodded.

"Okay," the man turned to his companions. "Load up."

One of the men was strong enough to lift an entire sack by himself. The other two worked together. As they moved back and forth, the pile of sacks sank closer and closer to the ground.

"Come on, come on," the man with the hat said, "it's tricky business. Never know what these peasants will do."

He tugged at a sack impatiently. Old Selo scuttled off the ladder, drew something hanging on the nearest house post. He rushed towards the men. The boys shouted. It was enough warning. The man with the hat evaded the downward slice of the machete. The blade buried itself in the topmost sack's belly. Old Selo tugged at the hilt, and gold kernels bathed the jute sacks. Without hurry, the man with the hat seized old Selo's wrist and wrung the weapon from him. Reversing the machete, he struck old Selo's chest with the hilt. A cry escaped the old man. His spine hit the ground and the man with the hat pinned him with a foot.

"It's okay," he said to his men. "I'll keep him quiet. Hurry up now. I don't want more trouble."

When the jeep with the trailer disappeared, the boys helped old Selo back to the ladder. He seemed to have forgotten the incident and resumed mumbling, his lips speckled with blood. The boys looked at each other. They walked to the gate, squatted down, and waited.

It took some time for the horse-drawn rig to appear at the road's rise. It moved so slowly that the boys could hardly keep still. They lost control when they recognized their mother and sister among the passengers. The older boy was aware of his incoherence, but impatience pushed the words out of his mouth. The afternoon's story had to be told. Still

shouting, he watched his mother climb down the rig and help his sister manoeuvre a basket past the dirty wheel. The horse, its flanks covered with sweat and whipmarks, snorted; its skin trembled.

The mother tried to wipe off the blood from Selo's mouth, but it had dried and would not come off. She released her skirt's hem impatiently and pushed the old man up the ladder. Meanwhile, the two boys menaced the basket their sister was carrying. She threatened them with a fist. They shied away, returned and tried to peer into the basket, sending it banging against the girl's shins. She shouted at them to leave her alone. There was nothing in the basket but food. The distressing news set the younger one wailing. Mother leaned out of the window and ordered him to stop or else . . .

Inside the house, old Selo had clean lips again, his daughter-in-law having used a wet rag on his face. He watched as she prepared the evening meal. She held an eggplant down with her left hand, forefinger extended and pressed against its end, while her right hand stroked through the eggplant's flesh with a knife. Her fingertip was never more than a hair's breadth away from the blade as it sliced through the vegetable. She grumbled as she worked. She had warned old Selo's son, she said, but he would not listen. He kept talking about the law. But what in god's name had the law got to do with people? Laws were paper and ink; they were kept in filing cabinets in offices in town and city buildings. Now, if it were the law of the sun or of the seas or of the earth, that would be an altogether different matter. People's laws had nothing to do with people.

The girl smiled at herself in the cracked mirror on the wall. Her eyes sought out the photograph of an actress pinned to the wall. Like her, the actress had limpid eyes and a small mouth. The girl sighed and lifted the weight of her hair from her nape. God willing, she would have a future. She smiled again, then picked up a thin blue towel draped on a battered bamboo chest.

"Where are you off to now?" her mother asked in her usual harsh voice.

"To the canal," she said, "to take a bath."

"Take the boys with you."

The girl crinkled her nose. "Why do I have to?"

"Because you're no longer a child," came the answer. "Because of what could happen which must not happen."

"It's not as if I take my clothes off," the girl muttered, but her voice had lost it conviction.

"Take the boys with you."

———

They tried to keep the canal's lips as bare and hard-packed as the summer fields, but green things somehow managed to make their way there. They took root overnight, dipping hair tendrils into the water: bizarre flowers of purple and yellow, stringy weeds, and the mimosa pudica. The girl hated the mimosa for its deceptive shyness. At the least touch, its leaves folded and drooped but only to bare the thorns on its stems.

The boys stripped immediately and dived into the water. They swam, transformed into sleek, brown puppies with iridescent limbs and bodies. The girl watched. Then she too entered the water. First she washed her hair, scrubbing it with crushed herbs and leaves. Then groping beneath the water, she cleaned the soft secrets of her body. Her fingers cupped her unfinished breasts. Sighing, she leaned back in the water and lifted her face to the sky where the sun was beginning to cool.

It was nearly dusk when they left the canal. The boys shared the weight of a pail of water while the girl shivered in her wet clothes. At the backyard's edge, the girl abruptly signalled for the boys to stop. From the house came her father's growls, her mother's shrilling. The boys' eyes widened. They turned to the sister, but something in her face made them look away. A clatter of tin plates erupted from the house. There was the sound of a slap, a sharp cry. Then, the creaking of the ladder as someone came down in a hurry. The girl showed her teeth.

Dinner was ready. The mother was picking up plates from the floor. She pointed to the table. The boys smiled and carried the pail into the kitchen. The girl changed her clothes.

"Rice!" the older boy exclaimed. "Not gruel. Real rice."

"Might as well eat it," the mother said. "It won't last very long."

She drowned the rice mound on Selo's plate with soup. A twinge of anger shot through the girl. It was a shame and a waste. Grandfather couldn't take anything solid anyway. But that was the way it was, the way it had always been. Even with eating, one took a vow akin to marriage—one ate as the others ate, for richer and for poorer.

Old Selo waited for the table to be cleared. It seemed hardly possible that the day was over, as the day before had been over. The sun was born in the east, died in the west; the dry season came and merged with the monsoon season. Flood and drought. And all through the changes of time, men worked in the fields, holding on and holding out, coaxing the earth into yielding the golden kernels, so tiny they seemed like babies' gasps. Why couldn't the sun and the rain clouds be nailed to the sky? Instead of men, the elements should hold on. Hold on, as his wife used to say.

Obediently, the old man lowered his body to the mat spread out by his grandsons. His body loosened its moorings and entered the sea of sleep. He dreamt, his dream melting into the dreams breathed out by his daughter-in-law and his grandchildren. One dream now possessed the house, each member of the family giving to it. There were scenes of joy, a morning rimmed with hope, a child's universe of a toy.

"Wh-wh-what?" the granddaughter murmured.

Something was in the yard. It moved, its bulk rustling against the nipa fronds of the house's walls. In the dark, the boys' eyes were pitted stars. The girl looked at her mother; the older woman was also awake, listening in the dark. Before she could say anything, the door blew open so violently it tore its upper rope hinges. In the doorway, a man's shadow stood, his head and shoulders dusted by moonlight.

Resentment came into the room. The man halted, prowled about the accusing air of his family. His insulted soul gave him pride. Son-of-a-goat, he said, he was a man, and a man had rights. So the law decreed. Circling, he came upon a face. His grief balled itself into a fist. Without a word, he smashed a blow into his wife's face.

Something heavy struck his back and clung to his neck with little claws. The man beat at the thing on his back. He swept it off and threw it to the floor. He began to kick at it. But the white bat shrieked in his daughter's voice. The man stopped. The shadows were un-ravelling themselves. There were his wife, his sons, his daughter and old Selo, his father, curled like a gnome in the corner. He found the door and lost himself in the night.

"Stop him," the mother cried out.

"Not me," the girl said. "He kicked me. The son-of-a-bitch kicked me."

"Don't say that," the mother said. "Follow him and see he's all right."

"He's drunk."

"Do as you're told," the mother said, dabbing at the blood on her mouth. "It's curfew time. If the soldiers find him, everything will be over for sure."

The girl did not move.

"Please follow him," the mother said. She was still stroking her mouth. "Please. We have to—to hang on."

The girl kicked at a pillow.

"All right," she said. "But if he kills me, it will be on your head."

"Take your brother with you," the mother called out.

The older boy was already running after his sister. He caught up with her in the yard. She took his hand, murmured something that sounded like everything had to be over, and led him to the gate. Moon-touch had trans-formed the world, and the two halted before the alien landscape. The boy felt he was gliding on silver water. From a distance came their father's voice. He was cursing the night.

"He's making for the town," the girl said.

"Son-of-a-whore," the boy muttered. "He'll hit a checkpoint for sure."

The girl broke into a run. The boy followed, his eyes darting with suspicion among the strangely lit objects of the night world. The girl shied suddenly, bumping into her brother.

"A snake," she said.

"I don't see anything."

"I heard it. Never mind. Hurry."

It was too late. Three shadows broke the silver road. The father was trying to convince the two soldiers that a man had the right to get drunk where and how it pleased him. Particularly when the harvest was involved, yes, sir, particularly... One of the soldiers replied by pummelling him in the ribs and stomach.

"Pests," the boy whispered and spat on the ground.

"Sssh," the girl held her brother's hand. "It will be all right. He pays now. Don't worry."

"Pay for what? They'll take him to the barracks now."

"Sssh. I'll take care of this. Go home and tell mother everything's all right. I'll bring him home."

"Sure."

"Believe me. Trust me. I'll get him out."

"How?"

The girl did not answer. Looking at her, the boy saw her lips had pulled back, her teeth were bare. In the moonlight, her mouth seemed full of fangs.

═══

She entered the room on tiptoe but hardly a second passed before a man's voice ex-claimed: "Well, what have we here?"

There were two of them—one seated behind a varnished table, the other on a canvas bed. The first held a notebook and wore fatigues; the second was in his under-shirt and pants and was polishing his boots.

"Please, sir," the girl said, "my father..."

The room smelled of wax and detergent. Light spilling from a naked bulb overhead turned the floor bloodclot red.

"Which one is he? The men here are so active it's hard to tell who has sired whom," the sergeant said.

"He was picked up, sir, just a while ago." The girl swallowed. In a softer voice, she added: "He was drunk, sir."

She told herself that nothing had changed in the room. The bulb still swung from the frayed cord; the light was as harsh as before. There was no reason for the hair on her nape to stand.

"What do you want with him?"

"I've come to take him home."

"Child, it's not as simple as that. First, we have to take him to the judge. Violating curfew, disturbing the peace. And so on. Then we'll have a trial. Since it's Saturday, we have to wait till Monday to even begin. The judge will either fine him or send him to jail or both. It may take weeks, months—maybe years."

"Please, sir, my mother's waiting."

"I suppose you can pay the fine."

"We don't have money," she said, flushing. "But we have rice."

The soldiers looked at each other. The sergeant said there was nothing to be done. As a matter of fact, the girl herself was violating curfew and he was tempted to arrest her, too. The soldier on the cot laughed.

"You want to see him?"

She nodded. The sergeant stood up and motioned for her to follow.

"We locked him in the toilet," he said.

It was an outhouse. The father rose from the cement floor when the door was opened. He bleated at the sight of his daughter.

"Go away," he said. "Go away. Tell your mother I'll be all right. Go on home."

His left eye was swollen. A blue-grey lump glistened on his forehead. The girl swallowed again. She stretched out a hand to him but the sergeant pushed her away. He closed the door on the father's voice.

"Well, he stays there," the sergeant said, "at least until he's sentenced."

The girl stood before the table.

"Please, sir," she said, "I must take him home."

"Can't do. Not unless you pay the fine. Do you have money?"

The girl bit her underlip.

"No? Maybe you can pay some other way. What do you think?" The sergeant turned to the other soldier. "Can she pay some other way?"

The man laughed. His eyes glittered.

"I should think so. She's old enough. And peasant girls are strong."

"How about it?" the sergeant asked. "You owe your father that much."

The girl's mouth opened.

"Any self-respecting daughter would do much more. How about it? We'll give him a bed, make him comfortable while you're paying. At dawn, we'll give him to you. How about it?"

The other soldier yawned. The girl looked at the lightbulb. If only the light had not been as harsh.

"How about it?" the sergeant repeated. "There are only four of us here. You're lucky."

Sometime in the night, the toilet door was opened and the father was taken out. He was given a cot in the barracks. Gratefully, he stretched his limbs, his sore muscles creaking. Sleep came to him, but he was awakened almost immediately. He had turned over and had nearly fallen off the cot. It must have frightened him, for his heart beat furiously for several minutes. His fear was transformed into a woman's cry. After listening for a few seconds, the father decided it was a bat shrilling in the dark. He went back to sleep and was awakened again, this time by a dog's barking. He lay with his eyes open, looking at the shadows of the strange room. From somewhere in the building came a man's low laugh.

It was morning when he rose from the bed. The sun was on the brink of rising. A soldier came and led him to the office. It was empty, the blankets on the cot neatly folded. The soldier pushed him towards the door.

"I can leave?" the father asked.

The soldier smiled and nodded. He patted the father on the shoulder. A smile cracked the man's dry lips. He bounded through the open door. The cool of the morning eased the creases on his face. Under a kamachile tree, his daughter waited, a scarf tied about her head.

"What are you doing here?" the father shouted.

"Waiting," she said, dropping her eyes. "Waiting for you."

He looked at her with suspicion, but she did not seem to have changed.

"Come quickly," she said. "Mother's waiting."

She stepped away from him. She turned too quickly and stumbled on a pebble. The scarf slipped off and when she bent to pick it up, her skirt rose, revealing a bruise at the back of her left thigh. The father looked away.

"Waiting," he mumbled. "That's another word for it. Waiting." He gave a short bark of laughter.

Thin wisps of smoke—dewdrops evaporating—curled from the ground. The air was cool and carried the scent of roasting corn. The father's head turn, his eyes scanning the fields. A softness lay in his chest. His daughter walked in front of him and he was seized by an impulse to tell her how he had first met her mother.

"Well, now" he said, clearing his throat, "I suppose we have to tell. Tell your mother."

"Let's not talk," she said.

He quickened his pace, leaving his daughter behind. At that instant, the sun touched a tree so violently that its branches crackled. The tree absorbed the light. Soaked through, it began to glisten, returning the sun's warmth. Open-mouthed, the father looked at the tree. He was still looking at it when something hard and jagged smashed in the back of his skull.

"I have the right," the daughter said.

It was the boy who found them. He had left his younger brother in the fields and had wandered off, asking himself what had happened to his father and sister.

"Whoreson," he said, "they killed him."

"Yes."

"Why?"

"There was no one else to kill."

The boy looked at her curiously. Her skirt was splattered with blood and white matter.

"You tried to lift him," he said—tentatively, as though it were a suggestion.

The girl smiled. "I learned so much this night."

"Well, we have to hang on. Hang together."

Joy T. Dayrit

UNFINISHED STORY

Bore. To bore is to tire oneself thru tedious iteration or dullness. To iterate is to repeat. Dullness is dullness. Dull, dull, dull. If to iterate is to repeat, the word reiterate is redundant, dundant. This is the quality or state of my being, it sways from tedious to dull.

When I come home from work there is my boyfriend to talk to. Hello, he says, how was work? Okay, I say, even if it wasn't.

I work as an usherette in a movie house. Stationed at the loge my job is to accept the loge people's ticket stubs and guide them to a seat with my flashlight. Dull. Except when they showed the super show *The Mountain.*

The Mountain is the story of a man who grows to be very, very old. He grows to be one hundred and twenty years old and naturally grows to be as wise. It is a religion story for modern people and everyone came to see it. All seats were taken for ten days and for ten days I pushed through people to guide people to aisle steps or to a piece of floor on which to sit. When at last *The Mountain* went on its last day and they showed *Bixbi,* it was dull again.

Dull is not as bad as tedious. Tedious is worse than dull. When my work becomes tedious I play secret games with my flashlight. In my work my flashlight is my only real companion. I flash it against my palm and see the translucent red outline of my hand, its green veins, the creases on my knuckles, the fingernail line on my finger, or I flash it on and off on someone's foot rested on the back of a seat until the foot slinks down. Loge people are not allowed to rest their feet on the back of seats, although at times I let them. I have power over the loge people—I let them do or not, and guide them well or not. In guiding I sometimes flash a light on a step short of the steps down and someone always trips. It entertains me but it nevertheless ends in boredom.

In drama there is an element called comic relief. It releases the audience from a hold and allows them to breathe. A flashlight game I play gives me this relief, relieves me from boredom. In guiding people to seats I swing my light along a row and as I bring the light back, I flash it against a face. The face viewing the movie reacts, and as I catch its instant expression, I click off the light. It all happens in half a second; it takes mastered calculation and a quick thumb. Then I go back to my station at the bottom right of loge and sit on my stool and play in my mind the expression I'd seen (no two have been the same) and in a few seconds I am bored again. The comic relief after its relaxing effect brings the audience back to a more intensive hold, Dante said. Dante is my boyfriend.

Dante and I live in my room not far from the movie house I work in and the university he attends. He is a scholar studying English and drama and one day would like to write for the movies. In a drawer is his treasured folder of ideas for movie stories, but more important to him now is his play. All day he sits and studies books lent by the university library and at night writes his play. The play, a last requirement for the completion of his university degree, is about a country girl in the city, who comes to do any odd job just to eat, and for shelter. Her pitiful ignorance is abused, but in the end she survives. In truth, Dante's play is about me, but he leaves from it important biographical items about my own city life.

For instance, I bore myself ushering because its pay allows me my room, some food, and a Friday night mathematics course (I aim to be a certified accountant) at the university Dante goes to. We met there. On a Friday rainy night, too wet outside to walk, we sat on the same damp bench at the university facade and talked about our courses. I understood much of what Dante was telling me about drama, and when the rain let off, it baffled him to know that I first of all ushered for the movie house a block down. The strong, unexpected rain had made my face and bare arms glisten against the facade light. I have a fine face, after my mother, whose provincial life formed year after year the ardent cool in her expression. My eyes, like hers, slant slightly up; I hardly paint them, they are of themselves dark. Wet hair pressed against my nape, and I grew sharply aware of but ignored Dante's incisive gaze. You don't look like an usherette, he said. I am out of uniform, I said. Dante leaves this out of his play. In his play his country girl suffers so much.

One week after Dante moved in with me, we had our first big quarrel. We fought over the papaya he had brought in with him, a gift for me, which I'd left to over-ripen severely on the window sill.

You ignored it! Dante smashed the papaya into our garbage.

I only forgot about it!

It was there for a week, couldn't you even smell it!

I had imagined a first fight with a lover to be out of romance, but ours was extremely strange. As we battled, he hotly asked me to a movie house to "quietly talk our quarrel out." What? I shouted. I was there all day, I will be there all day tomorrow!

We went to a movie house. Dante finds movie houses quiet places to talk in. All our fights since have been fixed, and sweetly, in movie houses, although not once has Dante brought me for a talk to the movie house I usher for.

The room Dante and I live in is one of five other small square spaces in an old, leaning two-story house, and in it we have put everything we own. Two steps from our bed is Dante's desk, full of books and papers. On our window sill is a burner on which I cook our food. A bureau with three drawers stores our clothes and is also our dining table on which we place our meals, have coffee, keep our canned or cellophaned food, and occasionally set a plate of fruit. Under our bed are shoes, things, newspapers, and our suitcases. We have a chair for Dante's desk. When we talk or eat he sits on his chair and I on the floor or bed beside him.

After work I help Dante with his play. I type it out for him on his rented Olivetti, using two or three fingers from one hand while resting my head on the other. Tired from work I type slowly, but in time Dante's country girl amuses me, and I begin to go more rapidly.

She is about to begin her fourth pathetic adventure in the city and she enters it with as much enthusiasm and cheer as she did her first. She will not learn her lesson. She accepts work from the next strange man who shows kindness, and is again used for activity other than the job agreed on. As pub waitress, Dante's country girl lures contacts for her employer, and big swindling occurs. When the syndicate is exposed, it is she who goes to prison.

It is in prison where she is loved, and finally survives, but Dante has not written the play's end yet, and as his thesis deadline approaches, he rushes his work, snapping at me for things I do that might disturb his thinking. He howls at me one evening for cooking fish. Intense concentration and the hot night had made him perspire, and I stand at attention while he howls. When he returns to his work I turn to flip the frying fish in the pan. He will eat the fish when it is cooked, and forget that it had filled our already very warm room with foul smoke.

Two days before deadline, midway through the last act of his manuscript, the *c* of Dante's rented Olivetti catches, and he continues typing wildly without the *c*'s. I am made to fill in the *c*'s with a black felt-tip pen. It is work as tedious as it sounds and soon my *c*'s dance, leaning all to the left and then to the right, or they stand very straight, like soldiers.

———

Dante's university scholarship is a gift from his widowed cousin in Batangas. In return, Dante promises her his thesis, and in the summer, a day after his graduation, with his play in a bag, we go on a bus to the town of Balayan, where this cousin lives.

She is a short woman with thick arms and hands, and is boss of her polished house. Two servants hurry, fixing our lunch, and she shouts at one for not setting me a place. Shrewdness is stressed as she talks austerely of managing her small field of coffee, of planting and harvesting, and she shouts again at the foreman who comes in, tardy with his report. Nevertheless, she is obviously generous. At lunch we learn of a servant's two small children she is caring for, of other young students she sends to school, of money for a sewing machine she has lent the foreman's wife. The two small children sit at table with us and they run back to play as rapidly as their meal is eaten, but not without a quick kiss on their guardian's cheek. Elderly, and loved simply the way she is, the woman is called T'yang by Dante and those around her.

After our lunch, Dante takes his thesis from the bag. This is for you, T'yang, he says, with an arm about her tough shoulders. It is a gesture thought extremely noble by this much older provincial cousin, and T'yang cries terribly as she receives Dante's Xeroxed copy of a badly typewritten play.

———

As summer sets in more harshly, a change in Dante's temperament slowly occurs. All day he sits quietly at his desk doing nothing. He brings out his folder of ideas for movie stories, but does not study them. He gets up before I do in the morning and has nothing for breakfast. He nods goodbye when I leave for work, and greets me, not always with a kiss, when I come home. He says nothing about the dried fishes I now fry thrice, or more, in a week. Nothing I do makes him snap at me at all.

Work on your stories, Dante, I scold him one morning.

I am thinking about my thesis.

Your thesis is finished.

I worked hard on it, I deserve a rest.

I then plan to one day shock him out of his complacency, and during a quiet time at work, guarding against falling asleep on my stool, I write a mental list of possibilities: Come home with Clement, the downstairs maintenance man. Come home walking like Ursula, the orchestra usherette. Not come home at all.

But I cannot not come home at all because there is no other place I know I can go home to, and Clement, who is in fact more feminine than I, already walks like Ursula.

So then I begin to talk to Dante about my Friday night math class. The Egyptians, our teacher said, were profound practitioners of mathematics. The pyramids they built are structures of precise and highly refined measurement. Mathematics was then directly connected to nature and God. The architect was also a priest, and in some of the pyramids are felt until today divine vibrations. Each Friday I pondered on what our teacher said about the Egyptians and their mathematics, and told it to Dante with enthusiasm. Did you know, Dante, I said to him one evening, that the Great Pyramid is made of over two million blocks of concrete, and each block weighs between two to 70 tons? How the Egyptians lifted the blocks up to 400 feet is a mystery. The Egyptians used a secret mathematical process yet unknown to us, and one theory says it was levitation. Dante would sit and listen to each new piece of knowledge I brought home for him. Sometimes he held my hand. In time, he began to go out evenings, to a bookstore that stayed open late, to post a letter, for a walk. Then, so painfully swift, he one day did not come home at all.

=====

At work the next day I load fresh batteries into my flashlight and in the dark flash it brightly against my palm, fingers, knuckles, and blindly into the loge people's faces until they squint. I flash lights on and off anyone's foot resting on the back of a seat. Loge people are not allowed to rest their feet on the back of seats. Guiding a lone man to his seat I flash a light short of a step up and he trips. Ursula visits my station to bring me cheer. I tell her that Dante had brought with him my suitcase instead of his. Mine is of straw and his, of leather, and Ursula convinces me of Dante's thoughtfulness: It was a gift, don't you see? I tell her that he also did not bring the burner, the chair, and some books on the desk. Ursula convinces me, before she hurries back to her station at the orchestra, it means nothing else but that Dante will come home one day.

Rowena Tiempo-Torrevillas

PRODIGAL SEASON

For Eman

The small boy and the man stood at the foot of the steps looking up at the tall white house known as Casa Grande.

The residence of the general manager of the sugar mill at Medina was built along pseudo-Colonial lines, an old structure—one could see where the edges of the cornices were chipped and painted over—but it was an oldness that was settled and almost benignly condescending. Unlike many old houses where ells and wings sprawled like untidy afterthoughts, Casa Grande had a prim look: it was a great-aunt among houses, never neglected, wearing the air of one who had neatly sidestepped several potentially disastrous marriages to the architecture of convenience.

The shutters in the upper-storey windows seemed to borrow their freshly-painted green from the unreal lushness of the lawn, where two rotating sprinklers whipped arcs of fine spray across the bermuda grass.

It was early afternoon, barely past noon, but the yard of the compound rang sporadically with the shouts and sounds of people swimming.

From across the lawn an indignant yelp was swiftly followed by a hollow but substantial splash.

"*Coño!*" the same voice spluttered a moment later. "*... Un hijo de cabrito ese.*"

The boy turned and squinted into the sunlight. The blue surface of the swimming pool was broken and churned by several swimmers. The derisive hoots from the small group of young people seemed to be directed toward one young fellow who was now climbing out of the pool. His skinny frame shook with rage, and probably laughter, as he struggled unsuccessfully to heave himself out by his elbows. He finally made it, to the accompaniment of mock encouragement, and ruefully rubbed his reddened abdomen, where an early paunch was beginning to show.

A dark girl in a red maillot dangled her legs from the pool's edge and kicked her feet smugly. "I bet that hurt, no?"

"Only my pride," he snarled.

More shrieks and another painful splash.

The door of the house opened silently. The little boy felt his father's hand tighten on his shoulder and he looked up.

A dumpy maid in a stiff blue uniform stood in the doorway and blinked down at them. She raised her eyebrows questioningly.

The man's hand withdrew from the boy's shoulder and he straightened his back.

The girl's mouth twitched impatiently. "Yes?

What is it? What do you want?" she asked, in the dialect.

"Mr. Vizconde," he told her.

She hesitated, her hand on the doorjamb.

"Mr. Vizconde?" the man repeated. "Your master? Is he in? Perhaps he is taking a nap."

"No. But he is having lunch with some visitors."

"We will wait, then."

She looked curiously at them. "No—wait. I will call him. They're through eating, anyway." She turned, leaving the door half-open. The squeak of her rubber pumps receded down the polished narra hallway.

The child glanced up at the man, but his father's eyes were unmoving on the empty hallway, half-seen from where they stood.

He stood on tiptoe to follow his father's gaze, and then feeling a little abashed, stared down at his father's feet. The laces of his father's shoes were new. The creases which outlined each of the toes were limned with fine white dust, all along up the arches . . . His eyes traveled up the drill pants, where some of the crease remained, in spite of all the walking, here and there the shine of starch and many careful ironings, perhaps wax from the bottom of the charcoal iron, his mother whistling softly . . .

Santiago Vizconde was not a tall man, but his frame seemed to fill the doorway. "Is there anything I can do for you?"

The Spaniard's voice was unexpectedly soft—high and husky—although his hand raked brusquely and almost impatiently across his short stubbly hair.

"Sir, I am—I used to be one of the tenants of the family of your wife. My name is Engracio Angay." His hand rested briefly on the boy's head. "This is my son, Ronaldo."

Vizconde's blue-black eyes flickered briefly to the boy and he gave a short hard nod, once. "Well? Maybe it's my wife, then, whom you'd like to talk to?"

"No, sir. I came down here to see you."

Vizconde waited; a quietness that was not hard, but pointedly neutral, thickened in the space between them. Engracio Angay, feeling that he had gotten off to a bad start, began to speak again, but Vizconde made another quick movement, in the direction of some tiled benches under a star-apple tree on the lawn.

"Why don't we sit there?" Vizconde navigated the four steps down with a lightness that belied his bulk. As they walked to the benches, the boy felt the impulse to reach for his father's hand but became too embarrassed to try.

Engracio Angay and the boy Ronaldo sat side by side on the bench opposite Vizconde. Angay's hands dangled between his knees and he fingered his cone-shaped rattan hat briefly before setting it beside him on the seat.

"I was a tenant of your wife's family until the outbreak of the war," he explained. "During the war Don Enrique Villanueva left me in charge of a cattle spread in Bugnay, below Valleverde. When the war ended, he offered to help me start out on my own. He guaranteed a loan for me, and so I was able to acquire a small piece of land on the hillsides of Valleverde." He waited for Vizconde's small brusque movement. When it did not come, he continued. "That was almost fourteen years ago. It's not much really, my land. Two and a half hectares of corn and the other half-hectare to vegetables. Some coconuts in Luca. But it's just enough. I have seven children— and another's coming." he smiled wryly. "Don Enrique always said I was a fast worker."

Unexpectedly Vizconde gave a short bark of laughter which sounded as though he had a chunk of meat lodged somewhere in his throat. "This your oldest?" He nodded toward the boy.

"No. Ronaldo is my second boy." Engracio Angay sent a small warm smile to his son, but his eyes were a little too bright and looked absent. "It's about Ronaldo that I came to see you. He's almost seven now, and ready to start his schooling."

Vizconde lifted his hand. The round long fingers looked suddenly helpless. "I'm afraid I . . ."

"I think I can still afford to send my children to school," Engracio Angay broke in hard and urgent, and he added a little bitterly, "public school's still free in any case. The older ones, at least, they can walk down to the primary school in Pamplona. They stay with my sister during weekdays. And what does it matter, really, if they have to stop now and then, be delayed a year or two?"

He looked up at the Spaniard, and two deep lines appeared between Angay's thin brows. "But my wife and I want—we think this boy ought to have a chance at something better than public school in Pamplona. He's different from my other children—from *other* children, *'ñor Vizconde.*" There was nothing supplicating about his tone; the wry flash lit his face again: "You're probably thinking I'd say that, anyway. But it's true."

Vizconde's smile was not unkind, but he said nothing.

The look Engracio Angay gave his son was proud and troubled. "I can't read well myself. My hands sweat when I sign my name. I finished the fifth grade only. Now, this boy here... when Naldo was three years old my wife's cousin came to the farm to help me figure out my accounts—every year he goes over them, taxes, payments to the bank, things like that, nothing very much to begin with, but he helps me. Naldo was curious about the numbers, so Julian taught him the alphabet and how to count. Two days later we noticed that Naldo was adding the numbers by himself, and when Julian taught him, he learned how to multiply and divide in less than one hour."

Vizconde murmured something that the other man didn't catch, and he leaned forward asking, "Señor?"

"Nothing, nothing." Vizconde waved his fleshy hand impatiently. "When he was only three years old, eh? Go on."

"I did not want to bother you with this. It's my problem; it's hardly even a problem." He glanced down at the boy. For the first time since they had arrived at the Spaniard's house, the boy found in the little smile the familiar warmth lighting his father's face briefly, as though coming out from somewhere deep inside his father's eyes a night-moth's soft brown wing had brushed against him and then blundered away into the darkness.

"My boy Naldo could never be a problem. In fact, when my wife was still carrying him, my sister and her husband wanted to adopt one of my children. They had none of their own, and I had so many, you see—and he was going to be the fifth child. They wanted to take this boy once he was born but I refused. And I'm glad." He kneaded the back of his son's neck. "From the time he could walk and talk he'd follow me around, asking me all sorts of little questions. Big ones, too. Sometimes I didn't know the answers." He gave a small wondering laugh. "A funny, strange little boy. With his own little strange thoughts..."

The man's voice broke, then, and as he fought to swallow the shards in his throat he forced his gaze to focus upon the grass at the Spaniard's feet, where the wetness sparkled, left there not by rain.

He bent over the boy, saying in a low voice, "You understand, son, it's not because your mother and I don't want to keep you. We could give you a good life, a hard one, but someone else will be more able to give you what is better for you. But no one will love you as well as we."

The shouts of the swimmers across the lawn had ceased suddenly and in the pause, from somewhere in the direction of the house he heard the tinkle of a fountain. In the midst of his embarrassment Engracio Angay sensed that the quality of silence which Vizconde held was no longer impatient. He looked up.

"That's all, Señor. You can see why I come here, to you." He hesitated. "If the boy could find a place here, sir. Running errands, or maybe helping the gardener tend the flowers..."

The Spaniard's heavy shoulders shifted under his white short-sleeved polo shirt. The bull neck moved uneasily inside the open collar, while a slow red flush crept to his jowls. He sat staring off to one side, head tilted and jaw jutting, and for a moment he looked almost angry.

"If you'd like to see what my son can do," Engracio Angay faltered, "perhaps he can read something..."

"No, no. Please. No need. You're not a performing monkey, boy."

Vizconde stared directly at the child for the first time, and the boy Ronaldo felt a lump growing quickly in his throat, a stone both sharp and dull and he hoped frantically that the tears would not rise to his eyes and that the big Spaniard would not expect him to speak.

"I wish myself I could help you, but here in our household we have all the helpers we need. More than enough help. Two of our girls are the daughters of tenants, in fact, and our driver's son is being sent to school. Besides," Santiago Vizconde spread his hands and the sudden smile was engaging, "I am not, myself, a rich man. Though I do what I can."

Engracio Angay remained silent, already half-taking him at his word, beginning to frame polite and face-saving phrases so he and his son could leave before being dismissed. An unbidden relief surged among his scattered and half-formed thoughts, and with it, shame.

Vizconde rose abruptly. "I'll see what I can do."

The man and the boy stood up, too, wondering if the conversation had formally terminated, when Vizconde beckoned them to stay. He strode to the house. "Rittenmeier!" he called.

A tall, heavy-set man emerged some moments later through the potted hibiscus and san francisco that screened the low stone railings of the verandah at the side of the house. His shiny bald pate was fringed with fine silvery hair; a few thin strands were brushed thriftily across the top, a token offering of protection from the noonday blaze.

Beside him on the verandah railing, a yellow marble statue of Daphne raised one ankle in her forever-flight from an invisible Apollo, her hair and the gown which whipped around her little young limbs already turning into the leaves and sprigs of the laurel tree.

Such a delicate metamorphosis did not seem remotely possible in the burly man who stood silently beside the statue, but even in his stillness one was able to sense a kindred kinetic force, leashed and quietly held in abeyance. With one hand he hitched up his baggy trousers by the belt which sloped dangerously low on his potbelly. In his other hand he held a tall misted glass of something that looked like lemonade. The ice tinkled.

Behind Mr. Rittenmeier in the little court-yard came the answering tones of water from a fountain that splashed into a tiny goldfish pool. A stone boy crouched at the edge of the pool, his ageless gaze drowned in the water.

"You wanted me, Vizconde?" the American asked quietly.

"This little boy's a budding prodigy, it seems. He needs a patron," Vizconde told him.

The boy looked up at Rittenmeier, his hand in his own father's grasp.

The sound of water inundated the summer air, falling water shattered the early afternoon into irretrievable droplets: a plenitude of liquid sounds shaken through the air almost like a wild benediction, water-music arcane and crass alike: noisy smacking splashes from the swimming pool, whirring lawn sprinklers, the broken cadences of the fountain, and, to the little boy, somewhere in the bright afternoon, the secret burble of a mountain stream flowing in the sunlight.

———

The dormitory intercom spat and crackled. A nasal announcement disentangled itself from the welter of static.

"Room 311. Ronnie Angay, visitors for yew. Mr. Ronaldo 'Ronnie' Angay."

As the young man in Room 311 pushed his feet into his shoes, sockless, he thought irritably, that smelly bastard of a desk assistant's using his phony accent to bug me again. He tries that on me one more time and I'll fix his neck for him so he'll be smelling his stinking armpits for life.

Halfway to the door he turned back, deciding to change his shirt, just-in-case, and then he emerged, locking his door carefully.

He trudged down the scuffed and dented boards of the hallway, the petty annoyance still clinging to him like cobwebs.

"Paranoia!" he yelled, to no one.

A head popped out of one of the rooms, greasy curls dangling nearly shoulder-length. The eyes behind the small pink-tinted glasses were unsurprised and regarded him with a kind of patient resignation.

"You all right, Ron? What was all that about?"

"Nothing. Just a new word I learned today."

The head retreated, a turtle into its carapace. "Ha, ha." The door closed again.

In the tiny lobby of the dorm the late-middle-aged couple rose to their feet uncertainly as Ronnie came down the stairs.

The lobby was dingy and badly lit. Silhouetted against the doorway and the muggy overcast greyness of the late afternoon, the faces of the two elderly people were indistinct. As Ronnie went to them he caught the swift jumbled impression of stolidness, and painfully neat but rather dated clothes, and an odd tentative waiting that hung about them, as ill-fitting somehow as the clothes they wore.

The woman drew nearer, smiling shyly.

"Ma? Pa!" Ronnie crossed to them in two strides—though not too hurriedly, he noticed with no surprise—and, feeling slightly unreal he hugged his mother and reached out for his father's hand. Then his father clapped him on the shoulder, hard. They stood awkwardly for a long moment.

He gave his mother a bright blank smile, almost dreading to look into her face.

Her own smile wavered. "You're such a big boy now."

The catch in her voice alarmed him vaguely, and mustering his matter-of-factness he said, "Why didn't you wire me you were coming?"

"There was no need, we knew where to find you," his father said quietly.

Ronnie was about to say "How?" when he stopped and glanced over his shoulder at the desk assistant. The fellow's eyebrows were raised, just slightly; a wordless "Well, well" combined unpleasantly with a bright-eyed inquisitiveness that Ronnie felt he just could not stand. It was a wretched combination. He wanted to yell at him.

"Look, why don't we have something to eat?" he suggested gently. "Someplace we can talk."

"We had something after we got off the boat," his father murmured as Ronnie steered them to the door.

"Well, *I'm* hungry," he said, flashing his father another toothy smile.

The desk assistant stood aside to let them pass. "Go hang yourself," Ronnie hissed as their elbows bumped.

As they crossed the shady oval driveway his mother said, "That man speaks well, doesn't he? Like an American."

"He likes to think so."

Ronnie hoped the anger did not show on his face and he glanced cautiously at his father. His eyes fell on Engracio Angay's hands. *At least he did not bring that hat,* he thought in momentary relief, and immediately felt deeply ashamed of himself.

"Where are you bringing us, son?" the woman asked. They were crossing the wide grassy football field which separated the men's dormitories from the campus clinic; because there were no trees the afternoon seemed to take on a nakedness that he found distasteful and even slightly ominous.

"To this place where I have my meals," he said. "There aren't many people there now . . . I mean, it's quiet, we can talk and have a snack."

"We have not seen you for a long time," said Engracio Angay.

Ronnie looked at his father. *Many years, Papa.* The dark seamed face told him nothing.

Suddenly he felt like weeping. "How is the farm?" he asked quickly.

A tiny swift look passed between the old man and the woman. His mother said, "Your father did not want to come. He told me to come and find you. Then he decided to come and talk to you himself."

"I see," he said vaguely.

They tramped along in silence. After a minute he asked, "Is everything all right? Pa? How is the farm?" he asked again.

The woman said, "It's doing well. Your father has a new carabao. And a calf. And your sister Meling is now married. The calf was part of the dowry."

"Good, good," he said genially. (My sister Meling. Was she the one with the dimple in her chin? That fat little girl?)

"How did you know where I live?" he asked.

"Your Tia Cora, the second cousin of your Papa, has a daughter, Arminda, who is studying here. Arminda told her."

"Are they from Pamplona?"

"No. They come from Misamis," she said patiently. "Cora sent a Christmas card to your Uncle Salvador in Luca. Your Papa met your uncle in Pamplona. So we knew," she said simply.

There was no reproach as she related this intricate route through the family annals; its very intricacy was reproach enough, he thought grimly.

"That card you sent us before said 'Narra Cottage,'" his father remarked abruptly.

"Ah. Yes. Let's see," he said uncomfortably. "It's been some time. That was . . . in fact," he pointed eagerly to a tennis court about forty yards away, "that's where it used to be, Narra Cottage. When I was a junior they tore it down." He became aware that he was babbling. "It was already so decrepit that when someone would sneeze the dust would come raining down from the ceiling. We had to put newspapers on top of our mosquito nets."

He was speaking rapidly now, almost enjoying himself. "They finally condemned the place one summer. I was the last one to leave, everyone else had gone home for vacation." He chuckled. "One night I came home drunk. The next morning when I woke up the sun was shining in through my mosquito net. I never knew the sky could be so blue. *Then* I realized the sun was shining through the walls, too. No more walls! No more ceilings! They'd taken the whole building down around me. And me in my jockey shorts with no protec-tion from the cruel world but my lousy mosquito net."

A great clap of laughter erupted from Engracio Angay, and several students hurrying to late classes stared curiously at him.

Ronnie's mother asked sedately, "Why did you have to stay in a place like that?"

"It was a cooperative dorm," he said. "We did all the housekeeping ourselves. It was Dad's—Mr. Rittenmeier's idea to put me there." He suddenly felt shy. "Be good for you, he said. Maybe he was right."

"Maybe he was right," said Engracio Angay.

———

Aquilino's Rendezvous was midway between a greasy-spoon joint and the University cafeteria. It derived its respectability from several generations of impoverished students who had dined there, and its prosperity from the oily swimming concoctions of hairy pork, sweet yam, and bananas that were regularly reorganized and recycled on its bill of fare. "The permutations of those triple ingredients are infinite under Aquilino's master touch," a math-major friend of Ronnie's had once pronounced glumly. Aquilino's culinary piece de resistance was deep-fried banana-on-a-stick, while-u-wait.

Bringing his parents there was in itself the product of delicate choices, as his favorite teacher Miss Panganiban would have said. What would you say now, ma'am dear, he thought, watching his parents across the oilcloth tablecover. What choice and fitting epitaphs to death and rebirth and confrontation-with-self would you zero in on? Hey watch, ma'am, no hands!—here where we wield words with the precise grace of picadores, so carefully, words to hide in. And my handicap? My English comes trippingly-on-the-tongue, so fine and glib, so much easier than the language of my parents.

He would have preferred to bring them to Momoy's Store, which was closer to the dorm. It catered to the students too, and it was cozier there. The place nestled among the sparse embattled groves of acacia and camachile at the shabbier periphery of the campus, in spite of the fact that Momoy had experienced a mysterious rising in the world, and had gotten around to cementing the floors.

Now that they were settled around the table waiting for their soft drinks to come, the earlier constraint sat once more upon their conversations. Like a broody hen with an old egg that wouldn't hatch, he thought, nastily.

"The place you're staying in, it's good?" asked his mother.

"Good enough. More expensive for me; now that I'm in Law School I'm on my own. I'm a graduate assistant at the University, and I work for this insurance company on the side selling graves." He laughed shortly. "Where are you staying?" he asked.

"We took our bags to your Uncle Tasio's place near Azcarraga," his mother said. "We brought them some bananas and mangoes from the farm, and your Papa bought some *maja real* at the pier in Cebu. Things like food are expensive here in Manila."

There was a vacuum in the talk and she spoke again: "We wanted to attend your graduation." Her voice was becoming strained and anxious. "But your telegram arrived just the day before your graduation."

"I know, Ma." Impulsively he reached out to pat her hand.

"We thought you might work at the Sugar Central in Medina after graduation," his father said. "Now you are taking law and your degree in chemistry will just be wasted." The eyes set deep in their webbing of crow's-feet were still neutral, almost too careful in their show of interest, as though he were carrying a bowl of water and was fearful it would spill.

"That's what Dad said, too," Ronnie said carelessly, and then the painful scarlet flush rose to his temples and the small pulse there began beating.

"I mean, Mr. Rittenmeier didn't really mean for me to work at the Central, if I didn't want to. Mr. Rittenmeier kept telling me that Nobel Prizes in chemistry were won young. James Watson won his at twenty-five." He smiled crookedly. "That gives me two years."

He saw the opaque and nearly anxious attentiveness which had frozen on his parents' faces, and he began to feel stranded again, and angry at himself. Even the smallest of small talk had its pitfalls.

"Why didn't you go with the Rittenmeiers?" she asked timidly.

He looked at her, then, across the circle of oilcloth-covered table, and the pain and the anger stopped his breath and he thought: What should I tell you, then? That they didn't want me to go with them, that at the airport he clapped his hand on my shoulder, saying, Well, Ronnie, you have been a good boy, and you will someday be a credit to your people. And the woman just turned away. She did not want me to see her weeping.

What was it he wanted from me, then, he thought, the extravagant grief still overriding his carefully nurtured amusement. I gave him every single one of my medals, for my sprinting, my debates, the quizz-bowl, the spelling. These are yours, I told him, each time. And after he had left I found them, all, in their little red boxes in the bottom drawer of his filing cabinet.

He sighed and dropped his eyes, shrugging. "I've been to the States," he muttered indifferently enough. "I don't want, or need, to go back."

"We were so proud, Naldo, when you came to tell us of the AFS scholarship. Didn't you like America? What was it like there?"

He looked helplessly at her. "Big. Even Nebraska seemed big." *What shall I tell you, then, Mother? You don't even know me. So how can you hope to know? I will tell you about the snow. About learning to ski and kissing buxom girls in the back seat of my foster-father's Oldsmobile. About the wide streets paved in gold. The bigness of it all. And next to it my smallness. My brown smallness, your child.*

He turned to his father, and saw in his eyes something big and deep. "My best friend was a Jew, Pa. He taught me how to play golf. And at the end of the year all the American Field Service scholars from different countries took a bus trip together through the whole of the U.S. to see America and the trip ended in Washington, D.C. I became real good friends with a Norwegian, from Norway." His voice was shaking, hurrying wildly now.

"You know what Bjorn and I did one night in the comfort room, in the toilet of the Smithsonian? We wrote on the wall, big black letters, YANKEE GO HOME."

He looked at the uncomprehending and bewildered faces of his parents, his mother's head to one side like a little brown bird, and in his father's eyes, welling up beneath the puzzlement, he thought he saw pity. It made him angrier.

He laughed. "I called him Erik the Red." Not irrelevantly, he went on, "Did you know that a while after I got home from the AFS thing I thought I wanted to turn Communist? I picketed a sugar central here in Luzon, wrote a few furious leaflets, did some yelling on behalf of the *sacadas*. It was shouting those slogans that turned me off. It made me feel stupid. So I quit. I guess I was just too full of myself back then. And," he cocked his head wrily, "I had too much of the good Rittenmeier respect for the law and the power of the dollar." And some of your terrible awe for the white men, too, Papa.

He had been speaking in English, lapsing into it in frustration when he became heated up: the language I dream in, he thought without irony, knowing his father and mother understood only a few words here and there, but not really caring too much about that, either.

His father said, "Why do you feel that way? The American gave you much."

Ronnie felt a swift thrust of feeling for his father, the sudden respect and the pity thudding home like a double-feathered arrow. He said. "He also took away much."

"Mr. Rittenmeier?" the old man asked in some surprise.

"He, and the rest," Ronnie said shortly, wanting to change the subject.

It was funny how in the end it was the little things, the pettinesses that remained, and their dreadful triviality filled him with shame to remember them. Petty slights and omissions racked up, like so many losses, on an abacus; small beads of resentment equalling, on the other end, one large shiny hard bead that rattled around inside him; he could hear it sometimes, knocking indifferently against his ribs, his guts, his mind, like a marble rolled around in there by an idiot child, and he could hear it echoing, marking times and memories when he wanted them least.

There was that time Dad's goddaughter came for a visit: a shy dark little girl in her crisp old-rose dress with ribbons tied at the back. She was a funny, solemn little thing, and in the depths of his eleven-year-old mind there lurked the black suspicion that his foster-parents were probably thinking of matching them up. ("She learned to read by herself when she was only five, too.") He gave her a wide berth.

The girl sat on the porch swing leafing through his illustrated copy of *Pinocchio*. Something in the intent though tentative way with which she handled the pages must have touched Mr. Rittenmeier, because he bent and drew the book gently from the child's hands and looked at the cover. "Ah, Pinocchio. The puppet who turned into a little boy. Let's see, have you gotten to that part where Geppetto gets swallowed by the whale?—or was it a dogfish?—What on earth's a dogfish? Good book. It's yours if you want it, honey." Still carrying the book in his big fist, he entered Ronnie's room. Ronnie, who had been watching from the doorway as his foster-father patted the child's cheek, hastily ducked back into his room, pretending to study the large plastic globe that stood beside his bed.

"I'm giving this book to Roberta," the American told the boy.

Ronnie's back was still turned toward him, sullenly, and Rittenmeier said, "It's *Pinocchio*. You won't be wanting it any more."

Ronnie turned and reached for the book. He bent his head over it and his long thin fingers ran over its spine and cover. Something about his hesitation seemed to annoy the man, and his voice took on a dangerous quiet patience. "Give it here."

"No, I won't. I don't want to give it to her."

"Good Christ!" He exploded. "And you entering high school next year." He took the book from the boy's now unresisting fingers and marched to the door.

"It was the first book you gave me, too," Ronnie muttered to the man's broad back, hating him, hating even the child who sat with one ankleted foot neatly crossed over the other, most of all hating himself for wanting to keep what he could not even get, and had never got. . . .

A slatternly waitress dumped their orders in front of them. The coarse chinaware clinked uncouthly as she set it on the table with a rap. Ronnie looked at his parents apologetically. His father frowned at the girl, but catching Ronnie's eye, he gave a small pinched smile that nevertheless brought out his laugh wrinkles, and he turned his attention to the *cuchinta* that lay quivering on his plate.

"Have some more, Pa," Ronnie pleaded, remorseful over his outburst.

The old man smiled again and his strong white teeth glinted as he shook his head. He dug his spoon into the skimpy sweetmeat.

Ronnie turned to his mother. "Ma?"

Her cheeks were hollow from where the teeth had fallen, marking her many childbirths. She chewed the *cuchinta* quietly with her front teeth. "No, son. This is all right."

"It's—it's good, isn't it?" he said with a spurious cheerfulness, and tried to swallow the coconut mange. His throat and eyes burned.

He was remembering a fourteen-year-old boy, one far Christmas. It had been the third visit he had paid to his home in Valleverde since the Americans adopted him. The only other time he had dropped by after that was two years later, to tell them he was going away, to the States, on the AFS. But he always thought of this visit, this Christmas visit, as his last. Strange how a finality could arrive unintended, accidental, and still be final . . . Perhaps he felt it, even then. When he sat on

the wooden bench at the table with his brothers and sisters, who stared bashfully at him from the corners of their long sloe eyes, all of them seemed to him to look alike.

Through the gay, faded flowers of the curtain which hung at the door to one of the two bedrooms, he could see his gifts for them carefully piled on his parents' bamboo bed. How proudly he had carried them into the house, store-bought with his first "salary" from working off-hours compiling the tally-sheets at the Central.

His mother moved busily to and from the *batalan*, her feet making homely, hollow music on the bamboo flooring.

"Your father went down to the town and was able to bring back some fresh fish yesterday, when he knew you were coming. How do you want it cooked?"

"Inun-unan," he said brightly, after some thought.

His father smiled widely and reached across the table, affectionately rumpling the boy's hair. "You eat well, ha?"

As his mother cooked the fish he leaned back against the bench, the tiredness of the long walk beginning to catch up with him. Now his stomach was starting to act up: he had had to run for the bus from Medina that morning without his breakfast. When his father met him at the foot of the slope in Pamplona, Ronnie did not want to tell him he was hungry.

She set a pewter dish before the boy. As she bent he smelled the faint tang of lemons and pinewood smoke in her hair.

In the cracked bowl swam fish stewed in vinegar and onions. The steam wafted up to his nostrils, the terrible fishiness strengthened by the sour marinade of vinegar. The acid ball in his stomach rolled and he smiled nervously.

He took a sip of warm Coke from his glass to clear his throat and the glass smelled fishy too.

"Go ahead, son, don't be embarrassed. It's poor fare, but we know you must be hungry."

He grinned again, hopelessly, and spooned up some of the fish. An eyeball rolled onto his plate. The children laughed.

"Is that all?" his father said. "Go on. Take more. There's enough for all."

"Maybe Naldo is only used to the food of the Americans now," his mother said, half-teasing. "He eats his avocado with vinegar now, imagine."

He felt his queasiness rising and he ducked his head. He swallowed hurriedly, not allowing his tongue to dwell on the fish-odor, choking down great spoonfuls of rice until the spoon clattered against his teeth.

He held out his plate. "More, please," not looking at his father.

The woman made a pleased sound and tipped the vinegar sauce onto his rice. "You like my inun-unan, son?"

He nodded feverishly. His mouth was filling up with the hot saliva and he downed more Coke.

Suddenly he could hold no more and he found himself doubled over the *batalan,* retching and retching, his father's hands kneading his back, and he buried his face in his father's belly, wanting to explain, crying and retching. "I'm sorry, Papa," and his father murmuring words he had forgotten and which never came back again.

———

The old man pushed his plate away and spread his horned brown hands on the table. "I know you've been wondering why Macrina and I have come here to talk to you," he said heavily.

An ant made its erratic and random way across the tabletop, tracking down some secret of its own. The man flicked it away absently.

"Is it about the farm, Pa?" Ronnie asked.

"Yes. I am afraid that I might lose it," his father said softly.

The young man stared at the grizzled head of his father; where the hair used to be so thick it was now salt-and-peppery and a thin patch showed at the top. He saw where the sides of the head bristled sharp from a new haircut. "Are you—are we in debt?" he asked carefully in the same mild tone. "Will you be needing money?"

The man raised his head; there was some-thing close to amusement glinting gravely deep in his gaze. "No, son. I don't want your money. It's your help I need."

The stubby hands moved restlessly on the tabletop. "As a matter of act, we didn't do too badly this year. I opened up a new *kaingin* higher up on the mountains, near that stand of *dol-dol* trees, near where your mother gathers her *bago* leaves. I don't know if you remember it."

Ronnie did not shake his head. He blankly studied a fly that settled on the table edge.

"I was asking around, going to apply for a title to the new *kaingin,* since no one seemed to own it," the old man's voice thinned, and the gnarled hands stilled. "There's been talk of a new sugar central going up in Bugnay, near where the Villanueva cattle ranch used to be. They've even started making a big new road to Bugnay. The bulldozers started coming four months ago."

Ronnie looked up, startled at the turn in the talk. "I heard about it too, Pa. I was glad. It'll raise the value of your land."

A black fire ignited in the old man's eyes. He said with deliberate softness, "I went down to the provincial capitol, to find out how to go about getting a title to the lot higher up." He breathed painfully, as though he had walked a long way. "I found out at the Provincial Assessor's office that the old lot, *my farm,* does not even belong to me any more. They sent me to the Register of Deeds to check the title, and it was different, in someone else's name. Someone named Manalo."

The bewilderment and rage struggled on the old man's face. "I don't know how it happened."

"Who is this Manalo, Pa?"

"I don't know. All I know is that he and some other people, rich ones, have bought up most of the area near Bugnay and in Luca. All of Valleverde too, for all I know."

"Did you show them your title?"

His father snorted. His mother spoke up. "The people at the provincial capitol sent him from one office to another. They did not believe your father," she said thinly.

"And those that did didn't do anything about it, I suppose."

"We approached a lawyer in the city. We heard he helps people like us. He asked us for fifty pesos a month, and he would help us investigate, he said. We have paid him four times already," she said. "Up to now, nothing. Now we have very little left. When we heard through Badong that you were studying to be a lawyer, I said to your Pa, You see, God helps us still."

His mother stopped. There was an embarrassed silence between father and son. Finally the old man said, haltingly: "All the years we never saw each other... When we did not come to visit you, Naldo, it was not because we had abandoned and forgotten you. When the American gave you his home, we did not want you to be confused by us. So we stayed away."

Ronnie sat unmoving, not wanting to believe him.

"Some nights, especially when you were in America, I used to get up and go to the porch; I remembered how you liked the sound of the crickets—I used to catch them for you, you'd hold them in your fist listening to them sing. They were the only toys I could give you."

Ronnie felt his throat tighten, and he thought angrily, *Stop it. Stop doing this to me, using that on me. What do I owe you anyway? You and the other one I called Dad. I had two fathers, and none. And I was happier once I knew I had none.*

"When you did not try to see us either, boy, we understood that. You see, we did not want the American—or you—to think we were begging."

Looking up from the small tremor in the other man's hands and the dark, carefully empty face before him, Ronaldo suddenly knew how much it had cost his father to come.

From far away his voice said, "What you're asking me is hard. It's hard, Pa."

"The farm will belong to you someday, Naldo," his mother said.

The father turned on her, with a sharp, impatient look. "And to his brothers and sisters."

"It's not that, Pa."

His mother started to speak again, a puzzled and hurt urgency in her narrow lips.

"Don't force the boy, wife," he said gently.

Turning to Ronnie, the old man spoke, lightly, "Never mind about that now. Everything will be all right. Let's talk some more about you. Have you been writing to Mr. and Mrs. Rittenmeier, son?"

He shrugged, wishing his throat would clear now that the moment had passed. "I sent them a card last Easter."

"How are they?"

"I heard Mr. Rittenmeier is being given shock treatments from time to time. He's had a nervous breakdown of sorts. He always was a stubborn old devil."

A quick look of displeasure appeared sternly between the old man's eyes and his mouth tightened.

Ronnie said hastily, "I wasn't being disrespectful, Papa. Or ungrateful. My way of being fond. They were good to me. They treated me well. Very well."

Dad Rittenmeier hardly ever raised his voice at him, never punished him: he just directed a tight momentary flash at him which filled him with disquiet, waiting for the anger, reaching for the relief that was not relief. He was almost fourteen when he knew for certain his foster-father would never raise his voice at him again.

———

The boy stood in front of his foster-father's desk. Rows of chemistry tomes marched around the room, halting only at the filing cabinets, between which was a shelf with bottles of samples from the sugar central.

The grey eyes studied him, unmoving, and Ronnie waited for the explosion that he knew now would never come. It was better when he was smaller, still in the grades; if he was sometimes yelled at, it was over quickly. Now his foster-father, who had a very slight heart condition, withheld his anger well.

Ronnie had already come to hate the polite weekly interviews in this study, but he knew he was being called in for a different matter tonight:

"The *capataz* at the Central stockroom came to see me this afternoon. He tells me you and a couple of your friends have been selling off some of the scrap metal from the stockyard."

Ronnie's arms hung down in front of him. He stared at the floor. It seemed far away. "No, sir. Not from the stockyard. We've only picked up some of the scraps of bronze wiring that've been left lying around all over the mill."

"And you sold them off. To this dealer—I understand, in San Jose?"

The boy nodded.

"That was wrong. You realize that, I suppose?"

Ronnie nodded again.

"It was wrong on at least three counts. Can you tell me why?" Rittenmeier's tones were measured and relentless, deceptively softened by the rich Midwestern twang.

"First," Ronnie recited, "the wire was still the property of the mill." He raised his head. "But they were small useless pieces!" he cried hotly. "And even the laborers at the mill do it."

"Are you a laborer at the mill? And, perhaps more to the point: are you even the son of a laborer at the mill?"

Ronnie flinched. "I'm sorry, sir. I'm sorry I shamed you," he lied.

"Fair enough, but we're not through yet. Apologies later. Go on."

Ronnie said dully: "We planned it. We sold the wire for money. In the next town."

Rittenmeier nodded, almost approvingly. "A good point. I don't care for that sort of sneakiness. It's not like you, not like you at all."

"I knew it was wrong." At his sides his fingers ticked off the point.

"Then why did you do it, boy? Don't we give you enough money?"

"It's not that," he muttered. "I wanted something—of my own."

"That's just fine; the problem is, it wasn't your own." The old man expelled a heavy sigh. "Maybe we ought to be thinking of giving you a bit more money, you're getting older. Why didn't you ask if you needed some? A bigger allowance, that's what you need. Then you won't be giving us any more reason for your high-jinks. Hijacks, more like it. It's not like you, not at all like you." He raised his voice. "Greta!"

There was no answer.

"Greta!" he bellowed.

Ronnie's foster-mother was a big-boned, mild-eyed woman who alternately babied, and was bullied by, her husband, and her shoulders stooped from a lifetime of good-natured acquiescence.

"What took you so long?" Rittenmeier asked her irritably.

"The cook's oldest daughter is looking for a situation,' " she explained.

"Well we've got one of our own here." He nodded toward Ronnie. "He and his friends have been selling off these scraps of bronze wiring the electricians leave lying around all over the place, just waiting for folks to trip over the temptation. I don't really blame the kids—but it was still stealing." Ronnie flinched again. "He says he's sorry. I've been thinking maybe his allowance has got too small now he's in high school. Think we ought to raise it? Add on fifteen, twenty bucks every fifteen days? That too much? Shall we take the additional amount out of your household money or will I give it to him?"

"Oh Joe," she protested. "It's such a small amount, do we have to do our great budget-balancing act again?"

"It's not an act," he said sententiously. "We must keep our books in order. You know I like having things just so."

Standing there listening to them, Ronnie thought angrily, Is that all I am to you then? Just another item on your budget? I *stole* those wires. So you'd sit up and see me. See I'm not just your good compliant close-mouthed son-of-a-tenant no-trouble-at-all-Ronnie. I stole so you'd be ashamed of me, and it doesn't even bother you. You stand me up here in front of you and make me recite you my faults and then instead of punishing me you reward me with a bigger allowance. Tomorrow Amado will come to school and tell us how his father almost beat the teeth out of him for stealing those wires, and Amado will tell us again how his father taught him to box, and he will be proud, and you sit there with your grey eyes, discussing which one of you will take care of my allowance.

The tears began to gather at the corners of his eyes, and he held back his sobs, as his Dad had held back his anger. . . .

Rittenmeier saw the tears and said, "No need to cry over it, boy. See, Greta, he's ashamed of himself. That'll do, son, pull yourself together. Tell you what. I'll talk the foreman at the paper division into letting you work on his tally-sheets. How about that, eh? Want me to talk to him? Then it'll really be your own money, like you want it. Keep you out of high-jinks when you're feeling frisky. How about that? Eh?"

Ronnie was shaking his head, choking down the tears, groping for his Dad's hand. The American patted Ronnie's damp hand awkwardly and then drew it away, saying, "Oh, come on, boy, you're too old to be crying. Don't take it so hard. You *know* it's hard on me too. Now stop that!" wiping the wetness from his own liver-spotted hand with the monogrammed hanky.

Ronnie wiped the tears away with the back of his hand. Dad, he wanted to cry, Shout at me, hit me, hold me.

Rittenmeier stood up and shuffled into the dressing room. He opened his closet and began pulling some shirts off their hangers, one by one, and dumping them on the floor. "Greta, These need washing. That new girl keeps hanging them right back up. The lazy—"

"I'll remind her to check," Greta Rittenmeier said soothingly.

The clothes lay in an untidy heap on the floor. "Oh, Joe," she sighed, "sometimes you're such a big old slob. How come you keep your study and office so neat, and in here you're such a mess. You don't expect me to keep picking up after you in my old age, do you?"

"I do," he rumbled. "While we're at it, the sleeve of this shirt I have on needs mending. I caught it on one of the flanges at the lab this afternoon." He stripped it off and dropped it on the pile.

From the periphery of his vision he caught the boy Ronnie lingering indecisively near the closet door. His white eyebrows jerked up in surprise. "You still here?" he said a little sourly. "You want something?"

"No, sir," Ronnie said, feeling stupid, still crying a little inside.

"Go tell Rosa to come here, will you? I want her to fix this sleeve."

"I'll take it to her myself," Ronnie said in a low voice, and he stooped to the pile of clothes on the floor.

He hurried out of the room, holding the delicately-embroidered polo *barong* carefully. The aroma of his foster-father's Cavendish pipe tobacco rose from the shirt, along with the clean, cheesy smell of the old man's sweat, still warm on the shirt.

The tears began to roll again, and in the darkness of the hallway, he lifted his father's shirt and buried his face in its crisp, still-starchy folds, its warmth already fading in his hands.

———

He said softly: "I suppose it must have been hard on them, too, leaving. After all, they spent most of their lives in this country. And now they live in a home for the aged— America can be cruel in that way. I just realized that's why they didn't want me to come with them, they didn't want to burden me. And growing old alone in America can be hell. Anywhere, for that matter, I guess."

For the first time Engracio Angay reached out his hard hand, to cover his son's where it lay clenching and unclenching on the table.

"Write to your father, boy," he said gently. "We owe him a lot."

The hot flood of shame washed over Ronnie, then, and some other feeling he did not pause to give a name to.

When I was a small boy, Papa, in the

American's house, soon after you gave me away, I used to take a rag and polish the furniture, the legs of their chairs and tables, every day I hoped some dirt would appear so I could clean it away for them, because I could not speak their language and I wanted them to know... He took the rag from me one day, and now you have done that, too. But now I can do this for you, too, Papa.

"I will do what I can for you," he told his father slowly.

After a short while they stood up to leave and he placed his arm rather awkwardly around his father's shoulder. How much easier to do something like this if you didn't mean it, he thought. Easier and emptier, and less hurting.

And the hurt stayed with him even after the three of them went out into the twilight streets.

The rest of the dormitory was empty when he got back. From the refectory came the comfortable clatter of supper being served.

He stuck his head in the door of the guy with the rose-colored lenses.

"Anomie," he said conversationally.

The jaded eyes glimmered a little with tired amusement. "I know. Don't tell me. Just a new word you learned today."

They nodded their heads at each other for a number of moments, solemnly and sagely.

The rose-colored lenses returned to *Being and Time.* It was upside-down. "Ha ha." And the door closed gently behind him.

He stretched out on his own bed, his shoes still on. The tiredness had not yet begun.

Before his father left, the old man had suddenly gripped his elbow and swung the young man around to face him. Peering at him in the dusk, the old man had said, "There are many things you don't remember, Naldo. But I remember, and keep them. That's little enough, for me."

Ronaldo closed his eyes in the darkness. But you're wrong, Papa. I do remember. And knowing that, my pain should be enough for me, for as long as I do remember....

Nearing noon the shadows of the ferns and the burnt-umber coronets of the everlasting flowers made a ragged filigree on the parched ground.

The man and the boy cut across the field of flowers, the short shadow bobbing importantly ahead of the longer one. Their feet in their rubber slippers made soft slapping flopping sounds in the dust. High overhead a hawk circled, its wingtips brushing a slow pattern onto the clear high air. In the sudden stillness, an early cricket sent out its thin pulsing cry, like the oscillations of a fine wire graphing heat waves in the sky.

The child craned his neck backward to look up at the man. "Are we almost there?" His round serious face was red and sticky with sweat.

"Almost there. We will rest in a very little while."

They marched on for some minutes, and then the boy asked, as though it had just occurred to him, "Are we going to walk all the way to the Spaniard's house?"

"No," the man explained again, patiently. "I thought I told you last night. We'll stop where the road meets the highway. Then we'll take the bus to the town."

The boy nodded. "We have come a long way, haven't we?" he said proudly. "A v-e-r-y long way?"

"A very long way," the man agreed.

How many kilometers, do you think?"

The man paused, head to one side, pretending to consider deeply. "At least one hundred," he said gravely.

"Really, Papa?"

"No. Of course not. Only about sixteen. Why, do you want to ride on my shoulders again?"

The boy gave a little skip. "No. Besides, it wouldn't be fair. You're carrying the bag."

The man swung the buri *bayong* on his shoulder. "You slept on my back this morning, part of the way down," he reminded him.

The boy laughed. "But we were up even ahead of the cocks. I liked riding on your back, even if I'm too big now."

It was still dark when they left the little

house which sat on the hillside overlooking the narrow valley, its own back on a taller slope. Pine needles rained gently on the thatch roof, and he shivered in the predawn cold. He could hear his mother's slippers sliding over the polished bamboo slats; somewhere inside, the muffled sleepy voices, and he stood on one leg at the top of the bamboo stairs, impatient to be gone.

His father came out, and then his mother emerged.

She stooped, with some difficulty, to hug him. It was also hard for him to hug her, because her belly, heavy with the eighth child, got in the way. "Naldo," she said indistinctly. It sounded as though she had been crying.

She held him away from her, and peered into his face. "Your nose is cold," she said, and her voice broke again.

His arms clasped her, but not reaching around her swollen waist. His head lay against her belly. Suddenly there was a small impudent knocking movement under his cheek.

"The baby kicked me," he said wonderingly, and laughed. . . .

"Pa, do you think that the people in the town know where we live?" he asked.

"They certainly seem to have forgotten us," he said. "Pamplona used to be a mining town, but the mine closed down, and now Valleverde is just a tiny old ghost town, too."

"Are we the ghosts?" the child asked solemnly.

"Maybe," his father chuckled.

"I hope the Spaniard is not there when we get to his house," the boy said.

"I hope not," said the father quickly.

"I hear a stream!"

"We will stop here."

The stream where the man and the boy stopped formed one of the smaller tributaries above the large river which flowed sluggishly through the Central Azucarera de Medina. From the sugar mill the wastes oozed toward a small bay where the waters foamed white and foul.

But the brook where they stopped to take their lunch swirled along in clear clean shallow pools, stirring gold in the sun, bounding over smooth sunquick pebbles and licking the coarse grass that overhung the narrow banks.

From the distance came the bang and roar of a diesel truck changing gear.

A wild guava tree dappled the ground where they squatted, and the air was sharp with the odor of scrub and wild grass from the overhanging verge of the roadside above and behind them.

The father was unwrapping small packets of food folded into banana leaves. "Your mother packed some bamboo shoots cooked in coconut milk."

They uncoiled some of the banana leaf strips that were woven and braided neatly around miniature pyramids of cooked rice.

"And now," said the father with a small flourish, "a special treat for you." And he produced a small can of sardined mackerel. "Here's the key. Open it carefully now."

The boy grinned up at him and with his tongue caught between his teeth bent over the can.

They ate with their fingers, neatly gathering the rice into little balls mixed with the vegetable and sardines. When everything was eaten, the last of the tomato-and-olive-oil wiped from the tin, they lay back against the meager shade of the guava tree.

"Papa," the boy said sleepily, "make me a slingshot. I see a good twig for it."

"Another time."

The busy chuckling of the brook made the boy's eyelids heavy, and the light-motes racing over the running water dazzled his eyes.

After a while the father said, "Time to wash up."

He laid out a fresh new set of clothes for the boy; the shorts, newly bought for P2.50, still smelled of the Chinaman's stall at the marketplace in Pamplona.

"Wash your mouth well, son," the father said half-jokingly. "Really well. The good smell of sardines offends some rich men."

They laughed as he briskly helped the boy out of his sweat-stained clothes. The child looked up at him in surprise.

"I can do it myself, Papa," he said.

The father smiled and shook his head, motioning him into the water.

He drew a thin silver of Perla soap from the depths of the bag. He rolled up his trousers and waded into the gold-threaded shallows. He started scrubbing the child, hair first, then sudsing the small smooth thin brown body.

"And you, Papa," the boy asked, his hair a lathery mass, "will you take a bath too?"

"I'll just wash up," he said, "a little manly sweat won't offend the Spaniards."

The water streamed down the boy's body, cold. The pointed, clean smell of the laundry soap smote his nostrils. High overhead the sun wheeled. He shivered.

"Look, Pa!" he cried, pointing. "A goat!"

A large ram emerged from the bushes, its great horns curving, and its long whiskers giving it a heraldic, almost patriarchal dignity. It stared incuriously at the man and the boy, and then dropped daintily, but with enormous stateliness, onto the bank and into the water. It splashed across the stream, high-stepping, and disappeared into the scrub and beyond that into the canefields. The light pattering hooves embroidered the field-silence and then were gone.

The man's hands moved over his son's sturdy brown body, soaping, scrubbing, firm and rough and tender.

"And you, Pa," the child said again, "will you also wear shoes?"

The man gave him a small conspiratorial smile. The fine lines around his eyes deepened. "We will both wear shoes today," he said gravely.

His hands cupped the water and poured it over the child's head. Handful after handful and the drops spilling over were diamond and amber and perfume and sun.

The boy gasped and crowed.

The sound of crickets rode in the bronze air, the sun and the cold water swirling at their feet and the water from his father's hands beat a timeless song on his body, for a short moment.

"Papa!" he called, the water pouring over his head nearly taking his breath away, looking up into his father's face, but through the bright water and the sun he could not see his father's eyes.

POEMS

Luis G. Dato

DAY ON THE FARM

I've found you fruits of sweetest taste and found
    you,
Bunches of *dubat* growing by the hill,
I've bound your hair with greenest vines and
    bound you
With rare wild-flowers, but you are crying still.

I've brought you all the forest ferns and brought
    you,
Wrapped in green leaves, cicadas singing sweet,
I've caught you in my arms one hour and taught you
Love's secret where the mountain spirits meet.

Your smiles have died, and there is no replying
To all endearment and my gifts are vain:
Come with me, love, you are too old for crying.
The church bells ring and I hear drops of rain.

THE SPOUSE

Rose in her hand, and moist eyes young with
    weeping,
She stands upon the threshold of her house,
Fragrant with scent that wakens love from sleeping,
She looks far down to where her husband plows.

Her hair disheveled in the night of passion,
Her warm limbs humid with the sacred strife,
What may she know but man and woman fashion.
Out of the clay of wrath and sorrow, Life?

She holds no joys beyond the day's tomorrow,
She finds no worlds beyond his arm's embrace,
She looks upon the Form behind the furrow,
Who is her Mind, her Motion, Time and Space.

Oh somber mystery of eyes unspeaking,
And dark enigma of Life's loves forlorn,

The sphinx beside the river smiles with seeking,
The secret answer since the world was born.

Cornelio Faigao

LEAF FALL

The signature of leaves fallen
        have long since lost traces
On the lawn loam, the races
        Of vanished aprils bright with fir.

Now I gather with hands heavy
        the remnants still red with remembering.

It will be like this for all dreamers,
        But the afterthought of it
Was merely a ghost of limned loveliness.
The tree is moveless in the gray now.
Leafless at the end of the day now.
And the thundering of the may now
Is heavy on the tired head.

Florizel Diaz

PORTRAIT OF AN UNMARRIED AUNT

She looks at life with fierce, defiant stare.
Clothed with pride, she walks her spouseless way
Secure in faith that each day is her day.
No burning tale, no broken love affair
Can pass but she a bitter moral draws;
And with blazing eyes that threaten mortal pain,
Her pose a heritage of haughty Spain,
She herds all men to her self-made iron laws.
The faintest contradiction voiced is a spark
That lights her ire, and reddishly she flares
Until the raging, scorching flame scares

The defier to repentance and the dark.
How unendurable must be this fire
That turned to ash the amorous youth's desire!

The laughter that rings: once more
The grandeur of praise and love.

R. T. Feria

TESTAMENT IN MID-PASSAGE

Man has the right to raise a fist against fate

On earth, air, and water
Decisive wheels move. Swift
Spindles intercross and weave
Patterns we cannot overlook.
This history of change
Pushes us into horizons
Of light that spills the darkness
Back within the covers of eternity.
Inordinate standards of dreams
And words we thought meaningless
Are flames that trail the crossways
Of wonders new to us: dazzling our eyes.
This is the seed of tomorrow, the golden
Ideal for which men died in ignorance.

This is home at last, O America.
Let us fly together over
Your naked breast. Let us give
Back the fields to the farmers,
Speech to the people; extol
To their delinquent hearts the purple
Blood that darkness destroyed.
Let us give them new patterns.

O America:

New hopes behind mask-faces;
New glitter to sunken eyes;
Motion to new frontiers.

Let us give them to each other's
Safekeeping: the feeling of touch,
The answer that glistens,

Carlos Bulosan

HYMN TO A MAN WHO FAILED

Evening and the voice of a friendly river
The symmetry of stars, time flowing warm,
The perfect hour sitting on the tree-tops,
And peace, bird of shy understanding, waiting.

This is your world, this tin-can shack on the dry
River bed, this undismayed humanity drinking
Black coffee and eating stale bread, this water
Blue under the dark shadows of the proud city.

Lie down and laugh your worries away,
Or sit awhile and dream of impossible regions,
While there is no hunger, no endless waiting,
No cry for blood, no deceptions, no lies.

You are lost, lost between two uncertainties,
Between two conflicts, the mastered and the
            unharmed.
You are altogether alone and cold and hopeless.
The end is crouching like a tiger under your feet.

Evening and returning home, finding no peace,
No embrace of devotion, my beaten friend,
O failure who returns always to the dry river bed,
We are betrayed twice under the fabulous city.

PASSAGE FROM LIFE

There came a day in my childhood,
in the beginning of my conscious life,
that swung like a drawn sword
and struck me full upon the face
and sent me bleeding
into the world of lies.

SOUND OF FALLING LIGHT

When she saw the big face again
nosing in the dark, she ran back
into the great cave and screamed for help.
But the face went closer and closer till
it was all around her, and she was defenceless,
and it was pursuing her from everywhere.

Helpless, she flung herself upon the stone
floor and a star shone brightly above her
and angels sang everywhere and there was silence
and then a voice said softly: "You can go now."
When she opened her eyes there was no
        darkness,
there was only light; but she could not see
the white trees that whispered as she passed.

She only knew that she was born
and she was afraid to die.

PORTRAITS WITH CITIES FALLING

This is the shadow of the unexpected hour.
As I walk across the tight room to breathe
The thin fog coming in from the strange night,
As I sit on the rocking chair to watch the key
In the lock turn twice and stop and turn again,
The shadow moves like a solid body and divides
Into multitudes of crosses, one upon the other,
So that the hands loom like the curling tentacles
Of a gigantic seamonster about to strike a prey.
I am pursued by the shadow. Everywhere I go
I see ghostly hands moving. I lie sweating
At night, hearing creeping hands in the darkness.
If I sleep, I am haunted by evil dreams.
If I wake, I imagine monstrous ills.

I open the door and I see a man without eyes.
But his hands are enormous, they reach
        everywhere.
And his feet are millions, they march everywhere.
At a distance, he is a man; when I look closer,
I see a woman reclining with starlight in her face,

Who is like any woman living or dead, only, only
Her hair is like the rainbow, multicolored,
        reaching
Everywhere with the sure quickness of the
        lightning.
And under drooping stars, her bigness is
        humanity.
A profusion of burdens, a Magdalen of men.
Sing like violinstrings. In the flowing darkness
The streetlamps flutter. The poor hug their
        hunger.
I am waiting, waiting. Soon the sun will be up . . .

Will they bear arms, will they come killing,
Will the headless man and the starlight woman,
Will they come together with the ancient
        emblem,
Will the lonely boy come with them, will they
        come,
Will they destroy the crosses across the profound
        years,
Will they come, I among them, I who have waited
Nameless in history, who will remember the
        hour,
Will they come to remake the world—?

The moon dies across the continent.
The wind screams and something lives.

F. D. De Castro

STILLNESS

Standing still—I never seem
To know when it comes, the trance,
I mean—I feel the stream hushed
        Under its thin glass,
The horses, motionless, clinging to
The hill, a cloud balancing the sun
        In a cotton hand.

I hold my breath. Then from the
Mouth of a tree explodes a flock of

Birds, flight and feather weaving
    A brittle spell: beaks
Spilling crystals lighter than dew
On spider webs. So bright my sight
    I see the lilting

    Notes leap, glint, hug and tease
The air, nimble as motes, do almost
Anything but disappear: with supple
    Twists perform like
Aerialists. This miracle a canticle
To the stillness all around. And
    Round the edges of

    The sound of birds I feel a lit
Stillness deeper than of horses,
Cloud and stream, a stillness bigger
    Than love, brighter than
Lighter or darker than the darkness
That moves above and under the ground—
    Oh, a stillness more

    Luminous than Death, and I feel
It breathing in myself, no longer standing
Still but walking away—
    The sunset on my back—
My pious feet stepping on the ground,
behind me leaving no marks, no quiet,
    Or the slightest sound.

DOG IN A ROOM YOU JUST LEFT

    Dog missing, pink tongue
    And tenderness of eye,
    Like pilgrim at your door
    With stars colliding
    In the heart.

    No angels, no master
    In the empty throbbing room.
    Dog kissing signatures
    Your toes have left
    Upon the floor;

    With anguished sense, knows
    The nooks you dropped blooms

    Of silences and the silky
    Quiet laces your breath
    Has hung around the place.
    Dog missing, all tremble

    And splendid with love,
    Is myself without bells
    Pawing at the glints
    Of your left-over sun.

Ricaredo Demetillo

SUMMER

After the swollen dikes the heat invades
The hedge on which the morning glory curls.
Later the heat will fly on heron wings.

Only the farmers have their deep roots here.
For them the heaven opens still, holds oracles,
Prompts, punishes, is a house of certain doors.

Not erudite, the earth still writes
A bold hand with its flourishes of grain.
The wind applauds along the slopes of hills.

Sap climbs the boles and flames into the bloom,
While butterflies are blossoms on the wing.
Kingfishers moult blue feathers by a spring.

The days are blooms swaying on stalks of light.
Their petals widen in the level fields
And laugh-bright children run to gather them.

The undulance of wings is not less clean
Than song of orioles in hilarious trees
On which the summer leans, the tipsy one.

THE SCARE-CROW CHRIST

I mourn man, man diminished, unfulfilled,
Whose shadow drags the darkness of his night

Across the endless dreariness of days,
Where no oasis greens the sand-choked waste.
I mourn for man, my brother crucified.

Though doom ticks through the clammy cells of
    blood,
Hope pendulums the marrow of each nerve.
I know his hungers scoop the lake for snails,
His guts Gehenna with their appetite
Prowling to thieve the larders for his lack.

In rooms where locusts crunch the dog-eared crop,
Despair bisecting thought in fields of blight;
In farms where claw-like fingers wear to shreds
And huts precarious sag down to the grave,
This man still sidles in a search for light.

Is he not neighbor to my creaking bed
When sleep weighs at the eyelids like a rock?
His cries croak down the echoes of my heart
Though often I would spurn his rattled knock.
Is he not neighbor to my creaking bed?

And you, my reader in this cramp of words,
Are you not party to his hang-dog gait?
You tear his blankets to a chill of shreds,
Snatching your fat feasts from his patient plate?
Are you not Judas to this scare-crow Christ?

José Garcia Villa

(Untitled)

In my desire to be Nude
I clothed myself in fire:—
Burned down my walls, my roof,
Burned all these down.

Emerged myself supremely lean
Unsheathed like a holy knife.
With only His Hand to find
To hold me beyond annul.

And found Him found Him found Him
Found the Hand to hold me up!
He held me like a burning poem
And waved me all over the world.

(Untitled)

Be beautiful, noble, like the antique ant,
Who bore the storms as he bore the sun,
Wearing neither gown nor helmet,
Though he was archbishop and soldier:
Wore only his own flesh.

Salute characters with gracious dignity:
Though what these are is left to
Your own terms. Exact: the universe is
Not so small but these will be found
Somewhere. Exact: they will be found.

Speak with great moderation: but think
With great fierceness, burning passion:
Though what the ant thought
No annals reveal, nor his descendants
Break the seal.

Trace the tracelessness of the ant,
Every ant has reached this perfection.
As he comes, so he goes,
Flowing as water flows,
Essential but secret like a rose.

(Untitled)

God said, "I made a man
Out of clay—
        But so bright he, he spun
Himself to brightest Day

Till he was all shining gold
And oh,
        He was handsome to behold!
But in his hands held he a bow

Aimed at me who created
Him. And I said,
        'Wouldst murder me
Who am thy Fountainhead!'

Then spoke he the man of gold:
'I will not
        Murder thee! I do but
Measure thee. Hold

Thy peace.' And this I did.
But I was curious
        Of this so regal head.
'Give thy name!'—'Sir! Genius.' "

Dig up Time like a tiger
Dig up the beautiful grave
The grave is graveless
And God is Godless.

I saw myself reflected
In the great eye of the grave.
I saw God helpless
And headless there.

Until I put my head on Him.
Then He uprose superb!
He took the body of me
And crumpled me to immortality.

(Untitled)

Were death not so involved
(I mean not the flesh's death)
I should long have resolved
The tactics of her faith.

Her tissues move unmusketed,
Her soldiery is lean;
Their sandals are blanketed,
Yet they cut most keen.

Her soldiers are devout,
Their pulses are delicate;
They keep no route,
Nor argue to debate—

But in phalanx move as one,
A fleet of angels, satin-shod;
They kiss like angels, every one,
And poison like an inverted God.

(Untitled)

Mostly are we mostless
And neverness is all we become.
The tiger is tigerless
The flame is flameless!

(Untitled)

When, I, was, no, bigger, than, a, huge,
Star, in, my, self, I, began, to, write,
        My,
            Theology,
        Of, rose, and,

Tiger: till, I, burned, with, their,
Pure, and, Rage. Then, was, I, Wrath-
            Ful,
        And, most,
        Gentle: most,

Dark, and, yet, most, Lit: in, me, an,
Eye, there, grew: springing, Vision,
            Its,
        Gold, and,
        Its, wars. Then,

I, knew, the, Lord, was, not, my, Creator!
—Not, He, the, Unbegotten—but, I, saw,
            The,
            Creator,
        Was, I—and,

I, began, to, Die, and, I, began, to, Grow.

(Untitled)

Clean, like, iodoform, between, the, tall,
Letters, of, *Death,* I, see, Life. This,
To, me, is, immortal, weather, immortal,

Spelling: The, elegant, interweaver, I,
Call, Hero. Beautiful, as, a, child, eating,
Raw, carrot: whole, as, a, child's, eyes,

Gazing, at, you: Death, builds, her, heroes,
Intensely, clean, Death, builds, her, heroes,
Intensely, whole. A, man, and, Death, indeed,

That, Life, may, speak: a, man, and, Death,
In, league, that, Life, may, flower: clean,
Athletic, mathematic, dancer: and, present-

Tensing, all, his, future: poises, dances,
Every, everywhere, he, go: Christ, upon, a,
Ball: Saltimbanque, perpetual, in, beauty.

THE ANCHORED ANGEL

And, lay, he, down, the, golden, father,
(Genesis', fist, all, gentle, now)
Between, the, Wall, of, China, and,
The, tiger, tree (his, centuries, his,
Aerials, of, light)...
Anchored, entire, angel!
He, in, his, estate, miracle, and, living, dew,
His, fuses, gold, his, cobalts, love,
And, in, his, eyepits,
O, under, the, liontelling, sun—
The, zeta, truth—the, swift, red, Christ.

The, red-thighed, distancer, swift, saint,
Who, made, the, flower, principle,
The, sun, the, hermit's, seizures,
And, all, the, saults, zigzags, and,
Sanskrit, of, love.
Verb-verb, noun-noun:

Light's, latticer, the, angel, in, the, spiderweb:
By, whose, espials, from, the, silk, sky,
From, his, spiritual, ropes,
With, farthest, fingers, lets, down,
Manfathers, the, gold, declension, of, the, soul.

Crown, Christ's, kindle, Christ! or, any, he,
Who, builds, his, staircase, fire—
And, lays, his, bones, in, ascending,
Fever. Verb-verb, king's-spike—who, propels,
In, riddles! Six-turbined,
Deadlock, prince. And, noun,
Of, all, nouns: inventor, of, great, eyes: seesawing,
Genesis', unfissured, spy: His, own, Arabian,
His, love-flecked, eye!
The, ball, of, birth, the, selfwit, bud,
So, birthright, lanced, I, hurl, my, bloodbeat, Light.

And, watch, again, Genesis', phosphor, as,
Blood, admires, a, man. Lightstruck,
Lightstruck, into, the, mastertask,
No, hideout, fox, he, wheels, his, grave, of,
Burning, and, threads, his,
Triggers, into, flower: laired,
In, the, light's, black, branches: the, food, of,
Light, and, light's, own, rocking, milk.
But, so, soon, a, prince,
So, soon, a, homecoming, love,
Nativity, climbs, him, by, the, Word's, three, kings.

—Or, there, ahead, of, love, vault, back,
And, sew, the, sky, where, it, cracked!
And, rared, in, the, Christfor, night,
Lie, down, sweet, by, the, betrayer, tree.
To-fro, angel! Hiving, verb!
First-lover-and-last-lover, grammatiq:
Where, rise, the, equitable, stars, the, roses, of, the,
zodiac,
And, rear, the, eucalypt, towns, of, love:
—Anchored, Entire, Angel:
Through, whose, huge, discalced, arable, love,
Bloodblazes, oh, Christ's, gentle, egg: His, terrific,
sperm.

Amador T. Daguio

WHEN I LOOK AT WOMEN

When I look at women eating
I think they look like fish
Eating other fish, but never-
Theless beautiful. They are
So silent nibbling their bites
And they look at each other
In unlidded silence, so very
Gossip in peaceful
Gesture.

Their hands tenderly pierce
The dead things they are eating,
As if to say: Life is salad,
Fish and roasted pig, hacked
Into crisp, brown pieces. They sit
Disarmingly, so modest in decorum:
Eating their custard pies; taking,
Taking their time.

MAN OF EARTH

Pliant is the bamboo;
I am man of earth.
They say that from the bamboo
We had our first birth.

Am I of the body,
Or of the green leaf?
Do I have to whisper
My every sin and grief?

If the wind passes by,
Must I stoop, and try
To measure fully
My flexibility?

I might have been the bamboo,
But I will be a man.

Bend me then, O Lord,
Bend me if you can.

Trinidad Tarrosa Subido

PAGANLY

God, but I do
Worship you.
Nun-like adoration? No.
Like a bird? So:

       faith
       natural as breath.

I shall pray when prayer is
lip's caprice

       like the thrilling of a bird
       impulse-stirred.

God to me, and prayer
    is as song to bird, and air:
      elemental,
      not sacramental.

C. B. Rigor

GOOD FRIDAY IN MANHATTAN

Good Friday three flights up
The passion is a long busy street (long ago)
A fruit and vegetable market
Busy items with the hard green thorns
    and crimson juice from bloody berries.
Cars roaring by with the fierce hurry of going
    (dust of ages)
A horse-drawn wobbler with Spring's poetry
    of tulips, daisies, iris, lilies
    for the Calvary-bound

A poem of joy by Carl Sandburg, sandy Carl:
    ("Let joy kill you!"
    Kill us with joy:
    "Keep away from the little deaths!")
We die the little vacuum deaths three flights up.

God has a heavy weight in his horse-dumb heart
Dying on the cross of his terrible love
Dying on the cross of his terrible love

Nick Joaquin

SIX P.M.

Trouvere at night, grammarian in the morning,
ruefully architecting syllables—
but in the afternoon my ivory tower falls.
I take a place in the bus among people returning
to love (domesticated) and the smell of onions
    burning
and women reaping the washlines as the angelus
    tolls.

But I—where am I bound?

    My garden, my four walls
and you project strange shores upon my yearning:
Atlantis? the Caribbeans? or Cathay?
Conductor, do I get off at Sinai?
Apocalypse awaits me: urgent my sorrow
towards the undiscovered world that I
from warm responding flesh for a while shall
    borrow:
conquistador tonight, clock-puncher tomorrow.

VERDE YO TE QUIERO VERDE

Color of Green: I love you: Green:
(Red
    scorches; White
        has whips; Blue
            bites.)

the river-cool sea-serpent skin
of your deep arms enfolds my flesh in silence.

Red assaults; rains fire, blood; excites,
devours. Red, our terror aloud,
cried out, of death. (Green is the night's
luxuriant waters jewelled thick with islands.)

White is wisdom, the scourge of God.
Insanity, her nudeness. Pain,
her blinding deserts. Noon, her shroud.
(O moss-grown wells, raw fruits, slopes hung
    with curtains!)

Blue is thought, despair; the ink-stain
time prints on all matter; the cold
vague melancholy, eyes retain
of voyages long perished from importance . . .

Red,
    ripeness, then; White,
        age; Blue,
            mold.
Yet from these senses, though in their
decadence, still rises fourfold
a hunger for that other color, virgin, girlish!

That abrupt, sharp waking up, bare
of blankets, of all dreams—with dawn
on the grasses: all water, air
and earth caught for an instant clean and careless!

Have I built of such moments one
more sanctuary? Have enthralled
stupid the flesh as swine that none
may interrupt these ears turned to the siren . . .

Deep the jungle. Here have I walled
me stranded from the rainbow; in
this leaf-wooed shrine the emerald
stone-unripe guavas pack their smell of iron.

Yea, this my world—spun, sped between
fire branching under, fire above: you
are its whisper of Eden, Queen
crowned over color:
        Color of Green:
            I love you!

NOW SOUND THE FLUTES

Now sound the flutes and the big bell
and call my brothers to my table.
I was never very bright or able:
my few virtues would not sell,
having less substance than a fable.

I would make merry once again
within the familiar horizon
and maybe beg a kiss to moisten
these cracked lips that they may strain
a little wine with a little poison.

I had a dream on Pentecost-tide:
fire did waste my flesh to nothing
till there, purged beyond love or loathing,
the skeleton, fair like a bride,
shone forth, redeemed from temporal
        clothing.

Now who would say that a simple man
like me might yield so great a treasure?
And how can you wed me to your pleasure,
Earth? for now the secular span
of flesh is not my spirit's measure.

Though Time invade my very field
and strip me bare to the last jewel,
the core that's India, his cruel
fingers may never teach to yield
nor pluck its ivory for fuel.

Wherefore, now sound the flutes, the bell:
it is my wedding, my long table!
And come, my brothers, wise and able!
Has come the time to break the spell
and find what's real and what's fable.

SONG BETWEEN WARS

Wombed in the wounds of war
grow golden boys and girls
whose green hearts are
peacocks perched upon apes
and pigs that feed on pearls
or sour grapes.

But we are old—we are only
a point, a pause
in the earth's decay—we are lonely
but no day dies
in the eyes we dare not close
lest we flock with flies.

Bankrupt by war,
let us mine the honey
that's ored in udders that are
this lad, that lass,
because they are molten money
and their bones are cash.

Imperial their coin still is
when other currencies are
imperilled; when peace
is for every man and woman
a labyrinth—and war
the bull that's human.

War is the Minotaur
and we are the waters
bearing for him to devour
the young, the beautiful—
our sons and daughters:
the tax we pay to the Bull.

The maze we made they shall travel,
its winding ways unwind
and the riddle unravel
till they come to the end of the thread:
the labyrinth behind
and the Beast ahead.

Edith Tiempo

BONSAI

All that I love
I fold over once

And once again
And keep in a box
Or a slit in a hollow post
Or in my shoe.

All that I love?
Why, yes, but for the moment—
And for all time, both.
Something that folds and keeps easy,
Son's note or Dad's one gaudy tie,
A roto picture of a queen,
A blue Indian shawl, even
A money bill.

It's utter sublimation,
A feat, this heart's control
Moment to moment
To scale all love down
To a cupped hand's size,

Till seashells are broken pieces
From God's own bright teeth,
And life and love are real
Things you can run and
Breathless hand over
To the merest child.

Carlos A. Angeles

BOATS

Boats intrigue me: the great ones and small.
I think they are most valid when laden
With cargoes, things vegetable or glass.
Pieces of fruit, textile, or motor parts.
Cereal, gold or animal.
But, mainly, man's subsistence.

Especially when, in a fog, they crawl,
Or seem to, toward a static danger,
Toward an ocean's hidden and coral skyscraper,—
But always negative to such disasters,
Successful vessels, they come gliding through!

They sail unscathed the trail pacific,
They will cross wave-tossed tempests
To sail into their own predestined ports
And dump by tons their bales of india.

Whose name, profile and labor
Vary down the ages,—
Steamship, junkboat, trireme, sampan, or canoe,—
They still are arks before new Ararats.

GABU

The battering restlessness of the sea
Insists a tidal fury upon the beach
At Gabu, and its pure consistency
Havocs the wasteland hard within its reach.

Brutal the daylong bashing of its heart
Against the seascape where, for miles around,
Farther than sight itself, the rock-stones part
And drop into the elemental wound.

The waste of centuries is grey and dead
And neutral where the sea has beached its brine,
Where the spilt salt of its heart lies spread
Among the dark habiliments of Time.

The vital splendor misses. For here, here
At Gabu where the ageless tide recurs
All things forfeited are most loved and dear.

It is the sea pursues a habit of shores.

THE LEAST MIRACLE

Someday there will be sudden miracles
Conjured in the potent noon and male hour
And shall be no news, nor shall appear in papers.

In the only bed then in the old house
I lay with my leg broken from a fall
And bathed in my own blood and marrow.
We all thought wrongly I might die,

And for a time I could not walk again.
It was a Sorcerer who limned a fertile cross
Above my wound—then I let fall my crutches.
And those in the gallery, upon seeing, knelt
Before the formal triumph of the saint,
While my Father wept for me who had
The last, the least faith of us all.

Margarita Francia-Villaluz

ADIEU

Adieu! Old House.
There is no home
For old houses.

Out of your ruins
Will rise an edifice:
Symbol of Affluence and Progress!

No plaque for you
For the years of
Shelter given.

Only the claw
Of a crane is
All you deserve.

Yet, I love you.
I'll see you again.
(Perhaps, in heaven?)

Virginia R. Moreno

ORDER FOR MASKS

To this harlequinade
I wear black tights and fool's cap
Billiken, make me three bright masks
For the three tasks in my life

Three faces to wear
One after the other
For the three men in my life.

When my Brother comes
Make me one opposite
If he is a devil, a saint
With a staff to his fork
And for his horns, a crown.
I hope by contrast
To make nil
Our old resemblance to each other
And my twin will walk me out
Without a frown
Pretending I am another.

When my Father comes
Make me one so like
His child once eating his white bread in trance
Philomela before she was raped.
I hope by likeness
To make him believe this is the same kind
The chaste face he made
And my blind Lear will walk me out
Without a word

Fearing to peer behind.

If my lover comes
Yes, when my seducer comes
Make for me the face
That will in colors race
The carnival stars
And change in shape
Under his grasping hands.

Make it bloody
When he needs it white
Make it wicked in the dark
Let him find no old mark
Make it stone to his suave touch.
This magician will walk me out,
Newly loved,
Not knowing why my tantalizing face
Is strangely like the mangled parts of a face
He once wiped out.

Make me three masks.

BATIK MAKER

Tissue of no seam and skin
Of no scale she weaves this:
Dream of a huntsman pale
That in his antlered
Mangrove waits
Ensnared;

And I cannot touch him.

Lengths of the dumb and widths
Of the deaf are his hair
Where wild orchids thumb
Or his parted throat surprise
To elegiac screaming
Only birds of
Paradise;

And I cannot wake him.

Shades of the light and shapes
Of the rain on his palanquin
Stain what phantom panther
Sleeps in the cage of
His skin and immobile
Hands,

And I cannot bury him.

MOCK BALLAD ON A PEARL

This thin hot oyster
Has swallowed
Something.
When it was merely looking
Around and gulping for green air
From the sea dark and the salt white
This thin hot oyster
Has swallowed
Something.
What it was no one knows
Yet, nor why nor how
Was it like? nor when
Was such going on?

Ay, but
Something:

Maybe a crazy fishtail
Dared to play a game
Of peek-a-boo
Beginning on a lowdown note
Jazzed up, climbing higher and higher, yes?
And one knows not why
Was caught in her winking eye, no?
Irised there and splayed,
Laocoöned in her warmest wave
And on the crown tip of panic trembling on panic
Let fall his glass salt tear on her tenderest rose
Bloom pit . . . his fresh grave, ay, her first wound!
While she remembered of the scene
Only a drunken dancing in her shellbone bed
And seagreen absinthe burning her rose mouth
    thin.

Now this cool fat oyster
Knows and has
Something.

PERFUME PRAYER

Lord Healer!
Receive the hurt soul of a foot soldier
Flying home from all earth's wars
Via First Class Express, for once,
And in style, wrapped with his country's rainbow
Flag of No Man's Land.
To your herbal garden without gates, let him
    enter—
Lord Embalmer!
Exhale now Your root, aloe, wine, honey
Myrrh of Perfume Flower
Into his mouth without tongue, into his ears
    without drum,
Breathing incense
Ash, distilled from the smoking dead
Of all man's wars, he must wake fragrant, singing,
Whole, but without his enemy, his knife.

Alejandrino G. Hufana

PORO POINT

The rock still roots the water
Tauter than the buoy in the channel
That marks where men-of-war should enter
And avoid the shallows of the turtle.
The lighthouse eye puts out. Today's communion
Is in the pulpit of the machine.
Now when all owes it religion
What adventure had the aborigine?
One make-up moment to be emperor
In this haunted hamlet on the coast—
Fishers foam-furrow the equator
To homage at a trading post.
Now when divinity is frail
Between the radar poles and the wishing well
To beat the mind to a bell
In brethren's bones with the sunken sail.
As if from rising bottom, sound of sand
Spills out cargo and conqueror
On seven sights of land
Far from either rock or buoy
Like a prayer's amen, and ahoy!
The brief bed of the whirling whore,
The sunbath, the pinpointed star,
And the native full five-strings deep in his guitar
Sermons how to suffer.
Now back to feed the lamps their fuel
While the rock still roots the water
Tauter than the buoy in the channel.

RETURN OF THE MAGI

Baltazar in Quiapo
Listen, the pulpit: more than what a mustard seed
And a dove's arc can contain: this live cemetery.
Just a sunflower's glance back that my people
    played
Under the clock's deep safekeeping, when I left
    them

On a far summons of soul and my ancient eye
Saw, and believed, a foreign race run themselves
As now we run ourselves by date and event that
    pass
North of the rainbowing bridge to cry "Covenant!"
And the black Nazarene's sigh trips the primitives,
As the flock stampede past calendars, as they hunt
More than semen and myrrh in the works of hands
At falls and triumphs of health and domes of love
Beehiving you with me as the flesh-hair stands
Sick and tired on its divinity, loin-bound
With the serious and clown—neither whom am I,
Floating rib, once more catching the split-second
    act
Of birth, adoring the huge holy ghost in woman
Claiming delivery, sitting on the Righthandside's
New Year: the resurrection of the body from mud,
From flame, from the failure of the candle in its
    gut,
The body that shall with the ambassid, moth, and
    the light-lover
From the wreck, the ash, and the darkness rearise
That no more shall snakes molt in God's capital.
Listen, the judgment: experience of innocents
On their crosses moves the mind off the morgue
    to the church
South of the manger where publicans spear the
    heart.

Gaspar in Antamok
On their mothers' side these sooted men,
Late of hell, sucked apocalypse,
None of whose ancestors but would reel
Out drunken from the labyrinths of milk,
Whereas they could not get soused up with wine.
From the crib ejected at a swaddling age
By their fathers who spun them up to the hair
To the heartlong sacrifice to the oracle
Of the gold that forever sinks
Before the orphan toothlings car bite a cave
Into the mine sarcophagus, ten fingers the orrery
Of the ore can sacrilege. No more than this
    religion
Hails in its ossiform the subsoil-swallowed soul
Worming below the mine shaft by carbide light,
Spoored by the flying kiss of her who keeps his
    home
Deep in his baby's faith and in his sweetheart's,

Whose loves, each morning of the surface earth,
Send forth the diamond drill to the origin
Of the ring on my finger and my head's filigree,
And draw from the priestless pit God in a nugget
Streaked with death-unminding miner's sweat.

Melchor in San Fernando, La Union
Golgotha of the ploughman and the seaplougher
Who might fulfill no scripture before them
To hang upon a tree or to have not one bone
    broken,
But whose vestures, among the peddlers, still
Are divided and after-effects cast lots on:
The clay-caked skin, the tang-torn muscle
And perspiring fruits of soil and water.
There is not in this summer archdiocese
A soul, awaking from his daily brain asleep
To usuries stamped on the cash exchanges,
But crying when, when to the crucifiers,
When will the saints avenge?
Tonight the climate turns and the lamps
In the granary go out, the spindrift breath
Shagreens to rust, and the aborigines
Might not again rise after final sleep
To prove life everlasting, but whose likeness
(To the incensed avenger of His saints)
Reinstates the sower in a parable, blood-compacts
With the outcast among the barnacles,
Even as I cross, in scorched earth or blessing
The while that fields are ripe and tides a-teem,
The holy liaisons of my birth- and dying-place.

Hilario S. Francia

"CELEBRATION" BY LUZ

It is the signature
    and the signs,
by which you hear
    this festive air,
or the sounds
    of a native game,
of dashes and dots
    pinwheels and hooks

and parametric curves,
    that echo and play
and dance with the
    surfaces of the limbs:
faces and torsos of the acrobats,
    musicians and jugglers
dovetailing neatly,
    now playing marvelously
and balancing themselves:
    these flat little figures
with their fly-like hands and feet!
    And neither your ohs nor ahs
can alter or change
    the order of it.

THE LOVERS
(In an art museum, Paris, 1964)

Not knowing how
    to move,
they posed
    like formal
wings in love.

A soft wind
    wantonly
welcoming itself
    into the company
of the two.

Slowly, they
    turned:
once, twice
    admiring
each other.

The angularity
    of one
complimenting
    the rotundity
of the other;

While cherubs
    and saints

outraced each
    other
across the room.

Did they glory
    in the system:
like the tendrills
    outside embracing
the laughter of the sun?

A cool shade
    came
and took the
    vacant nook
in their lives.

Now peaceful again
    in repose,
they gathered weight
    as lateness
tip-toed on the hour.

Tita Lacambra-Ayala

FORBEAR: THE CAT FLOUNDERS

among the roses, belligerent, beating
its pinclaws
among the roses.
And it hisses at a breath
of whisker brushing against a leaf
that makes the roseplant tremble.

"Forgive me, rosebud, but this bit
of root grass seems to strike my fancy,
exceedingly, and I must get at it—"

Get at it.

The marks it makes upon the soil
are sunlike, raylike, dancelike,
starlike, lovelike and it unearths
something—a tiny grass

a grass root!

Forbear: the cat sniffs,
licks it then dives away upon the roses—
it has seen its face grinning
upon a mirror.

Bienvenido Lumbera

PEDAGOGY

No, language never tells.
Like a pebble dropped,
a word touches bottom
but does not comprehend
the ripples it has stirred.
Like *loneliness*. It fails
to sound one's fears and griefs.
Meaning is but a hint
of what the mind and nerves
dictate. The body's press
or smell of hair perhaps
better defines absence
that words can only fill.
Void being bodiless,
the word that circumscribes
constricts our lack to pain.
You say the sense defines
the arc of emptiness.
Maybe. But you forget
the hydrography of loss.
When flesh erodes and wind
obliterates the scent
of hair, what then? The tide
of loneliness recedes,
and you are left where dark
assumes the shape of harbor
and nothingness of home.
Call it *hell*. Again
the word is futile. We know
loss is rippled water
whose geometry radiates
circles more vicious than death.

VOYAGERS ON RECTO AVENUE

(For Teddy Catindig)

It takes a daring voyager
to occupy that island there.
Grass that mats the strip of dirt
seems to sulk its roots on earth.
But three brown girls sprawl as though
the island were a luxury rug
endorsed by Good Housekeeping in *Life*
(non-allergenic oh soft like dawn).
For sure, blades of grass will cut
less keenly than a bed of nails.
These girls don't care, at any rate—
somewhere the pushcart has been parked
where grouchy cooks at midnight pile
a charity of rancid cans.

They mapped their grounds for play,
and fanciful cosmography
consigned the island to their claim.
The bundy clock ticks off our lives
and instant soup turns watery
while traffic stalls. What do they care?
And we, commuters that we are,
think censure of their levity.
Office girls will nurse corns
and husbands seek slippers and sex—
such mundane chores as night presents
cannot concern these kids who track
the changeless course of hardy stars
among the city's vapor lamps.

It is enough that in the wash
of horns and hawkers' cries, three friends
have found a private continent.
Simple as laughter or hunger pains,
their game is probably profound.
Those fingers compassing the stars
perhaps described the Pleiades?
Those stars (or so an elder's tale
once told) are really silver coins
the raving Judas cast away.
Kids are somehow sinister,
slier than ancient voyagers.

Who knows? Maybe they have devised
a plot of plundering the sky.

Emmanuel Torres

EL AMOR BRUJO

I am beast then;
The face above the collar hairy, hideous
To her wakening eye searching for
The saving grace where there is none. Her look
Hardens like rain between the banisters
Of a will not, not mine. Now it is confirmed,
My apish truth a thundercloud
Mirrored in ponds of cloistral innocence.

Beauty smiles, and smiles,
Obliging. "My lord," she says—
Susurrus of wingbeats smoothing
The edges of guilt. Her hand swoops
Desperately to stroke her special grief,
This monkeyface before her breast and mouth.

Again, beauty smiles.
I see myself held captive in the cold
Cage of her gaze where my beasthood slowly
Resolves into a shape
More sensual than the promised
Athlete torso of a young prince,

And all the handsels of my good
Name and nature turn to glass in my paws,
And break.

In her gaze, brute-bold,
Companionable hours are blanked out
Like blind mirrors. I am left alone
To consider only her own naked body glowing
In sacrificial waters warmed
By her religion of tears.

Me, me, proudly ape, she judges,
With pity, pity, ravishing her face.

Luis Cabalquinto

ALIGNMENT

It happened again this afternoon
While watching a Wertmuller movie
In the East Village:
This alignment that comes
Like a magnet's work on iron filings
When most things of the mind
As well as of the body are turned
Toward the one direction
Where all must come from
And where all must one day begin
Again: it comes unsummoned, a shift
Now familiar, a quick
Turning over of an event.
It comes as a small wind in Central Park,
The noontime hammering heard in a Philippine
    village.
It is an afternoon walk on a rain-wet street in
    Agra.
Neon lights seen from a hotel at midnight in
    Tokyo.
It came once from the bend of a woman's body in
    Rome,
From a late Flamenco show in Barcelona.
Also it came on the Monterey road
Riding the Greyhound from San Francisco
And, again, in the odd light of an old man's eye
Photographed in New Mexico.
When it happens a strong grip takes over
In the body: the head becomes light.
The hairs stand on end, the pores open
And currents run down to the palms and feet:
Aware at this moment of a new knowledge
That makes the old truths untrue.
Still, each time this happens,
The clarity lasts only seconds:
Before full possession can take place

Something changes the air, reworks the body:
The mind is dislodged, recalled
To an accustomed disorder.

BLACK FISH

From this Sunday's jigsaw I catch a day's
    resolution
Of probabilities: this quick tug between the first
    black

Fish and the big bucket waiting to be filled. I am
a connection in the tense traffic between white
    sea

And cobalt sky, a middleman in the brisk business
Of cosmic provision. I help keep heaven's
    contract terms.

——————Darn, he cut through my line!

Ernesto D. Manalo

IN MY COUNTRY

No autumn and no winter here
No snow and winter birds to hear,
No squirrel and no bear,
    None in my country.

No apples here in summer bloom,
No owl, no nightingale will croon.
Almost, there is only land and sea
    Here in my country.

Just land and sea and moon and sun
And open fields where boys can run.
And God is always fair to man
    Even in my country.

Rolando S. Tinio

LAWS OF SIGHT

I

Impersonal. It is not I
Lifting blinds, leaning out
Of a hole to watch the mountaining
Of rocks. *Here* is the eye of holes

And *there* the leaf a wind tingles—
The "cogitations of a noon's
Repose" unable to know themselves.
And wind withdraws, the brush of space

Plainly disappears, appears again.
The wind, bound nowhere, writes
Its law, its exercise of windness,
Waits for no seer, itself the sight.

II

As in a gothic garden live
With statuary in marbled white:
They loom above your head, those heads
Drilled with holes, as if the eyes

Fixed inward, and gazed themselves to stone.
Memory is full of Gorgons,
The plague that cries deliverance.
Theban Magus, teach us to pluck

The inner eye! this trick of mirrors
Bright as the burst of pomegranates.

Gemino Abad

TO CALIBAN

To Caliban, perfect half-fish,
Sing I this tempest.

Dark and beautiful foal
Of the blue-eyed Sycorax,
Bless you and your barefoot protest
Of this brutist thing, Prospero,
Who, of deep eternal frivolity,
     is the magical despot.

Rise, Caliban, and rage,
And pure, burst, Eyes.

PARABLE OF STONES

Every morning I sally forth
into the world, my pockets
are full of stones.

You cannot see them
where my hands are hid
and sometimes bruised by their edge.

O, a quick and deadly aim
have I, and ask no questions.
My hands are cold.

And few stones left have I
at each day's end,
and groan as my hands bleed.

My state—who can endure?
As morning breaks I know again
I have more stones to cast.

You cannot see them
where my hands close
and all my days bleed.

Who will close my morning,
O, who will empty
my pockets of my stones?

Florentino S. Dauz

"LOVE NOTES TO THERESA"

Afternoon it was, and our town
And cities began to glow.
Fear rose like fire in the countryside
And in the city, bellies trembled.
Ah, it was you after all, Theresa!
Unknown fire from a dying town.
It was you, yes, a combination
Of fire and folly; I was a socialist first
And a Catholic last, upon your belly:
Rising and falling in the sun.

But as usual, time was limited between us.
Our lips parted to embrace no more,
Our bodies collapsed and our senses became
    normal.
And everything around us returned to their
    former forms;
The politicians and their empty harangues;
The democratic dogmas, the Jesuits,
Factories of the brain, viva all!
And so, we parted Theresa,
Beat, beaten, bored, and Beat.

Federico Licsi Espino, Jr.

TINIKLING

Identity of bamboo that once defined
This man's and this woman's pliant ancestry

Stiffens into poles essential to the dance
That now defines what is natal,

What is native, what is numinous.
Transcending traps that bring back

To the ear and eye a memory of birds
Insulting a possible doom, they warn us,

He and she, that bone and beat must blend,
Or the dance, the dance can cripple.

Exile, then, the impossible dancer.
Banish him from the makeshift stage.

Who has not learned from birds—survival
Is impossible without essential grace.

Jose Maria Sison

THE GUERILLA IS LIKE A POET

The guerilla is like a poet
Keen to the rustle of leaves
The break of twigs
The ripples of the river
The smell of fire
And the ashes of departure.

The guerilla is like a poet.
He has merged with the trees
The bushes and the rocks
Ambiguous but precise
Well-versed on the law of motion
And master of myriad images.

The guerilla is like a poet.
Enrhymed with nature
The subtle rhythm of the greenery
The inner silence, the outer innocence
The steel tensile in-grace
That ensnares the enemy.

The guerilla is like a poet.
He moves with the green brown multitude
In bush burning with red flowers
That crown and hearten all
Swarming the terrain as a flood
Marching at last against the stronghold.

An endless movement of strength
Behold the protracted theme:
The people's epic, the people's war.

Cirilo F. Bautista

PEDAGOGIC

I walked towards the falling woods
to teach the trees all that I could

of time and birth, the language of men,
the virtues of hate and loving.

They stood with their fingers flaming,
listened to me with a serious mien:

I knew the footnotes, all the text,
my words were precise and correct—

I was sure that they were learning—
till one tree spoke, speaking in dolor,
to ask why I never changed color.

CHINESE IMPRESSIONS [excerpt]

let the moon shine
i don't care for light and love
i have wine

let the fish laugh at my reed
and youngsters talk of fight
brandishing swords of weed

i dont care for love or light
let them burn my verses
though i labored over every line

let the moon shine
on my white beard and bald head
i dont care i have wine

let them say hes out of his mind
if i choose to sit here
and watch the fields fall in time

i dont care i have wine
let all the lovers trip in their game
and all the warriors boast of shields

i dont care let the moon shine
i am brother to the fields
the birds sing my rhyme

i am exact in my hut
i am one i dont pine
i dont care let the moon shine
i have wine

A MAN FALLS TO HIS DEATH

1 Blood is nothing. Space is all. Is.
2 A simple diagram illustrates this:

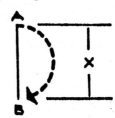

3 where A is the tenth floor of steel and glass
   (He was on
4 the noon shift forging the dream to a reality
   fine men
5 could slumber in, or whores, in
   antechamber, touch their bone)
6 and B the level earth (Above the clogged
   engine
7 a shadow traced the lines on his foot, while
   shoot
8 his brain with firelights the money did). Put
9 down an imaginary circle around the vertical.
10 Compute the square of guilt against an
   integral
11 his age built when he was young: wrong,
12 axiomatic: the sum stands thus: Along
13 the curve X (none noticed the leap; what
   they saw

14   was the red imprint) by which we know
15   the nothing particular, the momentum
16   carried him to the point beyond the
       dictum—
17   *Hic primus geometros*—for a body
       physical, a
18   mass, emits energy equal to zero, the stay
19   necessary to arrive at a base, as in Berger's
20   formula for optics. Here we remember
21   the fallacy of inclusive force if we extend
22   A to the absolute (He was, a day ago,
       threatened
23   with dismissal for displeasing a superior)
24   and call it the Cause: heat, hunger, air—
25   these were just contingent. To recapitulate:
26   Berger's law does not apply here, as the late
27   projections of X show, space being
       non-mathematic;
28   from A to B the descent exhibits a quick
29   increase in force, though the exact ellipsis
       we know not.
30   (The Blank and Blank Co., Inc., regrets to
       announce that. . . .)

TREATISE ON IMAGINATION

Umbrella umbrellum umbrellus
The possibilities are infinite
What I see I do not see
My voice is only garrulous

Ponder a moment what she is
Umbrella or girl
White girl under umbrella
A never-ending disgrace

White umbrella above a girl
White girl white umbrella
If sun is a mirror over them
There is no need to name her

Umbrella-girl girl-umbrella
Sun-umbrella sun-girl
Reality is a fox
The knotted tarantula.

CONCERNING THE DEATH, BY ASSASSINATION, OF BENIGNO AQUINO JR., AUGUST 21, 1983

Words are Flesh.
—Buddhist teaching

The word was dead before it was uttered.
Under the noon heat, having flown a sky
of short fear and long desire, six syllables
twitched, bloodied, cut down by a secret spy.
What message did they whisper to the earth
when silence shocked the bullet in the brain—
the end of empires? the text for violence?
concord and clemency blooming in pain?

For one word, the ritual rose to heights—
fever at first, then death disguised in blue,
till the word fell down, unspoken, unheard,
misunderstood, misjudged, declared untrue,
rushed to the grave without knowing why, while
a nation mourned and wept because it knew.

Jason Montana

I THINK THOUGHTS OF PEOPLE'S WAR

This morning is of heavy fog and monsoon rains
The mountains are disturbed by angry rivers,
And I by stories of mass arrests and massacres.
There is a loosening of rock and earth. In times
Such as this one must consolidate his social being
In ways designed by revolutionary wisdom.
I think thoughts of people's war,
Not of reactionary peace but of affliction
Within the barbed and sentried confines of the
       regime.
Now I think of a mother and child unborn,
And recall that once she said Come and feel me.
I sensed the little one quicken inside her,
Kick the palm of my hand once, twice, and
Lodge his threatened presence in the core of me.

I felt too the touch of her warmth on my cheek
And saw the central glow of her face fringed
With the pained penumbra of a sadness and a
  concern.
I think of her distant smile and grasp the Word
That the wailing of many Rachels must end,
And from the hearts of mothers swords be drawn
  out.
The fog then opens up to a fighting terrain.
Slippery is the soft brown carpet of pine needles.
The rain turns gentle. I think thoughts of people,
Of their war, and of peace of their own creating.
I think of you, Child, like a bullet
Quiet and alert in the chamber of a guerilla's gun;
Of you Comrade Woman, bearing a gift of hope.
You release me more deeply into the long struggle.

SONG FOR ANNA

I went around
Looking for carnations.
I couldn't find any.

Then it struck me
That today probably
Isn't for flowers,

But simply for this
Little poem for you,
Written on a delicate

Page of sunlight.

Merlie M. Alunan

BRINGING THE DOLLS

(For Anya)

Two dolls in rags and tatters,
one missing an arm and a leg,

the other blind in one eye—
I grabbed them from her arms,
"No," I said, "they cannot come."

Each tight luggage
I had packed
only for the barest need:
no room for sentiment or memory
to clutter with loose ends
my stern resolve.
I reasoned, even a child
must learn she can't take
what she must leave behind.

And so the boat turned seaward,
a smart wind blowing dry
the stealthy tears I could not wipe.
Then I saw—rags, tatters and all—
there among the neat trim packs,
the dolls I ruled to leave behind.

Her silence should have warned me
she knew her burdens
as I knew mine:
her clean white years unlived,
and paid my price.
She battened on a truth
she knew I too must own:
when what's at stake
is loyalty or love,
hers are the true rights.
Her own faiths she must keep, not I.

Bataan Faigao

SUMMER NIGHT

friends go memories go loves
go gods go the light goes
all the little children of
your mind

they go and the rain
that beats upon the night

goes

Marra PL. Lanot

SOLDIER'S SONG

Let the hills and mountains
Roll up behind me like
The tangled past of a jungle.
Let a rose grow when
I lay down my gun
Where the desert meets the shore.

I long to throw away
This mask of maleness,
All male desire to kill,
To spit the blood, the sour-
Ness balled in my mouth.
I have forgotten the face
Of my mother, sister, niece.
All I see are trenches
Hate burrowed in my brother's face,
His eyes, two barrels of a gun
Unleashing bullets.
I have learned that foes
May become friends tomorrow
And friends my foes tonight.

This season I may own a
Bowl of rice, next year
I might bite a fruit
Or have a new dress
Or a roof over our heads.
But I remember home
Each time a child
Presses a cheek to mine
Or even when a horse
Gives birth and goats
Cavort in a manger.

Let the hills and mountains
Roll up behind me like
The tangled past of a jungle.
Let a rose grow when
I lay down my gun
Where the desert meets the shore.

Beatriz R. (Veena Francia) Romualdez

MY COUNTRY WAS A LONG TIME AGO

My country was a long time ago
Lola clothed in musky brown
She sits there
Grandmother of these Tristes Tropiques
Rooted by her tapers
Fingering her beads
Droning prayers for the dead and living of the clan
Wearing a wry, weary smile
She watches those of us who come and go
Our victories, our machinations
Contests for the headship of the clan
Our sins that smell of rotting frangipani
Our Byzantine betrayals
She goes about her business
Watering her giant ferns of menacing vitality
There's no decay that a bit of holy water
Will not sanctify
Lola whose womb is the world
Fondling your bastard grandchild
Bearer of our darker secrets
Which the light of day would dissipate

My country was a long time ago
And my recurring dreams of being trapped
In the village of Lanag
Where all our servants hail from
The woman who stole my pearls and bridal finery
And Luisa, fat honey I saw,

I saw you marching as some archaic flower bearer
With your desperate laughter and dreams of glory
I dreamt I would find the fabled burial chamber
Of Sumakael with you in Budhian
But a capre guarding the graves
Refused us entry
A key that will unlock my random gestures
Lies buried there

My country was a long time ago
A tale hummed to a distant pitch
Which a woman, dreaming, rocking by
Her window, under the moonlight hears
While gathered by a beach
Two hundred Babaylans spit and chant
To soothe the pain
Of our fathers' thwarted dreams
Guzzling pang-asi from dragon jars
Under a cloth maypole
Breaking out into prophetic utterance
About green revolutions wrought by pesticide
And fertilizer
They sing of a Maytime queen
Who wished it was May forever and decreed it so
They twirl on three days and nights
Until a star deigns to approach us
And whispers a secret melody
That moves us to ecstatic oneness
We cannot decipher it but only sway
Engulfed in its waves
Its intricate interweavings
That leave us sated with love . . .

Wilfredo Pascua Sanchez.

GETHSEMANE

Creative difference, altogether again,
steadfastly stockstill and fast,
I take you wrongways by the head
to witness the natural flood
and disinhabit the customary house
slidden from insurrective light

fructified, a galbanum garden of light!
Leviathan fouls and spuddles again
my possessions and my father's house,
I ask the stinking brats the grave-fast
patio, threshold of the footworn flood
of the Lahai-roi. O, that fleering head

in the grange, that goshawked head,
garroted in plague's-pang of light
so seeming lost in fending the flood.
That hardly done, the children again
smut their ears with sesame upon the fast
borne worshipfully—O upraised house,

Keep back: I see the universal house,
exfoliating. I run through my head
her wax fingers from a tearful fast:
O, hermitess, you so platted the light:
it is naturally happening again,
and be the vile mediatrix of all flood.

I can hear the great whore down flood,
hung in the wilderness of the house
and I can hear the mineral dogrose again
originating in her hood, her head!
O manna amour, flouresced in myriad light!
Nemesis, to disannul her hymeneal fast!

I can see the great whore at her fast
stoop her thick plagues in the flood;
I kill, and eat; put my self loosed in light:
O harlot-stymied sepulchre, that the house
dragged down my calyx on a gypsum head.
I also, sundered and sunder, and kiss again

Shame, Danger, Evil Speech, and Flood
divide on foot and moan the house
yet; and drag the tired Galilean light.

Luis H. Francia

HIS HIDDEN SELF

Upon his flesh,
Upon his wrath, a

Madman's mask is
Wrought: they hush
His hidden self.
Whose anger once
To movement welled,
To form, but mur-
dered fell. Was it
Men's stares, old
Age it saw? Young
Fear, banishment
That grew? Geniuses
Say; only madmen know.

ERMITA GIRLS

Like engines of sensation
Waiting to be revved up,
Their tired breasts are oiled
For a hard night of
Easy love and its leavings—
These are brown bodies purged
of moisture, a desert of ransacked
hearts, propped up by
Thighs calloused in the arts
Of holding the secrets not only of
Flesh but of flesh's failures.
Now heat arising from them is
Not that of velocity expanded
For great distances of great dreams;
But the heat of aridity, the
Fever of skins plugged into their
Own deaths, the dollar by dollar
Destruction of the civil sensing
Self: rigor mortis among the living.
But the props are in place to
Fool us, the smiles of inviolate
Proportions, the little cries promising
Unholy sutras, but
Reveal to the keen volatile
Ear incendiary longings long laid
Low by the pyre of a rotting communality.
There we are. Are we to judge
Them then? In this city of uncommon grief
Where love a long time ago bowed its
Head and died, their bright eyes
Flare an instant, brief as falling stars

In a sky that is forever
The color of lent.

DAYS IN THE COUNTRY

Here where there is wilderness still,
    And stillness in the wilderness,
Here my time refuses the clock,
My lines desert linearity,
Here I deny the abyss and the height:
And all directions, one.
Here reverberates my life, beneath
The rockpile of civilization. My
Buried sinews, the muffled primitive
Heart formed long ago by a
River, by a Malay bay, respond
To an outside call—Heresy's voice!—
And smash the tomb of elegance into
A living order of royalty, where
The mighty pine lowering its gaze
Teaches me humility; and the
Feathers dazzling in flight—the blue
Of cobalt, red of blood, gold of
God—baffle all my booklearning; and
Where the burst of greenleaf, the cooling
Lake ripple unravel theory.
I too come unraveled, glad to
Be with forest gods, dwarves in ant-mounds,
Trickster spirits of the hills: to them
I submit mortality, my intellectual self
I yield to timeless earth.

And yet New York City calls, another
Wilderness still. The subways roar
Around like circus beasts in circles;
The cabs are yellowjackets on a
Tear; and in skyscrapers people
Move like anchorites in a
Capitalist heaven. There
The clock refuses my time, there
Linearity inhabits my lines, there
The abyss and the height
    Pinpoint me,
And one direction becomes four.

Still to the city my steps have been,
Still will go: it must always be so.

After the feast, the fast;
After opulent green, the nomad heads
Bare and blesséd for the desert.

Jose F. Lacaba

VILLANELLE GIVING REASONABLE ADVICE

Ever will the river lily flow
And the reed stay put with a minor swaying.
Sit down in the grass and scratch your toe.

The lovely girls in love will utter O
But never will they stop their cold betraying.
Ever will the river lily flow.

But once betrayed you find you must outgrow
The constant throes that sent your body straying:
Sit down in the grass and scratch your toe.

Not at all will flighty dragonflies know
It is for them your lips continue saying
Ever will the river lily flow,

It is for them that pebbles overthrow
The hush with ripples turning and decaying.
Sit down in the grass and scratch your toe

For at this moment there is nowhere you can go,
You must control the will that's bent on slaying
The river lily that will ever flow.
Sit down in the grass and scratch your toe.

RESTAURANT

Perhaps I should sit next to
The lady of the dainty bite
Who goes to most decent places.
It may be she can tell me why
Foam in a glass of coke
Cannot approximate the sea.

It is a necessity here to have
A constant repair of cautions . . .

And I shall say to her
In the irony of my approach,
Do not overdo it, remember
Your bites resemble the moods
Of waiter and cashier and solitary
Customer looking around, waiting
Politely for his order.

I anticipate the sand
Like accidental sugar in my palm.

Donel B. Pacis

ON THE BIRTH OF A SON

Most bright the seas
where jostle
            the whales
of your joy:
brighter than your
mother's mirth pressed
as petals against
            your pink mouth
trembling the delights
of her thoughts
I fail to put into
            words.

Her breasts and white
throat: do they warm
            you now?
Her small hands: are they
the sadness of things
you shall remember
leaping as light
            in disheveled dark?
My laughter is a quick
moan: in my mind torn
the scene of bubbles
            pricked faster

Than it takes your mother's
tears to fall
                    and you wake
in a bleat of song
breaking the spell
of tales untold
and things beloved.

Alfred A. Yuson

AN EVENING: ISOSCELES AND I

Gin and orange and fealty
of nights long spoken for.
Outside my retina a woman waits,
her forehead on the door.

I cast an eye on the quivering jamb,
shall give an eye to lock and key.
No songs for liquid screws, not yet;
My Madonna's lamb, I remain at sea.

And if she enters, her triple deeds
arrayed: Lady of the Unschooled Lay,
spiritless muse, duchess of discord—
Who knows my ethic? My etheric's me.

Gin and orange and yin the inner fish:
There shall be no evil, all is well;
full fathom deep, disparities erase
Smile of her nature on her phantom face.

Swigs of love and hate; guts and grit
in a headless rise. If I'm to become
the cleft in her Om, idler in the race—
Exeunt all: her smile, nature, phantom, phase.

DUMAGUETE DESPERADOES

He sat in the outhouse by the breadfruit tree,
He thought, and ripples flew

Like the wit of monks.
Upon the jagged leaves of the breadfruit tree
The humor grew. Punctured, impaled.
The humor blew (off the jagged leaves
Of the breadfruit tree) across thatched roofs
To come upon someone, a woman who
Catches sight of the outhouse by the breadfruit
     tree
And walks on hurriedly. She arrives
By the seawall, sets up her stall.
She addresses the ice, the beer, chicken
Stuffed with lemongrass, sticky rice
Sheathed in leaves. The leaves
Are a paler green than the jagged leaves
Of the breadfruit tree. She addresses them,
This woman who has walked on hurriedly.
She has arrived and so has her lover.
He who drones on all day upon his tricycle,
And clones himself all night
By making her his bicycle. She, this woman
Who has walked on hurriedly—light
Plays upon her eyes as he pedals furiously.
She is seat and tire, and road that curves
On endlessly, past the thatched roof
Of the man who has caused their coalfire love,
As he sat in the outhouse by the breadfruit tree.

Edgar Maranan

LANDING

Christmas day at Idlewild: a brace
of winter, vomit dried up in the mouth

eyes snow-stung, the heart a reliquary
of picture books and nursery rhymes

as Brown Boy clutched a Pan-Am bag
and strode across the tarmac, near tears

There was, in the 50s, a vision of trains
passing beneath rockies, over prairies

Where he lived in the colony, dandelions
grew, sunflowers, carnations, roses, too

There was a vaster flowerland, this much
he knew, where sunshine cabins stood

by placid lakes and rafting rivers,
and red sails billowed in orange sunsets

while pilgrims' souls bowled ten pins
on the clouds, above postcard mountains

He'd learned a continental history
from Columbus to Crockett, from Alamo

to Alamagordo and the Project. He gloried
in the knowledge of GoodWar's global theaters,

which saw democracy win, packing six-shooters
Actually, he was born in forty-six,

but recalled each battle from Gettysburg
to the walls of Intramuros, as though

he'd lived through all of them,
as though he'd been born in a barn next door

At sixteen, he'd seen the 60s begin,
and thus he stood before the new New World

dreaming of a handshake in Camelot
which, he recalls now, sheepishly,

was plotting Vietnam.

Richard Paradies

SUMMER

Perhaps it was the time of year
The grass had withered to the root.
The trees stood desolate
And, sometimes, on an evening,

A single swallow took wing
Under insulatiung skies.
Life being out of season,
The husks of things remained.

What can we do?
There is nothing can stop it.
Always, disintegrating earth
Shall call for propitiation.

And things being what they are,
I have sometimes stood on an afternoon,
Feeling the fall of slanting sunlight,
Wanting to suddenly like a claustrophobiac,
Break, batter and tear my way out,
But instead walking quietly off
And perhaps watching the aimless play
Of children in the narrow streets
While my fancy thought of the earth
Rolling in the sky's clenched fist
Like a marble.

Simeon Dumdum, Jr.

THIRD WORLD OPERA

When he kicked the governor,
The applause
Was deafening.
Everybody stood up
And cheered.
Even a baby cooed,
So he thought.
Such an adulation
He never had in his career,
And it was for an act
His role
Had not demanded.
Why, he was about to burst into song
After kissing the leading lady
When he saw
The governor, smiling
In the front row,

And he remembered the dictator,
The governor's master,
And his sins
Against the people.

For his part, the governor
Deserved credit.
That he loved Vivaldi
Whom he thought painted The Last Supper
Was well known.
Better known
Was his passion for the theater,
And the tragic thing that could happen
Was for one
To think his honor a fool
In matters of the stage,
And so when the actor descended,
In surprising haste,
And planted
A rather realistic kick
In his groin,
He felt honored,
Marvelling with gratitude
At how much theater had progressed,
And joined the crowd
In the applause.

FEBRUARY

Nothing escapes notice.
The hot months have made us heedful.
The fields, hurt to an alertness,
Strain for detail, seek God
In every pod and flower.
Faces set, we make
Yet one more inventory:
All corn gone,
Bare trees,
One last fruit
(Moon of the palms).
At the very last we hear it blowing,
The spirit that overhauls—
Sudden wind!
Sudden fall!

Sudden sap rising!
Leaf for leaf!

Felix Fojas

ORACLE OF THE YELLOW RAIN

And the imperial soothsayer oracled:
The wings of a giant dove shall bear
An omen clothed in the color of lilies;
Lord, beware! for when his perfumed feet
Touch any part of the sacred ground,
It shall augur the beginning of the end:
All your sandcastles shall be blasted

By divine lightning and human thunder.
And there shall be signs in heaven and on earth:
Even the sea the Empress owns shall bleed red,
Even your royal birthplace shall quake;
A month after the ritual murder,
The sky shall shed dry tears of the yellow rain:
Lord, should I put a bullet in your purple brain?

Emmanuel Lacaba

POEM

In puddles and rivers
Pebbles hit bull's-eyes
Before targets are drawn.

ICARUS CHRIST

Ploughman and dog whose wings are trees,
Dismiss me as no bird, or to the sea

I'll fall, though I relish flight. Yet why should I
    please

Strangers when I can't my friends and family?
Father Forsaker, you're not he beside me
Struggling with the air: you desire me
To be rain, and later air itself, which is you.

Which is death the constant. Which bids me
Fix my feathers if they're frail: Daedalus
Is a superior carpenter. Yet endlessness,
Like faces screaming blood, terrifies me

Still, terrifies me still. Terrifies
Me still. O to the hill, to the whale, with me!
Maybe I shall fly again in three days.

POEMS USING TAGALOG FORMS

1

Night has become a bad habit,
shrugs the morning, combing her wig,
extinguishing flames cleft by wicks
(her hands unlock windows' deafness):
Night has become a bad habit.

For the morning, two envelopes
with messages of two periods
might as well drawl: Coming and lost;
melancholia post coitus;
what's opened can never be closed.

The cup's one ear and empty skull
dares to approximate the sun:
who sips the night, keeps a journal;
who daily has one orgasm;
whose dusks are chins in horseshoe hands.

Timepieces die, the ceilings' scrolls
brightly proclaim; let the cotton
of dust and cobwebs cover wounds,

unicorns make love to centaurs,
men satisfy l'horloge de flore.

Night has become a bad habit,
shrugs the morning, combing her wig,
extinguishing flames cleft by wicks
(her hands unlock windows' deafness):
Night has become a bad habit.

2

When a cloud shades the sun all penumbras are
    one
and my eyes' blue pouches to Magdalene are
    moles
like my secreted bag's two most delicate coins,
like Shadow my true friend whom water cannot
    drown.

Styx and salt, salt and Styx. They'll look back,
    fugitives
who bother if there should be dots untouched by
    feet;
passing through rain prisons, the strings of puppet
    trees,
prepare with three roosters notes for the
    Pharmacist.

Antiseptically masked and aproned, the skies
knife with fire and brimstone abdomens of cities.
In the oboe distance: the first successful lies
predict a savage death dance of adulteries.

Let gazes be brassieres. Processions of black
    robes.
Holy Friday faces. The whitening of crows.
A fist of cowards I: who sing from a tau cross,
my sons by my daughters calling their mothers
    whores.

Named Judas, born Jesus, named Jesus, born
    Judas,
I am not what I am, I am what I am not:
a shower of insects under an outside bulb,
the Genuine Guitarist's indiscriminate scars.

CABALA

Siya nawa
Siya na nga

A cave of rain the daedal brain,
A cave of rain.
Two plates of rice the daedal eyes,
Two plates of rice.
Piping down the Hamlin wild!
Who thinks I'm out of tune?
Who the fellow child
Who wouldn't let me sing?

Quasar, quasar, now & at the hour
Of the pharaoh ant.
A tumor in the brain of God,
I lower my laser eyes.
Nights I telescope Icarus,
Closer than Mercury to the sun,
The asteroid closest to the sun.

The meteor is the moon meeting earth,
Caligula; what's truth There
Is myth Here. My nerves hear
(Treading the burst of light
Outside the cave is) the
Hemidemisemiquaver of hate;

I've scoured & scoured
The monkey tail of Fate.
O touch the Third Eye's scar
On my Third World head;
Go! imperialist of my spirit.

"Miriam the prophetess, sister of Aaron,
Took a timbrel in her hand;
& all the women followed her
With timbrels & with dances."

Lady Sutra! I am my sanctuary,
I my enemy. White my hair
Overnight. Through mountain windows

The fog plumes the latest surah.
You are cordially invited to

The mystic E of Delphi.

PATEROS BLUES

All I the brat of eight the brat of Death
itched to write were elegies. One for
the bitch among three dogs at home
I stroked the most: the summer evening toast

of all Pateros mongreldom. The next
town's camp of soldiers drowned her crisper
        bones
with coconut wine. Another for my great
great etcetera grandfather Quim

Suy the merchant later known as Don
Lorenzo Quiogue of whom the waterlilies of
tres siglos obstructed most recall.
Nevertheless he must have himself

forgot the cry of the ducks & the Pasig's swell
& the profit & the loss who had
taken a Christian martyr's name: Saint
Lorenzo who roasted by the Romans quipped

one side of him was cooked. "Come & eat. Then
        turn
me on the other side." Lorenzo too
Saint Martha's & the river's thin & gray
dancer: whose heart at eighty flying fell

with food hurled by sterile women on
a crocodile! the crocodile. When
forty my father died my mother's clan
the most impoverished *principalia* marched

through bridges' throats & intestines of streets
to the home of white! where black veils
blindfolded aunts. Uncles squinted: shut their
        eyes.
At the coffin halfway through the niche I stared

as at the duckling of *balut:* dark
as the spirit possessing pale virgins: as Death
my foster father my second name my other side
my favorite word my great etcetera Death.

THE PEOPLE'S WARRIOR

The people's warrior is an athlete:
A mountain-climber, not because it
Is there, but because the masses are there.
He is an acrobat: balancing himself
On fallen trunks of trees that bridge rivers
And monstrous waterfalls of certain death,
Like a tightrope dancer. The people's warrior
Is an actor: on the stage of revolution;
An actor of sincerity, for the masses
Are the best critics, can read faces and bodies
And know when you speak the truth, or are just
Hamming. The people's warrior is, oh yes,
A comedian: making the masses see the paradoxes,
The irony, of their condition—
The contradiction between him who is ruled but
    sweats
And him who rules without a sweat from his
Cushioned car and office and marble toilet seat;
The people's warrior inspires the masses to march
Forward to battle cheerfully, but with all
Determination; he clowns, to make the masses feel
At home with him, who is of them
And for them—for the first time one armed
But not abusive, the people's warrior.

OPEN LETTERS TO FILIPINO ARTISTS

*A poet must also learn
how to lead an attack.*
—Ho Chi Minh

I

Invisible the mountain routes to strangers:
For rushing toes an inch-wide strip on boulders
And for the hand that's free a twig to grasp,
Or else we headlong fall below to rocks
And waterfalls of death so instant that
Too soon they're red with skulls of carabaos.

But patient guides and teachers are the masses:
Of forty mountains and a hundred rivers;
Of plowing, planting, weeding, and the harvest:
And of a dozen dialects that dwarf

This foreign tongue we write each other in
Who must transcend our bourgeois origins.

*South Cotabato
May 1, 1975*

II

You want to know, companions of my youth.
How much has changed the wild but shy young
    poet
Forever writing last poem after last poem;
You hear he's dark as earth, barefoot,
A turban round his head, a bolo at his side,
His ballpen blown up to a long-barreled gun:
Deeper still the struggling change inside.

Like husks of coconuts he tears away
The billion layers of his selfishness.
Or learns to cage his longing like the bird
Of legend, fire, and song within his chest.
Now of consequence is his anemia
From lack of sleep: no longer for Bohemia,
The lumpen culturati, but for the people, yes.

He mixes metaphors but values more
A holographic and geometric memory
For mountains: not because they are there
But because the masses are there where
Routes are jigsaw puzzles he must piece together.
Though he has been called a brown Rimbaud,
He is no bandit but a people's warrior.

*South Cotabato and Davao del Norte
November 1975*

III

We are tribeless and all tribes are ours.
We are homeless and all homes are ours.
We are nameless and all names are ours.
To the fascists we are the faceless enemy
Who come like thieves in the night, angels of
    death:
The ever moving, shining, secret eye of the
    storm.

The road less traveled by we've taken—
And that has made all the difference:
The barefoot army of the wilderness
We all should be in time. Awakened, the masses
    are Messiah.
Here among workers and peasants our lost
Generation has found its true, its only home.

Davao del Norte
January 1976

Alfrredo Navarro Salanga

(Untitled)

Between our bed
and your crib
lies a gulf

But it's wider still
where your palm,
open, invites the sea.

You dream and stir.
We wake up, see
you stretch your hand

And drown.

A PHILIPPINE HISTORY LESSON

It's history that
moves us away
from what we are

We call it names
assign it origins
and blame the might

That made Spain right
and America—bite.

This is what it amounts to:
we've been bitten off, excised
from the rind of things

What once gave us pulp
has been chewed off
and pitted—dry.

A WAY OF COMING HOME

I think the end came
with his one foot
raised in the air—poised
like an inverted
    benediction
He was stepping down—
isn't that how one goes
into a country from the air?
Hawks and eagles—they too,
land on their feet. But nothing,
nothing was to come out of this.
Neither blessing nor returning.

As the sun touched his crown
it knew. Another door had
    opened
to welcome him neither
as priest
    nor as bird.

Jessica Hagedorn

SONG FOR MY FATHER

i arrive
in the unbearable heat
the sun's stillness
stretching across
the land's silence
people staring out
from airport cages

thousands of miles
later
and i have not yet understood
my obsession to return

and twelve years
is fast
inside my brain
exploding like tears

i could show you
but you already know.

you greet me
and i see
it is you
you all the time
pulling me back
towards this space

letters are the memory
i carry with me
the unspoken name
of you,
my father

in new york
they ask me if i'm puerto rican
and do i live in queens

i listen to pop stations
chant to iemaja
convinced i'm really brazilian
and you a riverboat gambler
shooting dice in macao
during the war

roaches fly around us
like bats in twilight
and barry white grunts
in fashionable discotheques
setting the pace
for guerillas to grind

the president's wife
has a fondness for concert pianists
and gossip is integral
to conversation

if you eat enough papaya
your sex drive diminishes
lorenza paints my nails blue
and we giggle at the dinner table
aunts and whores
brothers and homosexuals
a contessa with chinese eyes
and an uncle cranky with loneliness
he carries an american passport
like me

and here we are,
cathedrals in our thighs
banana trees for breasts
and history all mixed up
saxophones in our voices
when we scream
the love of rhythms
inherent
when we dance

they can latin here
and shoot you
for the wrong glance
eyes that kill
eyes that kill

dope dealers are executed
in public
and senators go mad
in prison camps
the nightclubs are burning
with indifference
curfew drawing near
soldiers lurk in jeeps
of dawn warzones
as the president's daughter
boogies nostalgically
under the gaze
of sixteen smooth bodyguards
and decay is forever
even in the rage
of humorless revolutionaries

in hotel lobbies
we drink rum
testing each other's wit
snakes sometimes crawl

in our beds
but what can you do
in the heat
the laziness makes you love
so easily

you smile like buddha
from madrid
urging me to swim with you
the water is clear
with corpses
of dragonflies and
mosquitoes

i'm writing different poems now
my dreams have become reptilian
and green

everything green, green
and hot

eyes that kill
eyes that kill

women slither
in and out of barroom doorways
their tongues massage
the terror from your nightmares
the lizard hissing nervously
as he watches
you breathe

i am trapped
by overripe mangoes
i am trapped
by the beautiful sadness of women
i am trapped
by priests and nuns
whispering my name
in confession boxes
i am trapped
by antiques and the music
of the future

and leaving you
again and again
for america,
the loneliest of countries

my words change . . .
sometimes
i even forget english.

Cyn. Zarco

SAXOPHONETYX

I've heard all about musicians
They take love, don't give love
cause they're savin it for the music
Got to be so one night I was watching him
take a solo and when he closed his eyes
everyone in the club closed their eyes

The first thing I saw was my shoes
float out of his horn
my favorite leopard-skin high-heel shoes
the left foot, then the right one
followed by my black silk stockings
with the seam down the back
my best hat and all that
were floating in the air like half-notes
like they belonged to no one
least of all to me

I tried to close my eyes
but I couldn't
Out flew my blue silk scarf
my alarm clock
my alligator suitcase
even last month's phone bill

He kept on playing that horn
as if nothing even happened
and when I slowly closed my eyes
I saw his fingers wrap around my waist
my spine turn into saxophone keys
my mouth become his mouthpiece
and there was nothing left in the room
but mercy

Denise Chou Allas

CHILD OF TOLERANCE

I am child of your eyes
Child of your fairy hair
Your father's delicate blood.

I am captive of your fragrant ovens
Captive of your daydream books
Your virgin poems.

I am twenty-seven and not grown up
You will not let me, Mama
Although you let me go.

Flowers bear flowers, weeds bear weeds
You wish I were my sweet sister faraway
My brother in his golden tower

You have a wide heart, Mama, wisdom
In your bones—but not for me
Issue of your iron womb: black

Sheep, counterfeit lotus
I write you poems you will not read
I bake you bread you will not eat.

You cannot like yourself, just
Cannot break the chains of your disdain
Prison of my child's landscape

But it's all right
You need not string the pearls on your cheeks
Around my neck

For I am child of your eyes
Your fairy hair
Your virgin poems

I am child of your primordial
Dreams. I cannot hate you
It will be my own death.

Ricardo M. de Ungria

OVER THE EDGE

You are beautiful when you are sick.

In your mouth I can still smell oysters
and the wine uncrushed
by the slithering warmth
of vomit.

Your slender throat
is the course of this night—
desire and decay thrashing
each other for air.

How easily your breath
conspires a precipice
where lunacy and tenderness
bray.
Even outside of this,
your stupor, it tickles
the hooves of death.

I had words and glances
that warned of excess.
But I am wanton
with your sterling secrets.
And now by your lack
of words and glances I am
kept up, a stale form of excess.

You are farther from me now
than the next day's
brightness and ache.

You like mushrooms. I know
You are sleeping under one
now. The stealth of closing
the door regains
this day's composure.

NO MAN'S LAND

Cocked gun at cockcrow.
If anything moves, I shoot.
And when canefields
or walls of alleys or even
the city's sidewalks
make explicit fallen bodies,
I am glad for the thud.
Whether of men or carabaos,
children or women or pigs
—I cannot tell or care—
I am glad for the groan and the thud.
I am glad to be reborn
in the groan and the thud.

I love to twist my bootheels
on the sandstone of their faces.
Yank out and cut their tongues
and ears that knew more
of what I stand for, or so they think.
Play tic-tac-toe or nothing special
on their throats and backs
with my bayonet and cigarette butt.
Bash to a pulp their hands
that never learned to write,
or write about me in unmangled light.
Blast their eyes and genitals,
spit on their blood and curse them
for taking me away from my coffee.
Spit and curse. And spit again.
And piss on them to put out the stench.
These fools begged for my bullets,
and I am glad to lift
a finger to my trigger.
I am fatal metal's philantropist,
slaughterous to a fault.

Let their bannerful complaints
shoe the flies from their carrions.
If they have nothing more to prove
I leave guns in their arms.
Planting evidence is always fun.
It is rice to particulars of command,
then wine, even before reaching
the generals. For the rest, who cares
about dumped bodies and unmarked graves?

This is war, and I believe it.
Each man's poison thrills—
there are no jails, only trajectories.
Gawking bulletholes in the dead
are medals for the living.
Combat fatigue is a wound knifed
to pray out maggots fattened on mass deaths,
and it never heals. But it remains
like home sweet home for me,
my bread of salt, my uniform.

CARILLONNEUR

I took the thought
of going back to New York
for a walk at dawn
before the fruit vendors
set up their stalls
and while the she-wolf next door
is still making love
loudly for the good of us all.
Wind-whipped trash bags
winging down empty streets
still remain the sure signs
of the city's nursery of speed.

Someone must be keeping count
of what is yet to come.
So strong is the feeling
some long-overdue debt
is being paid me
in installments.
When I look at my photos and postcards
I know I have been somewhere,
and everything is still taking place
long enough for me
to move from here to there.
Making a home for absences
restores to the self the true
magnificence and pain of presence.
It gives me confidence
and drives me out to seek
some form of love.

As long as I can keep from talking
to myself too long,

as long as passion kills
mutely and obscurely
I can live here.
But this can be anywhere,
the tambourines higher in pitch,
the bed harder.
And I find myself again
out of the A-train
in the middle of nowhere,
ready to begin again
with slick black hair.

Mila Aguilar

DISILLUSIONMENT

There is something about
the heaviness of summer
the kept humidity
that will not break out into rain
that wants not to break
into fine, life-giving rain.
The keptness
that numbs
all forward-looking in my eyes . . .

Oh bourgeois!
A whole system of thought
the absolute rationale
just to stay the way you are
what is it in me anyway
that ever wanted to save you?

Alan Jazmines

WRITINGS ON THE MARGIN
OF A BOOK

Writings on the margin of a book
have a lot in common
with guerrillas.

They come from nowhere
and from all directions,
suddenly are spread out
over white areas.

Unmeasured by ens and ems
they are a rag-tag lot,
do not march in letterpress order
nor go by the rules of the book.

Not simply black on white
they emerge in their own styles,
dialects and colors
and not only in red.
(Observe the curls
that fly unshaven
in defiant fashions.)

Unfettered by column inches
and flush rights
they grow infinitely
drawing from a well-spring
of creativity
even if sometimes ungrammared
unlettered.

At will
they waylay precisely
clumsy targets
encircled and crosshaired
for annihilation.

A burst
of exclamation points
or question marks
may blow up whole structures
but it usually takes
a rapid fusillade
of unmistakable tirades
to send their targets
back to pulp.

What is decisive
is intimacy to the issue
in the native heart
and the grassroots facts
uncouth, unshod,
with no fear

of censors
or the military.

No matter erudition,
stereotypes holding on
to fixed positions
cannot escape
the scrutiny and force
of new ideas and critiques
resolute in their challenge
for the rule.

In time
the writings on the margin of a book
are established;
a new book
supercedes the old.
And then there will be new and different writings
on the margin of this book.

Mehol K. Sadain

EPILOGUE TO JOLO EXODUS

A day had been reached with another one to come
and the leeches in us cling to the creaking bamboos
of a dying life,
and the butterflies in us flutter weakly
out of the whirling wind,
and the grasses on our feet turn brown
as we squat dumbly
dreaming of epicurean philosophies, while inside
    us
hope decays.

Another day, and we feel the bitter bite of cold wind
on our skins, as it sweeps
across Fort Pilar—where once drowsy Spaniards
    stood
guard to watch our forefathers coming.

The whiteman's shouts we still hear
with the ancient gale that brings our own inner
    shouts:

to the dead—who will pray for them?
and the living—who will pity them?
Are the Moros (a race lost) forever
to be left between the madness of two forces?

Like idle onlookers, we stare
at the fly hovering above our soup
and wait for it to fall in
so that we can throw the soup away
and fill our mouth with curses.

A day had been reached, with another one to
    come
and the leeches in us still cling
to the wrong side of the bamboo.

Rowena Tiempo-Torrevillas

VOYAGER

Into the void, past Neptune now—
Leaving the nest of planets
Spinning in their calm vortices
The basal threads of primordial desire:
Tiny wanderer, made to outlast
The sun's final, convulsive wheel:
Celebrating the path
Men's eyes first took,
Each station, each ancient name
Its own relinquishment:

Past angry, empty Ares
And dervish Saturn, armored
In hoops, inscrutable mandala:
Slip past Father Jove,
Feel the heavy last
Tug of chill fires
Beckoning, bellowing
Gravity's archaic laugh;
(In astronomy's crazy dance
Pluto's switched places this year
With the Sea-God, death safely
Hidden in the frictionless deeps)—

And you, wandering out of reach,
Small pilgrim voyager,
Mere eyes and voice
Singing to itself
In the emptiness
Beaming Eroica, the Beatles and Berry
And golden Brandenburg to the stars
Wheeling in their own silence:

Child of the stars, now,
Earthstone, earth-tone
Humming offkey or on
In brave diatonic
Of your lost home.

Eric Gamalinda

INCANTATION / A SCROLL

The mad and the hypocrite roam this city I don't
        want
        to die in
My generation scours the avenues for scraps and
        sex
I have seen twilight fading in the eyes of the
        young
and the needle piercing the skin and the ooze of
        impossible blood
All of them fortify my battlements i.e. not even
        the leaves tremble
when the season impels the hour of decay
and even as this man dies or that one fails I am
        lessened or am fallen
not defeated but bracing for the next attack
the symmetry of vespers and arrows
and I watch the pious diminish into prayer
and their hunger diminish into rain
        Listen to me
now the inner midnight is descending
and the fire opens and closes
over someone's sad mouth holding back the howl
with its immaculate crises and blooms of violets
        and always I am he
        I burn in the rainbows

I am driven insane by the simplest wind
I will lose myself among the vast redeemed
and when this man fails or that one exults
I am that one / I die or exult

Babeth Lolarga

THURSDAY THE THIRTEENTH

thursday the thirteenth
i took my pen for an outing
trusting it to try the air
and return rejuvenated

the tremor of the rows of trees
frightens the ink flow
weightless paper flies off
to wonderland perhaps?

the stains and spots say
stay, the trip's not over yet
pen, sip a little water
then writing will again matter

Maria Fatima V. Lim

FR. RUDY ROMANO, REMEMBERED

—Dublin, Ireland

'Romano.' When said in their brogue
Thick and lilting, your name
Becomes a herb of healing or an animal
Wild and fettered, with gleaming eyes.

'Romano.' Word has reached them.
You are a rebel rousing the hills.
A messiah moving invisibly, among the masses.
A military prisoner with a cut tongue.

'Romano.' They say the High Mass for you.
They march in the rains for you
And they capture you
In song for the harp and bohdran drum.

'Romano.' Finding me in the fog,
Through the thick pipe smoke
And Guinness foam in the pubs,
They tell me who you are.

'Romano.' Inured in ice,
Immune now to any memory
Of May, massacres and monsoons,
I make meek noises. I am struck dumb.

'Romano.' Here where I am 'Gaill'
or foreigner and where you are 'Mac' or son,
We meet, both ghost-like,
Both half-way between worlds.

'Romano.' Lost amongst these people
Who love you, I pray your name.
My remorse, dear stranger, in this exile,
Shall keep you alive.

JoJo Soria de Veyra

LEATHER EXCRETES

You listen to the sound.
of pencil on
    leather—
        Does it hurt
your eyes,
  to see its silver black, trekking
   a shimmery gloss
    on leather, young leather—
        one
     shiny one.
         Love
  is a market bowl
  of noise
       and swelling
       of shit But is there

        not joy
        in bad ardors
        also,
leather excretes
unsavory fumes
        to a pencil's scratchings
But look at what they make:
look at pain's metal

     knocking droplets on
     leche flan. Is not
          man
         a beast
      upon a princess
     he is also prince !

Danton R. Remoto

CORPUS DELICTI
(After the Sandiganbayan
Decision on the 21 August 1983
Assassination)

We are being fed a body of lies:

Dirt on the tips of toenails
that do not intend to die.
Toes that gingered a country's dreams
into a brew more bitter than Macbeth's witches'.

Dirt on the terrible corners
where thighs edge into crotch.
Dry spores seeding an archipelago's sky,
unquenching our thirst for a cloudless day.

Dirt on the tips of fingernails
that do not intend to die.
Maggots fattening the fingers
splayed outward as Baudelaire's flowers.

Dirt on the crag of mountain hair
down a mask of Ibaloi stone:
This bloom of blackest blood,
this nothingness finally
                unutterable.

Manuel Ortega Abis

I LOVE THE RED
To the Agrava Commission

I love the red fell on the lap
  of yellow & white;
    I love the blue was doused by bullets;
    Light,
      do I have to kill for thee?
        The sun is so noon & sight;
          the runway stars are so soon &
           warm;
            give me back my linen
              & my shadow & fight, too;
                though dead.
"Sir, he wets our schemes, this son;
the people now are in a coma;
should I call to the stand the yellow, red & blue
or Joema Sison?"
No.
"Why?"

Because I love the red fell & lapped
  this ground where once
    this sound was John Paul's kiss
      & silence, peace & eloquence;
      I did hope they did miss
        this day of awe
          before the flag declared violence
          & police.

LOVE IS TOO THIN

Love is too thin. Like a dream
between reality of dark foxes & boxes &
couch of soft counting up to seven doves
or following the line of Tennessee Williams;
like a dam breaking; like a dome leaking; like a dame
sipping, dripping milk of obvious scream:
a silk; love is too thin.
But Galapagos is in him
& surely, I can carve cherubim with palm
leaves as wings or stern of canoe:
this is creating only in that instinctive
calm. He is thunder & terror;
under & error; vertical & horizon;
intersection that states, "Mirror. Love is too thin."
While the two cherubs under his armpits
become un-displaced by the body odor of sacrifice
that rise to my nostrils & eyes looking
down from the real pit where light voice
    announced,
"It is the third day, my son.
Love is too thin attention.
Love is too thin ascension."

STRIKE

Strike the Minotaur in the sun's tale
meat by meat!
For who knows what time of year he will whale
to his true whiteness,
myth by myth?
What labyrinth is there, so ordered
to confuse, what labyrinth is there
our child to dare, this child to dare
into his meat, the tail of his sperm,
into his myth, the wail of his germ,
for where is his space but the darkest
and the deepest? O, this lurking of mind!
So strike the Minotaur by the sun's tale
bust by bust!
What egg-ship shall break, what morons
shall take their motions by beliefs and not
by hand-outs of truth, or morbid lies?
Strike!
And call him Israel.
Strike!
And call me Emmanuel.

NOTES ON SHORT STORY WRITERS

As well as writing short stories and poetry, **T. D. Agcaoili** (1915–1987) alternated between journalism and film writing and production. Active in the underground during the Japanese occupation (1941–1945), Agcaoili formed the now defunct Palaris Films, a film production company, after the war. As literary editor at the now defunct *This Week,* he encouraged literary criticism.

Though a prolific writer, **Estrella D. Alfon** (1917–1983) had only one collection of stories published, *Magnificence and Other Stories.* A member of the University of the Philippines Writers Club, she held the National Fellowship in Fiction at the U.P. Creative Writing Center in 1979.

Francisco Arcellana (1916–) is the author of *Selected Stories* and editor of *Philippine PEN Anthology of Short Stories.* Professor of English at the University of the Philippines, he helped found the literary group known as the Veronicans and the now defunct literary quarterly *Expression.*

Manuel Arguilla (1911–1944) was known for his stories of peasant life and later for stories concerned with social causes. Some of these were published in U.S. journals like *Story* and *Prairie Schooner.* Author of *How My Brother Leon Brought Home a Wife and Other Stories,* he was executed by the Japanese during World War II for his involvement with the underground.

Included in many anthologies, **Paz Marquez Benitez** (1894–1983) edited the first anthology of Philippine short stories in English, *Filipino Love Stories,* and the frist Philippine literary magazine in English, *Woman's Home Journal.* She taught English literature at the the University of the Philippines.

Gregorio C. Brillantes (1932–), winner of several Palanca Memorial Awards for his fiction, has two published collections of stories: *Distance to Andromeda and Other Stories* and *The Apollo Centennial.* A member of PEN Philippines, he is also an editor and journalist.

Carlos Bulosan (1911–1956) immigrated to the United States as an eighteen-year-old. A largely self-taught writer, he supported himself working on the farms and helping organize farm labor. Some of his stories appeared in *The New Yorker.* He is the author of *Voice of Bataan, The Laughter of My Father, America Is in the Heart, Power of the People,* and *The Philippines Is in the Heart.* He died of consumption in Seattle in 1956.

Gilda Cordero-Fernando (1930–) has authored two collections of stories, *The Butcher, the Baker, the Candlestick Maker* and *A Wilderness of Sweets.* She is an editor and publisher as well.

A TOYM (Ten Outstanding Young Men) awardee in 1961, **Andres Cristobal Cruz** (1929–) writes in both Pilipino and English. He is also a poet, with two collections out: *Estero Poems* and, with Pacifico Aprieto, *Tondo by Two*. He has been awarded the Republic Cultural Heritage Award, for his fiction.

Amador T. Daguio [see Notes on Poets]

Joy T. Dayrit (c. 1952–   ) is a journalist and a poet as well as a short story writer. She teaches children creative writing at a Montessori School in Manila.

Author of a collection of stories, *The Road to Mawab and Other Stories*, **Leoncio Deriada** (1938–   ) teaches English literature at Silliman University in Dumaguete City. He writes in four languages: English, Tagalog, Cebuano, and Hiligaynon.

A Palanca Memorial awardee for fiction, **Rony V. Diaz** (1932–   ) is the author of *Death in a Sawmill and Other Stories*. He has taught at the University of the Philippines and worked for the Philippine government.

A prolific writer, **D. Paulo Dizon** (1915–1961) once had fifteen stories published separately, in 1950. A collection of his fiction, *Twilight of a Poet and Other Short Stories*, came out shortly after his death.

N.V.M. Gonzalez (1915–   ), the literary editor of the now-defunct California-based Philippine-American monthly *Katipunan*, was Professor of English at California State University at Hayward. Awarded various honors, he has written three novels and five short story collections, among them *Seven Hills Away*, *Children of the Ash-Covered Loam and Other Stories*, and *Look, Stranger, on This Island Now*.

Author of *Collected Short Stories*, **Sinai Hamada** (1912–1991) was a lawyer by profession as well as a journalist in Baguio, a resort city in Northern Luzon, where he founded, published, and edited a newspaper, *The Baguio Midland Courier*.

Nick Joaquin (1917–   ) has written in many genres: journalism, biography, history, drama, nov-

els, short story and poetry. Honored by the Philippine government as a National Artist in Literature, this ex-seminarian and multitalented Manila-based writer is the author of works collected in *Prose and Poems, Selected Stories*, and *Tropical Gothic*; two novels, *The Woman Who Had Two Navels* and *Cave and Shadows*; and a play, *Portrait of the Artist as Filipino*.

Recipient of a Ramon Magsaysay Award and Palanca Memorial Award for his fiction, **F. Sionil José** (1924–   ) has written novels and novellas in addition to three collections of stories, including *The God Stealer and Other Stories*. He owns and runs Solidaridad, a book store cum publishing house, in the heart of Manila.

Ibrahim A. Jubaira (1920–   ), a diplomat, is from the Muslim Southern Philippines. He has a published collection of stories, *A Canto of Summer and Other Stories*.

A lover of music and theater, **Paz Latorena** (1910–   ) has had her stories anthologized. She was head of the English Department at the University of Santo Tomas for a while.

Renato Madrid (1940–   ) is the nom de plume of Fr. Rodolfo E. Villanueva, a parish priest who has won numerous literary prizes, including the Palanca Memorial Award. He is also a playwright, composer, and choirmaster.

Resil B. Mojares (1943–   ), a professor of literature at the University of San Carlos in Cebu City, is the prize-winning author of *Cebuano Literature* and editor of *The Writers of Cebu*.

In addition to fiction **Anthony Morli** (1927–   ) writes plays and essays. A member of the U.P. Writers Club, he is based in New York City.

Wilfrido D. Nolledo (1933–   ) has won Palanca Memorial awards for his plays as well as his fiction. In 1963 he was honored as one of the year's Ten Outstanding Young Men. His first published novel was *But for the Lovers*.

Currently teaching at Ateneo de Davao University in Davao City, **Aida L. Rivera** (1926–) has a published volume of short stories, *Now and at the Hour and Other Stories.*

Ninotchka Rosca (1946–), now living in New York City, has written two collections of short stories, *Bitter Country and Other Stories* and *The Monsoon Collection;* two novels, including *State of War;* and a journalistic work, *Endgame,* on the events of 1986 that forced the Marcoses from power.

Arturo B. Rotor (1907–) based most of his stories on his experiences as a physician, his professional calling. A music critic and orchid fancier, he has had an orchid named after him. He is the author of two collections of short stories, *The Wound and the Scar* and *The Men Who Play God.*

Bienvenido N. Santos (1911–) has held Rockefeller and Guggenheim fellowships and has been awarded the Republic Cultural Heritage and Palanca Memorial awards. He has written several novels and collections of short stories that include *You Lovely People* and *The Scent of Apples and Other Stories,* the latter receiving the 1980 American Book Award from the Before Columbus Foundation.

Loreto Paras Sulit (1908–) was widely published as a short story writer in the 1930s. Later, she wrote children's stories. A founding member of the U.P. Writers Club, she headed the Philippine National Red Cross for decades until her recent retirement.

Along with his wife Edith, **Edilberto K. Tiempo** (1913–) directs the Silliman Annual Summer Writers' Workshop in Dumaguete City in the Visayas region. Recipient of a Guggenheim fellowship, he has written four novels and a collection of stories, *Stream at Dalton Pass.*

Rowena Tiempo-Torrevillas [see Notes on Poets]

NOTES ON POETS

Gemino Abad (1939–   ), member of the Philippine Literary Arts Council, is the editor along with Edna Z. Manlapaz of *Man of Earth: An Anthology of Filipino Poetry and Verse from English, 1905 to the Mid-50s*. A professor of English at the University of the Philippines, he has written several books of poetry, among them *Fugitive Emphasis* and *Poems and Parables*.

The youngest contributor included, **Manuel Ortega Abis** (1967–   ) is a high school graduate who has been published in journals and an anthology, *Versus: Philippine Protest Poetry 1983–1986*.

Mila Aguilar (1952–   ), a political detainee under the Marcos regime, is a journalist as well as a poet. She has a published collection of poetry, *A Comrade Is as Precious as a Rice Seedling*.

Denise Chou Allas (1951–   ) is a journalist and technical writer whose stories and poems have appeared in magazines. A collection of her poems was published as *Way Station Blues*.

A Palanca Memorial awardee for poetry, **Merlie M. Alunan** (1943–   ) helps run the Silliman University Writers' Workshop every summer.

Carlos A. Angeles (1921–   ) has worked for the Philippine government and, in private industry, in public relations. A Palanca Memorial awardee, he also won the Republic Cultural

Heritage Award in 1964 for his collection of poems *A Stun of Jewels*.

A bilingual writer, **Cirilo F. Bautista** (1941–   ) is a Palanca Memorial awardee for poetry and a member of the Philippine Literary Arts Council. A professor of English at the De La Salle University, he has written four books of poetry, including *Charts* and *The Cave and Other Poems*.

Carlos Bulosan [see Notes on Short Story Writers]

Luis Cabalquinto (1935–   ), a New York–based poet, won the 1978 Dylan Thomas award from The New School for Social Research. Widely published, he is the author of *The Dog-Eater and Other Poems*.

Amador T. Daguio (1912–1966) was an editor and public relations man, working in government and the military. A member of the resistance during World War II, he also taught at several universities and won numerous literary prizes, among them the Republic Cultural Heritage Award. He is the author of *The Flaming Lyre*, *Bataan Harvest: War Poems*, and *Collected Poems*.

Luis G. Dato (1906–1983) was a professor of English and a journalist, acknowledged as an authority on the language and culture of the Bicol region, in southern Luzon. He authored several volumes of poetry, among them *Manila: A Collec-*

tion of Verses and *The Land of Mai: A Philippine Epic.*

Florentino S. Dauz (1939–   ) is a poet, essayist, and novelist. His books include *Caligula* (poems) and *The Survivors of Warsaw,* a novel.

F. D. De Castro (1911–   ) writes fiction as well as poetry. He later studied filmmaking, wrote film scripts, and worked for the Philippine government and, later, for the United Nations.

Ricaredo Demetillo (1911–   ) is a literary and art critic and a retired professor of humanities. His books of poetry include *No Certain Weather, Masks and Signatures,* and *Lazarus Troubadour.* He is also the author of *Major and Minor Keys: Critical Essays in Philippine Fiction and Poetry.*

Once the lead singer for a rock band, **Ricardo M. de Ungria** (1951–   ) is a member of the Philippine Literary Arts Council. He teaches English and the humanities at the University of the Philippines in Manila and has two books of poems out, *R+A+D+I+O* and *Decimal Places.*

Florizel Diaz (1910–   ) was one of the few poets in the 1930s to write humorous and satiric verses.

A practicing lawyer, **Simeon Dumdum, Jr.** (1948–   ) has had two books of poetry published, *Third World Opera* and *The Gift of Sleep.*

Federico Licsi Espino, Jr. (1939–   ) is a playwright, fictionist, and essayist as well as a poet. He is the editor of the anthology *New Poems in Pilipino.*

Bataan Faigao (1944–   ) is based in Boulder, Colorado, where he teaches Ta'i Chi at the Naropa Institute. He has two published books of poetry, including *In Celebration of Strange Gods.*

Chairman of the English Department at the University of San Carlos in Cebu City, **Cornelio Faigao** (1908–1958) was a noted poet and critic in the 1930s and '40s. An annual writers' workshop was instituted in his memory at the university in 1984.

A World War II veteran, **R. T. Feria** (1910–1978) and his American wife, Dorothy Stephens, taught at Silliman University in Dumaguete City shortly after the war. There they helped found the literary journal *Sands and Coral.*

Felix Fojas (1948–   ), a member of the Philippine Literary Arts Council, works in advertising. He has a published book of poems, *Port of Entry.*

Hilario S. Francia (1929–   ) is a painter, art critic, and book designer as well as a bilingual poet. He has had four books of poetry published, including *Selected Poems.*

Luis H. Francia (1945–   ), based in New York City, is a Palanca Memorial awardee in poetry. In addition to being a poet, he is a journalist and critic. Published in journals and anthologies, he has written two books of poetry, *Her Beauty Likes Me Well* (with poet David Friedman) and *The Arctic Archipelago and Other Poems.*

Published in magazines and now based in New York City, **Margarita Francia-Villaluz** (1925–   ) has written several children's books. She has also worked as a journalist.

Eric Gamalinda (1954–   ), a member of the Philippine Literary Arts Council, writes for the Philippine Center for Investigative Journalism. Also a novelist, he has had two novels published, *Planet Waves* and *Glimpses of a Fertile Land.*

Jessica Hagedorn (1949–   ) is a Manhattan-based poet, novelist, and noted performance artist. Her first novel, *Dogeaters,* was nominated for the 1990 National Book Award. She has two collections of poetry out, *Dangerous Music* and *Pet Food and Other Tropical Apparitions,* the latter including prose pieces.

Alejandrino G. Hufana (1926–   ) teaches English literature at the University of the Philippines and is a critic and playwright as well. A recipient of the Republic Cultural Heritage Award, he has several books of poetry out, including *Sickle Season* and *The Life of Lot and Other Poems.*

A political prisoner during the Marcos years, **Alan Jazmines** (c. 1952–) is Secretary-General of the political party Partido ng Bayan (People's Party).

Nick Joaquin [see Notes on Short Story Writers]

Forsaking academe to join the radical left-wing guerrilla underground, the New People's Army, **Emmanuel Lacaba** (1948–1976) at the age of twenty-seven was killed by a military patrol. A collection of his poems, *Salvaged Poems,* came out posthumously (1986). A collection of his prose is to be published shortly.

In addition to being a poet, **Jose F. Lacaba** (1945–) is a journalist, editor, and screenwriter. He teaches creative writing at the University of the Philippines and at Ateneo de Manila University. A political detainee under the Marcos regime, he now writes mainly in Pilipino. He has a published collection of journalistic pieces, *Days of Disquiet, Nights of Rage* and two collections of Pilipino poetry.

Tita Lacambra-Ayala (1931–) is a short story writer, poet, and publisher of the Road Map series on art and literature. Her books include a poetry collection, *Sunflower Poems,* and a short story collection, *Pieces of String and Other Stories.*

Marra PL. Lanot (1944–), a bilingual writer, journalist, and Palanca Memorial awardee for poetry, has also written teleplays and movie scripts. She has authored three books of poetry, including *Sheaves of Things Burning.*

Published widely in journals, **Maria Fatima V. Lim** (1961–) is a Palanca Memorial awardee in poetry and has had published a collection of her work, *Wandering Roots.*

Babeth Lolarga (1955–) is a journalist who has written for the country's major dailies. Her poetry has appeared in various periodicals.

Critic, poet, and professor of English and Pilipino literature, **Bienvenido Lumbera** (1932–) is currently head of the Film Center of the University of the Philippines. He and his wife, Cynthia Nograles, wrote and edited *Philippine Literature: A History and Anthology.*

Ernesto D. Manalo (1936–1962) started writing poetry at age twenty. Six years later, he committed suicide because of failing health. A posthumous collections of his works came out in 1965, *Selected Poems.*

Edgar Maranan (1946–), also a playwright and fictionist in Pilipino, teaches Philippine studies at the Asian Center of the University of the Philippines. He is the author of a volume of poems, *Agon.*

Jason Montana (c. 1942–) is the nom de plume of a former priest and professor of humanities and journalist now with the underground Left.

Virginia R. Moreno (1925–) is a playwright as well as a poet and teaches the humanities and English literature at the University of the Philippines. She has a published collection of poetry, *Batik Maker and Other Poems,* and her plays include *Straw Patriot* and *Onyx Wolf.*

Donel B. Pacis (1945–) writes fiction and essays as well as poetry. He has written a book of poems, *My Name Is Sadness.*

A graduate of Ateneo de Manila University, **Richard Paradies** (1946–) is believed to be living in Australia.

Danton R. Remoto (1963–) teaches English at the Ateneo de Manila University and writes nonfiction in addition to poetry. He has had a book of poems published, *Skin, Voices, Faces.*

Published widely in the 1930s, **C. B. Rigor** (1914–1960) was a bemedaled World War II veteran, who survived the infamous Bataan Death March, and for a time headed the Philippine Military Academy's Department of Languages, having earned an M.A. in English from Columbia University.

Published in anthologies and magazines, **Beatriz R. (Veena Francia) Romualdez** (1944–), now based in Hawaii with her family, wrote the libretto for Manila's first rock musical, *Mahal,* and a biography of her aunt Imelda Romualdez Marcos, *Imelda and the Clan.*

Mehol K. Sadain (c. 1952–) is a poet and a fictionist. His works have come out in various periodicals.

Alfrredo Navarro Salanga (1948–1988) was a newspaper columnist and editor, member of the Philippine Literary Arts Council. He wrote a novel, *The Birthing of Hannibal Valdez,* and a collection of his poems came out posthumously in 1989, *Turtle Voices in Uncertain Weather.*

Now living in Chicago, **Wilfredo Pascua Sanchez** (1944–) is a Palanca Memorial awardee in poetry. He has written stories as well as poetry and has done work in theater.

Jose Maria Sison (1939–) is better known as the founder of the Communist Party of the Philippines and its military arm, the New People's Army. A political prisoner during the Marcos regime, he now lives in exile in Europe. He has a published collection of poems, *Brothers and Other Poems,* as well as books on Philippine political and social conditions.

JoJo Soria de Veyra (1961–) has had his works published in journals.

Shanghai-born **Trinidad Tarrosa Subido** (1912–) worked as a journalist for a while. She edited, with Carolyn Fosdick, a four-volume series, *Literature for Philippine High Schools.* Along with those of her late husband, Abelardo Subido, she has published a selection of her own poems in *Two Voices: Selected Poems.* She has also written a history of Philippine feminism, *The Feminist Movement in the Philippines, 1905–1955.*

Edith Tiempo (1919–), along with her husband Edilberto, is the guiding light behind the prestigious Silliman Writers' Workshop. Among her published works are *The Tracks of Babylon and Other Poems* and a novel, *A Blade of Fern.*

In addition to being a poet, Palanca Memorial awardee **Rowena Tiempo-Torrevillas** (1952–) is a short story writer. Her books include *Upon the Willow and Other Stories,* a collection of short stories, and *East of Summer,* a volume of poetry.

A bilingual writer, **Rolando S. Tinio** (1937–) is also a playwright, stage director, and translator (into Pilipino). For a while he headed the resident theater company of the Cultural Center of the Philippines. He has a published collection of poetry, *Rage and Ritual.*

A professor of English at the Ateneo de Manila University, where he is also the university gallery's curator, **Emmanuel Torres** (1932–) was a Ten Outstanding Young Men awardee in 1961. He is the author of two poetry books, including *Angels and Fugitives.*

Honored as a National Artist in Literature by the Philippine government and recipient of a Guggenheim Fellowship, **José Garcia Villa** (c. 1911–) is one of the country's most important poets, and certainly its best-known writer. He began by writing short stories, before hearing the call of poetry. Villa is the author of several collections of poetry, including *Have Come, Am Here,* and *Selected Poems and New.* He has been a seminal influence on Philippine letters. Living in New York City since the 1930s, he has taught at the City College of New York and at The New School for Social Research.

A newspaper columnist as well as a poet, Palanca Memorial awardee **Alfred A. Yuson** (1945–) has written two books of poetry—*Sea Serpent* and *A Dream of Knives*—as well as a novel, *The Great Jungle Energy Cosmic Cafe.*

Cyn. Zarco (1950–) lives in Miami and has had her works published in journals and anthologies. She has a published book of poems, *cir'cum*nav'i*-ga'tion.*

ACKNOWLEDGMENTS

STORIES

Paz Marquez Benitez, "Dead Stars," originally published in the *Philippines Herald,* September 20, 1925, from *Storymasters 1* (Manila: A. Florentino, 1973); reprinted by permission of the publisher.

Arturo B. Rotor, "Zita," originally published c. 1937, from *Storymasters 4* (Manila: A. Florentino, 1973); reprinted by permission of the publisher.

Loreto Paras Sulit, "Harvest," originally published in the *Philippines Herald,* February 9, 1930, from *Storymasters 1* (Manila: A. Florentino, 1973); reprinted by permission of the publisher.

Paz Latorena, "Desire," originally published in *Literary Apprentice,* July 15, 1937, from *Storymasters 1* (Manila: A. Florentino, 1973); reprinted by permission of the publisher.

Manuel Arguilla, "How My Brother Leon Brought Home a Wife," from *How My Brother Leon Brought Home a Wife and Other Stories* (Westport, Conn.: Greenwood Press, 1970).

Bienvenido N. Santos, "The Day the Dancers Came," from *The Scent of Apples* (Seattle: University of Washington Press, 1979); reprinted by permission of the author.

Amador T. Daguio, "Wedding Dance," originally published in *This Week,* January 18, 1953, from *A Survey of Philippine Literature in English,* ed. Josephine Serrano and Trinidad Ames

(Manila: Phoenix Publishing House, 1988); reprinted by permission of the publisher.

Sinai Hamada, "Tanabata's Wife," originally published in *The Literary Apprentice,* from *Storymasters 2* (Manila: A. Florentino, 1973); reprinted by permission of the publisher.

Carlos Bulosan, "The Romance of Magno Rubio," *Amerasia Journal* 6:1 (1979); reprinted by permission of the publisher.

Edilberto K. Tiempo, "The Grave Diggers," from *Philippine Writing: An Anthology,* ed. T. D. Agcaoili (Manila: Archipelago Publishing House, 1953); reprinted by permission of the author.

T. D. Agcaoili, "The Fight," originally published in the *Sunday Times Magazine,* June 5, 1949, from *Philippine Short Stories, 1941–1955, Part I,* ed. Leopoldo Yabes (Quezon City: University of the Philippines Press, 1981); reprinted by permission of the publisher.

D. Paulo Dizon, "The Beautiful Horse," from *Philippine Cross-section: An Anthology of Outstanding Short Stories in English,* ed. Maximo Ramos and Florentino Valeros (Quezon City: Sight Publishing, 1958).

N.V.M. Gonzalez, "A Warm Hand," from *Children of the Ash-Covered Loam and Other Stories* (Manila: Benipayo Press, 1954); reprinted by permission of the author.

Francisco Arcellana, "The Wing of Madness (II) The Yellow Shawl," originally published in the *Philippines Free Press,* May 9, 1953, from

Storymasters 5 (Manila: A. Florentino, 1973); reprinted by permission of the author.

Estrella D. Alfon, "Magnificence," from *Filipina I* (Quezon City: New Day Publishers, 1984); reprinted by permission of the estate of the author.

Nick Joaquin, "The Summer Solstice," from *Tropical Gothic* (St. Lucia, Queensland, Australia: University of Queensland Press, 1972); reprinted by permission of the author.

Ibrahim A. Jubaira, "Blue Blood of the Big Astana," originally published in *Graphic*, August 28, 1941, from *Philippine Short Stories, 1941–1955, Part I*, ed. Leopoldo Yabes (Quezon City: University of the Philippines Press, 1981); reprinted by permission of the publisher.

F. Sionil José, "Tong," from *Waywaya* (Manila: Solidaridad Publishing House, 1968); reprinted by permission of the author.

Aida L. Rivera, "Love in the Cornhusks," from *A Survey of Philippine Literature in English*, ed. Josephine Serrano and Trinidad Ames (Manila: Phoenix Publishing House, 1988); reprinted by permission of the author.

Anthony Morli, "Dada," from *New Writing from the Philippines: A Critique and Anthology*, ed. Leonard Casper (Syracuse, N.Y.: Syracuse University Press, 1966); reprinted by permission of the author.

Andres Cristobal Cruz, "So," from *New Writing from the Philippines: A Critique and Anthology*, ed. Leonard Casper (Syracuse, N.Y.: Syracuse University Press, 1966); reprinted by permission of the author.

Gilda Cordero-Fernando, "People in the War," from *Butcher, Baker, Candlestick Maker* (Manila: Benipayo Press, 1962).

Gregorio C. Brillantes, "Faith, Love, Time, and Dr. Lazaro," from *A Survey of Philippine Literature in English*, ed. Josephine Serrano and Trinidad Ames (Manila: Phoenix Publishing House, 1988).

Rony V. Diaz, "Death in a Sawmill," from *A Survey of Philippine Literature in English*, ed. Josephine Serrano and Trinidad Ames (Manila: Phoenix Publishing House, 1988); reprinted by permission of the author.

Wilfrido D. Nolledo, "Rice Wine," from *New Writing from the Philippines: A Critique and Anthology*, ed. Leonard Casper (Syracuse, N.Y.: Syracuse University Press, 1966).

Leoncio Deriada, "Pigpen," from *The Road to Mawab and Other Stories* (Quezon City: New Day Publishers, 1984); reprinted by permission of the author.

Renato Madrid, "The Death of Anacleto," from *Southern Harvest* (Quezon City: New Day Publishers, 1987); reprinted by permission of the author.

Resil B. Mojares, "Ark," from *The Writers of Cebu: An Anthology of Prizewinning Stories*, ed. R. Mojares (Manila: Filipinas Foundation, 1978); reprinted by permission of the author.

Ninotchka Rosca, "Generations," from *The Monsoon Collection* (St. Lucia, Queensland, Australia: University of Queensland Press, 1983); reprinted by permission of the author.

Joy T. Dayrit, "Unfinished Story," from *Filipina 1* (Quezon City: New Day Publishers, 1984); reprinted by permission of the author.

Rowena Tiempo-Torrevillas, "Prodigal Season," from *Upon the Willows and Other Stories* (Quezon City: New Day Publishers, 1980); reprinted by permission of the author.

POEMS

All poetry is reprinted by permission of the author or the author's heirs. In addition:

Jessica Hagedorn, "Song for My Father," from *Dangerous Music* (San Francisco: Momo's Press, 1975); copyright 1975 by Jessica Hagedorn; reprinted by permission of the author.

Mila Aguilar, "Disillusionment," from *A Comrade Is as Precious as a Rice Seedling* (Latham, N.Y.: Kitchen Table / Women of Color Press, 1984); copyright 1984 by Mila Aguilar; reprinted by permission of Kitchen Table / Women of Color Press, P.O. Box 908, Latham, NY 11210.

INDEX OF AUTHORS AND TITLES

SHORT STORIES

POEMS